Ann Quinton is m̲ ̲ ̲ ̲ ̲ ̲ ̲ ̲ ̲ ̲ ̲
daughter. She live̲ ̲ ̲ ̲ ̲ ̲ ̲ ̲ ̲ ̲
and collection of Siamese cats in a small Suffolk
village. She worked in the library service, both in the
County Library and in a Scientific Research Station
where she met her husband, before leaving to have
her family.

A Fatal End is her third crime novel.

Also by Ann Quinton

To Mourn a Mischief
Death of a Dear Friend

A Fatal End

Ann Quinton

HEADLINE

First published in 1992
by Judy Piatkus (Publishers) Ltd

First published in paperback in 1993
by HEADLINE BOOK PUBLISHING PLC

10 9 8 7 6 5 4 3 2 1

ISBN 0 7472 4004 3

Printed and bound in Great Britain by
HarperCollins Manufacturing, Glasgow

HEADLINE BOOK PUBLISHING PLC
Headline House
79 Great Titchfield Street
London W1P 7FN

To Melanie, my favourite cellist

I should like to thank the many people who helped me with my research for this book, in particular Fred Ferry, Simon Grew, Dr Donald Mitchell, John Smith, Dr Jeremy Trowell and Maureen Woodcock.

"This night I'll spend
Unto a dismal and a fatal end"
Macbeth, III, v

Prologue

He lifted the manuscript out of the dingy green folder and carefully laid it on the bed and with the tips of his fingers reverently stroked the pages, as if by so doing he could coax to life the written symbols. He lightly traced the line of dedication at the beginning. The black, crabbed writing was starting to fade but was still perfectly legible. The person for whom it had been written had never seen it; what had happened to him? He must be dead by now. He had disappeared on that fateful day seventeen years ago, dropping into obscurity, never to be heard of again. Perhaps he had been hounded to death by the authorities he had flouted? The same authorities who had undergone such a volte-face over the last few years.

A light breeze from the open window caught at the curtains and lifted the corners of the manuscript and the man shivered and tidied the sheets back into the folder. There would be no mistake this time, he would manage things better. There would be no problems now over leaving. They had miscalculated; he hadn't come up to their expectations and was instead an embarrassment. They would welcome his absence, would be relieved at losing someone who had become a liability. His new life beckoned and the contents of this folder would

1

be his passport to it. He would be the one to cash in on its value.

There was the sound of footsteps approaching along the corridor outside the room and he hurriedly swung the heavy suitcase on to the bed and stowed the folder inside. The suitcase was a relic from the Belle Époque and the cracked black leather, shabby and greying, only hinted at its former glory. Somehow it had survived a revolution and two world wars, a reminder of the days when such cumbersome, handsome baggage was evidence of a family's wealth and importance and when there had always been a fleet of servants and porters to deal with it. He locked it and buckled the straps and heaved it back inside the wardrobe. The manuscript was safe in there and he would produce it on his own terms; if they wanted it they must have him too, neither one without the other.

There was a knock on the door and he shot a quick look in the mirror, tweaked his tie into place and flicked an imaginary scrap of lint from his cuff. He must appear as normal when he joined his colleagues at dinner. They must not suspect the action he intended taking in the near future. He opened the door and smiled at his companions as he joined them in the corridor.

Chapter 1

'Your new husband is a policeman, isn't he? Tell him he ought to investigate. There's something fishy going on.' The elderly woman put down the binoculars through which she had been scanning the scene beyond her window and turned back to the heavily pregnant woman sitting opposite.

'You can tell him yourself, Aunt Nell. We're going to a concert at the Maltings on Saturday and we'll call in and see you beforehand. It's time you met James.'

'Should you be gallivanting about to concerts in your condition? You ought to be resting.'

'I'm fine. Everything's fine. And it's hardly energetic to spend a couple of hours sitting in a concert hall.'

Ginny Roland regarded the speaker with exasperated affection. Aunt Nell was not a real relation but the godmother of her long-dead mother. She had re-appeared in Ginny's life a couple of months ago when she had moved back into the area to take up residence in one of the new block of retirement flats built on the outskirts of the village. These were luxury apartments built round three sides of a southfacing courtyard which was furnished with garden seats, tubs of riotously blooming annuals and a square of velvet lawn, in the middle of which a fountain trickled into an ornamental pool. The most sought after flats overlooked this courtyard but Ellen Gascoigne had preferred one at the back, upstairs, facing north and overlooking the river. From the window of her sitting room she could see across the road that ran past the building to the near distant river bank and towpath and the river beyond.

Ginny Roland heaved herself to her feet and joined her companion at the window. The tide was out and the water was a thin blue line beyond the glistening mud flats. In the far distance the wooded slopes on the other side of the river shimmered hazily in the August sunshine. To the right, several dinghies lay beached and oddly-angled by the retreating tide but to the left, where the channel had been dredged and there was always deep water, a colony of houseboats was moored. Beyond them, the river bent sharply and curved inland, out of sight, towards the old maltings at Blund which had been turned into a prestigious music centre.

It was these houseboats, or rather the occupants of one of them, that were exercising Ellen Gascoigne's imagination at that moment.

'That one on the right,' she said, pointing through the glass, 'it's Dutch and comes and goes at all times of the day and night.'

'I thought that they were permanent fixtures.'

'Not all of them. That one has a mooring here but it is always sailing off.'

'How do you know that it's Dutch?'

'It's got those side paddles, all Dutch barges have them, and I've heard them talking.'

There was no way conversation from the barge could

be heard in the flat. Aunt Nell had obviously been investigating at closer range, thought Ginny, but she humoured the older woman.

'But just what are they supposed to have done?'

'They're drug smugglers, of course.' Ellen Gascoigne looked surprised at Ginny's obtuseness. 'Holland's supposed to be the centre of the European drug scene. They nip backwards and forwards across the North Sea and no one's the wiser. And not only that – they get visits from other smaller boats. I've seen people boarding them from other craft in the middle of the night.'

Ginny forbore to ask what her aunt was doing, up and snooping in the small hours. She was rather amused. Who would have thought that an intelligent, shrewd woman like Nell Gascoigne, retired primary school headmistress, would have let her imagination run riot to such an extent, spinning fabrications, libellous ones at that, about the passers-by beyond her window? She was probably bored, thought Ginny, and filled in her time by inventing scenarios that owed more to television escapism than real life.

'I'm sure there's a perfectly innocent explanation but I'll mention it to James.' She sought to change the subject. 'Have you settled in and made friends with any of the other occupants yet?'

'I'm getting acquainted with one or two but some of them are very doddery and decrepit, especially the widow women. They seem to go to pieces when they're left on their own. I'm glad you've remarried. You're young enough to be independent but a boy of Simon's age needs a man's firm hand behind him. Do they get on all right?'

Ginny's first husband had died nearly four years ago leaving her with an eleven-year-old son. Simon had at first bitterly resented the advent of James into her life, even the prestige of having a Detective Inspector from Felstone CID as a stepfather had not overcome his feeling of betrayal, but since the wedding he seemed to have accepted James. An uneasy truce now existed between them and Simon, much to her surprise and relief, actually seemed to be pleased about the forthcoming baby. She realised that the other woman was regarding her rather oddly and pulled herself out of her reverie.

'Oh, yes, they get on fine and James is very good with him.'

'And what about the new baby? You're old to be having another child.'

'I'm only thirty-four,' protested Ginny. 'Nowadays a lot of women don't have their first until they're into their forties.'

'Very foolish. The older you are the more likely you are to have a handicapped baby.' Although firmly entrenched in spinsterhood, Miss Gascoigne had plenty of opinions and advice to give on all aspects of marriage and parenthood.

'This baby is all right.' Ginny hesitated 'I've had the amniocentesis test.'

'So you know what sex it is?'

'No. I don't want to know. James and I shall be quite happy whether it's a boy or girl.' But secretly she hoped for a girl. It would not be so likely to put Simon's nose out of joint and she was afraid that if it were a boy James might not be able to help feeling favouritism towards his own son in preference to his stepson. Perhaps that was why she had refused the knowledge that could have been hers. She preferred to live in ignorance a little longer.

'You're happy, aren't you? He's making you happy?' persisted the older woman. 'Policemen work funny hours. You must be alone quite a lot.'

'I'm very happy,' said Ginny firmly, 'and I knew all about James' work commitments before I married him. I'm trying to get on with my own painting now that I've left school.'

She had been head of the art department at the local comprehensive and when she had stopped working had intended passing the intervening months until the baby's birth by developing her own painting skills, but somehow it hadn't worked out like that. Women were reputed to become light-minded and bovine in pregnancy, she reflected, and it was certainly true in her case. It was usually just too much effort to set up her easel and prepare her canvas and brushes; instead, she lolled around, lapped in complacency, the perimeters of her world shrunk to the business of childbirth and motherhood. How dull and boring she had become. Was James bored with her?

'Are you staying to have lunch with me?' Ellen Gascoigne asked hopefully.

'No, thanks very much. I have to get back. Simon's going off to camp this afternoon and I've got to sort out his food and laundry.'

A short while later Ginny Roland manouevred out of the car park and set off home. As she drove past the block of flats she glanced up at her aunt's window and was momentarily blinded by the light reflecting off Ellen Gascoigne's binoculars. The elderly woman was once again at her favourite occupation, scanning the riverside from the comfort of her home.

Blund Maltings had been built in the 1850s on the banks of the river where it curved inland, almost doubling back on itself, and the tall brick buildings had stood sentinel ever since against a background of reedbeds and farmland, a landmark for miles around. The business had thrived, employing as many as one hundred and fifty men in its heyday, and the repeal of the Malt Tax in 1880 brought further prosperity. Barges had plyed the busy waterway and as many as half-a-dozen at a time could have been seen tied up at the quay, their tawny sails silhouetted against the vast Suffolk skies. But in the early years of this century the river had started silting up; the reedbeds encroached, nibbling away at the channel, and mudflats and salt marshes, interspersed with lagoons, colonised the once open stretches of water. An earlier attempt to bring a branch line of the old LNER railway into Blund had failed and these transport difficulties, exacerbated by the agricultural recession and drift from the land which meant that less and less barley was being grown locally, brought a reversal in fortune to the Maltings. The Second World War had brought about a temporary revival but afterwards the company found itself unable to compete with the new modern techniques and machinery which were being developed in the malting industry and production had gradually run down. By the 1950s the business had ground to a halt and the navigable river had shrunk to a narrow channel meandering through a sea of reeds.

The buildings had fallen into decay, the village of

Blund having turned its back on the source of its former livelihood, and it wasn't until the 1960s, when a business entrepreneur with connections in the music world had had the astute idea of turning the old Maltings into a concert hall complex, that prosperity once more returned to Blund, putting it firmly on the cultural map. Today the Maltings enjoyed an international reputation, hosting what had come to be known as the Blund Festival, organising series of concerts and musical workshops and gathering about itself an attendant community from the world of arts and crafts. Apart from the concert hall itself, the complex encompassed a music school and residential quarters, a library, an upmarket restaurant and snack-bar, a craft centre and art gallery, and a shopping arcade which surrounded the old stableyard and consisted of a bookshop, a piano workshop, a small garden centre which sold locally-grown produce, a boutique selling hand-knitted garments and leather goods, and a health food store.

Laura Nelson was the manageress of the latter. She was a tall, slim young woman in her early twenties with limp fair hair and an intense manner. Normally she enjoyed her work but today she was pre-occupied, longing for the lunch hour when she could join her colleagues in the snack-bar. As she screwed the lids on the jars of pulses and replaced them on their shelf she sneaked a glance at her watch: nearly twelve-thirty. Once the customer she had just served had left the shop she would lock up and go, but the said customer showed no willingness to exit. She dawdled round the store, inspecting the merchandise; poking her fingers into the bowls and baskets overspilling with pot-pourri and dried herbs, turning the pages of the cookery and natural history books and scanning the collection of upmarket kitchen equipment, loth to venture out of the cool interior into the intense heat of an August heatwave.

Laura Nelson sighed and drummed her fingers on the counter. She should be using the time to make out her weekly orders but today her mind was on other things, or rather other people, and one person in particular at that: Jonathan Cade. She spoke the name under her breath, lingering over the syllables. Jonathan Cade, who had appeared on the scene a couple of months ago, taking over as the manager of the art gallery and studio when the previous manager had been forced to retire suddenly on health grounds. Jonathan Cade, who was the nearest thing to God's gift to women that she had ever set eyes on. He was tall with an unruly mop of tawny hair and hazel eyes, but although he had the physique of a Greek god, there was something gentle and disarming about him. He didn't trigger off that feeling of revulsion that so many men aroused in her. She felt safe in his presence and knew that he was a person she could trust.

He was an artist who freely admitted that he had only taken on the job in order to earn his bread and butter until he should become established in the art world. It was either that or teaching, he had explained to Laura, throwing out his arms in a dramatic gesture. And who could teach anyone to paint? The gift was either there or not and he had no intention of prostituting himself, spending his time nurturing non-existent talent in snotty little schoolkids, didn't she agree? By this time she was so hooked on him that she would have agreed with anything he said.

10

His paintings were an exaggerated extension of himself, bold and colourful and full of nervous energy; large abstracts in which the build-up of paint and impasto owed more to knife than brush-work. Very different from most of the artwork on sale in the gallery, which consisted mainly of easily-recognised local landscapes aimed at the tourist trade. Jonathan sneered at these but apparently didn't consider that the selling of them in any way impaired his own integrity. He had been living in a local holiday flat but only this week Laura had learnt that the owners were returning for their annual month's holiday and Jonathan was looking for other accommodation. She intended offering him digs in her own cottage.

A Victorian brick and tile building, it was dark and pokey but there were several rooms and also some potentially useful outbuildings. She had lived there on her own since inheriting it from her maternal grandmother, the last of her relations, who had died three years ago. Her own parents had been elderly when she was born, her mother over forty and her father nearer fifty, and as an only child she had had a lonely, repressed childhood, detached from her contemporaries. Her parents had been old fashioned and strict, religious in a bigoted way, and when they had died within a year of each other while she was in her late teens she had felt guilty that she could not mourn them. At school she had found it difficult to make friends. Her parents had discouraged her from bringing her school-mates home, and they in turn had jeered at Laura's prim and proper ways and laughed at her unfashionable clothes. The only person who had shown her any interest or affection had been *him* and look where that had led to . . .

She dragged her mind back to the present. There was plenty of room in the cottage for a lodger, but how horrified her parents would have been at the thought of her sharing her home with a member of the opposite sex; modern conventions had passed them by altogether. She couldn't make up her mind whether Jonathan was interested in her or not; he was certainly aware of her and displayed a casual affection when they met which she was afraid he bestowed on all his acquaintances. Still, if he took up her offer – no strings attached, she would make that quite clear – they could develop their friendship and then – who knows? She hoped to see him in the snack bar that lunchtime when she intended making her offer.

There was a click as the tardy customer shut the door behind her and Laura grabbed her handbag from under the counter and prepared to leave herself. She displayed the CLOSED side of the card on the door, turned the key in the lock and stepped out into the blinding sunshine.

Jonathan Cade grabbed at the plate of salad sliding off his tilting tray and edged his way between tables and chairs towards the girl sitting in the corner.

'Hi, Laura! Hot enough for you?'

'And how. Are you going to join me?'

'Sure, if I'm not queering your pitch. You look as if you're waiting for someone.'

'Yes . . . no. Who would I be waiting for?'

'I dunno – the boyfriend?'

'I haven't got a boyfriend.'

'No? I don't believe that. I bet there's half-a-dozen men hanging out for you.'

'Don't be ridiculous. I meant that I haven't got a special boyfriend.' She felt the colour rising to her cheeks and sought to change the subject. 'Have you been busy this morning?'

'I've sold three prints of Woodford Mill and a couple of sketching pads and, believe it or not, Stella has off loaded a Harris tweed cape.'

Stella Lingard managed the craft shop which formed an extension to the art gallery.

'Trust her. Stella could sell the proverbial fridge to an eskimo.'

Laura moved further along the bench seat and made room on the table for his tray. He flung himself down with a sigh of relief and sorted out his cutlery.

'So, what's new?' He jabbed his fork into a tomato and jerked back as a stream of juice spattered his shirt front.

'Nothing much,' she handed him a paper napkin, 'but I hear that you've lost your flat?'

'Well, it was only a temporary arrangement. I knew all along that I should have to find somewhere else.'

'I've had an idea, Jonathan. You can move in with me. There's plenty of room in my cottage.'

He look taken aback and she hurried on: 'Until you can find somewhere permanent.'

'It's sweet of you Laura, but I couldn't impose . . .'

'You wouldn't be. It's far too big for one person and you could use one of the outbuildings to work in, turn it into a studio.' She was aware that she was gabbling but couldn't stop herself.

'We could share the cooking – take turns at preparing meals.'

'I'm a veggie.'

'That shouldn't present problems – I'm that way inclined myself. Look, if you're worried about the legal side of it, we could get an agreement drawn up by a solicitor. I'll be your official landlady but your rights will be protected.'

She had meant it as a joke and smiled at him expecting an answering chuckle but he was looking embarrassed.

'I appreciate the offer but I've . . . I've already made other arrangements. I've moved in with Barry.'

'Barry? but he lives on a boat!'

Barry Spender was the genius behind the piano workshop. He was a gifted craftsman who tuned, reconditioned or rebuilt the many keyboards that came into his hands. He lived on an old houseboat further down the river, not far from the new part of Blund village that was developing eastwards towards the coast.

'Yes, well, it makes a change. You'd be surprised at how much room there is below deck, and besides . . .'

'What?'

He looked thoughtfully at the young woman opposite him and shrugged.

'Oh, nothing, it doesn't matter.'

The cafeteria was filling up and Jonathan Cade hurriedly demolished his cheese salad and glass of lager and checked his watch.

'I shouldn't be here really. I've got to meet this chap in Woodford to finalise details of an exhibition of his work. I should just about make it and get back in time for afternoon opening.' He pushed back his chair and got to his feet.

'Are you coming now?'

'No, I think I'll hang around a little longer.'

'Bye then, see you around.'

He moved off, leaving his tray, and Laura gathered up his dirty crockery and tried to quell her disappointment. She had left it too late. Whilst she had dithered and pondered on the best way of approaching him, he had casually moved in with someone else. Perhaps she had appeared too eager. Maybe he had thought she was making a dead set at him and it had scared him off. But surely not? People thought nothing of sharing accommodation these days. One of her few friends, a girl who had been at school with her and had recently qualified as a vet, had spent her years at university living in digs or rented houses with various permutations of students, male and female. It was quite the norm these days. Just because *she* hadn't been in such a situation before . . .

She stared after Jonathan Cade in frustration and dumped his tray at the end of the table.

Dennis Coleman locked the door of the reference library, re-set the alarm and descended the spiral staircase to the main library floor. He frowned as he caught sight of the pile of orchestral scores lying on a table waiting to be shelved and brusquely informed his assistant that he was taking his lunch-break. He was a sparely-built man of medium height who looked older than his forty-two years and had about him a look of perpetual harassment. He blinked as the sunlight caught him full in the eyes, momentarily blinding him.

He hesitated and then, drawn by the sound of the music, turned towards the concert hall. A rehearsal was in progress and he slipped inside and took a seat at the back of the darkened auditorium.

The St Petersburg Philharmonic Orchestra was rehearsing for the final concert of its current tour. It had been in the country since the end of June and Blund Maltings was the last venue on its itinerary. It had given a performance here the week before and in the intervening period between that and its farewell concert on the coming Saturday various leading members had been involved in workshops in connection with the summer Music School. Dennis Coleman leaned back and prepared to enjoy a short musical interlude in his busy day.

The orchestra had been founded in St Petersburg in the middle of the last century and by some curious anomaly had retained its original name despite the revolution and the dark days of Stalin. Things were of course different now, he reflected, what with Perestroika and all that; very different from the last time the orchestra had visited in 1975. Then members had been strictly segregated from their British hosts, guarded almost like prisoners, whereas now they seemed to have complete freedom of movement.

Take Mikhail Rabinovich, the cellist, for instance, who was at that very moment playing the solo part in Tchaikovsky's 'Variations on a Rococo Theme'; he was a gregarious chap who had made himself quite at home in the Maltings, striking up friendships with many of the personnel and delighting in the variety of goods on offer in the shops. His English was good and he had shown a great interest in both the library and the piano workshop.

The students liked him too, pondered Dennis Coleman; reputedly he was a good teacher though he personally thought he had gone off a lot in recent years. He was a competent player, good technically, but he seemed to lack that certain touch that marked out the genius from the merely good. At one time he had looked set fair to become a second Rostropovich but that prophecy had certainly not come true; in fact, you could almost plot his decline from the 70s visit here. Hadn't he been taken ill then? Dennis Coleman searched his memory. Yes, that was right, he had been stricken by some mystery illness at the end of the tour and had faded from the musical scene for quite some time. He had emerged again a few years later but had never regained his former stature. Still, that often happened; musical genius was a precarious thing and often those who had shown great promise in their youth had burnt themselves out by the time they reached middle age.

He shrugged and got quietly to his feet, leaving as the orchestra reached a crescendo.

Laura Nelson withdrew from her absorbed contemplation of the scene beyond the window and looked up as the librarian stopped at her table.

'Hello, Laura, you look as if you've lost a pound and found ten pence.'

'Nothing so simple, I'm afraid.' She gave him a weak smile. 'Do you want to sit here? I'm just leaving.'

'Stay and keep me company. You're not in a hurry, are you?'

'No. There are things I should be doing in the shop but it's too hot to concentrate.'

'Too true, but don't tell me it's just the heat that's making you look so miserable.'

'I'm not miserable, just . . . just . . . Oh, it doesn't matter.'

'Come on, confide in Uncle Dennis. What's wrong?'

'There's nothing *wrong*. I've just been rebuffed.'

'Rebuffed? That's an old fashioned word. I take it we're talking about your love life?'

'Or lack of it. How do you find Jonathan Cade?'

'Jonathan Cade?' Dennis Coleman paused in the buttering of his roll and looked at her warily. 'He's not my type, dear. I'm not into that scene.' He gave a little giggle.

'What do you mean?'

'Look, what about Jonathan Cade?'

'He's just been turned out of his digs so I offered him rooms in my cottage but he's moved in with Barry Spender on his houseboat.'

'Two of a kind. You *have* got your wires crossed if you're interested in our Jonathan.'

She stared at him. 'What are you trying to say?'

'Laura, my sweet, surely I don't have to spell it out? They're a couple of gays together.'

She blanched and then the colour flooded into her cheeks. 'I don't believe it! You're having me on!' And then, as he regarded her wryly, 'How do you know? You know what they say – it takes one to know one!'

'Don't be absurd, though I sometimes wish my proclivities did run in that direction.'

'Oh, Dennis, I'm sorry. How is Helen?'

Helen Coleman, Dennis' wife, suffered from Multiple Sclerosis. She was confined to a wheelchair and the

18

disease had embittered her considerably. It was common knowledge that she led Dennis a hell of a life.

'Much the same as usual. This weather makes her life a misery. It brings it home to her all the more when she sees holidaymakers swimming and sailing and playing tennis.'

'Yes, it must, but doesn't she go swimming? I thought the local club for the handicapped . . .'

'Yes, they do very well, but she doesn't really enjoy it. She says she feels like a landed fish, being hauled in and out of the water in what she calls a ducking stool. It's the feeling of helplessness, having to rely on other people all the time, it destroys what little confidence she has.'

Privately Laura thought that whatever else Helen Coleman suffered from, it wasn't lack of confidence. She made her presence felt and she made you feel guilty. You felt as if you had to apologise for being fit and well.

'It must be very difficult for you Dennis, but to get back to what we were discussing: I'm sure that you're mistaken about Jonathan. Oh, I know it's pretty obvious that Barry is that way inclined but I'm sure this is just a business arrangement. He's just helping Jonathan out of an emergency.'

'You're one of life's innocents, Laura. Well, don't say you haven't been warned. If you have ideas in that direction you're going to be disappointed.'

Detective Sergeant Patrick Mansfield lumbered to his feet and swatted ineffectually at the wasp buzzing round the CID general office at Felstone Police HQ. He swore as it zoomed upwards and landed in the top right-hand corner of the window, out of reach.

'Having problems?' James Roland paused in the doorway and poked his head into the room.

'Bloody thing. Don't know where it gets the energy from in this weather.'

'You're not nimble enough on your feet, Patrick.' He regarded the bulky figure of his colleague with a grin. 'How's the diet going?'

'Don't talk to me about diets,' growled the older man. 'Do you know what Jean's latest idea is? To have only two meals a day.'

'I shouldn't have thought that she needed to lose weight.'

'She's doing it to keep me company, she says, but God knows what she gets up to when I'm not there. She's probably nibbling all day long.'

'Envy will get you nowhere. How's that report coming along that the Super's been shouting for, the one on the Colby case?'

'Finished and on his desk. At this rate we'll soon be out of a job.'

'Yep, I've never known such a lull in business. One advantage of this heatwave – the criminal fraternity seems to have gone on leave.'

'Famous last words! You'll live to regret them.'

'I'm sure I shall, but as long as there's no action this evening I shan't mind. I'm taking Ginny to a concert at Blund Maltings.'

'How is she keeping? It's not long now, is it?'

'She says everything's okay and I suppose she should know . . . Don't look so smug. I know I'm coming late to the parenthood stakes.'

'It catches up with all of us in time.'

Patrick Mansfield grinned at his superior. He himself had a son in his early twenties and a daughter in her late teens but Detective Inspector James Roland, a dozen years his junior, had had a disastrous first marriage which had produced no offspring and had only married his second wife the year before. Ginny Dalton, his new partner, had figured in two of the murder cases they had worked on in previous years and since her advent into James' life he had sobered down considerably. With his dark good looks and sensual temperament he had had a bad reputation with women but Ginny appeared to have tamed him.

'She's certainly educating you. I didn't know you were into music.'

'There's a lot you don't know about me,' said James Roland coldly. 'Anyway, I called in to tell you I'm closing shop for the day.'

'I didn't know that concerts started so early, or are you doing a Glyndebourne and picnicking on salmon and champagne first?'

'God, no! We've got to visit this long-lost relative of Ginny's. She's moved into one of those new luxury flats that overlook the river near Blund and, according to Ginny, passes her time keeping surveillance on the houseboats moored nearby. She's convinced there's some skullduggery going on.'

'You're joking? You don't think there's any truth in it?'

'Of course not, but Ginny thinks a few apt words from me will sort her out.'

'And since when have the resources of the CID been focused on the fantasies of a little old lady?'

'This is not official, you idiot! She's a relative and I'm doing it out of the kindness of my heart.'

'Well, you never know, perhaps she's uncovered the scam of the century; smuggling, drug-running, corruption . . .'

'Don't *you* start!'

'You see, young man, I have a perfectly good view of what's going on.'

James Roland blinked at Ellen Gascoigne's term of address but agreed that she had a good prospect of the river and its environments.

'I'm sure you're being a good citizen in reporting what you think is suspicious behaviour, but . . .'

'You think I'm making it up, don't you?' said the elderly woman in distress. 'I may be in my late seventies but I'm not gaga yet!'

'James doesn't mean that at all,' said Ginny soothingly, 'but he has to have some real facts to go on. He can't take action on conjecture.'

'Does that mean you're not going to investigate?'

'I promise you that I shall look into it,' he said, 'but I can't promise any results. I say, that dog looks as if it knows where it's going.' He pointed to the large black dog that was trotting purposefully along the towpath.

'That's Reuben. He belongs to the people who live in that green boat. They've trained him to take himself for a constitutional all by himself.'

'Is that a fact?'

'Yes. Three times a day, regular as clockwork, he walks from their boat up to the old mill and back again. He's so regular that you could set your watch by him and he never deviates, straight there and straight back,

22

and he never takes any notice of anything he might meet on the way.'

'Programmed like a robot you might say.'

'Yes, not like that other dog, the one off the Dutch barge. That's always getting ashore and causing trouble. Not a bit disciplined.'

'Dutch barge?' asked James Roland sharply. 'Are you saying they've got a dog that's allowed to roam around?'

'Yes, it's a Dutch barge dog, a keshund I think it's called – grey, a little like a chow, with a tightly curled tail.'

'How often does this happen?'

'Well, I don't really know. The barge isn't here all the time as I told you. Is it important?'

'I think you have just given me a very good reason for investigation, Aunt Nell.'

The Rolands spent longer with Ellen Gascoigne than they had intended and as a result were almost late for the concert.

'Thank you for humouring her, James,' said Ginny as they parked the car and hurried towards the concert hall. 'Are you really going to do anything about it?'

'You and I know she's just talking moonshine, giving in to her imagination, but I'm certainly going to look into that business of the dog. If it is being taken across to Holland and then let free over this side they're contravening the rabies law and it could be serious.'

'Rabies?' Ginny shivered and clutched her husband's arm.

'It need only take one incident like that to start an

epidemic here. It's indigenous over on the other side of the Channel. It's only surprising that we've kept free of it so far.'

'Horrible thought. Perhaps Aunt Nell has done some good after all.'

The concert drew to a close and the encore brought tumultuous applause from the audience. It was a full house and the tightly packed auditorium throbbed with heat and excitement.

'Are you okay?' James Roland looked anxiously at his wife who was perched uncomfortably on the edge of her seat, fanning herself with her programme.

'Yes, I'll be fine when I get out in the open air, it's rather oppressive in here.'

'The air conditioning must be on the blink. I think it would be wise to get out now before everyone is on the move.'

'We can't go yet,' hissed Ginny, 'they're going to play another encore. We'll disturb everyone along the row.'

'Too bad, come on.' He put his hand beneath her elbow and helped her past the still applauding audience.

Outside, the sun had long gone down and all that remained of the sunset was a red glow in the western sky. This was echoed in the turgid water that lapped the quay. It was a deep garnet colour and looked to Ginny like congealed blood. She shuddered.

'Are you sure you're all right?' The baby's not started?'

'It's just given me a hefty kick,' she lied, telling herself not to be so fanciful. 'What did you think of the concert?'

'I enjoyed it, especially the Beethoven. Did it come up to your expectations?'

'Mmm, yes. I don't know what it is but these continental orchestras certainly seem to have the edge over our British ones.'

'I wouldn't exactly call a Russian orchestra continental.'

'No, well, you know what I mean. They seem to be just that much more professional and they're so smartly turned out, tails and all. When do they go back?'

'Tomorrow, I suppose, or early next week. It says in the programme that they've been on tour for three months, finishing here.'

They had reached the car and he unlocked it and carefully handed her into the front passenger seat.

'Are you sure you're okay? You wouldn't like to just check with the doctor?'

'Of course I am. Don't be ridiculous, James, we wouldn't be very popular at this time of the evening. Don't fuss so.'

'Right you are, Ma'am. Let's go.'

He reversed the car out of the car park and they set off home. The narrow road wound between stands of Forestry Commission firs and gleamed dully silver in the light of the half moon that sailed the skies ahead of them. A little farther on the headlights picked up the glint from a dozen pairs of eyes. A small herd of deer waited passive and immobile on the grass verge. As he accelerated away from them he looked in the mirror and saw them glide silently across the road to be swallowed up by the dark, massed trees.

Back at the concert hall, the orchestra filed off the stage and returned to their dressing rooms. The success of the programme and the response of the audience cast a warm, congratulatory ambience round the musicians as they cased their instruments and prepared to spend their last night on British soil. There was to be a fork supper, a farewell reception, for them later that night and many of the members intended returning to their hotel first to wash and tidy up before attending this.

Mikhail Rabinovich wiped the sweat off his brow and checked his watch. The Orchestral Manager was in heated discussion with the Leader and around him his fellow musicians were absorbed in their own affairs. He picked up his cello and sauntered towards the door muttering 'See you later' to anyone who happened to be listening. At the doorway he hesitated and looked back, running his eyes over the men and women who had been his friends and colleagues for so many years. Tears filled his eyes and the figures blurred and merged forming a black and white kaleidoscope that whirled before him. He swallowed and took a hold of himself, fumbling in his pocket for a handkerchief. He blew his nose violently, then humped his cello once more and walked out of the door.

Barry Spender lay sprawled at ease on the hatch cover, his eyes half-closed as he listened to the music seeping out of the cabin. There was something faintly simian about him; squat, muscular torso, short legs and powerful arms that were just too long to be in proportion with the rest of his body. Close by, Jonathan Cade perched on the transom, his arms clasped round his knees, his head bowed, as the haunting notes of Miles Davis' trumpet spilled out into the still night air. The only other sound was the gentle slap of water beneath the timbers as the full tide nudged at the moorings.

'Are you sure you've made the right decision? No regrets?' The older man fixed his companion with a shrewd gaze. Jonathan Cade lifted his head.

'Yes and no. I feel as if I've come home at long last.'

'That's a lovely thing to say.'

'I've been so mixed up before. There have been girls . . . but it never seemed right, and then we had that discussion the other week and everything clicked into place.'

'That's how it sometimes happens. Some fellows know right from the start and others eventually arrive there after much aggro and heart-searching.' He got to his feet and clapped his companion lightly round the shoulders. 'I think this calls for a celebration. What shall it be, red or white?'

'Just a moment, someone's coming.'

The two men looked towards the towpath. A heavily laden figure was struggling along the bank; they could hear his ragged breathing and the rustle of dried grasses beneath his feet.

'You're not expecting company, are you?'

'No, but whoever it is, he looks as if he is coming for a month.'

The figure reached the rickety gangplank and looked up at them. His broad, swarthy face gleamed in the moonlight.

'Why, it's the Maestro! I thought you'd already left?'

'Shh, don't make the noise. Please to help me?'

Barry Spender shrugged at his lover and the two of them manhandled the luggage aboard. Only when case and cello were safely carried below did Mikhail Rabinovich look round the cabin with a beaming smile and announce with bravado: 'I have come to stay!'

Chapter 2

'But your tour is over. I thought the orchestra was leaving immediately for Russia?'

'I do not go with them. I stay here.'

'You mean you're quitting?' The two Englishmen looked at each other.

'*Da*. That is right. I wish to stay here in this country.' Mikhail Rabinovich sat down and fiddled with the clasps of his suitcase as if everything were settled.

'But you can't stay here,' said Barry Spender. 'If you really want out you'll have to go to the police or the Foreign Office or whatever and give yourself up and ask for asylum.'

'He hasn't committed any crime,' pointed out Jonathan Cade. 'But you certainly must go through official circles. Won't they look for you if you've suddenly gone missing?'

'We have freedom now, it is different. I wish to join a western orchestra. I stay here until they are safely returned so that they are not embarrassed and then I apply to your Home Office for the official papers. It must not happen like last time.'

'Last time? Look, Mikhail, are you really serious?'

'*Da*, I have worked out the plan. Tomorrow they go back to London. Tomorrow night they fly back to

Moscow. I stay here one week, two week, and then I go to your authorities and join a British orchestra.'

'Okay, so you don't have to defect nowadays if you want to live in the West, but surely if you go missing tonight they will search for you, if only to make sure you haven't met with an accident.'

'I have friend in orchestra who will cover for me. He tell them I go to London tonight to see friend and say farewell – woman problem – and will join them at airport. When I do not arrive it is too late, the plane is leaving, they have to go without me.'

'You're not being very consistent. You say there will be no problem about your leaving the orchestra so why the secrecy? Why does it have to be a hole in the corner affair?'

'Please?'

'Can't you just apply for an exit visa or emigration papers or whatever?'

'You don't understand. I bring something with me.'

By this time the Russian had unlocked his suitcase and opened the lid. He fumbled amongst the clothes inside and drew out a package wrapped in newspaper. He unwrapped this to reveal a dirty green folder, bulging and dog-eared. He clasped this to his chest and said with reverance: 'Shostakovich's 3rd Cello Concerto!'

'But he didn't write a third cello concerto,' said Barry Spender sharply whilst his friend looked on uncomprehendingly.

'He did. It was last thing he finish before he die. It is dedicated to me.' He pointed to the faded writing on the cover. It was in Russian and he read it out proudly: '"To my dear friend M.R. with my very best wishes, Dmitri, June 1975."'

'Are you saying this is a new work by Shostakovich that nobody knows anything about?'

'*Da*, that is so.'

'But how come? How long have you had it? Why have you kept it secret until now?'

'Dmitri died in August 1975. This was the last composition that he completed. At the time of his death the St Petersburg Orchestra was in England on tour. When we return I find this has been left for me.'

'And you did nothing about it?'

'It was to be premiered in the West, that was always his wish. So I keep quiet until the time is right.'

'Do you mean nobody knew that he had been working on it prior to his death?'

'It was rumoured at the time but the authorities never found it.'

'But what about his family? Surely they knew? He has a son, Maxim, the conductor and pianist – doesn't he live in the States now? Surely this belongs to him?'

'*Niet*. It was written for me,' said the Russian mutinously, clutching it tightly to his chest. 'I was to play it in the West, in England, that was his wish.'

'And you've been sitting on it how long – sixteen, seventeen years?'

'I wait. Now the orchestra comes to England again I decide to take my chance. There is nothing for me in Russia now. I will become famous. All the orchestras over here will want for me to join them when they know that I have this.'

'Have you no family left behind?'

'No, I never marry and my mother – she die in the spring.'

'Look, this is all rather above my head. I've heard

of Shostakovich – I don't know much about him but he was quite a famous Russian composer, wasn't he?' Jonathan Cade, who had been listening to the exchange in a bemused manner, broke into the conversation. 'If this is the real thing it would be dynamite. Can it be authenticated?' He pointed to the folder.

'Authenticated?' squeaked the Russian.

'I mean, can you prove it was written by him?'

'It is easy to prove. It is all here, in his writing. The experts will agree, no problem. You can read the music.' He turned to Barry Spender. 'See here.' He rifled through the pages in the folder. 'Here is the beginning of the second movement – where the cello take up the theme – you play it on piano.' He nodded at the large upright piano that took up a great deal of space in the cabin. Jonathan Cade has been very puzzled as to how it had been manouvered aboard and down into the cabin until he had discovered that it had been brought on to the barge in pieces and assembled in situ.

His friend took the sheet carefully and propped it up on the piano. With one hand he picked out the notes written there; one phrase repeated three times.

'Well?' demanded the cellist.

'It's his theme certainly,' said Spender who seemed suddenly rather shaken.

'What do you mean?' demanded Jonathan Cade.

'He had a theme, a motif, that he repeated over and over again in his works: D, E flat, C, B.' As he spoke he depressed the relevant keys again and the foreboding notes rang round the cabin.

'But surely that doesn't prove anything. Anyone could use that. In fact, it would be the obvious thing to do if you were trying to fake a piece of music by him.'

'Fake? This is no fake! You do not believe me! I tell you this is genuine, I have it with me all these years. It is very valuable.'

'It would be, wouldn't it?' enquired Jonathan of his friend.

'Well, yes, I suppose so if it's the real McCoy. Okay, Mikhail, what do you want us to do?'

'I can stay here? On this boat?'

'Won't that put us in the firing line?'

'What you mean?'

'I mean we don't want the police or the Home Office investigating us.'

Mikhail Rabinovich turned pale. '*Niet, niet.* I have done nothing wrong, you would not be involved. I just wish for somewhere to live until it is settled. Please to let me stay?'

'Do you mind if we just discuss it in private?'

Barry looked at Jonathan and jerked his head towards the door and the two men went up on deck, leaving the Russian behind.

'What do you think?'

'I don't know, it's your boat. Do you think he's genuine?'

'Well, we know who he is, but whether he's telling the truth about that manuscript is another matter.'

'You think he may have stolen it?'

'God knows, but if it is genuine and he's hung on to it all these years one must suppose that no one else knows of its existence.'

'Surely the Russian authorities will search for him? Even with all the Glasnost and Perestroika they aren't going to just let him walk out without doing anything about it?'

'He seems to think he'll get away with it. Shall we give him the chance?'

'We could let him stay for a few days and see what happens.'

'Right, but any trouble and he's out double quick. Let's make sure that he understands that.'

Mikhail Rabinovich was still sitting hunched on the bunk when they went down below again. He looked up eagerly as they descended the companionway.

'Okay, Mikhail, you can stay until you feel it is safe to give yourself up but we don't want any trouble with the police – yours or ours.'

'No trouble, I promise. Nobody know I am here.'

'People are going to see you. What explanation shall we give?'

'I am your friend. I come for a holiday.'

'Well, yes, all right. But what are you going to do with yourself all day long?'

'I practise.' He indicated his cello.

'That will draw attention to you straight away. How do you rate in the cooking stakes?'

A week later Mikhail Rabinovich was still living on the houseboat and the St Petersburg Orchestra was back in the USSR enjoying a well-earned rest on the shores of the Black Sea. There had been no mention in the press or media that one of the members had decided to stay behind and take his chance in the West and as far as his hosts knew no attempt had been made to find the missing musician. However, the news of his presence aboard Barry Spender's *Painted Lady* had infiltrated the Maltings complex in the way that rumours do in a tightly-knit community. Some of the people who worked there knew that the Russian cellist was still amongst them and there were also rumours concerning a valuable musical score. The man himself seemed content to bide his time. He had discovered the delights of fishing and was to be seen most days, trailing a line over the side, engrossed in the changing colours and patterns of river and shoreline. Dennis Coleman, the music librarian, had been shown the score and had professed great interest and excitement, but the management committee who ran the Maltings and its director remained in ignorance of the interloper in their midst.

Detective Inspector James Roland was returning from a meeting in Woodford when a distant view of the river reminded him of his undertaking to Ginny's elderly relative. He swung the car left at the next junction and detoured down to the waterfront, where he parked the car behind some old warehouses and set off on foot along the river bank. The weather was still fine but there was a light breeze blowing off the water and the heat was not so oppressive as it had been of late. As he neared the moored houseboats he dropped down from the towpath and walked along at the water's edge, scrunching dried seaweed, driftwood and tiny bleached crab shells underfoot.

He could see no sign of the Dutch barge and cursed under his breath. It looked as if she were off on one of her mysterious voyages and he wondered if there could possibly be any truth in Ellen Gascoigne's surmises. At that thought he looked across at the distant apartment block and wondered if he were, even at the moment, under surveillance by a sharp pair of elderly eyes. If he were, then at least she would know that he had kept his promise. He could see no signs of life aboard any of the moored boats and was just about to turn back when he noticed the head and shoulders of a man framed in the porthole of a houseboat that was moored a little further upstream, apart from the others. He raised his arm and hallooed and had the brief impression of an expression of alarm flickering across the broad features before they disappeared from view.

Roland waited, expecting this person to come up on deck in response to his shout. When nothing happened, he walked along to the boat. At one time it had been painted scarlet but the paint had faded to a rusty pink and in many places was peeling off altogether revealing the bare timbers underneath. The name *Painted Lady* was picked out in black lettering on the stern and below it fluttered a couple of painted butterflies whose bright primary colours recalled no living butterfly to mind. He paused at the shore end of the gangway and shouted again and when he received no answer, crossed over and boarded the boat. It certainly appeared to be deserted. There was no sign of life and he banged on the cabin door without getting a reply. Strange, he could have sworn that he had seen a figure on board; maybe he was imagining things. He shrugged and made a quick detour of the deck. If there was anyone lurking in one of the cabins he was definitely not at home to visitors and, short of breaking down the door, there was little Roland could do. His business was not to do with the occupants of this boat anyway. The Dutch barge was missing and there appeared to be no dogs on any of the other boats.

He re-crossed to the shore and retraced his steps. He

would come back another time, but first he would have a word with Customs.

Laura Nelson was shopping in the local supermarket when she spotted Stella Lingard over on the other side of the shop and hurried after her.

'Stella, you're just the person I was wanting to see.' Her trolley rattled against the other woman's. 'Has Jonathan said anything to you about their mysterious visitor?'

'My! Word does get round.' Stella Lingard looked up from her shopping list. 'Just what have you heard?' She was an attractive, vivacious divorcee in her mid-thirties who had a great mass of hair in an improbable shade of red and a penchant for rather arty, peasant-type clothes. Today she was wearing a vividly patterned cotton skirt that trailed her ankles, an emerald green camisole top and a pair of flamboyant earrings that resembled miniature chandeliers. Beside her, Laura felt pale and insignificant.

'That one of our Russian friends has decided to stay behind and is camping out on Barry Spender's houseboat.'

'The little bird you heard that from was correct but not very discreet. It's supposed to be a big secret.'

'Well, Jonathan's obviously told you all about it.'

'We do work together and he dropped so many hints that I put two and two together and made half-a-dozen so he had to put me right.'

'Who is it?'

'Mikhail Rabinovich, the principal cellist.'

'And he didn't come empty-handed?'

'Now what do you mean by that?'

'Something about a hitherto unknown manuscript, a musical score by a famous composer that he's smuggled out with him.'

'That *is* news to me. Who told you that?'

'Dennis Coleman's been dropping hints. I think he would like to secure it for the library.'

'I bet he would. Did he say who the composer was?'

'I think Shostakovich was the name mentioned.'

'Oh!' Stella Lingard looked disappointed. 'I thought you meant someone like Beethoven or Mozart. Still, I suppose it would cause ripples in musical circles. I wonder if he'll be head-hunted?'

'So the three of them are living together on the *Painted lady*?' Laura Nelson was not interested in the musical side of the situation.

'Yes, I've heard of a ménage à trois but not quite like this. I wonder if he's a poof too?'

'I'm sure it's not like that. Why does everyone think Jonathan's gay?'

'There's a simple answer to that, my dear, but I agree he's a great loss to our sex. He's one of the handsomest men I've set eyes on for a long time.'

'I'm sure it's only a temporary phase. He's been seduced by Barry Spender but he'll get over it. He's mentioned girlfriends,' said Laura rather desperately.

'He could be bisexual,' agreed Stella Lingard, 'but that's bad news for us women. You'd get no joy out of a relationship with a bisexual, believe you me. I didn't realise you were so smitten with him but if you want my advice, forget him. There's plenty of other fish in the sea and I'm afraid you've completely mis-read the signals if you hope to make it with Jonathan Cade.'

'You're very free with your advice for someone who hasn't exactly made a success of her own lovelife.'

'You mean because I made a mess of my marriage and am not doing much better with my new relationship?'

'Oh, Stella, I'm sorry! That was unforgivable of me. I didn't mean it.'

'You did, and it's true,' said the other woman calmly. 'I'm a fool as far as men are concerned but you must admit that Nick is quite something.'

Nick Blackstone was a freelance journalist who was currently living and working in the area. Stella was known to be crazy about him but he was playing hard to get. Laura did not find him at all attractive and thought that he was sponging off her friend.

'He's not my type, but I suppose you know what you're doing.'

'Actually I'm shopping now for a little, intimate dinner party à deux tonight. You know – candlelight, soft music, the works. What do you think of these melons? I could do a Florida cocktail for starters with this and some grapefruit and orange segments, and I thought about poached salmon for the main course.'

'You spoil him.'

'I know. I'm trying to follow the old adage about the way to a man's heart being through his stomach. The trouble is, there are other parts of his anatomy that I'm far more interested in and vice versa! I don't know what I shall do if he goes back to London.'

'Is he likely to?'

'He keeps threatening it. Says there's no copy to be got locally and he needs to be in the centre of things if he's to earn his crust that way.'

'Well, there's a nice story for him to follow up now,

isn't there? A Russian who's decided to stay in the West and the valuable manuscript he's brought with him, something to really get his teeth into.'

'Why didn't I think of that! Laura, you're a genius, you've made my day! I shall mellow him with food and wine and then drop all sorts of mysterious hints and innuendos into his ear. He won't be able to resist the chance of an exclusive story. I must rush – 'bye!'

Laura Nelson continued her own shopping in a much happier frame of mind. There was more than one way of rocking the boat.

Unbeknown to them another woman had been listening in to their conversation from behind a food stand that hid her from view. Màrta Rakosi helped out in the boutique. She was Hungarian by birth, in her mid-fifties, and had been living in England since escaping from Hungary in 1956 as a teenager. Besides working part-time in the boutique she also made some of the beautiful hand-embroidered sweaters that were sold there, utilising a craft she had learned in her native village as a child. She had thick grey hair which she wore in an untidy knot on top of her head and a very strong accent which she had not lost although English had been her first language for over thirty years.

As Stella Lingard and Laura Nelson parted she twisted back an untidy wing of hair behind her ear and wondered whether to go after them in the hope of learning more. She hesitated and then realised that the older woman was already going through the check-out leaving Laura Nelson behind. She did not like the younger woman; she was too aloof and stand-offish for the likes of Màrta Rakosi who, with her excitable temperament, could not understand the reserve of the English girl. She decided to leave it alone for the time being and keep her ears open in the hope of hearing more from other sources. Instead, she would hurry home and tell her husband. He would be astounded. On the other hand, perhaps she wouldn't mention it yet; he got so upset when anything connected with his past came up.

She thrust the packets of tea and biscuits back on their shelves, dropped the wire basket on to the floor and left the shop empty-handed.

'You've no idea how awful my life is!'

Helen Coleman tapped her fingers on the arm of her wheelchair and stared accusingly at her husband.

'I should do, you tell me often enough.' The retort was out before Dennis Coleman could prevent it and he groaned inwardly, knowing that any such remark was always seen by Helen as sheer provocation and would set her off on a tirade lasting for hours.

'That's typical of you,' she snapped, 'you're out all day living your own life and I'm not allowed even to mention the fact that my life is over!'

'I'm sorry, Helen, I didn't mean it. Have you had a bad day?'

'When do I ever have a good one?'

She was a dramatic-looking woman with pale skin and jet black hair cut in a sleek cap. She had once been beautiful but that had been a long time ago, before the illness had ravaged her limbs and poisoned her mind. Her skin was unnaturally pallid, etched with lines of discontent, and her dark eyes glittered with malice. As someone had once said when they had got on the wrong side of her tongue – in the olden days she would have been put out of her misery by being burnt at the stake as a witch.

'Is the heat getting you down? It's supposed to turn cooler in the next few days.'

'Pam has her grandchildren staying with her. She has to take them to the beach.'

So that was what was bugging her, thought her husband, pleased that it was no deed or omission on his part that had triggered off this latest burst of ill-temper and self-pity. Pam Maudsley lived in the next road. Her children were all married and off her hands and her husband was a long-distance lorry driver spending periods away from home so she filled in her time by helping out with several local families. She was officially employed by the Colemans two mornings a week during which time she coped with the basic housework but she dropped in most days to see Helen, either as a purely social occasion or to take her to the local shops or help in some project. She was a placid, cheerful woman who was quite impervious to Helen's sharp tongue and tantrums.

'Does that mean that she's unable to come this week?'

'No, she's doing her usual mornings but she can't spare the time to bother with me apart from that.'

'Well, it's understandable if she's got her hands full with her grandchildren. We're lucky to have someone like her.'

It was Dennis Coleman's greatest fear that Pam Maudsley would get fed up with Helen's behaviour and simply stop coming. He didn't know what he would do then. He was wrapped up in his work as librarian at the

Maltings and, apart from needing the salary, he craved the hours spent away from home; they enabled him to survive the stress of living with Helen. For a few hours each day he could lose himself in another world and re-charge his batteries. With no Pam Maudsley and Helen's disease getting progressively worse he could foresee a time when he would have to give up his job and devote himself to looking after her full-time. It didn't bear thinking about.

Whilst Helen moaned that if only they had more money she could have more labouring-saving devices and gadgets for the handicapped, he thought of riches in terms of a residential nurse to look after her. Perhaps then he might even get away for a holiday – a musical break in Salzburg or a week in Sussex taking in Glyndebourne.

'To think that I have to rely on the goodwill of someone like her to relieve the boredom of my days. I don't get many visitors.'

This was only too true and entirely her own fault but Dennis made a valiant effort to steer her away from this topic.

'What are we having to eat tonight? Did you manage to prepare the vegetables?'

'Yes, and I cut my thumb – look!' She held out her pale, still graceful hands and her husband was moved to pity. He suddenly remembered her in the corps de ballet as she had been in the days of their courtship when he had fallen in love with those elegant hands and wrists. Multiple Sclerosis was a cruel disease to happen to anyone but it was doubly ironic when it struck a promising ballerina.

'Oh, Helen.' He lifted the limp wrist and planted a

kiss at the base of her thumb. 'I'm sorry.' He wasn't sure what he was sorry about but he felt a sudden surge of tenderness for his stricken wife. 'Tomorrow we'll eat out – in the Maltings restaurant. How would you like that?'

'How can you bear to be seen consorting with a cripple?'

'Don't be silly. We'll have an early meal and come back and watch TV – they're doing "Giselle" tomorrow on BBC 2. You'll enjoy seeing that.'

'You must be mad! I can think of no crueller punishment than having to watch my former colleagues *dancing*! How could you be so unfeeling?'

Dennis Coleman sighed and reflected that coping with Helen was like trying to negotiate a minefield. To distract her he told her about the Russian cellist and the music he had brought with him.

'I shall miss this when I'm back in town.' Nick Blackstone scraped the last of his brie on to a piece of roll and bit into the creamy richness.

'Are you referring to me, the setting or the food?' asked Stella Lingard tartly, pushing back her own plate and scrunching up her napkin.

'Aren't they indivisable?' he teased. 'A charming setting, a beautiful woman and a gourmet meal . . . what more could a man ask for?'

He was a tall, well-built man in his late thirties with close-cropped curly hair and a droopy moustache which should have looked dated but somehow didn't. He wasn't yet running to fat but the warning signs were there; the incipient double chin, the bulge at his waistline not quite hidden by the loose shirt. He was easy-going and good-humoured. He made Stella laugh and he was an experienced lover.

'And what do I get out of the bargain?'

'Me, all me. I'm yours to command.'

'I thought you were talking about removing yourself from my presence?'

'Ah, now, I thought we were talking about this evening, not the unforeseeable future.'

'Your future may be unforeseeable but mine isn't. I have planned my life and I know where I'm going.'

'Here, in the backwater of Blund? Burying yourself away in deepest Suffolk, wasting your talents? You should be more ambitious.'

'Why, Nick, are you suggesting that I join you in the big city?' She spoke lightly, mockingly. It would never do to let on just how much she would love such an invitation.

'Come on, sweetheart, you know our pact: no commitment. You know you'd hate to be tied down as much as I. You've tried it once and it didn't work out. You're not hankering for another bite at the cherry?'

'I've no intention of marrying again. Once bitten, twice shy, if we must talk in clichés.'

'Do I detect a little aggro there? How's Andy Pandy?'

'I don't know why you call him that! When last heard of he was living in married bliss with his second wife.'

'You're well rid of him. I can't see how you, Stella Polaris, could have tied yourself down with a nine-to-five accountant.'

'I wish you wouldn't call me that. It makes me sound cold and frigid.'

'Far from it. Stella Polaris is the pole star. The one,

immovable, immutable star around which all the rest of the galaxy revolves. That is how I prize you.'

'You mean I'm always here to fall back on!'

She got to her feet and stacked the dirty plates. She was wearing gold-printed culottes with a low-cut black vest top and her sunburned feet were thrust into flat, embroidered Arabian Night slippers. He watched appreciatively as the gauzy material swirled round her calves. When she bent over the table her breasts threatened to pop out of their nigrescent confines. She was not wearing a bra.

'Shall we have coffee outside?' She was well aware of the effect she was creating. 'It's still very warm.'

'Afterwards.'

'Afterwards?'

'After the next course, the main course, the bed course.'

'The coarse course.'

'La, a wit! The lady plays on words.'

'Later, Nick.' She brushed aside his exploratory hands and carried the tray through to the kitchen. He followed and leaned against the door jamb as she busied herself with coffee pot and cups and saucers.

'It's rather late in the day to play hard to get.'

'What do you mean?'

'You know you want it as much as I do.'

'Surely it's worth waiting for?' She dodged his lunge and laughed as he slammed his hand against the table and swore. 'Tell me, when does your friend Toby return?'

Nick Blackstone was house-sitting for his friend. Toby was a freelance photographer currently working on an assignment in the Far East and Nick was looking after his house for him in his absence. Stella was pretty certain he had snatched at this opportunity in order to escape a love affair that had threatened to get out of hand. Perhaps there was an irate husband on his trail or a clinging woman. He really was a skunk, she thought, but even knowing this she was his current willing victim. Whatever the cause for his expedient departure from London, he must think the danger over if he were planning to return.

'Sometime in the autumn – he wasn't sure exactly when I heard from him last.' He accepted temporary defeat and helped himself to some grapes from a bowl on the dresser.

'So you intend returning to London before he gets back, leaving the house unattended?'

'I really can't think that it will come to any harm. It's not as if he had it stuffed with valuables, but I may stick around . . . depends on whether I can write and flog many more scintillating articles on little ole Suffolk. There's a limit as to how much rural whimsey my readers are willing to digest.'

'I think I may be able to help you there.'

'You mean you'll do your siren act and lure me so completely that I forget all about my work?'

'I can do better than that, I'll do a Scheherazade. Later tonight I shall beguile your ears with a tale that will really grab you.'

'It had better be good.'

'In the words of my nephew, you'll be gob-smacked!'

The weather broke the following day. There was a violent thunderstorm at midday with torrential rain that caused flooding in many areas. The ground, hard as frost-bound soil from the long drought, could not soak up the excess water and it lay around in pools, silvering the bleached grass and turning minor roads into fords. At Blund Maltings it lapped the concert hall itself and the Henry Moore and Elizabeth Frink sculptures that dotted the lawns were isolated islands, awash in a shallow sea. The car park was under water and it was feared that the remaining concerts in the Summer Proms Season might have to be cancelled. Now that the storm had changed the weather pattern it was thought likely to herald the end of the summer weather, but the pessimists were proved wrong. Although it turned considerably cooler the sun came out again and the weather in the next few days alternated between sunny periods and heavy showers.

Mikhail Rabinovich viewed it with detachment. He had heard tales about the vagaries of the English climate and had been surprised at the heat and continuous sunshine which he had experienced since setting foot on English soil – until this last week. The weather was now behaving in the way that he had expected and it didn't bother him. He was used to extremes of temperature in his native Russia. What was bothering him was his complete failure, so far, to establish himself officially in this country. To use one of the idioms he had eagerly picked up from his new friends, he had not yet managed to get a foot in the door.

The Home Office – and what a funny name that was when it dealt with foreigners rather than its own nationals – was not being encouraging. A middle-aged, mediocre musician was not welcome in this country and he had fears of being deported back to the USSR. Unless he could persuade one of the English orchestras to take him on, this was surely what would happen and his fellow countrymen wouldn't welcome him back into the fold either. He had not lived up to his potential; he had been groomed for the job but had been unequal to the task. His former employers were probably relieved at his departure, it had saved them the business of getting rid of him. No, they certainly wouldn't want him back. He had to get employment here so that the British authorities would allow him to stay.

He sighed. He had no illusions either about the standards required of English orchestral players. He would have no hope at all if it weren't for his possession of the Shostakovich manuscript. It was his bargaining point; if they wanted that they got him too, that would be the deal. He would get in touch with a contact he had in the BBC Symphony Orchestra and put out some feelers . . .

He withdrew from his reverie and squinted up at the sky. The rain clouds were piling up in the west again, black and purple layers hovering over the fawn reeds which marched in fallow symmetry towards the horizon. Soon there would be another deluge, he could see the curtain of rain moving steadily before the wind and switched his attention to his rod and line. The fish were supposed to bite in the rain but he had had no luck so far. As the first stinging drops swept across the deck he reeled in his line and went below.

A few miles away Ginny Roland was caught in the same shower as she was walking home from an ante-natal class. After their wedding, the Rolands had moved to an old Edwardian house on the outskirts of the village of Wallingford, which was situated between the village of Croxton where Ginny and Simon had lived, and the coastal town of Felstone where James had had a house. They had decided that it was better to start their new life in a different home and not in either of the ones that had been shared with previous partners. Simon had been quite happy with this decision, partly because the new place had attics which had been turned over to him so that he had his own bedroom and a second room in which he could entertain friends and make a noise without disturbing the rest of the household.

Detective Sergeant Mansfield also lived in Wallingford and Ginny was walking down their road towards home when the heavens opened. Unable to hurry due to her condition she was soon drenched and when she realised she was passing the Mansfields' house she pushed open the gate and staggered up the path. Jean Mansfield answered the bell.

'Why, Ginny! You're soaked! Do come in.'

'If I may, until the storm has passed.'

'We must get you out of those wet clothes. Come into the lounge and I'll find you a towel.'

Jean Mansfield was in her mid-forties. She was a small, dark, dynamic woman who channelled her energies into many local activities, most of them worthwhile, charitable and unpaid. She had long ago come to terms with the mores of her husband's occupation, and had in fact in the early days of her marriage given up her career as a social worker because of a possible clash of interests. She was very fond of the younger woman who, with her tall, normally slim figure, long strawberry blonde hair and odd-coloured eyes, had brought James Roland to his knees. And not before time in Jean's opinion.

'Are you sure you're not busy, that I'm not inter-rupting anything?' Ginny took the proffered towel and rubbed her hair which flew into a riot of curls.

'No, of course not, it's lovely to see you. I'll get you Patrick's dressing-gown to wear whilst I dry your clothes – you won't get into mine – and then I'll make us a cup of tea.'

A short while later Ginny Roland put aside her cup and saucer and grinned at her hostess. 'Whatever will Patrick say when he learns that two people have been sharing his dressing-gown?'

'I'm sure he'll be flattered. You're looking well but the heat can't have suited you, it's been very trying.'

'Too true! I've found it very oppressive these last few weeks. I shall be glad when it's over. I feel like a top-heavy galleon in full rig and I keep mis-judging distances.'

'I can remember feeling exactly the same; still, it isn't long now, is it? How is James enjoying the idea of fatherhood?'

'He's thrilled and very matter-of-fact about it all but underneath I think he's scared stiff, though he won't admit to it.'

'Has he been to any of the classes with you?'

'Yes, he came to the prospective fathers' evening and managed to carry it off with equanimity. He's convinced that nothing to do with the actual birth could be more gruesome than one of his murder cases.'

'He's going to be there?' Jean Mansfield showed her surprise. She could well believe that James Roland was proud of his forthcoming fatherhood but could not see him at Ginny's bedside doing the soothing the fevered brow bit. He must have mellowed considerably more since his marriage than she had credited him with.

'Yes, he's going to be in at the birth. Wouldn't miss it.'

'Don't be surprised if he chickens out at the last moment and uses work as an excuse.'

'He's promised,' said Ginny firmly.

'Well, let's just hope that no stray corpse turns up on their patch at the appropriate time. If it's a case of bodies or babies, I know who'll miss out!'

The body turned gently in the swell. It had gone into the river at high water, when the flood tide was on the turn, and the sudden surge and play of cross-currents had carried it out of the channel and through the narrow inlet into the tidal lagoon that crept inland behind the village of Blund.

The receding tide beached it on a mud bank where it lay hidden from sight amongst a bed of pale, rotting reeds. It continued its journey on the next incoming tide, nudged from its resting place by the greedy, capricious eddies, and as it was swept along towards the head of the lagoon the underswell tugged at the flacid limbs, giving the impression of voluntary movement. A heron flying overhead, alerted by the glint of a wristwatch, dipped lower to investigate; but the water was deep, too deep for a wader, and it veered off from the cumbersome object wallowing beneath the surface and flapped lazily towards the shore.

At the far end of the lagoon a group of dead oak trees, victims of the 1953 East Coast floods, clung to a bank that was now partly submerged and suffering from erosion. As the sand had been washed away so the roots of the oaks had been exposed; a forest of thick, knarled fingers clinging to their precarious hold and reaching down into the brackish water. Behind this grill of twisted roots a vast colony of shore crabs lived in the watery cavities.

The body entangled itself in this root maze and was gradually sucked down. It could have remained there undetected for weeks or even months if it hadn't been August and the school holidays. A gang of boys armed with forked sticks, jam-jars and string baited with bacon rinds and crusts converged on the bank for a morning's crabbing. They clambered over the roots and dangled their lines hopefully into the murky water. The crabs were not interested; they had far richer pickings.

The leader of the gang, a tow-headed youngster of twelve, scrambled lower through a cleft in the roots and poked his stick into the cavern behind. As the water cleared a round, moon-shaped object swam up at him. The sightless eyes stared into his and a myriad of tiny crabs scuttled across the pitted features.

Chapter 3

James Roland stared down at the body lying on the bank.

'You say he was trapped behind those tree roots?'

'Yes,' said the uniformed sergeant. 'Some lads crabbing found him. They had the sense to run back to the village and report it straight away.'

'They didn't try and get him out?'

'No way. They put as much distance between him and them as possible. You can't blame them. I've got a WPC with them and their parents at the moment – if you want to see them?'

'Later.' The detective inspector dropped down beside the body and examined it carefully. It was a middle-aged man, below medium height but stockily built, wearing a navy kagool over jeans and a striped tee-shirt. There was a dirty handkerchief and a pencil stub in one of the pockets but nothing to aid identification. He was wearing ancient sneakers on his feet and there was an ugly contusion on the back of his head.

'Been in the water some time, I should imagine, the crabs have started on him. Well, Patrick,' to his sergeant who had accompanied him, 'was he pushed or did he fall?'

'You mean that wound on the back of his head?

Could have been caused by bumping against those tree roots, I suppose, they're very knotty.' DC Mansfield looked at the roots in question.

'Why should he just be marked there, in that one place? No, I fear he may have been helped into the water. Have we any idea who he is?'

'No, sir, none of my men recognise him,' said the uniformed sergeant. 'And of course the young lads didn't get a proper look at him. I don't think that he is local.'

'Hmmm. Perhaps we shall know more when Doc Brasnett has had a look at him. He should be here at any moment.'

Whilst they waited for the pathologist to arrive, Roland and Mansfield explored the immediate area. The dead oak trees, long stripped of their bark, stuck starkly out of their crumbling anchorage, their bleached, peeled limbs etched against the blue sky looking surreal.

'Plenty of footprints,' Roland nodded at the muddy bank, 'too many. What with the kids and the local police puddling around it's going to be almost impossible to detect an alien print. Still, I suppose we'll have to try.'

'You think he went in here?'

'Probably not. He could have slipped in as you suggested and bashed his head on one of those protuberances and got sucked behind into the cavity, or he could have been knocked on the head and toppled into the water and then hidden behind the roots. On the other hand, he could have gone into the water somewhere else and just fetched up here, or he may have been killed on dry land miles away and his body dumped in the river. We need to know about currents and tides.'

'So you think he was murdered?'

'God knows. If he was, we're going to have a job proving it. There's certainly no murder weapon lying around.'

'If he was hit over the head here with your blunt instrument, his attacker would probably have chucked it into the river.'

'Yes, we'll have to get the divers in on this.'

'There's no need, if you'll excuse me, sir,' the local sergeant had rejoined them. 'The tide's going out fast. In another couple of hours the water will only be about two feet deep at the most.'

'Is that so? Thank you, Sergeant, it will be quicker to wait for low tide than alert the frogmen. Where has Brasnett got to?'

'Isn't that his car coming past that row of trees?' asked Mansfield.

'Yes, I believe it is.' They watched as the car drove down the sloping track and stopped beside the other vehicles. 'He won't like getting his feet wet.'

Dr George Bransnett got out of his car, exchanged a few words with those scene-of-crime officers who were nearby, and started along the footpath towards the two detectives. His rotund body was dressed in immaculate cream flannels and pristine shirt, reminding Roland yet again of his likeness to Tweedledum.

'I didn't know he played cricket,' said Mansfield.

'He doesn't. I believe it's croquet – a nasty, vicious game or so I've been told.'

As Brasnett drew closer they could see that he was

annoyed; his round, perspiring face was set in a scowl and he carried his case as if it were a suspect bomb. He nodded curtly at the two men.

'Really, James, I'm sure this isn't necessary. If you're going to call me out each time you fish some poor drowned fool out of the water . . . I can attend to them in the mortuary. He's already been pronounced dead, hasn't he? I don't see why I have to be dragged out to the scene of crime.'

'I don't know if he *has* been drowned.' Roland indicated the abrasion on the back of the corpse's head and the pathologist became more businesslike. He opened his case, took out and donned thin plastic gloves, then squatted down beside the body. He looked up at the other man through his thick hornrims.

'He was found in the water here?'

Roland explained the circumstances and Brasnett made a quick preliminary examination.

'Well, what do you think?' asked the detective.

'What do I think about what?'

'Did that blow on the head kill him or was he alive when he went into the water? Or to put it another way, could that wound have happened by his body coming into contact with something in the water after he had drowned?'

'I know that I'm a brilliant, overworked, under-rated man but you're asking the impossible. You know that death by drowning is one of the hardest things to establish.'

'Give me a break. If you find diatoms in his bloodstream that will surely prove that he was drowned?'

'I often wish the big police machine had never heard of diatoms. You know what they say about a little knowledge being a dangerous thing? If, after I have done the autopsy, I find diatoms in the bone marrow I shall know that he drowned, but absence of diatoms doesn't mean that he didn't drown, as you know all too well. He could have suffered dry drowning – died of shock as soon as he hit the water.'

'But the wound on the head – can you tell if it was inflicted before or after death?'

'Not here, I can't. Perhaps after I've had him on the slab I may be able to ascertain more facts.'

'Right, but can you say how long he has been in the water?'

'Quite a while, he's got washerwoman hands – look.' Brasnett indicated the wrinkled hands. 'Has your photographer finished? Can I take his temperature?'

Roland replied in the affirmative and helped the pathologist to ease down the sodden trousers which clung tenaciously to the dead limbs. Brasnett wielded his rectal thermometer and checked it carefully before grunting and turning his attention to the temperature of the water in the creek, which was slipping away, visibly shrinking in front of their eyes.

'Hmmmm. Body temperature has reached the same temperature as the water so he's been dead more than twelve hours. There's some distension of the abdomen with bluish discolouration in the flanks – see? – due to early decomposition but rigor mortis is still present in the legs. Therefore, in view of the warm water, I'd say he's probably been dead about forty-eight hours. He hasn't been there all that time, though.' Brasnett squinted down into the water, at the hollow behind the submerged roots where the crabs and seaweeds held sway.

'Why do you think that?'

'The crabs have been at him. See how pitted he is around the mouth? He's been down there several hours but no longer or the damage would be far worse. It's strange that. One would have expected him to have lain face downwards where the sand and grit would have caused excoriation, but you say he was face up?'

'Yes, according to the local sergeant. They'd got him out of the water before we arrived.'

'Well, for what it's worth, I reckon this chappie's been travelling before he got wedged in his watery grave.'

'So he could have gone in the water just about anywhere.' Roland walked back to the uniformed policeman. 'Do any of your men have any local knowledge of currents and tide drift?'

'You want to talk to PC Scoggins, sir, that's the bloke over by the squad car. He does a lot of sailing and fishing here-abouts; he's the man if you want to know where things are likely to end up if they go in the water at a certain point.'

PC Scoggins was a large, placid young man with a deliberate manner. He pondered Roland's question slowly but when he eventually answered it was in a confident manner.

'He would have fetched up here on an incoming tide, of course, but there's not many places round this creek where there's easy access to the water. It's thick mud and swamp in most places. He may have gone in off a boat.'

'Yes, I had thought of that possibility. Do you get many craft up here?'

'Not a great many. It's very shallow, not much

draught for anything sizeable, and at low tide you lose the water completely except for a narrow channel.'

'Could he have gone in in the main river?'

'Not very likely. It's a very narrow inlet and I wouldn't have thought there was enough impetus to carry something like a waterlogged body through.' The young constable looked thoughtful. 'Yet it would be possible at a certain stage, with certain tides.'

Roland cocked an eyebrow and he continued: 'With a flood-tide when it's just about on the turn you get a disturbance like a miniature maelstrom at the mouth of this inlet. I've known a small dinghy get swept through, out of control.' He paused. 'And yesterday there was a full moon so there was a very full tide . . .'

'Thank you, that's most useful. I may need your help with some experiments later.'

Roland rejoined Mansfield and Brasnett. The pathologist was making a futile attempt to wipe the mud off his shoes. They were two-tone, tan and white, and looked like something out of a nineteen-thirties gangster film.

'As I thought, he could have gone in just about anywhere – from the river bank itself or off a boat. We're going to have our work cut out trying to pinpoint the location. I don't think there's much more we can do here. I'll arrange for the body to be taken to the mortuary, Doc. You, Mansfield, had better stay here with the team just in case something shows up at low tide. I'll go and interview the kids who found him.'

'Get one of your men to get me a sample of the water down there,' said Brasnett, grimacing maliciously at Roland. 'You know, to check the local diatoms!'

* * *

The next day found James Roland in the mortuary where he had been attending the autopsy. George Brasnett sluiced his hands and arms vigorously at the sink and beamed at the detective over the top of his glasses.

'Well, there you are, James. I think we can safely say he drowned. Air passages and lungs full of what you, a layman, would call frothy fluid and a little blood-stained fluid in the chest cavity. Voluminous lungs weighing about 1 kg each which release fluid and air bubbles when squeezed after cutting.' He grinned at the detective.

'Don't look so squeamish, James. There's something else you'll be pleased to learn – I found diatoms in the bone marrow and blood stream. But not the same little fellows as are floating about in the sample taken from the creek where he was found, so you can assume that he went in elsewhere.'

'And the blow on the head?'

'It certainly didn't kill him but probably knocked him unconscious.'

'So he received it before he went into the drink?'

'There's bleeding into surrounding tissues and bruising of the brain so he certainly received it before he died, but whether it was by human agency or something he bumped against when he was in the water – well, that's your business.'

'Thanks a bundle. At the moment I can't even establish whether it was murder or an accident. But to come back to the wound. Surely if he struck his head on something as he entered the water, it would be more likely to be the top of his head or his forehead where the injury would be?'

'He needn't necessarily have gone in head first. He could have slipped in feet first and tipped sideways at an awkward angle. If you can find out where he went in you may find all manner of submerged objects that could have been the culprit, but why should I tell you your business?'

'So far we've drawn as much of a blank about that as about his identity. There are no reports of anyone local going missing and if he came off a boat – well, no wreckage or empty drifting vessel has been sighted. Anything else you can tell me?'

'There is a little partly digested food in the stomach but no alcohol. He hadn't been drinking so he didn't fall because he was one over the eight.'

Brasnett removed his rubber apron and hung it up. 'I'll tell you something – I don't think this chappie was of English extraction.'

'You mean he's a foreigner?'

'I'm going to be fanciful now. I reckon Genghis Khan looked very much like this.' He went back to the table and uncovered the head of the victim. 'Look at the broadness of the skull and the tilt of the eye-sockets. And then, of course, there are the teeth and the jaw.'

Roland joined him at the table. 'He reminds me of someone or something . . .'

'Give him long hair and trailing moustaches,' continued Brasnett ignoring the interruption, 'and clap a helmet on his head, and what have you got? A typical Tartar.'

'I thought Genghis Khan was a Mongol.' Roland was sidetracked although still trying to grasp at something that hovered on the perimeter of his memory.

'Tartars, Mongols, the same difference.' Brasnett

shrugged. 'They over-ran parts of Russia in the thirteenth century and the eastern influence can still be seen in the local physiogonomy today.'

'Are you saying he's Russian?'

'Well, he's more likely to be Russian than Outer Mongolian or Tibetan, wouldn't you say? But perhaps not, given world trade and the way the world is shrinking today.' The pathologist started to draw up the sheet.

'Wait a moment! I've *seen* him somewhere!'

'You'll be telling me next that he's a personal acquaintance.'

'God, I've just remembered! I must be losing my touch. *And* he was on a boat!'

'You know who he is?'

'No, but unless I'm hallucinating or off my trolley I think you may soon be able to tie a label on him. Thanks, Doc, and hang on to that water sample.'

Roland nodded to the mortuary attendant and the other policemen present and hurried off to find his sergeant, leaving an astonished and disgruntled pathologist behind.

As they drove out of Felstone, Roland put Mansfield into the picture.

'You remember my telling you about this elderly aunt of Ginny's who has this bee in her bonnet about suspicious goings-on on one of the houseboats near her flat? I went there and had a poke around the other day and, needless to say, nothing doing. The Dutch boat in question was missing, there was no sign of any dogs – did I tell you that I think they could be contravening the Rabies Act? None of the occupants of the other boats was at home, but there was another old houseboat moored a little further along the bank and I saw this fellow looking out of one of the portholes watching me.'

'You think he was our stiff?'

'Yes. I only saw his head and shoulders, but, thinking back, I remember at the time being aware that there was something different about him. Call it hindsight if you like, but subconsciously I noted that there was something foreign-looking about him. Anyway, I hailed him and he skeddadled out of sight. I expected him to come up on deck so I waited around and when nothing happened I actually boarded the boat and had a quick look around. The cabin doors were all locked and there was no sign of him, so I gave up and came away.'

'You didn't follow it up?'

'Christ, Patrick! I didn't know he was going to turn up on the mortuary slab a short while later. I was interested in a dog and a Dutch barge, neither of which appeared to have any connection with that particular boat.'

'Are you going to check on ownership?'

'Not now. We're going straight down there. If there's no one at home today, then we'll have to run a check on who lives there.'

'But if he lived on his own – and surely he must have or someone would have reported him missing by now – I can't see much point in this journey.'

'I don't think he did. I think he could be an illegal immigrant and somebody was aiding and abetting him, which is why they haven't reported his disappearance. That or they had a hand in it.'

'Maybe Ginny's aunt is right in her suspicions and there's an illegal immigration racket going on under our very noses. Hell, it's getting parky! I wish I'd put on my jacket.'

It was decidedly cooler that day. As they had driven round the outskirts of Woodford, Roland had noted that the holidaymakers were not as much in evidence as of late and those they had seen had been huddled in cardigans and sweaters. Down by the river, kagools and heavy Guernseys were the order of the day. The halyards of the sailing dinghies moored in the yacht basin snapped and hummed metallically in the strengthening breeze and a cat's paw snaked across the water.

'Aren't those the houseboats the local council was trying to get moved last year?' asked Mansfield as they made their way along the river bank.

'Yes, they'd had complaints about them being an eyesore, but nothing came of it. Personally, I think they fit in far better with the surroundings than those modern fibreglass superyachts in the new marina downriver. Mind you, the one we're interested in could do with a good lick of paint but one presumes it's watertight.'

'There's a lot of litter about.' Mansfield swore as his feet became entangled in a length of abandoned fishing line and he had to stop and free them.

'Yes, but I bet the houseboat owners aren't responsible. Now, if you were a bird, Patrick, that would have been curtains for you!'

Barry Spender tilted the pan, swirled the fat around and broke two eggs into it; he added a couple of rashers of bacon and a halved tomato and nearly dropped it as it sizzled and spat over his hands. He lowered the heat on the calor stove and pushed open the galley door. Hell, he must get rid of the smell before Jonathan returned, *and* dispose of the bacon wrapper. This vegetarian lark was all very well but you could get fed up with hamster food. Still, he would make up for this lapse by cooking Jonathan a special meal that evening: a mushroom and broccoli crumble with his speciality Gazpacho first, well laced with garlic. He hummed as he ladled the fry-up on to a plate and sat down to eat it at the small table in the corner.

It was good to have the boat to themselves again though it was odd the way the Russian had taken himself off without even saying goodbye or thank you. Damn' rude really, when you remembered how they had put themselves out to help him. One moment he had been there, enjoying their hospitality, and then the next time they had come home he had gone without even leaving a note behind. Presumably he now thought the time was right to sort out his position with the Home Office; well, good luck to him. Now Barry could concentrate on Jonathan.

Was he being premature in believing that at the age of thirty-eight he had at long last found someone to replace the love that he had lost through bereavement? He had never felt like this since, had never wanted a permanent commitment with any of the men with whom he had had fleeting affairs since Stephen's death. And what about Jonathan? He had only just come to terms with his own sexuality. Would he really be content to throw in his lot with Barry who was, let's face it, ugly, short, and considerably older? Jonathan was handsome, could have his pick of the fellows.

Barry's appetite vanished. He pushed away his plate and went over to the piano. He sat down and crashed into a Rachmaninov prelude. He concentrated on the fortissimo chords and the music vibrated round the confined space, bouncing off the walls; he did not hear the footsteps on deck or the pounding on the door. It was the sudden reduction in light that alerted him. He dropped his hands from the keyboard and spun round to see two figures framed in the doorway.

He knew instinctively that they were policemen although they were not in uniform; he had had too many brushes with hard-line coppers in the past not to recognise one face to face; but he had done nothing wrong, they weren't coming to harass him this time, it must be about the Maestro. He got to his feet and waited for them to speak.

'Are you the owner of this boat?'

'I may be. Who wants to know?'

'Police officers. I am Detective Inspector Roland and this is Detective Sergeant Mansfield of Felstone CID. May we come in?'

Without waiting for a reply, the two detectives ducked and entered the cabin.

'To what do I owe the pleasure of this visit?'

'We'll ask the questions. What is your name?'

'Barry Spender. And, yes, Inspector, I am the owner of this vessel.'

'Do you live here on your own?'

He hesitated. 'No, a friend lives with me.'

'And would that friend be male?' asked Mansfield.

'Yes, Sergeant, how did you guess?'

In the same way that the pianist had recognised the Bill, Mansfield had immediately known that Barry was 'one of those', as he put it. He strove hard to carry out his work fairly and without prejudice but when faced with a gay man suffered a gut reaction that was quite involuntary. Roland knew this and hurriedly took over the questioning.

'Do you know why we are here?'

'I presume you are checking up on our Russian friend? He has been living here, I freely admit it, but it seemed perfectly harmless and now he's asked for asylum I can't see why we have to be bothered.'

'We, Mr Spender? To whom are you referring?'

'The person who lives with me. My friend, Inspector.'

'He has a name?'

'Jonathan Cade. What has this got to do with Mikhail?'

'Mikhail? And would Mikhail be this Russian you were alluding to?'

Barry Spender stared at Roland. 'Are you playing games with me?'

'As I said, we'll ask the questions. Suppose you sit down and tell us just what has been happening?'

'If that's the way you want to play it.' The other man shrugged but did as he was bid. In a few succinct sentences he told the two detectives about the Russian cellist coming to live on the *Painted Lady*.

When he had finished, Roland asked sharply: 'When did you last see him?'

'Tuesday lunchtime. But surely you know all this if he's asked for asylum? You must have questioned him.'

'What makes you so sure he *has* asked for asylum?'

'Look, I don't understand. As I've just said, he asked if he could stay with us for a week or two whilst he sorted things out with the Home Office. When he cleared off the other day, we presumed everything was settled.'

'Mr Spender, I know nothing about Home Office activities in connection with your Russian. We are here because we are investigating the suspicious death of a man whose body was taken out of the river yesterday.'

'Taken out of the river! But I don't understand . . . you're not suggesting its Mikhail Rabinovich? But that's impossible!'

'Is it? You say you left him here when you returned to work. Is it not possible that he fell overboard? It was nasty weather, very wet. It would have been slippery.'

'I can't take this in.' Barry Spender looked stunned. 'You mean, he never left? He accidentally slipped overboard? No, I can't believe that.'

'Why not? Why are you so sure that he couldn't have had an accident? Why are you so convinced that he left of his own free will?'

'Because . . . because he took all his belongings with him.'

'Are you sure?' asked Roland sharply.

'Of course I'm sure. He hadn't got much personal baggage, just a very ancient suitcase and his cello, but they've both gone. He left nothing behind.' Barry Spender gestured round the cabin. 'It's just as if he had never been here. We thought it strange . . . that he just upped and left without a word.'

Roland and Mansfield exchanged glances. If their body was this Mikhail Rabinovich, then it was beginning to look increasingly likely that his death had been no accident. They must get an identification.

'But why are you so convinced that the body you've found came off this boat?' continued Spender who had got over his initial shock and was beginning to reason things out. 'Where exactly did it turn up?'

Roland ignored the last question. 'We had reason to believe that a stranger was staying on one of these boats. Perhaps you'd like to come with us to the mortuary and see if you recognise the body.'

'What, me? You mean now?' he was shaken.

'Yes, please, Mr Spender.'

'You want *me* to identify the body?'

'If it is your Russian friend you would be the ideal person for the job. Who else would you suggest? Would you rather we pulled in your friend – Jonathan Cade, I think you said his name was?'

'No, no . . . I'll do it. It's just that I've never done anything like this before. I mean . . . a dead body! Is it very nasty?'

'We manage to survive this occupational hazard, but don't get too upset. He hadn't been in the water long enough for the fish to have made a meal of him.'

Barry Spender gulped and looked rather wildly round the cabin.

'All right, I'm ready.' He grabbed an anorak from a locker under the seat and shrugged into it. Roland noticed that he made no attempt to lock or even shut the cabin door behind them, though whether this was by accident or design he didn't know.

As they stepped ashore Roland glanced over at the only building nearby: the block of flats where Ellen Gascoigne lived. Although he could see the upper storey from here he guessed that a clump of scrubby willow effectively hid this boat from prying eyes at the windows. What a damn' nuisance! She had a grandstand view of all the other houseboats but this one, the significant one, was hidden from her sight. Just his luck. He also noted that the riverbank curved

71

sharply away at this point so that the boat was equally secluded from the towpath and the other houseboats unless you happened to be right on top of it. If their stiff had fallen or been pushed off the *Painted Lady* there were unlikely to be any witnesses to the deed.

Barry Spender was very quiet on the journey back to Felstone. He appeared to be steeling himself for the ordeal ahead and whilst Roland had plenty of questions he could have put to him, he was glad he didn't have to parry any enquiries at this stage. Time enough for a real interrogation if he got his identification from the decidedly worried man.

At the mortuary Spender waited in trepidation as the attendant wheeled out the body. He was loth to approach it and Mansfield reckoned he would have turned tail and bolted given the slightest chance. Was this through guilt? Could he have been the one who had bashed the dead man over the head? Or was it natural squeamishness?

'Well, Mr Spender?' Roland drew back the cover, exposing the face.

'Yes, yes, that's him.' The other man glanced at the corpse quickly and then looked hurriedly away, his eyes flickering around the cold, white room, looking anywhere except at the waxen figure lying on its clinical catafalque.

'Are you sure? Please have a good look and take your time.'

'Yes, that's Mikhail Rabinovich. There's no mistaking him. He was of Tartar extraction, said he was born in Tashkent.'

Bully for Brasnett! thought Roland, ushering him out of the room.

Once outside, away from the morbid surroundings, Barry Spender recovered his aplomb. 'Perhaps you could drive me back to Blund Maltings, Inspector? My lunch hour is up.'

'All in good time. First, I'd like you to come along to the Station to answer a few questions.'

Spender looked affronted and suspicious. 'I really can't think why, it was nothing to do with me, and I don't understand why two CID officers are involved in investigating an accidental death.'

'What makes you think it was accidental. You were the one who pointed out that he couldn't have fallen overboard because his baggage is also missing. We have reason to believe that Mikhail Rabinovich was attacked before he entered the water; there is a nasty wound on the back of his head.'

'You mean he was murdered!'

Roland ignored this. 'Please get in the car, Mr Spender.'

'You're arresting me?' Barry Spender had paled at the information but now the blood flooded back into his face and he looked belligerent.

'Arresting you? Whatever gave you that idea? You are the only link with the dead man that we have so far. I just want to know everything you can tell me about him – surely you want to get it cleared up? It shouldn't take long if you co-operate.'

A short while later, back at police HQ, Roland and Mansfield were trying to piece together a picture of the dead man's last few days.

'Let's get this clear, Mr Spender. You run the piano workshop at Blund Maltings and your friend is in charge of the art gallery – how long has he been living with you, by the way?'

'Three weeks and four days,' said Spender promptly, and then looked annoyed.

'Not very long, hardly longer than our Russian. I hadn't realised this was a recent arrangement.'

'I've known him much longer but he didn't move in until three and a half weeks ago.'

'Perhaps you had another co-habitee before that?' put in Mansfield.

'Perhaps I hadn't! Look, I can't see what my private life has to do with all this.'

'Keep your cool, Spender, we don't know yet.'

'You both work at Blund Maltings but you live here on your houseboat away from the village,' said Roland, throwing a warning glace at his sergeant. 'Mikhail Rabinovich was a member of the St Petersburg Orchestra which has been on tour in this country and was staging a series of concerts and workshops at the Maltings.'

My God! he thought. Ginny and I went to the final concert! I must have seen him play – I should have recognised him from that, but I suppose we were sitting too far back to take in individual features.

'He decided to walk out – why did he come to you? Why not go to someone in authority at the Maltings, the Director or one of the management committee?'

'Search me. I think he wanted to keep it low key, at least for the time being. Although he seemed to think the Russians would have no objection to his staying in the West, I think there was still some residual fear. He was one of the old school, he remembered the purges of the past and couldn't quite believe that they would let him go just like that. But why come here? Well,

I suppose we'd got quite friendly in the ten days he'd spent here with the orchestra. They had complete freedom of movement, all the members, and he was very interested in the work I was doing on my various pianos in my workshop. He'd been over to the *Painted Lady* several times and we'd had musical sessions, me on the keyboard, he on his cello. When he decided to make a break for it I reckon he thought this would be as good a place as any to stay whilst he applied for his papers.'

'Can you think of any reason why he should have been attacked?'

'You mean the Russians may have had something to do with it?'

'I think we can safely discount that. We're living in the 1990's, the Cold War is over. We have to look for other motives. Did he ever hint that he could be in danger from some other quarter?'

'No, he was a funny old codger, only interested in his music.'

'So you have no idea who would want him out of the way.'

'No . . . Good God! The manuscript!' Barry Spender looked startled. 'I'd forgotten about that.'

'Manuscript?'

'Yes, he'd brought an original score out with him. Claimed it was the 3rd Cello Concerto by Shostakovich and that it had been dedicated to him. Dennis seemed to think it was the real thing, too.'

'Dennis?' asked Mansfield with raised brows.

'Dennis Coleman, the librarian at the Music School. He examined it and he knows what he's talking about.'

'You're saying that Mikhail Rabinovich had an original – I take it this was unknown and unpublished –

manuscript by Shostakovich? It would be very valuable, wouldn't it?'

'Priceless. It would really take the music world by the ears. I think he was convinced that it was his passport to the West – that it would give him the entrée into any musical circle.'

'And how many people besides you, Mr Cade and the librarian know about this manuscript?'

'I don't know.' He looked blank.

'Let's try it from a different angle: who knew about Mikhail Rabinovich leaving the St Petersburg Orchestra and staying with you?'

'Quite a few. None of the officials as far as I know but certainly several of my colleagues who worked at the complex. We obviously didn't broadcast it but there seemed no need for secrecy. We certainly didn't hide him away incommunicado on the boat.'

'And would all these people have known about the manuscript?'

'Some of them certainly did.'

'I shall want a list of everyone who knew about your visitor.'

'You don't think one of them knocked him off to get their hands on the manuscript?'

'Mr Spender, we don't know yet that he *was* murdered. He could have slipped and struck his head on a submerged object as he entered the water, but the fact that his suitcase and cello are also missing looks highly suspicious. How security-minded are you? Do you usually keep the cabins locked?'

'When there is nobody on board, yes. But while Mikhail was there we didn't, of course.'

'Where did he keep his manuscript?'

'In his suitcase when he hadn't got it on the piano picking out themes from it.'

'We shall have to make a thorough search of your boat. I take it you have no objection if the team goes on board?'

'No, I suppose not. What will they be looking for?'

'How do I know until I find it? But they will check for fingerprints and evidence of intruders. Don't worry, they'll leave your boat in ship-shape condition.'

A little while later, after having told the two detectives all that he knew of Mikhail Rabinovich, Barry Spender was taken back to the *Painted Lady* by DC William Evans to await the arrival of the Scene-of-Crime team. These were given a quick briefing by Roland and were later joined by members of the Underwater Search Unit. With Spender safely out of the way Roland and Mansfield drove over to Blund Maltings to interview Jonathan Cade.

'I thought you would want to be around whilst the SOCOs are going over the boat?'

'This won't take long but I want to talk to Jonathan Cade before Spender has a chance to warn him.'

'Do you think they could have done it?'

'If we do decide that it's murder then they have to figure on our list of suspects. They knew about the score and would have had ample opportunity to tap him over the head and tip him into the river. I must say Spender doesn't strike me as a villain, he seems genuinely shocked and bewildered, but on the other hand he may be a very good actor and not as ingenuous as he appears – though I think he rather under-played this business of the manuscript.'

'How do you mean?'

'He was late in bringing it to our attention. If it's as valuable as all that do you think he had really forgotten all about it and only remembered it as an afterthought when questioned? It will be interesting to hear what Cade has to add to the story.'

'I bet he'll be a real little nancy boy,' said Mansfield gloomily, 'poncing about his art gallery.'

'Sergeant, I didn't hear that! Perhaps I should have left you behind and brought Evans with me.'

Afterwards, Mansfield had to admit that he had been wrong in his assumption but the truth seemed only to irritate him further.

'What's a young chap like that doing getting himself involved with someone like Spender? I bet that Trog has seduced him.'

'Trog?'

'Troglodyte. They were squat, dark hairy beings who inhabited caves or lived underground.'

'Pat! I've never known you to be so fanciful before.'

'Jane had a book when she was younger,' said the older man, looking rather sheepish. 'It was all about hob-goblins and troglodytes and the like. I used to have to read it to her every night and the name and the description stuck in my memory. We had a family who used to live near us in Wallingford and they were small and dark and secretive. Jane always used to refer to them as the Trogs – I think they were Welsh.'

'It's a good thing Evans can't hear you!'

They had found Jonathan Cade in the office of the art gallery sorting through a drawer of catalogues.

As he unfolded his long limbs and got to his feet, Mansfield had done a double-take. He looked to him exactly like that actor, whose name he couldn't for the life of him recall, who had recently starred in a TV serial set in India. When he had learned that they were police officers he had looked apprehensive but had displayed no sign of guilt or evasiveness as they had explained the reason for their visit; shock, disbelief, all the emotions one would expect from someone who had just been told that an acquaintance had been found dead in suspicious circumstances, but no guilt. Unless he was an even better actor than his lover.

'But are you sure this dead man is Mikhail Rabinovich?'

'Mr Spender has just formally identified him.'

'Barry? Hell – how awful for him! Is he all right?'

'Mr Spender or Mikhail Rabinovich?'

Cade looked reproachful but he was more concerned about his friend than the Russian.

'It must have been a terrible ordeal for him, I must go back . . .'

'Later Mr Cade, when you've answered our questions.'

'Surely Barry has told you everything already?'

'As you have realised, he is rather distraught so we want to make sure we have our facts right.'

'Double checking to make sure we're both telling the same story, you mean? Okay, you have your job to do and I suppose you have to check us out. Where was his body found?'

'Some way from the *Painted Lady* but consistent with the state of the tide at the approximate time that he entered the water. Don't worry, Mr Cade, we shall be

able to prove where he went in. I have frogmen searching the area at this moment.'

Jonathan Cade's story matched that of his friend. The
two detectives learned nothing new about the Russian
except that Cade had got the impression that he had
left the orchestra under something of a cloud, but he
couldn't enlarge on this and admitted that he might
have been mistaken.

'Right, Mr Cade, that will be all for now but we shall
need your fingerprints to match them up with those of
yours on the boat.'

'I must get back there now, Barry . . .'

'Can you close the gallery at this time of day? What
about your customers?'

'I won't shut shop, I'll get somebody to stand in for
me – the woman who runs the craft centre.'

'By the way, how do you and Mr Spender get from
here to your boat? Do you drive? It must be at least
two miles.'

'It's only a mile by the footpath that runs across the
marshes. That's the way we usually go, either by foot
or by bike – I have an ancient cycle – we neither of us
runs a car.'

As the two detectives made to depart, Cade walked
across the gallery and went through the archway leading
to the craft centre. They could see him in animated conversation with the woman who was setting up a display.

'Isn't she someone who's on our list – Stella Lingard?'
asked Mansfield.

'Yes, she was one of the people Spender mentioned
who knew about the Russian.'

'Are we going to interview her?'

'Not now, I want to get back to the houseboat.

Cade's already spilling the beans by the look of it, she can wait.'

'It will be interesting to see how long it takes Cade to get over to the *Painted Lady*,' said Roland as they drove in that direction themselves. 'I wonder if he's using his bike today or Shanks's pony.'

DC Evans was waiting for them when they arrived back at the *Painted Lady*. The Scene-of-Crime team was hard at work and Barry Spender, looking very subdued, was sitting hunched up in the cockpit.

'Have they found anything?' asked Roland. 'No, don't tell me, I expect the place is covered with fingerprints. They seem to keep open house. What about the divers?'

'They've only just got here, sir. Apparently it's pretty murky down there.'

'If they find the weapon it's not going to have any prints left on it now, is it?' said Mansfield, wandering over to peer into the water.

'No, but I'm hoping they'll find something else.'

Roland asked one of the men to get a sample of the river water. He swirled the water round in the flask he was given. 'Let's hope that analysis will show that the diatoms in here match up with the ones found in our stiff's blood stream.'

'Hallo, here comes Cade,' said Mansfield looking across at the tow-path where the figure of Jonathan Cade could be seen wobbling along on a cycle. 'Pretty good going, nearly as quickly as motoring by road.'

'I wonder how many of their visitors know about the footpath and use it regularly? I should think it gets like a quagmire in bad weather.'

'Have they got a dinghy? That's something that should be checked.'

Jonathan Cade had reached the *Painted Lady* by now. He threw his bike on the matted grass and hurried across to the boat. He was stopped by the man on duty from stepping on to the gangway.

'It's all right, Officer, he lives here,' said Roland, and after a dismayed glance at the police officers swarming over the place, Cade stumbled on to the deck and joined his friend.

'Are you okay? what a terrible thing to happen – I can't believe it.'

'If you stay around here you will,' said Spender sagely, looking warily at the detective who was approaching.

'Do you have a dinghy, Mr Spender?'

'Not now. I used to have one but it broke adrift and sank last winter and I've never bothered to replace it. I live on the water but I don't go far. There's too many weekend sailors and ignorant landlubbers afloat these days. The river's getting more like a marine Clapham Junction every day.'

'Tell me, did Mikhail Rabinovich stay below deck, out of sight, whilst he was here?'

'No, emphatically not, Inspector. He spent a great deal of his time fishing over the side – not that he ever caught anything, mind you.'

'So he would have been in full view, much of the time, of other passing vessels?'

'He wasn't at all bothered about being seen,' said Jonathan Cade after a quick glance at his friend. 'It's my belief that all this business about dropping out of sight whilst he sorted out his affairs was all eyewash

– he just wanted a free meal ticket and we were good for a touch.'

'I see.' Roland searched his memory and remembered the other point that had stuck in his mind as being wrong. 'When he was found he was wearing jeans, a navy and white striped tee-shirt, and a navy kagool. I would not have expected a middle-aged Russian to possess a pair of jeans.'

'Too right, he didn't. That's just what I mean. He took advantage of our hospitality by borrowing our clothes.'

'The jeans were mine,' said Spender. 'He got a kick out of wearing western clothes. And the tee-shirt sounds like yours Jonathan.'

'And the kagool?' asked Roland.

'There's always a couple of old ones stashed away in one of the lockers, it was probably one of those. Do you want me to check?'

'Yes, please, but first – do you know if he made contact with anyone whilst he was staying here? Did he receive any letters or did he go ashore at all?'

'As far as I know he didn't receive any post but I believe he was putting out feelers to several British Orchestras so he must have been writing letters and going to the Post Office. I really don't know how he passed the time – apart from fishing. I suppose he could have got up to all manner of things without us being any the wiser.'

At that moment there was a buzz of excitement from the shore. William Evans, his carrot hair aflame in the afternoon sunshine, bounded on deck.

'The divers have found something, sir.'

Roland and Mansfield hurried across to the section

of riverbank from which the frogmen were operating. They watched as the large black object was lifted dripping from the water and laid on shore.

'A black leather suitcase. I think we've found our man's luggage,' said Roland, bending over it.

'They'll be no dabs after being in the drink all this time, will there?' said Mansfield.

'Not a hope in hell. Was it far from the boat?' he asked the diver who was preparing to re-enter the water.

'No, just behind the stern. There's something else down there, sir.'

'That figures. I think you'll find it is a musical instrument.'

A short while later another large black object joined the battered suitcase and Roland felt a glow of satisfaction.

'Well, that clinches it. Our Ruskie didn't go of his own free will, nor did he accidently fall in. Where are our two friends?'

Evans fetched Spender and Cade. The former viewed the sodden, cased cello with horror.

'Did these belong to Mikhail Rabinovich?'

'Yes, they were his. That cello . . .' Spender was anguished. '. . . it was a beautiful instrument, quite priceless.'

'And its owner was a living human being until a short time ago.'

'Quite, Inspector, I didn't mean . . .'

'Are you quite sure these were the property of Mikhail Rabinovich? Are you prepared to swear this in a court of law?'

'Yes, they're his all right,' said Cade. 'There's no

mistaking the suitcase. It looked as if it came out of a museum – genuine pre-World War One vintage leather.'

'The manuscript was kept in this suitcase?'

'Yes, but it will be waterlogged . . . ruined by now,' said Spender sorrowfully.

'You don't think we're going to find it in here, do you, Mr Spender?'

The opened suitcase revealed saturated clothing and few personal effects. There was no manuscript.

Chapter 4

'There's no doubt in your mind, James, that he was murdered?'

Superintendent Bob Lacey tapped the report in front of him with a podgy finger and looked at his detective inspector out of shrewd pale eyes. These eyes, almost hidden between the craggy brow and bulging cheeks, always reminded Roland of a pig's and Mansfield had confessed to him long ago that the Super closely resembled a hog his family had once owned when he was a kid. The superintendent's eyes could glitter malevolently, convey cunning and express stubborness, as had this pig's. As he had remarked to Roland, it had been a real swine of a swine and had terrorised the entire household until it had met its timely end in the abattoir. Today, the Super's eyes looked almost benevolent as he regarded the man sitting across from him.

'You have the facts, sir. There is no doubt in my mind that he was killed in order to gain possession of the manuscript.'

'Ah, yes, the manuscript. Have we proof that it actually existed, apart from hearsay?'

'Several people at the Maltings knew about it and at least one person actually saw it, apart from Spender and Cade.'

'They're the two queers? What have we got on them?'

If Mansfield's prejudice was latent, Bob Lacey's was overt and militant.

'I don't think that is relevant, sir, to our investigation.'

'Don't you indeed, Inspector? I stand corrected. How valuable would this manuscript be? Not having had your university education I don't know how world-shattering this work by an obscure musician would be.'

Roland tried to quell his annoyance and told himself not to rise to the bait.

'Shostakovich was an eminent composer. I haven't got any figures yet but I'm sure it was well worth killing for.'

'Are the Press on to it yet?'

'The activity down by the river didn't escape their attention,' said Roland diplomatically. 'I issued a statement to the effect that a man's body had been found and we weren't ruling out foul play but that his identity was so far unknown.'

'And we must keep it that way as far as the Press and the Media are concerned. I don't like this at all: a dead Russian, a missing manuscript – it sounds like something out of a spy thriller, but it could have nasty repercussions. I don't know where we stand on this but I don't want to promote an international incident.'

'We are going to have an official investigation?'

'When murder is committed on my patch I don't give up until I find the culprit,' growled Lacey. 'Any line on the weapon that was used to hit him over the head?'

'There were no submerged stakes or posts where he went in but the divers found several lengths of wood in the mud of the river bed that could have been used. Forensics are working on them now.'

'Hmmm. Well, it's your case, James, you haven't got anything else important on at the moment, have you? You've got Mansfield and Evans. Who else do you want?'

'I'd like DC Robert Lucas, please. He lives at Blund and knows all the local people.'

'I thought he was on leave?'

'He came back today.'

'Right. Well, good hunting, James, and remember – I want to be kept informed of every new development immediately. This is a delicate one to handle and I shall be in touch with the Home Office to find out exactly where we stand from the Russian angle. We've got a body, but who it belongs to and who is going to be responsible for burying it, always supposing the Coroner eventually gets around to releasing it for burial, well . . .'

Bob Lacey heaved himself to his feet. 'You've got two prime suspects already.'

Roland raised his eyebrows in enquiry.

'The two poofs. Maybe your stiff was one too and it was a crime of passion.'

'There was no sign of buggery, Brasnett was quite definite about that.'

'That doesn't mean anything, as you well know; if anyone had motive and opportunity it was them.'

'They certainly figure on my list of suspects, sir.'

As will most of the people involved in the set-up at the Maltings, thought Roland, once I start digging into possibilities. He bade his superior good morning and went in search of Mansfield.

* * *

'The director is Edwin Cheyney.' Roland was putting his sergeant in the picture as they drove over to Blund Maltings. 'He is responsible to the Trustees' Committee who run the whole caboodle on behalf of the Morton Greenacre estate. It's quite complicated. Morton Greenacre, the millionaire, started the whole thing and endowed it. When he died his entire fortune was left in trust to perpetuate it. There is also a Mrs Marilyn Proctor who co-ordinates the running of the complex.'

'So who is the boss out of those two?'

'They run in tandem. He is responsible for the musical side and she for the organisation of the place.'

'Do they know we're coming?'

'Yes, but not why. According to Spender, they're ignorant of what's been happening in their midst. I think we may be going to set the cat amongst the pigeons in more ways than one.'

'Talking of pigeons – look at those! They're pure white.'

They had driven across the river by the new concrete bridge which had been built to replace the old humped-back stone bridge a few years earlier against much protest from conservationists and the local history society. As they swung into a parking space on the quayside a flock of birds beat upwards and swooped in a pearl and silver curve against the dark massed clouds that were building up behind the concert hall.

'They're domestic doves. There's a large dovecote somewhere in the grounds, I remember seeing it.'

'They're going to get wet.' Mansfield nodded towards

90

the queue of people boarding the Thames barge which was moored a little further along the quayside.

'I think the trips are run mainly for the benefit of the birdwatchers and the like. They're not going to be upset by a little rain.'

'Pity they can't use the sails but I suppose there's not enough water to manoeuvre now. It can't be the same, chugging along under horse power.'

As they walked across the courtyard the first flurry of rain hit them and they made a dash for the old granary which housed the office block.

Edwin Cheyney was a tall, thin ascetic looking man in his late fifties. As he ushered them into his office he called out to his secretary to bring them coffee. He waved them to chairs and seated himself behind the enormous leather-topped desk that took up a good third of the room. The walls were covered with posters advertising past musical events and the desk was strewn with papers and folders. In the middle of it stood a pottery vase of corn marigolds, richly yellow against the sombre background.

'Well, Inspector, what can I do for you?' asked Cheyney after Roland had introduced himself and Mansfield. 'I'm a very busy man, as I'm sure you can appreciate, but I always endeavour to co-operate with the law.'

The secretary arrived with a tray of coffee and after she had departed and while Cheyney busied himself with cups and saucers, Roland told him the reason for their visit.

'But I find this incredible! You're asking me to believe that one of the members of the St Petersburg

– a principal member – stayed behind and has been murdered?'

Roland remained impassive and the other man continued: 'This is a fact? Mikhail Rabinovich did not go back with the orchestra, but remained here and has now been found dead?'

'Yes, Mr Cheyney. He stayed with Mr Spender, who lives on a houseboat on the river, and he was killed and his body went into the water. Mr Spender has formally identified him. You had no knowledge of his staying behind?'

'None whatsoever.' Cheyney took off his glasses and polished them vigorously before clapping them back on his nose. 'As far as I am aware the orchestra, in its entirety, went back to London after their last concert here a fortnight ago and from thence on to Moscow. I have certainly heard nothing to the contrary. The Russian authorities . . . I have heard nothing from them. There have been no repercussions.'

'Did you make all the arrangements for their stay over here?'

'I really think Mrs Proctor ought to be in on this. She deals with the running of things.'

'I want to speak with Mrs Proctor. Perhaps we can kill two birds with one stone. Will you ask her to join us?'

Marilyn Proctor's office was just down the corridor. She appeared almost immediately in answer to the summons, a comely, middle-aged woman of ample proportions. She was super efficient and somewhat domineering but hid these traits behind a pleasant manner. Roland summed her up as an iron fist in a velvet glove and nothing he learned about her later caused him to alter this first impression. She was as horrified and astonished as Edwin Cheyney.

'I'm not denying that what you're saying is true, but I find it almost impossible to believe. Nothing like this has ever happened before . . . Why did no one know about it?'

'Quite a few people did, Mrs Proctor, Mr Spender for one,' he prompted.

'Barry Spender who runs the piano workshop, you mean? So, this event took place and you're saying a lot of my colleagues were in on it, but it was kept from me?' She was highly indignant.

'That is what I'm asking you.'

'I certainly knew nothing about it, and neither did you, Edwin, did you?' This was a pronouncement rather than a question and Edwin Cheyney hurriedly agreed.

'And you're saying he has since been killed?' she continued.

'Yes, he met his death in highly suspicious circumstances.'

'You surely don't think it was the work of the Russian authorities?'

'Oh no, Mrs Proctor. We're not still living in the dark days of the Cold War. There are far more venal reasons for his murder. Mikhail Rabinovich brought with him, out of Russia, a manuscript which he claimed was the 3rd Cello Concerto of Shostakovich. He claimed it had been dedicated to him and entrusted to him to premier in this country.'

'You're joking!' If the Director had been surprised before, he was now flabbergasted.

'I can assure you I am not, Mr Cheyney. We have reason to believe this manuscript exists. Your librarian, we have been told, was convinced that it was genuine. We think that Rabinovich was killed by someone or some persons who wished to get their hands on it.'

'Dennis Coleman knew about this? And he said nothing?' Edwin Cheyney was outraged.

'He was shown it whilst the Russian was staying on Spender's boat and was sure that it was the real thing. I don't know how difficult it would be to authenticate something like that, but presuming it is a fact I should imagine it would be very valuable?'

'Dennis would know what he was talking about. He has copies of some of the original scores in the library and also letters in Shostakovich's handwriting.'

'And the value?'

'Priceless!'

'And how valuable is priceless?'

'Thousands. A hundred thousand? Two hundred thousand? Perhaps even more. Every performer in the world, every orchestra, every recording company, would give their eye teeth to get hold of it.'

He realised what he had said and looked aghast.

'You're saying someone *here*, someone in this little community, got to hear of it and killed him to gain possession?'

'That is what we believe happened.'

Edwin Cheyney got to his feet and mooched round the office, pausing to align a picture that was hanging out of place on one of the walls.

'I can't see, Inspector, that it would be of much use to him. I can't see how he could benefit from possessing it.'

'Would you mind explaining that?'

'You have the manuscript. Let's say, for the sake of argument, that it is authenticated and genuine. How are you going to prove ownership? Shostakovich's family are going to dispute it on principle. He has a son, Maxim, who now lives in the States, a fine conductor and pianist in his own right, and a wife and daughter still in the USSR. Mikhail Rabinovich might have been able to satisfy the authorities that the manuscript was gifted to him and he was the real owner, but if it turns up in someone else's hands there is no way this other person can claim it for his own – for one thing you would be on to him immediately as the Russian's killer. And then, of course, there is the matter of copyright.'

'Yes?' prompted Roland.

'The copyright of this manuscript would be the property of the composer's legal heirs – in this case, his family. As you know, copyright lasts for fifty years from the author or composer's death, which takes us up to the year 2025. All revenues deriving from the performance and publication of this work would revert back to them.'

'So you're saying that this manuscript, which the murderer has killed for, would be worthless to him or her?'

'I don't see how he could make use of it by publication or performance but there is another theory you could consider – he could sell it to an unscrupulous collector.'

Roland thought about this.

'I know it happens in the art world, but would anyone pay out a fortune for a piece of music? I mean, it's not like a picture where your art freak can gloat over it in

private. This is just a collection of squiggles on paper
– meaningless, I should have thought, unless you could
hear it played.'

'Oh, no, Inspector, your corrupt music buff would get
a great kick out of it. Imagine, he has in his hands – and
I'm taking it for granted that he is enough of a musician
himself to be able to read music and pick out the themes
and melodies – a composition that has never been heard
since the composer penned it. A large-scale work full
of new musical sounds that only he can appreciate and
which he is denying to the rest of mankind. I think there
is a certain type of person who would be really turned
on by such a situation. It would give him a feeling of
power, of being one up on everyone else.'

'You have me convinced, Mr Cheyney. Thank you
for your help.'

'Are you sure it couldn't have been another member
of the orchestra?' asked Marilyn Proctor. 'Someone
who could have known about the existence of the score
and took a chance when the opportunity offered?'

'We are not ruling out that possibility. We are following up many lines of enquiry. In the meantime, I
have told you all this in confidence. I don't want it to
become known to the public.'

'We certainly don't want any bad publicity,' said
Edwin Cheyney, getting to his feet to usher them out
of his office. 'Thank goodness he didn't get himself
killed here at the Maltings!'

'Eloquent gent, wasn't he?' said Roland as they walked
over to the library. 'He almost had me convinced for a
moment that he's laid hands on it himself.'

'Is it possible?'

'I hardly think so, especially as his secretary mentioned when I rang to make the appointment that he was in Paris at the time of the killing.'

'It's lucky we know just when Rabinovich was killed.'

'Yes. Knowing how long he'd been in the water, and also knowing exactly where he must have gone in to have ended up where he did, has pinpointed it nicely. I wonder what sort of alibis our suspects will produce.'

They met their first snag at the library. The assistant behind the loans desk told them that Dennis Coleman was not in that morning.

'I see. Is he on holiday? Or is he ill?'

'It's his wife,' said the young woman assistant who was greatly intrigued as to why two CID officers would want to see her boss.

'She's ill?'

'She has Multiple Schlerosis. Dennis . . . Mr Coleman . . . sometimes has to look after her in the mornings if she has had a bad night. He should be in this afternoon, shall I check with him?' She reached for the phone.

'No, we'll catch up with him at his home. Does he live far away?'

'No, in one of the new bungalows just over the bridge. Number seven Mill Close.'

'Thank you, Miss . . . ?'

'Carson. Emma Carson.'

'Have you worked here long, Miss Carson?'

'No, I'm a student, this is just a holiday job. I have four more weeks to do before I go back to college.'

'Would you have been here on duty last Tuesday? Is the library open every day?'

'It's open every day except Tuesday afternoon. I was here in the morning.'

'I see. And can anyone use the library?'

'Everyone involved with the Music School and any visiting musicians or scholars are allowed to use the lending library, but you have to get special permission and a pass to use the reference library.'

'Why is that?'

'There are some very valuable books and scores kept there.'

'Where is the reference library?' Roland looked around him.

'Upstairs, leading off the mezzanine floor. There are special security locks and alarms and it's temperature controlled.'

'Well, thank you, Miss Carson.'

'Are you sure there's nothing I can do for you?'

'No, you have been most helpful.'

'Are we going to see Dennis Coleman now?' asked Mansfield as they left the library premises.

'No, we'll leave him till later. Now we're here we'll check up on the others who work here. Let's go to the art gallery. Whilst I interview Stella Lingard you have a word with Jonathan Cade and see if he has an alibi for last Tuesday afternoon.'

'Don't you think you ought to have a chaperone? She looks a hot bit of stuff.'

'I could say the same to you, Sergeant. He's a handsome devil.'

Mansfield growled and took himself to the art gallery and Roland went through to the craft centre.

Roland had been here before with Ginny and they had been impressed with the diversity of goods on sale and the attractive way in which they were presented.

Someone who either had expertise in window dressing or artistic flair had arranged this display; he wondered if it were Stella Lingard. She was crouched down rummaging in a basket of ethnic printed scarves and all he could see of her at first was the top of her head and bronzed shoulders emerging from her peasant blouse. She sensed his presence and scrambled to her feet and they eyed each other appraisingly.

'Detective Inspector Roland, Felstone CID.' He flashed his ID card before her.

'Oh, my goodness, you've come about that poor chap who was drowned, I suppose? What a tragedy. They're saying he was murdered!'

'Who are saying?'

'You know how these rumours get around.' She shrugged and a further portion of suntanned shoulder popped out of her frothy embroidered blouse.

'Is there somewhere we can talk?'

'Yes, come into the office. I'll get Jonathan . . .' She looked through to the art gallery where Mansfield could be seen talking to Jonathan Cade. '. . . oh, you're after him as well? Never mind, I haven't got any customers at the moment.'

She led the way through into a little room that was hardly more than a cubby-hole and sat down in the sole chair. Roland was left looking down at her, aware that from this position he was seeing far more of the curve and swell of her bosom than was comfortable. He was also aware that she had deliberately contrived this and was enjoying his discomfiture.

'How can I help you?'

'We are treating Mikhail Rabinovich's death as murder. I am interviewing everyone who knew that he stayed behind after the St Petersburg orchestra returned to Russia.'

'Do you mean that I am a suspect?' The idea seemed to amuse her.

'You will appreciate that everyone who knew of the situation must be checked out if only to eliminate them from our enquiries. We shall require your fingerprints.'

'My fingerprints . . .' She stretched out her hands in front of her as if she expected them to be processed there and then and he noticed that whilst she wore several rings, her ring finger was bare.

'Are you married?'

'Divorced, Inspector. He got away, or rather I escaped before he could suffocate me completely.'

'Would you mind telling me all that you know about Mikhail Rabinovich?'

'That's not a great deal, I'm afraid you're going to be disappointed. Jonathan Cade told me that he had stayed behind and was living with them on the *Painted Lady*, but I never saw him.'

'Did you know about the manuscript he claimed to have brought out of the USSR?'

'Yes, I heard about it.'

'Mr Cade told you?'

'I think it was someone else. I can't remember.'

'I see. Well, perhaps you'll search your memory. Would you mind telling me what you were doing last Tuesday afternoon?'

'Is that when he was killed?'

Roland ignored this. 'Were you here?'

'Tuesday is early closing day here. As we keep open at the weekends – we get most of our custom then –

we close Tuesday afternoon. In fact, some of the units are closed all day on Tuesday.'

Damn! thought Roland, I should have checked that before. I wonder if it will help or hinder my enquiries?

'So you weren't here in the craft centre. Where were you?'

'I was visiting a friend who lives in Old Blund.'

'Presumably she can confirm this. May I have her name and address?'

'It's a he, Inspector. I don't suppose he'll mind my divulging his particulars. As far as I know he's not cheating on an abandoned wife.'

'Is he a local person?'

'No, he's looking after a friend's house for a few months whilst this friend is abroad on business.'

'So he is out of work?'

'I wouldn't say that. *I* keep him busy and he's a freelance journalist who seems to find plenty to write about in the area.'

A journalist – that was all he needed! Roland kept his voice deliberately neutral. 'You were going to tell me his name.'

'Yes, I was, wasn't I? I mustn't tease you, Inspector.' She gave him an enticing smile, and when he ignored it, continued cheerfully: 'He's Nick Blackstone and he lives in the Old Smokehouse in Findleys Drift.'

Roland noted it down. 'Does he know about Mikhail Rabinovich?'

'Naturally I told him all I knew – wouldn't you have? But he doesn't know about him being found murdered; he's been in London for the last three days on business.'

'When are you expecting him back?'

'I have no idea. I'm not his keeper.'

'Have you an address or telephone number where we can contact him?'

'No, Inspector. We don't keep tabs on each other, it's not that kind of relationship. Are you so anxious to prove my alibi?'

'Mrs Lingard, you have just told me that he is a journalist. I don't want this story to break in the newspapers yet.'

He could just see it: two-inch high headlines splashed across the front of the tabloids. It would severely hamper their investigations and Lacey would have an apoplectic fit.

'You're afraid he may be filing copy even now?'

'Is it likely, Mrs Lingard? Or wouldn't he tell you?'

'He was hoping to get a good story out of it, I admit, but he was still in the process of following it up. I don't think he will have tried publishing anything yet.'

Roland changed the subject. 'Are you familiar with the *Painted Lady*? Have you been on board?'

'I went to a party there once, some time ago, but I haven't been since – I don't believe in wasting my talents, Inspector!'

No, I bet you don't, thought Roland. Her sexuality was a tangible thing, permeating the small room like an animal odour. Perhaps he should have kept Mansfield with him after all.

'Thank you, Mrs Lingard, that will be all for now. I should like you to go into the station as soon as possible and make a formal statement and have your fingerprints taken.'

'Anything to oblige. Are they all as handsome as you?'

'Perhaps you will let me know the minute Mr Blackstone returns. You can leave a message in the station if I'm not there.'

Roland left the building feeling he had escaped a close encounter that a small part of him had not wanted to evade. Only a very small part, he admitted. Ginny was all he wanted, all he needed. Ginny was sanity, Ginny was everything. Even in her present bloated state she was more attractive than a hundred Stella Lingards. He loosened his tie and rejoined his sergeant.

'Any luck?'

'It was early closing day here, as I expect you've found out,' said Mansfield. 'Cade says that he cycled over to Woodford to do some shopping. He says a lot of people must have seen him but he can't produce any actual names. I suppose he could easily have popped back to the *Painted Lady*, done the dastardly deed *and* fitted in his shopping expedition. How did you get on?'

Roland filled him in and Mansfield exclaimed: 'Christ, a journalist! She's having a bit of nookey with one of the Gentlemen of the Press! I wonder where that leaves us?'

'I shudder to think, but I tell you something – I recognised his name and if he gets on to this we'll be up against opposition. He's the bloke who exposed the Dumford prison riot scandal – do you remember that – he's made a name for himself in investigative journalism and I don't like his being involved, not one little bit. Come on, let's go and find Laura Nelson. No, on second thoughts, we'll go and get a coffee first.'

* * *

The cafe was doing a steady trade. Roland presumed that most of the customers were visitors to the Maltings but some of them at least must be people who were employed in some capacity or other in the complex. He wondered if they would ever run to earth everyone who had heard the rumours about Mikhail Rabinovich. A place like this was a little town in itself, a miniature Vatican City where whispers and rumours circulated and everyone knew everyone else's business.

'A penny for them,' said Mansfield, as they took their coffee over to a table by a window.

'We have a list of people who definitely knew about Mikhail Rabinovich but what's the betting that a lot of other people, who we'll never know about, got to hear about it too?'

'We need a lead. Perhaps Forensics will come up with something.'

'We can always hope, but don't pin too much faith on it.'

Their window overlooked the river and reedbeds. The recent squall had departed as quickly as it had blown up and the sun had re-appeared, glistening on the wet rushes. A thousand drops of water spangled like a sea of sequins as a breeze snaked through, feathering them this way and that. A couple of mallards shot across the river skimming the surface and in the far distance a combine harvester moved across a golden field – a toy machine crossing a toy field.

'Beautiful now, isn't it?' said Mansfield, getting out his pipe and starting the complicated business of lighting up. 'I can't think why people hanker after mountains and lakes when they've got scenery like this.'

'You're prejudiced, Pat, because you're a Suffolk man, born and bred. Many people would find this flat and uninteresting.'

'They want their heads seen to.'

Part of the back of the shopping arcade could be seen over to the left of them and as the two men looked idly out of the window a woman came out of a door carrying a brush and dustpan. She threw the contents of the dustpan on to the scorched grass and immediately a flock of sparrows and pigeons fluttered to her feet, strutting and pecking at the bounty she had scattered for them.

'I wonder if that's Laura Nelson?' said Mansfield, straining to see which building she had gone back into. 'One of those must be the health food store.'

'Let's go see. Put that damn' pipe out before you set the place on fire. I'm sure this is a no-smoking area.'

'Wishful thinking.' The older man grinned as he tapped out his pipe in the large ashtray provided.

'I read a very interesting article the other day about passive smoking – I reckon my days are numbered. I ought to get danger money.'

'Bullshit!'

As they entered the health food store Mansfield tripped over a basket of apples that was standing on the floor not far from the door. They rolled over the stone flags and he cursed and bent to pick them up, helped by his companion. He had just put the last one back and replaced the card that stated they were organically grown when the young woman reached them from the other side of the shop.

'Can I help you?'

'Are you Miss Laura Nelson?'

She affirmed this with obvious apprehension and Roland introduced himself and his sergeant.

'We are enquiring into the death of the Russian, Mikhail Rabinovich. I have a few questions to ask you.'

She paled and stared at them out of wide, blue eyes. 'The Russian?'

'Are you all right, Miss Nelson?'

'Yes . . . I'm sorry.' She made a visible effort to pull herself together. 'It was just the shock of hearing you say that.'

'You did know about his death?'

'Yes, it was a terrible accident.'

'I'm afraid it was no accident. Mikhail Rabinovich was murdered.'

'Murdered? But how awful! Are you sure?'

'I think you had better sit down.'

'No, I'm all right . . . I'm sorry to be so silly. It's just that . . .'

'I know, it's the first time you've ever come up against anything like this,' said Mansfield soothingly. 'Don't worry, even us hardened police officers aren't immune.'

She flashed him a grateful smile. 'What do you want to ask me?'

'We're checking up on everyone who knew about him staying on the *Painted Lady* after the St Petersburg Orchestra went back to Russia.'

Roland took over the questioning. 'I believe you are one of those people?'

'Yes, I knew about it.'

'How come, Miss Nelson? Are you a friend of Mr Spender and Mr Cade? Did you actually meet Mikhail Rabinovich?'

'Yes, to both your questions.'

Roland and Mansfield exchanged a quick look. This could be crucial; someone who admitted to meeting the Russian apart from their two chief suspects.

'Would you please tell us all that you know about the situation? No matter how insignificant you may think them, the details could be important.'

'I learned about him from Jonathan – Mr Cade – in the first place, I think, but several people here knew about it,' she said rather vaguely. 'He was staying with them until he felt it was safe to go to the authorities and officially ask for asylum.'

'And you actually met him?'

'Yes, I was invited to a meal on the *Painted Lady* and he was there.'

'And?' prompted Roland.

'What do you mean?'

'I mean, what impression did you get of him? You are one of the few people who actually saw him. Your evidence could be important.'

'Well, he seemed a very ordinary sort of person. It was hard to believe that he was a well-known musician. He wasn't egotistical or puffed up with his own importance. And believe you me, Inspector, I meet a great many professionals working here as I do and many of them have very inflated egos.'

'I'm sure they have. Did he appear at all apprehensive or frightened?'

'No, the complete opposite in fact. He seemed very contented and at ease. He spoke very good English and was joking about the weather and English food. He really seemed more like someone enjoying a holiday than a fugitive.'

'Did you know about the musical manuscript he claimed to have?'

'The Shostakovich? Yes, he had it there on the boat.'

'You saw it?'

'Yes, it didn't look very impressive. Just an old green folder stuffed with loose sheets of paper. I thought it was rather careless – the way he left it lying around on top of the piano. Something as valuable as that should have been kept under lock and key. It wasn't fair on Barry, being responsible for something like that.'

'Do you think it was genuine?'

'It's no good asking me, I'm no expert, but he certainly thought so, he wasn't trying to pull a fast one.' She looked surprised. 'Haven't you had it authenticated? Who does it belong to now?'

'Miss Nelson, the manuscript is missing. I thought that you realised that.'

'Missing?'

'We believe that Mikhail Rabinovich was killed for that manuscript.'

She digested this. 'You mean someone who knew about it killed him to get their hands on it?'

The two detective remained silent and as the significance of what she had just said dawned on her, she continued in agitation: 'You suspect me? *I'm* one of your suspects?'

'Miss Nelson, I'm not accusing you of anything but you must see that we have to check out everyone like yourself in order to eliminate them, Perhaps you mentioned the matter of the manuscript to other people? It would make an interesting topic of conversation.'

'No . . . no, I'm quite sure I didn't.'

'Well, if you do remember mentioning it to anyone, perhaps you'll let us know. What were you doing last Tuesday afternoon?'

'Last Tuesday afternoon? Was that when he was killed? I thought he had fallen overboard and drowned.' She gulped. 'It was early closing day. I was hoping to work in the garden.'

'You live in the village?'

'Yes, in Keeper's Cottage in Bridge Lane.'

'And you spent the afternoon gardening?'

'I got very little done, we kept having heavy showers. I got fed up with popping in and out and gave up in the end and stayed indoors to write some letters.'

'Did anyone see you?'

'Whilst I was in the garden? I must have been in view of passers-by but nobody called out. Wait a minute . . . I saw the paperboy delivering the evening papers. I had a few words with him.'

'What time would that have been?'

'I'm not sure . . . mid-afternoon? He always comes earlier in the school holidays.'

'No doubt he'll remember.'

Roland gave her the same instructions about making a formal statement and having her fingerprints taken, and the two detectives left her to serve the customer who had come into the store.

'She seems a nice young woman,' said Mansfield as they left the Maltings to walk across to the librarian's house. 'Rather a nervy type, though. She seemed genuinely surprised to hear that the manuscript has gone missing. Did you believe her?'

'She would say that if she had taken it, wouldn't she? To try and throw us off the scent.'

'You think it could have been her?'

'You can't cross her off just because you think she's a nice girl, but I must admit she strikes me as the sort of person who would have difficulty in saying boo to a goose. But there's no reason why a woman couldn't have done it. It didn't take much strength to creep up on him unawares, tap him over the head with a handy weapon and tip him over the side. Let's see what Mr Coleman has to say for himself.'

There was a pause of several minutes before the door opened on what at first appeared to be an empty hall. Finally the two detectives lowered their gaze and realised that the person who had answered their ring was a woman in a wheelchair. There must be some sort of electronic device that allowed her to open the door without grappling with the handle, thought Roland, taking in her appearance. She looked like someone left over from the nineteen-twenties; that sleek cap of black hair, the white face, the red gash of her lips. A couple of his friends from the Squash Club, who collected Art Deco, had a mirror held by a figure whose face could have been modelled on hers.

'What do you want? I don't buy from door-to-door salesmen.'

The voice was at once querulous and authoritative. Roland introduced them and she narrowed her eyes and inspected them carefully.

'I suppose you've come about the Russian? It was obvious it would end in tragedy.'

'Is your husband at home, Mrs Coleman?'

'You'd better come in.' She backed down the hall and the two men followed her, wondering if they should offer to help when she appeared to get stuck in the doorway. However, with a quick turn of the wheel she manoeuvred the chair into the room and turned back to face them.

'You'd think I'd be used to handling this damn' thing by now, wouldn't you? I've been disabled long enough.' There was rage and frustration in her pale face and her hands shook on the arm rests.

'It must be very difficult for you.'

'You can have no idea what it is like, two hale and hearty men like you.'

'Yes, it must be hard to accept.'

'I don't accept it, Inspector. I never shall! Why is it that everybody expects a handicapped person to be all sweetness and light, grateful for any crumbs of comfort that may come their way? I shall never be resigned to my state and I don't want pity!'

'Your husband?'

'I'm sorry. You haven't come here to listen to the woes of a cripple, I mustn't embarrass you.' Roland was sure that this was just what she was trying to do. 'I'll call him, he's in the garden.'

The room they were in was a sitting room with french doors that stood open to the garden beyond. She wheeled herself over to these.

'Dennis? The police are here.'

Roland had followed her across the room and could see a figure amongst the runner bean rows at the bottom of the garden. He looked up, alarmed at his wife's voice, and pottered up the path, a trug of runner beans over his arm.

'You'd better sit down, Inspector, Sergeant. I don't like people looming over me.'

Dennis Coleman appeared in the doorway. He looked hot and dishevelled, his glasses were steamed up and shrivelled bean blossoms clung to his sparse hair and checked shirt.

'Dennis, these police officers have come to question you about the Russian.'

'Thank you, Mrs Coleman, this shouldn't take long. We don't need to detain you.'

'Dennis has no secrets from me, Inspector. He has told me all about this business.'

'All that I know,' corrected her husband, 'which isn't very much. Perhaps you had better leave us, dear? The inspector may have some details which are not nice hearing for a woman's ears.'

'Don't be ridiculous, Dennis, there's nothing he can tell you that I'm not able to cope with.'

Roland resigned himself to a participating audience.

'It was a terrible thing to happen,' said Dennis Coleman, setting the trug down on a coffee table and wiping his glasses, 'after all that plotting and planning. I wonder if they'll premier it themselves? I suppose if they leave a decent gap they'll hope that nobody over here will remember the episode.'

'I'm afraid you've lost me, Mr Coleman. To what are you referring?'

'He must have planned this for ages. He hung on to the manuscript all those years since Shostakovich's death, biding his time, and when the chance came he took it. But just when he thought he was safe, they caught up with him.'

'You think his death was engineered by the Russians?'

'It's obvious, Inspector,' chipped in Helen Coleman. 'Once they realised what had happened they couldn't let him get away with it. Believe me, I know what I'm talking about.'

'Really?'

'Yes. I was a ballet dancer in my youth. I know it's difficult to believe, seeing me as I am now . . .' she gave a harsh little laugh, '. . . but I was good, had promise as they say. Anyway, I've been to the USSR on tour and I know how they operate over there; how jealously they guard their artistes; how little freedom they have. They wouldn't let Mikhail Rabinovich leave of his own free will, especially if they knew about the score he was trying to smuggle out. As soon as they realised he had disappeared, wheels were set in motion and he was a doomed man.'

'I don't think things are quite like that these days, Mrs Coleman.'

'Aren't they? Then if it wasn't the Russians, who did it?'

'That's what I am here to find out.'

He had momentarily silenced her and took advantage of this to direct his questions at her husband.

'You know that Mikhail Rabinovich was living on the *Painted Lady*? I believe you saw him and actually examined the manuscript?'

'Yes, I did. I think Spender and Cade wanted to know if it was genuine without putting his back up.'

'And was it?'

'Yes. I think it was. I wouldn't be prepared to swear to that in a court of law,' he added hurriedly, 'on the brief examination I made, but it certainly looked like his handwriting, and the short excerpts they played me certainly sounded vintage Shostakovich.'

'Could you describe it?'

'There were about 150 sheets of music manuscript paper tucked inside a dirty old folder. All the parts were there – he'd written them all out for each member of the orchestra. There was some writing on the cover in what I could swear was Shostakovich's writing – I'm quite familiar with it, we have several samples in the library – and I know enough Russian to be able to translate it roughly. It was dedicated to Mikhail. To his "dear friend M.R.", I think it actually said.'

'Mr Cheyney, the director of the Maltings, thinks it could not be utilised by the person or persons who stole it. If it turns up in someone else's possession the family of Shostakovich would claim it, as they would all revenues deriving from performance and publication due to copyright. He thinks its value lies in how much an unscrupulous collector would pay to add it to his collection.'

'A bit far-fetched, I would have said, and you're not quite right about this matter of copyright.'

'What do you mean?'

'In this country, the PRS, the Performing Rights Society, collects the revenues accruing from performance, etcetera, and the composer or the composer's estate receives part of it back in royalties. When a Russian work is preformed in the West this revenue is collected and transmitted back to Moscow to the VAAP, which is the Russian equivalent of our PRS, but only a tiny fraction of this reaches the composer or his heirs. Most of it goes into the General Cultural Fund which was set up to support Soviet artistes and their families. Of course, you could say that they benefit indirectly but they don't get hard cash.'

Dennis Coleman leaned forward.

'Mind you, Inspector, things are changing in the USSR these days and I believe that there are moves afoot to bring the whole business more in line with western ways. No, I wouldn't mind betting the Ruskies have got their hands on it. Mark my words, in a few years time the 3rd Cello Concerto will turn up in the repertoire of a Russian orchestra.'

'This is most interesting, Mr Coleman. Would you mind telling me what you were doing last Tuesday afternoon?'

The librarian looked blank.

'It was early closing day,' prompted Roland.

'Yes, yes, quite. I stayed in my office. I was putting together a catalogue of all our Baroque chamber music and I wanted to get it finished so it could go to the printers.'

'Dennis works even on his day off,' said his wife bitterly, 'he always puts his work before me.'

'Helen!' exclaimed Coleman wretchedly.

'Were any of your assistants there with you?' asked Roland.

'No, I was on my own all the afternoon. I found it easier to get the job done without constant interruptions.'

'The inspector is trying to find out whether anyone can prove your alibi Dennis,' said Helen Coleman. 'I take it last Tuesday afternoon was when the murder was done?'

'I'm afraid you'll have to take my word for it,' said the librarian, even more wretchedly when Roland ignored his wife's question. 'I didn't see a soul the whole afternoon.'

* * * *

'Well, Patrick, what do you think of that little set-up?' asked Roland as they walked back to where they had left the car.

'If she had been the one to be knocked off you could understand who had done it and why. Poor chap, I feel more sorry for him than for his wife. She's really embittered, isn't she?'

'I reckon she has reason to be but it can't make life any easier for him. I should imagine her attitude drives away anyone who might give them a helping hand.'

'I suppose she couldn't have done it?' said Mansfield hopefully.

'Not if she really is crippled, and we must presume that is so. Perhaps they were in it together and she is the driving force behind it all.'

'Like Lady Macbeth, you mean?'

'I can certainly see her in the role of Lady Macbeth but he doesn't fit the bill. Well, so far none of our suspects can provide an alibi that can be substantiated. It's going to be one of those cases. I want you and Evans to come back here this afternoon and see if you can winkle out anyone else who may have got to hear about the Russian. You can also see if you can find anyone who can corroborate the two alibis we've been given so far.'

'Have we got one for Barry Spender?'

'He claims that he spent all afternoon in his workshop putting a piano together. Of course, according to him, he saw nobody and nobody saw him.'

'Maybe it's a conspiracy and they were all in it together.'

'You do your best to cheer me up, don't you, Patrick?'

* * *

Stella Lingard caught up with Laura Nelson at lunch-time as they were both crossing the courtyard at the Maltings and by mutual consent they sat down together on one of the rustic bench seats and discussed their experiences with the police whilst eating their sandwiches.

'It seems that anyone who admits to knowing about the presence of the Russian has come under suspicion,' said Stella, brushing away an intrusive wasp.

'I suppose they have to start somewhere,' said her companion, 'but they really latched on to the fact that I had actually been aboard the *Painted Lady* and met him.'

'So the wind still blows in that direction?'

'What do you mean?'

'That you're still trying to make it with Jonathan. You're wasting your time – forget him and find someone else. You wouldn't catch me hankering after someone like that.'

'No. Well, you're different.'

'Yes, I am, aren't I? But you're the one who's odd, not me. I wouldn't mind betting you're still a virgin. Are you, Laura?' Her eyes gleamed mischievously. 'Haven't you ever had it off with a man?'

The younger woman flushed scarlet and snapped the lid on her lunchbox.

'All you think of is sex!'

'It's what makes the world go round. I'm sorry, Laura, I shouldn't tease but you're an endangered species, you know. There's not many of you around.'

'I am *not* a virgin.' She stood up and collected her belongings together.

'Are you going already?' asked Stella Lingard, rather taken aback by the ferocity in her companion's voice.

'Yes. I find this a pointless conversation and my private life is no business of yours.'

As Laura walked back through the archway Stella stared after her in dismay. Help, she'd put her foot in it! Something was bugging the girl, she'd really got a hang-up. Strangely enough, Stella believed what she had said about not being a virgin; she hadn't been trying to climb on the bandwaggon by pretending to something she hadn't experienced. She must have had an unfortunate affair sometime in her past, a sexual experience that had gone wrong and turned her sour. Stella's thoughts ran riot. Perhaps she'd been the victim of an attack, even been raped. It might account for her being attracted by someone like Jonathan who was not a threat to her in that way. Subconsciously she had chosen someone who would not be sexually interested in her . . . But enough of these Freudian suppositions; she'd upset Laura badly and would have to try and put things right.

She picked up her bag and walked back to the craft centre. Thank God she was not repressed by any sexual inhibitions!

That afternoon, as Roland sat in his office trying to collate the evidence they had collected so far, the duty sergeant on the front desk rang through.

'I've got someone here, sir, who's asking for you. Says his name is Mikhail Rabinovich.'

Chapter 5

'Sir? Are you there, sir?'

'Would you mind repeating that?'

'I've got a bloke here who wants to see you, says his name is Mikhail Rabinovich. Do you know him?'

'Sergeant, Mikhail Rabinovich is tucked away in a mortuary drawer.'

There was a pause from the other end of the line, and then:

'He looks and sounds foreign, sir. I think you'd better see him.'

Roland slammed down the phone and pounded down the stairs, prepared to make short shrift of the joker who was wasting police time and resources. He ground to a halt when he saw the figure sitting on the bench and did a double-take. For a few seconds he thought it was the man he had last seen, very dead, on the mortuary table. Then the figure moved and turned to face him and he saw his mistake. There was a fleeting resemblance, they were of the same race, but that was all.

'This is the man, sir.' The sergeant came from behind the counter and spoke to the caller. 'This is Detective Inspector Roland, tell him what you have just told me.'

The man looked at Roland. There was the same tilt to his eyes but he was frailer and his black, stringy hair was liberally streaked with grey.

'I am Mikhail Rabinovich.'

'Mikhail Rabinovich is dead,' said Roland flatly.

'He is imposter. *I* am the real Mikhail Rabinovich.' He sounded very sure and very convincing.

'Look, we'd better have a talk, and I hope for your sake you're not wasting my time. Is there an interview room free?' Roland asked the duty sergeant.

A few minutes later he was installed in an interview room gazing at the little man who sat opposite him. The man returned his gaze serenely and waited for Roland to speak.

'Mikhail Rabinovich, who was principal cellist with the St Petersburg Orchestra, was taken dead out of a river near here last week. We believe he was murdered.'

'That was not the real Mikhail Rabinovich, that was an imposter.'

'Are you trying to tell me there are, or were, two of you?'

'Only one real one. I think I explain to you, Inspector.'

'I think you should, and it had better be good.'

'It is a long story and it start a long time ago but I swear to you it is the truth.'

Whilst thoughts of twins, mistaken identity and immigration fraud jostled around in Roland's mind, the man sitting opposite fixed him with a black glittering stare, like the Ancient Mariner's, and began to speak.

'I was principal cellist with the St Petersburgh Orchestra from 1969. There is much good times but I was not happy with the system. I try to conform but I am stifled – many, many restrictions. My good friend Mstislav Rostropovich, he get out in 1974 and go to live in West and I decide to follow him when is possible. My wife, she die soon after this and I have no children no family left in Russia. Then a year later, in 1975, the orchestra goes on tour in Europe. It play here at Blund Maltings for the final concert and I decide to leave, to stay here in England, maybe go to America later. My wife, she was Hungarian and she have relations here – a cousin who escape from Hungary in 1956 and come to live in England, they kept in touch. I arrange to go and stay with this cousin, she live in Essex. After the last concert I disappear and go to Màrta. She keep me hidden. We wait one, two, three days, then we go to the authorities and I give myself up.'

'The authorities? Are you talking about the Home Office?'

'Yes, the Immigration and Nationality Department in Croydon.'

'But if they investigated your claim, how come . . . ?'

'Please, Inspector, I explain.' He continued his story.

'I apply for refugee status and am given temporary admission. While I wait for my case to be assessed, I live with Màrta. One day I have accident – I am run over by bus and taken to hospital. It is not bad accident but I have neck injury – I fear I not play the cello again. While I am in hospital it is announced in the papers that Mikhail Rabinovich was taken ill at the end of his stay in England and is now in Moscow clinic having treatment for very serious illness. Màrta brings me this news and then the officials come to see me in hospital. They do not believe me because of this report and I panic and leave the hospital.'

'You mean, you discharged yourself?'

'Yes, that is so. I go to stay with friends of Màrta. They look after me and I lie low. I am afraid the British officials will hand me back to the Russians. I stay with them a long time. My injury gets better, it is fine. For you, for anyone else, it is alright, but for me, I am finished with cello.'

'You mean that for most people your recovery would be termed complete but it left you with enough of a handicap to prevent you playing the cello?' Roland was intrigued in spite of himself.

'You understand. For cellist a neck injury is the end. I can still play, I am good, but no longer can be concert cellist. That is finished.'

'Go on.'

'Màrta's friends get me some papers so I can stay here and work.'

'You mean, you're living here on forged papers?'

He ignored this. 'I re-marry and I make a new life for myself. I teach pupils to play the cello and I learn to make the string instruments – cello, violin, viola. And that is how it is, Inspector.'

He raised his shoulders in a very continental shrug.

'Oh no it isn't! What about this little matter of the other Mikhail Rabinovich?'

'Patience, I am telling you all.' He settled back and seemed to go into a trance. 'This is what happen. I live quietly in this country with my new wife. I expect to see, any day, an announcement from Moscow that Mikhail Rabinovich has died, but nothing happen. Six months pass, a year, two year – nothing happen, and then I read in papers that Mikhail Rabinovich has made a complete recovery from his illness and is once more lead cellist with the St Petersburg Orchestra. I am amazed! I do not understand! But later I see newspaper photograph of orchestra and I know what has happened.' He leaned forward and said dramatically: 'They put someone in my place!'

'You mean they substituted someone for you?'

'Yes, that is so.'

'But who was it? How could they hope to deceive anybody?'

'It was old colleague of mine: Mikhail Temirkanov. He is few years younger and play with the St Petersburg many, many years. He is good, but not great like me.' This was spoken as a fact, not a boast. 'We were not unalike, we were both natives of Tashkent, and the Western world does not notice the substitution.'

'But what about the rest of the orchestra and the Russian public? Why did the Russians do this?'

'You must know that this was very bad time for them. There had been many defections – musicians, ballet dancers, athletes – and they did not want to lose face further. When I did not appear in the West after my defection they must have thought that I was dead and they decide to take advantage of it by coaching someone to take my place and deceive the rest of the world. My fellow countrymen – they believe what they are told to believe!'

'So, you are asking me to believe that the Mikhail Rabinovich who has been with the orchestra since 1975 is an imposter?'

'Yes, it is truth, you must believe me.'

'And what about his part in this deception?'

'He would have been told I was dead. He would be flattered to get the chance to step into my shoes. He has much better lifestyle, it would be fine by him, but he didn't make the grade.'

'Make the grade?'

'Yes, that is right expression, is it not? If I were still cellist I would be famous by now, in demand all over the world. Mikhail Temirkanov is still only principal cellist in orchestra, he is not front rank.'

'So why, after all this time, did he too decide to defect to the West?'

'Perhaps they are dissatisfied with his performance? He think he can do better in the West and he get out while he still can.'

'Or perhaps he thought the manuscript would bring him fame and fortune.' Roland said it carelessly but watched carefully for the other man's reaction.

'Manuscript? What you say?'

'He had a manuscript which he claimed was the 3rd Cello Concerto of Shostakovich, written for and dedicated to him.'

The effect on the other man was extraordinary. He started to his feet and wrung his hands in jubilation whilst his voice soared in excitement.

'He kept his word! He finished it – my dear friend Dmitri! All these years I have wondered what happened to it. I think he don't complete it, for he was very ill towards the end – I think perhaps he never start it, it was just promise.'

'You know about this manuscript?'

'Why, yes, I tell you! Dmitri always say he write a third concerto.'

'Which he dedicated to you, and the bogus Mikhail Rabinovich tried to cash in on it!'

'Dedicated to me? Oh, no, Inspector, that is not so.'

'I have been told by those who actually saw it that there is a dedication on the cover: "To my dear friend M.R."'

'That is big joke! No, he write it for Mstislav Rostropovich. The first two concertos were also written for him. When last I see Dmitri he says he is working on a third concerto which he wish to be premiered in the West by Rostropovich. I was to bring it out.'

'Now, let me get this clear. Shostakovich himself told you he was writing this concerto and he wanted you to get it to Rostropovich, who, I believe, lives in the States? Did he know that you were going to defect?'

'We had discussed it. He knew I was very unhappy and it was his wish that I should bring the manuscript out of Russia when I go on tour. But things go wrong. Dmitri is ill for long time – bad heart. I do not see him, I do not know if he write the concerto. I come to England with the orchestra in the summer of 1975 and while we are here he dies. Is very sad. I think the music not written, or lost, but now . . .' he beamed at the detective and grasped his hands '. . . it has turn up! We have the last work of most brilliant composer of this century!'

Roland came within a whisker of being embraced in a bear hug. He side-stepped and waved the Russian back to his seat.

'Unfortunately we do not have the manuscript.'

'What you mean? You say Mikhail Temirkanov bring it with him out of Russia, that he wish to make money out of it?'

'I believe that the man whom I know of as Mikhail Rabinovich was murdered by someone who knew about the manuscript and killed him to gain possession of it.'

'Is so? How terrible!' He shrunk back in his chair, his euphoria completely evaporated, and gazed at Roland with tragic eyes.

'Tell me, how do you think he got hold of this manuscript in the first place?'

'Who know?' Perhaps Dmitri give it in safe-keeping to a friend before he die and it is left in my flat to await my return and Temirkanov find it. We shall never know now.'

Which just about summed it up, thought Roland, but there was something else puzzling him.

'Why have you decided now, after all this time, to come to the police?'

'Because he was imposter. *I* am Mikhail Rabinovich and I could not live the lie any longer.'

'And where do you live and what alias are you living under now?'

'In Woodford. I am calling myself Miklos Rakosi but my friends call me Mick – that is English name, yes?' He gave Roland his address and looked at him anxiously. 'What will happen to me now?'

'I really don't know. This extraordinary tale will have to be investigated. If you are telling the truth we should be able at least to check out this end of it, though there is the little matter of your living and working here as an illegal immigrant.'

'I can apply for the right papers, can I not, Inspector? It is not too late? I have been good citizen for these last seventeen years.'

'That's not for me to decide. In the meanwhile keep yourself available for further questioning and don't tell anyone else what you have just told me. As far as the public are concerned the Mikhail Rabinovich who was killed was the one and only Mikhail Rabinovich, do you understand?'

'I may go?'

'As long as you promise not to run away again.'

He got up to go and then hesitated. 'That manuscript . . . if only I could have seen it . . . played it. It would be very wonderful.'

'It may turn up. Let us hope the world has not lost a new masterpiece.'

Roland escorted his visitor out of the building. He had driven himself to the Station in an ancient Morris Minor which he had parked on the forecourt in total disregard of notices stating that it was for police personnel only, and the car was arousing great interest among a group of police cadets who were gathered round it. Roland cleared them away and waited whilst the Russian unlocked it and got into the driving seat. As he started up the engine the detective bent down and spoke through the open window.

'By the way, what happened to the Hungarian cousin you stayed with when you first came to England?'

'Màrta? But did you not understand, Inspector – Màrta is my second wife. She work at Blund Maltings.'

'You're having me on, this is some joke!'

'Check with the duty sergeant if you don't believe me. He walked in here as bold as brass and announced that he was Mikhail Rabinovich.' Mansfield snorted. 'And you believe him?'

'Yes, I think I do,' said Roland calmly. 'I've been in touch with Lunar House and they're checking their records and promised to get back to us as soon as possible.'

'It sounds too far-fetched to me, taking over another person's identity. How did he get away with the fact of looking different? Surely people would have noticed that it was a different man?'

'There is a superficial resemblance in looks and build. Don't forget they both came from the same part of Russia, and if anyone had thought that he looked changed – well, he was supposed to have been very ill for a couple of years which could have accounted for it. I think this is a case of fact being stranger than fiction, but where does it leave us?'

'With another suspect, I should say. How did he get to know about the other Russian anyway?'

'His wife works at the Maltings. She helps out in the boutique. She must have got to hear about it and passed it on to him.'

'And they decided to bump him off and steal the manuscript?'

'I'm convinced he knew nothing about the manuscript until I told him. His reaction was genuine, I'd stake my life on it; delight, and then disappointment when he realised that it is missing.'

'Well then, perhaps they killed him out of revenge.'

'That is a possibility, but if so, why bring his part in it to my attention? He claims that he wants to put the record straight, but after all this time it just doesn't ring true. I think they may have been rivals and there was probably bad blood between them which he has not admitted to, but there must be another reason for his suddenly coming to us, especially as it makes him a suspect. I wonder what it is? And where is the manuscript? If they didn't know that it existed they couldn't have taken it, but the fact remains that it is missing, someone has nobbled it.'

Mansfield sucked on his empty pipe. 'Have you thought that maybe his death *was* accidental? That maybe he slipped and banged his head on the side of the boat as he fell in and then drowned because he was unconscious? Spender and Cade may have gone back to the boat, seen signs of his fall and realised what had happened. They decided to cash in on it so they stole the manuscript, tipped his luggage over the side, and then pretended that they thought that he had done a bunk.'

'I might go along with that if I hadn't just received this.' Roland tapped the papers in front of him. 'It's the other thing that I wanted to tell you. Forensics have come up trumps. They found a tiny piece of hair snarled in the rough wood of one of those pieces of timber that were found in the river; it matches up with the victim's hair. There's no doubt – he was hit over the head before he entered the water.'

'So where do we go from here?'

'How did you and Evans get on with checking the alibis?'

'Nothing checked out. Dennis Coleman was pre-sumed to be in the library but nobody actually saw him there and nobody admits to having seen him elsewhere in the area that afternoon. Stella Lingard's lover-boy has not returned yet so we haven't been able to check that one but she was not seen around either. Cade was seen on his cycle leaving the Maltings at about one-thirty but God knows where he went after that. Evans is still checking the shops in Woodford which he reckons he visited. Spender, like Coleman, is supposed to have been closeted in his work-place and no one set eyes on him. Laura Nelson did speak with the paper-boy at about four-fifteen – we've checked with him – but that still leaves all the afternoon before that unaccounted for. Oh, wait a minute, we did discover one fact which may or may not be significant: Mrs Lingard says that it was Laura Nelson who told her about the manuscript but Laura told us that she hadn't mentioned it to anyone.'

'You didn't challenge her?'

'We interviewed Stella Lingard after Laura Nelson and we didn't go back to her.'

'We'll have to tackle her about it but she'll probably say she forgot. She was very flustered at that first interview and you know how muddled witnesses can get if they're agitated.'

'Any luck with fingerprints?'

'They've found Laura Nelson's and Coleman's on the *Painted Lady* which means nothing as they've both admitted to having been on board recently. Stella Lingard's haven't turned up which also tallies with what she told us. She'd only been on the boat once a long time ago, some party or other. They found a mass of prints all over the place, Spender is not the world's best housekeeper; he and a duster and polish are not on familiar terms. They did find a very good set of dabs on the outside of the cabin door which they can't match up with anyone so far, but that doesn't mean a thing.'

'Surely our murderer would have worn gloves anyway?'

'Yes, we're going to have to tackle it from another angle. I'm still waiting for a flash of inspiration.'

'What has the Super had to say about this latest development?'

'He doesn't know yet. He's up in Norfolk this afternoon at some meeting or other. He's not going to be very happy when I break it to him. He was jittery enough about one Russian being involved. When he learns that there are two and one of them is currently masquerading under a Hungarian alias, he's going to hit the roof!'

Ginny Roland sat on the sofa with her legs propped up on a stool and stitched listlessly at the baby gown she was embroidering. At the other end of the sofa Faience, the cat, stretched out on the bag of silks and regarded her mistress through half-closed amber eyes. She pricked up her ears and raised her head at the sound of movement in the hall. Simon burst through the door, clutching a pile of magazines and tapes.

'Isn't James home yet?'

'No, but he shouldn't be long. He hasn't rung to say he's going to be late. Are you going out?'

'I was going to Mark's but I can leave it till later.'

'Don't be silly, off you go.'

'But I don't like to leave you . . .'

'Simon, I'm perfectly all right, nothing's going to happen yet. You go off and enjoy yourself.'

He was a tall, gawky teenager who had outgrown his strength, all elbows and knees. His dark, unruly hair stuck up in a crest and he looked not unlike his stepfather, a fact that afforded Ginny much secret amusement. He came over and dropped down by his mother.

'How's Fred?'

'It's not Fred, it's Freda.'

'You can't call it Freda! You're not going to call it Freda if it's a girl?' He was scandalised.

'You know what we said – we won't decide on a name till after it's born – but what grabs your fancy?'

'What about Esmerelda?'

'So who's been reading *The Hunchback*?'

'Perhaps it is a bit fancy. How about Estelle? I think it should start with an E.'

'Why?'

'I dunno, there's a lot of nice names that begin with an E.'

'Like Ellen and Elaine and Eleanor . . .'

'And Edith and Erica and Edna . . .'

'And Eunice and Eugenie and Ermyntrude. And if it's a boy we'll call him Ethelbert!'

They collapsed in giggles and she ruffled his hair.

'That sounds like James now. I hope he doesn't have to go out again this evening.'

He had left the car in the drive instead of putting it away in the garage, an ominous sign. She smiled up at him as he came into the room and he bent down and planted a kiss on her upturned face.

'How are the two of us?'

'Fine and kicking well. What sort of day have you had?'

'Interesting. I'll put you in the picture later. How is that school project going?' He turned to Simon.

'I'm stuck. Can you help me with it later?'

'If I can. We'll go over it together and see what we can work out.'

'Stepfathers have their uses,' said Ginny with a smile

after Simon had left, 'that's one thing I could never have helped him with. Maths was never my strong point.'

'I thought it was a biology project?'

'It's a joint biology, history and geography project but he's stuck on the ecology side of it – something to do with measurements. I'll get you something to eat, what would you like?' She started to get up.

'No, don't bother, I had a meal at lunchtime in the canteen. I'll just make myself a cheese sandwich and a coffee. What about you?'

Whilst he was eating his snack be brought her up-to-date with the events of his day.

'You know, James, Patrick doesn't tell Jean anything about your work. She seemed very surprised to learn that you often discuss your cases with me.'

'Most policemen operate like that. We're not supposed to blab outside the station walls, but you've been involved in two of my cases and I know it won't go any further. Besides, I like to use you as a sounding board, try out my ideas and hunches on you.'

'I'm flattered.' She helped herself to a glass of milk and eyed him over the rim. 'This business of a new work by Shostakovich is really exciting.'

'Except that it's disappeared off the face of the earth. What is his music like, are you familiar with it?'

'Ummm. We've got some recordings.'

'We have? I didn't know.'

'They were mine. Shall I put one on?'

She searched through the cabinet and found a record of the 10th Symphony which she put on the turntable and the two of them sat together on the sofa as the powerful music surged round the room.

'Phew! I feel as if I've been on a roller-coaster,' he said when the record came to an end. 'He really was a haunted man, wasn't he?'

'Yes, I think he was. He was always coming up against the system. He fell foul of the authorities on several occasions but somehow appeared to conform and managed to survive but it all comes out in his music. You feel as if he were continuously searching for something that always eluded him. Do you think the new concerto will ever turn up again?'

'It could be in the States by now or somewhere on the Continent. All I know is that somebody did for the Russian and removed it from the houseboat last Tuesday afternoon. So far we haven't been able to trace anyone who was in the vicinity then.'

'What about Aunt Nell? Perhaps she saw something from her window.'

'I've thought of that but unfortunately the *Painted Lady* is not one of the gaggle of boats that you can see from her window; it's further up and hidden by a screen of trees.'

'She might have noticed something though. Someone behaving suspiciously along the river wall.'

'Yes, I suppose it's worth a try. I'll have to pay her another visit. I only hope it doesn't encourage her fantasies about the other boat owners!'

'Why for you go to the police?' Màrta Rakosi clapped her hands on her hips and rolled her eyes heavenwards. 'Men, they are crazy!' she shrilled. 'All these years I look after you, I hide you, I make you new life – and now you go blow it!'

'Màrta, don't excite yourself. I had to do it.'

'Had to? Sweet Mother Mary, this man who took your place – he has been murdered! They will think you do it, you will have the blame!'

'You exaggerate. Please don't disturb me, this is very delicate work.' Her husband bent over the strips of purfling he was attaching to the upper bout of a violin.

'You crazy man, they will put you in prison – you will make no more instruments, no more music!'

'Why?'

'What do you mean, why?'

'I have done nothing wrong.'

'Nothing wrong?' She searched for words and skewered a hairpin back in her chignon. 'You are emigré – you have the false papers, they take you away.'

'You got me the papers, it is your fellow countrymen who will be in the trouble, not me. The police tell me to come home.'

'What you tell them?'

'The truth. That *I* am Mikhail Rabinovich, that Temirkanov steal my identity. The world at last shall know what my country had done to me.'

'Oh, Miklos, why you do this to me?' wailed Màrta Rakosi, throwing herself down in a chair and fanning herself with her hands. 'We have good life here, we are happy, now you rock the boat.'

Her husband sought to distract her. 'You have not heard all. Temirkanov brought a manuscript of Shostakovich's 3rd Cello Concerto out of Russia with him.'

'Ah yes, the music – I have forgot to tell you that.'

'You knew about that as well and you did not tell me?' Her husband looked at her in amazement.

'It was not important, I think.'

'Not important? Now I know is *you* who is crazy! Did I not tell you when first I come to England that Dmitri promise new work for cello which he wish for me to bring to the West but I never receive it? It *was* finished but he not get it to me before I leave. Temirkanov find it and now after all these long years it turn up!'

'But now it is lost again. These English police will think you steal it. That you knock up Temirkanov to get the manuscript.'

'Knock off,' he corrected her automatically. 'I did not kill him so I have nothing to worry about, that is the famous British justice.'

'Suppose it is the Russians? Do you not think of that? They not let him get away and now you have gone to police and they know you are still alive they will come for you too.'

'No, Màrta, is not like that now. Do not worry so.'

'Someone has to worry, you are like big baby. What can I do with you?'

'Make me a drink,' he coaxed. 'It is hot today, I get thirsty. Some of your lemonade.'

Still muttering imprecations, Màrta Rakosi went into the kitchen. Her husband did not tell her that the police wished to speak with her and take her fingerprints.

Whilst Ellen Gascoigne was in her kitchen making him coffee, James Roland went over to the sitting-room window and picked up her binoculars. He focused on the river scene and grimaced. As he had thought, the *Painted Lady* was hidden from view by the little thicket of willow trees. All he could see was her bow mooring rope attached to a bollard on the towpath. He was wasting his time. Even if she had been able to see

136

what was happening on the houseboat, she couldn't be
expected to remember something that had happened
over ten days ago. But the elderly woman proved
him wrong.

'Of course I remember that Tuesday, James,' she
replied in answer to his question as she handed him a
cup of milky coffee and produced a biscuit tin. 'I have
good reason to remember. It was most annoying.'

'What was annoying?'

'We should have gone on an outing that day to
Oulton Broad and Lowestoft. The warden arranged
it and booked the coach, but when the weather broke
she postponed it. Ridiculous – we would have been
on the coach most of the time and we wouldn't have
melted in a little drop of rain, but she decided it was too
wet. As it turned out it was only showery. There were
sunny periods between the showers in the afternoon.'

'So you were here that afternoon. I don't suppose you happened to look out of the window with
your glasses?'

This was sure to be the one afternoon that Ellen
Gascoigne had not perused the river bank through her
binoculars. He was wrong again.

'I most certainly did but the Dutch barge wasn't
there. As you can see it's still missing, been gone two
or three weeks. I suppose they are cruising somewhere
on holiday.'

'It's not the Dutch barge that I'm interested in at
the moment, it's the houseboat that's moored further
up. But you can't see it from here, those trees are
in the way.'

'I know the one you mean. It's called the *Painted
Lady*, which is a misnomer if ever I came across one

137

because it's in sore need of a coat of paint! I've walked past it many times; it's owned by a man who works at Blund Maltings – a piano restorer, I believe. What has he been up to?'

'I'm not sure that he's been up to anything but I'm interested in any activity aboard or near that boat that took place that Tuesday afternoon. Pity it's out of view from here.'

'The boat may be, but I did see someone behaving very suspiciously near there that afternoon.'

Roland couldn't believe his ears. Excitement stirred but he kept his voice deliberately neutral.

'Just what did you see?'

'I saw this man. He was walking along the towpath in a most furtive manner.'

'But surely you see lots of people up and down there in the course of an afternoon.'

'Not behaving like that, I don't, and please let me continue. He was sort of skulking along as if he didn't want anyone to see him. He went on board and a few minutes later came back on shore and had a good look round as though he were making sure that no one else was observing him. Then he went back on board again and was there about ten minutes or so . . .'

'How do you know that he went aboard the *Painted Lady* if you can't see it from here?' interrupted Roland, risking her wrath.

'Because I can see the towpath beyond the *Painted Lady* and he certainly didn't carry on along that. No, I'm sure he went on board the boat and when he came back he was skulking in the same manner *and* he was carrying something.'

'What was it? Did you see?'

'A package of some sort about the size of a large book.'

'Are you quite sure of this?'

'Of course I'm sure. As I said, he was behaving in a most suspicious manner.'

'Are you sure it was a man?'

Ellen Gascoigne considered this. 'I thought it was a man because he was wearing trousers and one of those lightweight waterproof things – kagools, aren't they called? The hood was pulled up over his head, but I suppose it could have been a woman. So many of them wear trousers these days. Anyway, he or she was wearing glasses.'

'Glasses?'

'They could have been sunglasses. I saw them glinting in the sun – it had come out again by then.'

'And you're sure that this happened on that Tuesday afternoon?'

'Yes, I told you, we should have gone on this . . .'

'Yes, yes, I know. Well, this is very useful information, Aunt Nell. Could you identify this person if you saw him or her again?'

'You mean you want me to attend an identity parade?' Ellen Gascoigne was thrilled at the thought.

'No, I don't think it will come to that. I'm thinking of something along more informal lines. Suppose I arrange for you to visit Blund Maltings? Do you think you would recognise this person if you saw him in the course of your visit?'

'I'm sure I should, I watched him very closely as he was behaving in such a strange manner. I've always wanted to see round the Maltings. When can you arrange it?'

* * *

Roland had decided to enlist Ginny's help. He could not go round the Maltings with Ellen Gascoigne as he would be recognised by his suspects, and the same applied to any of his colleagues. Ginny in her present condition would arouse no suspicions even if she had to visit parts of the Maltings which were not open to the public.

'Are you sure that you feel up to it? If not I'll get someone else. It's not really fair to ask you to trudge round there – I know how tired you get.'

'I shall be perfectly all right. It's no more than walking round the shops and we can take our time. Where do you want us to go?'

Roland told her and gave her a list of people he wanted Aunt Nell to get a look at.

'And do I tell her which people you are interested in?'

'I've been thinking about that. If you don't tell her she'll be looking on everyone she sees as a possible suspect and she'll be punch drunk before she gets round the complex. There's sure to be masses of visitors milling around. On the other hand, I don't want to influence her memory in any way. I think the best thing to do is to take her in the places where the male suspects are: the library and the art gallery etcetera, and make sure she gets a good look at them but don't say anything. We'll have to try a different tactic for the women. She thinks it could have been a woman dressed in trousers and a kagool and none of them will be wearing that sort of outfit at work so you'd better make sure she knows which women to scrutinise. She mustn't indicate and give the game away if she thinks she does recognise someone – she can have a quiet word with you afterwards.'

'Where are you going to be, James?'

'Not far away. I'll treat you both to lunch but it had better not be in the Maltings restaurant. We'll go to the pub down the road, the Eel and Jug. I'll park the car there and go for a walk and we'll meet up there later. I should think you'll get round in an hour.'

'Do I get taken on the payroll?'

'I told you, a slap-up lunch. Aunt Nell is raring to go. I think she sees herself as a latter-day Miss Marple.'

'I bet she does. This is probably the most interesting thing that's happened to her for a long while.'

'This really is most exciting, dear,' said Ellen Gascoigne clutching Ginny's arm as they walked through the archway into the Maltings. 'I know I mustn't ask questions and I don't suppose that James has confided fully in you, but I do hope that I don't let him down.'

'Don't worry, Aunt Nell. Just relax and enjoy yourself, and if you recognise anyone just give my arm a squeeze.'

The elderly woman was dressed in what she termed her 'summer visiting clothes'. This outfit consisted of a red, white and green striped dress that bore more than a passing resemblance to a deckchair, a scarlet blazer and a panama hat of very ancient lineage into the band of which she had tucked some large artificial daisies. We are not exactly going to merge into the background, thought Ginny, who felt very conspicuous herself. I do hope that James knows what he is doing. She wore a green and blue smock dress and had piled her red-gold hair on top of her head. She was sure that she looked like a floral tank, and certainly felt like one.

'We're going to look at the pianos first. Have you played?'

'My dear, I was a primary school teacher. Everything from nursery rhymes to carols.'

The piano workshop was a vast cavern of a place, well stocked with pianos of various size and vintage. They were the only people there and there was no sign of Barry Spender but they could hear a tuning session going on somewhere in the background. Ellen Gascoigne stalked over to a grand piano in the middle of the room, sat herself down and plunged into a spirited rendering of 'Three Blind Mice.' It had the desired effect. A man appeared through a door in the far wall and came over to them.

'Can I help you, ladies, or are you happy to browse around on your own?'

'Nice tone.' Aunt Nell indicated the keyboard. 'But far too big for my flat. Have you got a Challen upright? I had a Challen once before, a good little piano.'

'If you're looking for something smaller, I've got something over here that might interest you.' Barry Spender led her over to the other side of the room and they were soon deep in discussion about over-stringing and under-dampening, with frequent sorties on different keyboards.

We're going to be hours at this rate, thought Ginny, she seems to have completely forgotten why we're here but she obviously hasn't recognised him. Some while later she managed to extricate her Aunt and manoeuvre her towards the shopping arcade.

'I really must see if I can squeeze a piano into my

flat. I hadn't realised how much I miss playing. He was a most helpful man, really interested in suiting me, not just in trying to sell any old piano.'

'I take it you didn't recognise him?'

'I thought he was probably one of James's suspects. No, dear, it wasn't him. He was altogether the wrong build.'

In the health food store Ellen Gascoigne bought oat cakes for herself and a jar of Suffolk honey for Ginny and spent a considerable time perusing the cookery books. At a prompting from the younger woman she looked closely at Laura Nelson and tried to imagine her in kagool and trousers.

'She's tall for a woman; I suppose she could pass as a man, but I'm sure it wasn't her. She doesn't move like a man.'

In the boutique next door Màrta Rakosi was also dismissed from the list.

'She's a foreigner. It certainly wasn't a foreigner.'

'But how could you possible tell from that distance?'

'They have an altogether different way of carrying themselves, more dramatic, more . . . abandoned. Look at her,' she said in a stage whisper as Màrta Rakosi walked across to the window to remove from the display a garment in which someone was showing an interest. 'She's *flouncing*. You could imagine her playing Carmen in her youth with a rose between her teeth. She would never skulk.'

From the shopping arcade they went across the courtyard to the art gallery and craft centre. Jonathan Cade was having an animated phone conversation in his office. They could see him quite clearly from where they stood by the poster displays near the open door;

his long legs propped up on the desk, gesticulating with his hands and arms.

'Is he the one you want me to look at?' Ellen Gascoigne studied him casually and looked worried. 'I suppose it could have been him. It's difficult to tell with him sitting down like that.'

As if on cue, Jonathan Cade put down the phone, got to his feet and sauntered out into the gallery. He saw the two women watching him and went over to them.

'Can I help you?'

'Er . . . yes,' Ginny racked her brains. 'Have you any Alphonse Mucha posters?'

'We did have but I think they've all gone. I'm waiting for a new consignment, they should be here any day now.'

He flicked through the racks and smiled apologetically, 'No, I'm sorry, not one left now but we have got some other Art Nouveau prints.'

'No, I particularly wanted a Mucha. Never mind, we'll try next time we are here.'

He moved away and Ginny turned to her companion. 'Well?'

'No, he's too tall and far too handsome. Are you all right, Ginny – you look tired?'

'I am a little weary but we're nearly through. Just the woman through there in the craft section and then we have to think of an excuse to get inside the library.'

The sight of Stella Lingard, as exotic-looking as the bunches of dried flowers and feathers she was arranging, brought an emphatic no from Ellen Gascoigne and they left the building and walked over to the library.

'It's not open to the general public, only the music

students and such like use it, so I don't know how we are going to manage this.'

'We can pretend we don't know and ask if we can borrow something. Who is it I am supposed to be looking at?'

'You'll know if you recognise him or her.'

The library was cool inside and had that hushed, reverent air peculiar to such places. The tall, high windows were filled with opaque glass and through them the sunlight fell in fragmented pools of light on the parquet floor. There was an elderly woman seated behind the loans desk, almost hidden by a pile of sheet music. Ginny and her companion went over to her and she looked up as they approached and regarded them suspiciously.

'Are you members?'

'No, I'm afraid we're not, but I wondered if it would be possible to consult one of your reference books?'

'This library is not open to the public, you shouldn't be here.' She was hostile and looked affronted by Ginny's condition.

'I'm sorry, I know this is an imposition, but if I could just have a quick look in Grove – to check something for my son, he's a music student,' lied Ginny. 'You do have Grove?'

'Of course we do,' said the woman coldly, 'but you cannot see it.'

'It would only take a minute or two,' she pleaded.

'No, I've told you, this library cannot be used by the public. If we once let someone break the rules we'll have every Tom, Dick and Harry in here.' Her voice rose in righteous indignation.

'Is anything wrong, Miss Parker?'

The voice came from the direction of the stairs and Ginny and Ellen Gascoigne looked up to see a man peering down over the banister.

'It's all right, Mr Coleman, these women mistakenly thought the library was open to outsiders.'

'I just wanted to check a reference,' said Ginny, and nearly cried out as fingers dug hard into her elbow. 'I . . . I . . . do you think I could sit down for a moment?'

'Are you all right?' The librarian looked at her anxiously.

'I just feel a little faint. If I could just rest for a short while . . .'

'Of course.' He produced a chair with alacrity and helped her to sit down. 'Miss Parker, fetch a glass of water – quickly.'

'I'm sorry to be such a nuisance but it has turned very warm again and I'm afraid in my condition the heat knocks me out.'

'Do you have any brandy?' demanded Ellen Gascoigne, who was fluttering round Ginny in a very convincing manner.

'No, but I'm sure we can run to a cup of tea.'

'No, a glass of water will be fine, thank you. I don't want to cause any trouble.'

The water was brought by the library assistant and Ginny sipped it gratefully.

'Are you sure you don't want any medical attention? I can ring for an ambulance from my office.'

'No, I'm fine now, it was only a temporary faintness.' She hauled herself to her feet and the librarian looked worried.

'What was it you wanted in the library?'

Ginny trotted out her excuse again and he said: 'As Miss Parker told you, this library is not open to the public but perhaps I could check your reference for you?'

'It's very kind of you but I really can't trouble you any further. My son will have to do his own dirty work and use his college library.'

'Have you got any transport . . . should you be driving?'

'My husband is picking us up shortly. We'll wait for him outside.'

As soon as the door had closed on them Ellen Gascoigne pounced on her companion. 'You weren't really feeling ill, were you?'

'No, I thought I would cause a diversion so that you could get a better look at him. You recognised him, didn't you?'

'Oh, yes, my dear, I've no doubts at all. As soon as he looked over that banister, the way he tilted his head and the light reflecting off his glasses, I knew that he was the one that I'd seen that day.'

'Let's get back to James. I hope he appreciates all the lies and subterfuges we've resorted to to get him his identification.'

'He seemed such a nice man, so concerned about you. I do hope he's not a real criminal.'

As they walked round the corner they nearly collided with a wheelchair being pushed by a middle-aged woman. Sitting in it was a painfully thin, black-haired woman who was swathed in a rug although it was well into the seventies. Ginny felt a pang of pity but the woman glared up at her and she changed her mind. She told James later that she felt as if she had been given the evil eye.

* * *

James Roland took the footpath that led in the opposite direction from the Maltings. It followed the river which was little more than a wide stream this side of the bridge and flowed sluggishly between reeded banks. The sun was in his eyes and the midges were biting although it was not yet midday, and he began to think that the walk was not such a good idea; he should have stayed in the pub, quenching his thirst with draught ale in the cool, dim interior. From somewhere a long way away came the drone of a combine as a farmer harvested the last of his wheat, but the birds were silent, lulled in noontide heat, not a cheap or trill disturbed the heavy air.

He came to a stile and straddled it, looking back at the distant Maltings. The tawny buildings huddled in a cradle of fawn rushes like a bird on a nest, the ridge vents emerging from the slate roof dazzling white against a cerulaean sky. Someone in that complex was a murderer, he was sure of it, but who? Would Ginny's and Ellen Gascoigne's visit prove anything or was it a wild-goose chase?

He sat on the stile and pondered the situation. The PRO Office at the Immigration and National-ity Department at Croydon had confirmed that a Mikhail Rabinovich had applied for refugee status in 1975 but had gone to ground and disappeared during the preliminary investigation into his case; so it would seem that the man now calling himself Miklos Rakosi had been telling the truth and was the real Mikhail Rabinovich. There had been no report of any commotion at Heathrow when the St Petersburg had flown back to Moscow. They had been booked on an Aeroflot flight and the Russians had not reported anyone missing, which left the coroner with an unclaimed body that had to be accounted for.

What was even more interesting was the latest fax message that had come through from Croydon. They had received, recently, an application from the false Mikhail Rabinovich and were not looking on it favourably. He wondered why. Was it because of the mix-up in the past or was there some other reason? Roland knew how sticky the Home Office were about immigrants in the current political climate, but surely an accomplished musician of some standing was not your run-of-the-mill penniless petitioner? This must be followed up, though to extract information from the Home Office was like trying to get blood from the proverbial stone.

He slapped at a gnat on his arm and checked his watch. Time to get back, the two women should be through by now. In the event, it was nearly three-quarters of an hour before they turned up. He had strolled back to the pub, ordered and drunk a beer and was just wondering whether he should mount a rescue operation when they joined him in the saloon bar. Ginny looked exhausted, he should never have asked her to do it, but she also looked complacent and Ellen Gascoigne was nearly beside herself with triumph.

'Ginny, are you all right? Come and sit down.'

'We've cracked it for you, James.'

'You look like the cats who swallowed the cream. What are you going to have?'

'Don't you want to know?' demanded the elderly woman.

'Let's order first, it's getting busy. You can tell me whilst we're waiting for the food to arrive.'

* * *

A short while later, seated at a corner table away from the hustle round the bar area, Roland handed Ellen Gascoigne the port and lemon she had requested and put down the tray.

'Well, Aunt Nell, I can see you're dying to unburden yourself. Did you recognise your suspicious character?'

'I did, James – it was the man in the library!'

Roland looked to Ginny for confirmation and she nodded.

'The librarian. Aunt Nell recognised him the moment she saw him.'

'Dennis Coleman. Are you quite sure?'

'No doubt about it, he was the one that I saw skulking about on the towpath that Tuesday afternoon. Will I have to give evidence in court?'

'I don't think it will come to that, but many thanks for your help.'

He steered the conversation into other channels as the three of them ate their lunch. He was itching to get away and pursue this new twist in the case. Coleman might have a perfectly legitimate reason for having been along the river-bank that afternoon but he had lied to the police in the first instance, insisting that he had spent the relevant hours incarcerated in the library; he would have difficulty talking himself out of that one.

They finished their meal and were about to depart when the door opened letting in a blinding shaft of sunlight and two late-comers who hurried over to the bar and engaged the landlord in backchat as he served them drinks. One of the couple was Stella Lingard.

She draped herself gracefully on a bar stool and lit a cigarette, blowing the smoke upwards towards the low beamed ceiling. Her companion was a tall, heavily-built man who leaned on the counter lazily and played with his companion's hand. So, loverboy was back in the sticks, another thread to unravel in the plot. Roland wondered how soon he could whisk Ellen Gascoigne home without causing offence; she was starting across the room with a perplexed look on her face.

'What's the matter, Aunt Nell, are you having second thoughts about your identification?'

'Oh, no, I'm quite sure that it was the librarian, but I saw *him* too, the same afternoon – that man leaning against the bar.'

She indicated Nick Blackstone.

Chapter 6

'Right, Patrick, we'll pull him in. Take Evans with you and collect him.'

'You want him arrested?'

'I want him pulled in for questioning. I'm going to scare the shit out of him. We've got no concrete evidence but I'm going to try and get him to confess.

'You really think he did it?'

'It's only circumstantial evidence. This old girl of Ginny's thought she recognised him but it would never stand up in court. That's why we need a confession. Don't let him know why we want to question him, just stress the gravity of it and let him stew.'

Dennis Coleman was a very worried man when he faced Roland and Mansfield in the interview room a little later and he tried to cover it with bluster.

'You've no right to arrest me and bring me here. I've done nothing wrong and I know my rights . . .'

'You are not under arrest as I made clear when you were cautioned. You have been brought here to answer some questions and it will be to your advantage to answer them truthfully this time.'

'I don't know what you mean.'

'No?' Roland stared at him thoughtfully. 'Let me jog your memory. Last time we met I asked you where you were on the afternoon of Tuesday 23rd August.'

'And I told you – I was working in my office in the library.'

'Tut, tut, Mr Coleman, stop wasting my time. I'll ask you again – where were you that afternoon?'

'In my office working, where else would I be?'

'Aboard the *Painted Lady*?'

'That's not true. Whoever told you that is lying!' He denied it vigorously but it was obvious to the two detectives that he was running scared.

'You were seen, Coleman, it's no good denying it.'

'I do deny it, you can't prove it! It's my word against whoever it is who's trying to throw suspicion on me.'

'You were seen on the towpath boarding the *Painted Lady* twice in the course of fifteen minutes.'

'It's not true – who told you that?' He shrunk back in his seat and licked his lips apprehensively. Roland ignored his question and Coleman made an effort at defiance. 'What am I supposed to have done?'

'I think we can work out a nice little scenario for your movements, don't you, Sergeant?'

'Oh, yes sir, it's quite obvious, isn't it?' replied Mansfield. 'A very nasty business.'

'What do you mean?'

Roland leaned forward and spoke softly but menacingly. 'I suggest that you saw Mikhail Rabinovich sitting up on deck and you crept up on him, having first snatched up a handy length of wood that was lying nearby. You bashed him over the head and pushed his body into the river.' He paused and Coleman stared at him like a rabbit mesmerised by a stoat. 'You then went ashore and had a good look around to make sure there was no one about and then went back on to the *Painted Lady*. This time you went below. You searched through the Russian's luggage and found the Shostakovich manuscript. You put this on one side and stowed all the rest of his belongings into his suitcase which you then took up on deck and tipped over the side. You did the same with his cello and then you went over the boat with your handkerchief making sure your fingerprints were not on anything. You then picked up the manuscript and made off along the towpath.'

'I didn't kill him! I swear I didn't! It was someone else!'

Roland and Mansfield exchanged a glance of satisfaction.

'But you were there, Coleman? You're not denying it?'

'All right I was there!' he cried desperately. 'And I took it – but I didn't kill him, I swear to it! You can't pin that on me!'

'Can't we, Coleman? Perhaps you'd like to tell us your version of what happened?'

The librarian had fallen to pieces. He seemed to have shrunk and turned a pasty white. His hands shook against the edge of the table.

'You've got to believe me, I didn't kill him! I saw it happen but it wasn't me!'

'No?'

'No! It happened like you said but it wasn't me that did it. Look – I can explain . . .'

'That's what I'm waiting for and it had better be the truth. You're in bad trouble, very bad indeed. I shouldn't like to be in your shoes.'

Coleman ran a tongue over his dry lips and blinked through his glasses.

'I was going to see the Russian. I knew he would be there on his own and I was going to try and persuade him to let me handle the business of exploiting the manuscript. I was walking along the towpath from Woodford and could see him sitting like you said on deck with a fishing rod. He had his back to the shore and was huddled in a kagool – it had been raining heavily a short while before, the path was a quagmire. Then this figure appeared. He must have come from the opposite direction along the footpath from Blund. He had this lump of wood in his hand and he crept on board and brought it down on the Russian's head. He slumped forward and toppled over the side into the water. His attacker threw the weapon into the river after him and bolted back the way he had come.'

'You saw this happen and yet you made no attempt to stop him or rescue the Russian?'

'It was too far away and I . . . I couldn't believe my eyes. I couldn't believe it had really happened, it was like watching something on television. It was all over so quickly that I began to think I had imagined it.'

'But you can tell me who this assailant was?'

'No, I can't!' the librarian burst out. 'He had his back to me all the time – he was wearing a kagool with the hood pulled up.'

'You're telling me that Mikhail Rabinovich, the mysterious assailant and you yourself were all wearing kagools at the time with the hoods covering your heads?'

'Yes, I am – you know what the weather was like that day.'

'So what happened next?'

'Well, I just crouched there on the bank stunned for a few minutes, then I realised that the . . . the murderer had gone and I pulled myself together and went along to the *Painted Lady*. I went on board and I looked over the side but there was no sign of the Russian. I had hoped that maybe he would be swimming in the water but he hadn't surfaced. It was high tide and the water was running strongly and I guessed he'd been swept quite a way by then. A plane flew overhead at that point and I suddenly thought that if I was seen by anyone I would be blamed for his death. I scrambled ashore and had a good look around but there was no one about and the boat is more or less hidden by that screen of trees. It was then that I had the idea of ste—. . . taking the manuscript. Believe me, Inspector, I would never have killed him to get hold of it but it suddenly seemed too good an opportunity to miss.'

'I went back on board and down into the main cabin. The manuscript was inside his suitcase and I took it out. I thought that if his luggage and instrument were missing, Spender and Cade would think that he had gone off of his own free will so I lugged them up on deck and tipped them over the side. Then I went below again and made sure that there was nothing else of his lying around and wiped all the surfaces that I had touched and brought the manuscript away with me.' He looked wildly at the two detectives who were listening impassively. 'You do believe me, don't you?'

'Would you if the situation was reversed, Coleman? You have an extraordinary imagination but we police-men deal in facts not fantasy.'

'God! That's how it happened, I swear to you! How can I prove that it's the truth?'

'For starters, where is the manuscript?'

'In the library.'

'The library?'

'I filed it away in the reference library amongst the other copies of scores of Shostakovich. I thought it would be so obvious that it would be overlooked.'

'Well, you were following a good precedent but I don't see how you thought you could possibly capitalise on it.'

'I was going to hang on to it until the heat was off and then sell it to a collector – an unprincipled one who wouldn't want to know where it came from. Oh, Christ! I must have been mad! I've never done anything like this before, I've never stolen anything in my life, but the temptation was too great. The money would make such a difference to Helen . . . Oh God, Helen! What will she do if I'm sent to prison?'

'Does she know what you did?'

'Yes, I told her everything. The hiding place was her idea. She'll never forgive me for making a balls up of it.'

'You're admitting that your wife was an accessory?'

'Oh, what am I saying! You can't arrest her too. It was nothing to do with her, you must believe me!'

'I'm prepared to believe that you didn't tell your wife that you had killed Rabinovich in order to get your hands on the manuscript.'

The librarian groaned and hid his head in his hands.

'Inspector, I swear to you that I didn't kill him.'

'If only I could believe everything that people swear to me. Countless suspects have sat on that chair just as you are doing and have sworn on their dead mother's body or their baby's head that black is white or night is day. In fact, the more they scream their innocence, the more guilty they usually are.'

'What am I to do?' Coleman looked across at the detective and there was a sudden shabby dignity about him. 'I know I didn't do it, but I can't prove it and you can't prove that I did.'

'I shouldn't be so sure of that.'

'You mean the person who said they'd seen me? Well, they didn't see me kill him. If they told you that they were lying through their teeth! Who was it?'

Roland ignored the question and got to his feet. 'Let's go.'

'You're arresting me? I demand to see my solicitor!'

'You will accompany us back to the library and produce the manuscript.'

'You're not arresting me?'

As Mansfield said afterwards to Roland, it sounded as if he almost preferred the idea of police custody to the thought of having to face his wife.

'Coleman, I could throw the book at you. Apart from the most heinous crime of murder there are countless other charges I could make stick, not least perverting the course of justice. Even if you didn't do the killing – and don't think I've given up on that – your failure to report the deed means you were actually aiding and abetting the murderer.'

'Oh, why did I get involved . . . what will happen to me?'

'I'm going to give you the benefit of the doubt. I shouldn't – my superintendent would roast me if he knew. He'd have you up before the magistrates on very serious charges here and now, but I'm going to be kind . . .' Roland paused and Coleman looked at him hopefully. '. . . I am going to let you go for the time being.'

'You mean, you're not going to charge me?'

'Don't kid yourself, Coleman, charges will be preferred, but I'm staying my hand until we know exactly how many to bring against you. I am giving you your freedom now on condition that you keep your mouth shut. I want no word of this interview to be heard outside these walls. If you didn't kill the Russian we still have a killer in our midst and I don't want him alerted. Do you understand? If any of this leaks out you'll be back inside here so fast you'll wish you'd been born without a tongue in your head.'

'I won't say anything. I swear it! I'll be as silent as the grave.' He spoilt his protestations by adding almost immediately: 'What about Helen?'

'What about her?'

'Do I tell her what has happened as she was in the know?'

'Coleman, you are responsible for your wife's silence as well as your own. You know her better than I.'

'I think she must remain in ignorance about this. She must go on thinking that I still have the manuscript hidden in the library.'

'I think you've made a wise decision. Let's hope that you can now produce it.'

The elderly assistant was on duty when the two detectives and Dennis Coleman went back to the library. The librarian made as if to go over and speak to her, changed his mind and took them over to the stairs and then changed his mind again and went back to where she sat behind the desk. He exchanged a few words with her which Roland and Mansfield could not hear and then rejoined them and led them up the stairs to the reference library. He switched off the alarm, undid the security locks and opened the door.

'You seem very security conscious, have you much of value in here?'

'Yes. We have some original Benjamin Britten manuscripts, also Vaughan Williams and William Walton and some valuable sets of orchestral scores and many rare books. It's temperature controlled, too, that's what that humming noise is.'

'So who is allowed to use this?'

'Not the students, apart from exceptional cases whom I personally vet. Well-known musicians and writers have to apply for a special pass and everyone is judged individually on their own merits.'

'Did Mikhail Rabinovich come up here?'

'No. He was interested and I probably would have shown him round if he . . . he hadn't been killed.'

The librarian mopped his brow and swallowed hard.

'Where is the Shostakovich manuscript, Coleman?'

He went over to a bookstack in the far corner which reached from floor to ceiling and with shaking hands removed a folder from the middle of a tightly-packed shelf and handed it to Roland.

'Yes, I see what you mean. It could easily be overlooked. So this is the magnum opus. Is it worth killing for?'

'I didn't . . . it wasn't . . .' Coleman looked utterly wretched.

'And this is how you found it?' Roland flicked

through it quickly, noting the cyrillic handwriting on the dog-eared cover. 'You haven't tampered with it?'

'No, I brought it straight up here and I've resisted the temptation to pore over it since.'

'You haven't approached anyone about selling it?'

'No, I told you, I intended waiting for a long time before I did anything about it.'

'We'll take charge of it now.' He zipped it into his briefcase.

'What will happen to it now that Rabinovich is dead?'

'That is hardly your concern, Coleman. This is vital evidence and as such will remain in police custody for the time being.'

'Of course, of course. I just meant . . . it is priceless, Inspector, you do realise that?'

'You think it would be safer here than at the station?'

'No, no . . . I . . . forgive me, I'm so overwrought I don't know what I'm saying.'

'Tell me, what time was it when you left the *Painted Lady*?'

'Between three and four o'clock, probably nearer four o'clock.'

'Did you meet anyone either on the way there or on the way back?'

'Well . . .'

'Think carefully about this, Coleman.'

'I didn't notice anyone but if I was seen then I must have done, mustn't I?'

'But you don't remember seeing anyone?'

'Not near the *Painted Lady*, but when I had got nearly back here, I thought I saw Barry Spender on his way home. I obviously didn't want him to see me so I kept out of sight once I'd spotted him but I'm pretty certain it was him.'

'I see. Will your wife be at home at this time of day? Presumably she doesn't get out much?'

'You're not going to interview Helen now? There's nothing she can add to what I've told you and I thought she wasn't to be told about this . . . this latest development?'

'We'll leave it for now but if a squeak of this gets out I'll pull you in straight away, and your wife too. In the meanwhile, if you remember anything else about that afternoon, no matter how insignificant you may think it, get on to us immediately.'

'Oh, I will, Inspector, and thank you.'

'Don't thank me, Coleman, you're not off the hook yet.'

'Well, I think that's sorted him out,' said Roland as they walked back to the car. 'He won't dare risk dropping any hints to anyone in case it gets back to his wife. She's really got him in a straight jacket, hasn't she?'

'Poor sod. What did you think of his story?'

'It would be tempting to think that we'd got the case buttoned up, that he was the killer and thief and that's the end of it, but unfortunately I believe he may be telling the truth. What do you think?'

'I'm inclined to agree with you. He's not the stuff of which villains or heroes are made. He's just a little man who has jumped in the deep end and discovered that he can't swim. But where does this leave us?'

'With virtually the same list of suspects as before, with him still near the top. Just because the killer didn't take the manuscript when he knocked the Russian off doesn't mean that that wasn't the reason for his murder. He could have heard or caught sight of Coleman and run off, intending to go back later and remove it. On the other hand, it could have been a revenge killing – one or other of the Rakosis acting on the spur of the moment. Or maybe it was either Spender or Cade fearing that the Russian was getting too friendly with his bed partner.'

'So where do we go from here?'

'Back to the station right now and get this under lock and key, then we'll try and catch up with Nick Blackstone. The old girl couldn't remember whether she saw him near the *Painted Lady* before or after she saw Dennis Coleman, but either way he's got a lot of explaining to do.'

Nick Blackstone was in his garden, or they presumed that it was he from what they could see of him. He was stretched out in a deckchair with a sunhat tipped over his eyes. At his feet was an empty glass, a pile of books and a portable typewriter. Although he must have heard the click of the gate and their footsteps on the path he ignored their presence and it wasn't until Roland stood between him and the sun that he came to with an elaborate start.

He snatched the hat off his face and said in a lazy voice that was belied by the shrewd gleam in his mud-brown eyes: 'Don't tell me, it's the flat-foots.' He made a pantomine of getting out of the deckchair to his feet. 'God, this is more an instrument of torture than a chair. You'd think my host would have run to a sun-lounger or something more suited to relaxation.'

'Detective Inspector Roland and Detective Sergeant Mansfield of Felstone CID,' said Roland, flashing his ID card. 'And you are Mr Blackstone?'

'That's me. You see me, Inspector, in the throes of creative activity.'

'Really? You could have fooled me, I thought you were asleep.'

'A common mistake. No, I was deep in profound thought communing with my muse. What can I do for you?'

'We are investigating the death of the Russian, Mikhail Rabinovich, and I have some questions to put to you.'

'Look, is this going to take long?'

'As long as it has to, Mr Blackstone,' said Roland impassively.

'Then we'd better make ourselves comfortable. I believe there's another of these contraptions in the shed,' he kicked the deckchair, 'but perhaps we'd better go inside.'

He sauntered across the lawn towards the house and the two detectives followed him. He took them through french doors into a sitting room that was large and untidy. The walls were covered with photos that Roland would have liked to examine more closely, they looked like the work of an expert in his field; there were books everywhere and the remains of a tray meal on the table. Blackstone waved them to seats and sprawled in an armchair himself, near the open doors.

'The love of my life said you were grilling people about the case. How is it coming along?'

'That would be Mrs Stella Lingard?'

'Spot on. I only have one at a time and she's

enough for any man to handle. You've met her, Inspector?'

'Let's get to the point, Mr Blackstone, I'm sure you're au fait with the facts or do I have to spell them out to you?'

'You mean the Russian's murder and the disappearance of a certain manuscript? Of course I know! It's my business to know. You forget, I'm an investigative journalist.'

'I haven't forgotten that at all. It's one of the reasons that I am here. I hope for your sake that you haven't leaked any of this story?'

'Hey, what do you mean? There is such a thing as freedom of the press! You can't stop me from publishing my story, you have no rights . . .'

'Mr Blackstone, you are involved in this case yourself; in fact, I could say that you are up to your eyeballs in it. If you persist in writing up your version I shall make sure that *your* name is splashed high in *my* account, do you understand me?'

'You're threatening me?'

'I'm just reminding you that if I were in your shoes I should be very careful of what I published. Do we understand each other?'

'So what is the other reason for your presence here?' asked Blackstone sulkily.

'Mrs Lingard claims that she spent the afternoon of Tuesday, 23rd August in your company.'

'Yes, that's right.'

'Would you care to be more specific?'

'Why not? We spent it in bed, Inspector. We were here, upstairs, in the back bedroom all the afternoon. Does that answer your question or would you like to view the mise-en-scène?' He made as if to get to his feet.

'That won't be necessary.'

'You relieve me, I thought all policemen were voyeurs.'

'Blackstone, how long were you together?'

'How do I know? We don't clock-watch when we're on the job!'

'But it was all afternoon?'

'I think we can account for three hours, between two and five o'clock. Does that satisfy you, Inspector?'

'It would if it were the truth.'

'What do you mean?' He sounded indignant.

Mansfield took up the questioning. 'I think you're telling porkies, Blackstone.'

'You mean, you don't think she could entertain me for three hours? You don't know the lady, Sergeant, she . . .'

'Cut the cackle,' interrupted Mansfield whose puritan soul was offended by the journalist's attitude of kiss and tell. 'You were not with Mrs Lingard all that time.'

'Did she say so? Why should she say that? It's her alibi you're trying to prove?'

'Mrs Lingard's story agrees with yours, but then it would, wouldn't it? The fact is that during that time you say you spent with her, here in this house, you were seen on the *Painted Lady*.'

'That's a lie!'

'Is it? We have it on good authority.'

'I don't believe it . . . Look, who told you?'

'Are you still denying it?'

Nick Blackstone ran his fingers through his hair and

his curls stood on end in an untidy halo, making him look like a debauched middle-aged cherub.

'Look, I don't know what you're getting at. I spent most of the afternoon here but I did slip down to the river for a short while later on.'

'When would that have been?'

'Fivish? Half-past five?' He saw their faces. 'All right, it may have been earlier.'

'So you admit that you were on the *Painted Lady* during the course of that afternoon? Don't worry, we can pin-point the time exactly.'

'Look, it was only for a few minutes. I didn't think that it was important.'

'Not important? Yet you were prepared to perjure yourself on the point! Stop playing games with us, Blackstone. We're giving you a chance to explain before we pull you in, so make the most of it.'

'Pull me in? What am I supposed to have done?'

'Don't play the innocent with us. You topped the Russian to get your hands on the Shostakovich manuscript. What have you done with it – is it here?' Roland looked round the room.

'Christ!' Blackstone was really shaken and his flippant manner disappeared. 'You're not serious? This is ridiculous . . .'

'Is it? Perhaps you'd like to tell us your version of what happened that afternoon.'

The journalist heaved himself to his feet and walked over to the window. He turned to face them and leaned against the sill, his hands in his pockets.

'Look, Stella had told me all about the Russian and naturally I was very interested. There was a good story there and I intended being the one to break it. Spender and Cade guarded him like a hawk, I knew that they would never let me near him so I chose a time when they were out of the way and went along to see him.'

'You chose a time which happened to be early closing afternoon when they could both have been expected to be around.'

'Yes, well, Stella knew their movements. She tipped me the wink.' He paused and shrugged his shoulders.'

'Go on.'

'There's not much to tell. I went along to the *Painted Lady* and he wasn't there.'

'You're quite sure?'

'Of course I am. I had a quick look around – the boat's not very large – but there was no sign of him.'

'So you admit that you searched the boat. Were you looking for the manuscript?'

'All I'm admitting is that I gave it the once over – wouldn't you have in my place? But there was no sign of him or any of his belongings. I thought he'd done a runner, moved on to another hiding place or given himself up to the authorities. I was damn' annoyed. I'd been back-pedalling on the story, using the softly, softly, catchee monkee technique, and now it looked as if I'd lost out.'

'Did you see anyone else near the houseboat or along the riverbank when you were in the vicinity?'

'It would be tempting to say that I saw all manner of Maltings employees acting in a suspicious manner, but no, I didn't. I'm not saying there wasn't anyone else around but I didn't notice anyone. Look, you do believe me, don't you? If he was killed that afternoon it must have happened before I got there. It was nothing to do with me.'

'I have only your word for it. Things look very black for you.'

The journalist mopped his brow with his handkerchief. 'Whew, it's hot. Would you like a drink? I've got some cans of beer in the fridge.'

Roland and Mansfield declined.

'You don't mind if I do? I've got a thirst on me.' He went through to the kitchen which led off the square hall and Mansfield followed him. The kitchen was reasonably-sized, a light airy room well stocked with modern appliances, but it didn't look as if Blackstone put them to much use. The sink was full of dirty crockery and the worktops littered with further pots and pans and food remains.

'Don't worry, Sergeant, I'm not going to do a bunk.' He bent down and took a can of beer out of the fridge and waved it at the detective. 'Are you sure you won't change your mind?'

Mansfield shook his head and after looking round futilely for an empty glass Blackstone opened the can and took a swig out of it. He wiped his mouth on the back of his hand and blundered back to the sitting room, clutching the tin to his stomach as if it were a talisman.

Roland turned from rapt absorption of the framed photos on the walls.

'These are good. Who's the photographer?'

'Toby Mannering, you must have heard of him? This is his house. I'm keeping an eye on it for him whilst he's away on an assignment.'

'Yes, I know all about that. You found it politic to shake the dust of London off your feet for a while.'

'Look, what are you getting at? I can work here just

as well as in town. I'm not a nine-to-five gent. I'm combining my work with a holiday.'

'Yes, it's a pleasant part of the country to be in at this time of the year but I believe you have been back to London for a short stay? What were you doing there?'

'Amongst other things, searching for Mikhail Rabinovich.'

'Really?'

'Yes. I've been in touch with the immigration authorities in Croydon to find out whether he applied for political asylum. So you see, Inspector . . .' his voice rose in triumph '. . . that proves that I didn't know anything about his murder or I shouldn't have gone looking for him!'

'It would be the obvious thing to do to try and throw us off the scent.'

'Christ! You've really got it in for me, haven't you? Look, I'm just an innocent bystander who happened to get caught up in it.'

'Who happened to think that he could make a great deal of money out of fabricating a sensational story around it!'

'I don't fabricate, the facts were there,' said Nick Blackstone, swallowing the remains of the beer and chucking the can into the wastepaper basket. 'Defectors are not news these days, not with the current climate in the USSR and Europe, but this was different. A long-lost manuscript by a famous composer being smuggled out to the West – it would make a riveting story.'

'What a pity you can't write it. I meant what I said, Blackstone. Any leak to the Press and I'll come down on you like a ton of bricks.'

'But I'm not the only journalist around here,' he protested. 'What about the local press? You can't nobble everyone.'

'If you know what's good for you, you'll do as you're told.'

Roland got to his feet. 'Now, Sergeant Mansfield will drive you over to Felstone Police Station where you will make a formal statement, sign it and have your fingerprints taken.'

'Right now?'

'Yes. There's no time like the present. You have no objection to having your fingerprints processed?'

'Why should I? I'm innocent,' said the journalist with dignity. 'Though I'm sure you'll find my dabs all over the *Painted Lady*.'

'I'm sure we shall. Now, if you're ready?'

'Let me just get my stuff in from the garden.'

Whilst he was collecting his typewriter and books Roland had a quick conversation with Mansfield.

'I want to have another word with Barry Spender. If Coleman was right, he also went back to the *Painted Lady* that afternoon, although he said he was working in his workshop all the time. I wonder how many more of our suspects were actually at the scene of crime that day? I can't believe that they were all milling around without seeing each other.'

'You think it was collusion?'

'No, I don't, but I don't think anyone has been honest about his or her movements that afternoon.'

'How are you going to get back?'

'Send Evans back to the Maltings in a Panda. I want to hear how he got on with Màrta Rakosi.'

Nick Blackstone dumped his belongings on the sitting

room table and picked up a linen jacket from the back
of a chair. As he put it on he appealed to Roland:
'Look, Inspector, when you've nabbed your man and
proved that I'm innocent, will you give me exclusive
rights to the story?'

'I don't make bargains with my suspects, Blackstone.
What makes you think you're going to be in a position
to write anything?'

Although he maintained a bored silence on the way
back to the station, beneath his flippant manner Nick
Blackstone was worried. What he had told the police
about visiting the *Painted Lady* and finding no one
there was the truth, but researching the story from the
London angle, he had uncovered an extraordinary tale
of deception and false identity. He knew that the man
the police thought was Mikhail Rabinovich had been
an imposter and it wouldn't be long before the police
also found out – it was almost unbelievable that they
hadn't done so already – and when they did and faced
Miklos Rakosi with the truth he would tell them about
the meeting he and Blackstone had had before that,
and the Dicks would wonder why he had kept quiet
about that and why also he hadn't told the Russian
about the manuscript. Why hadn't he? Because his
journalistic instincts had alerted him to another strand
in the story that needed following up . . . Miklos Rakosi
had revealed a deep hatred of Temirkanov which went
back to their early days in the St Petersburg Orchestra.
Blackstone feared that a confrontation between the
Russians had triggered off a vengeance killing. Miklos
Rakosi had killed his old rival; it had had nothing to do
with the manuscript – he had not known of its existence
– which meant that someone else had knocked off the

Shostakovich, and Blackstone intended finding out who and what had happened to it. He appeared to be a jump ahead of the police at this point, but for how long? And when they did catch up with the facts they would really have grounds for thinking that he, Nick Blackstone, had stolen the manuscript!

Barry Spender was up to his elbows inside a piano doing mysterious things to the strings with an equally mysterious tool. He straightened up when he saw Roland and wiped his hands on a rag that was hanging out of his jeans' pocket.

'Inspector, how are you getting on? Are you any nearer to finding out who killed Mikhail?'

'I might be progressing better if people would only tell me the truth.'

'Who hasn't been telling the truth?'

'You, for one.'

'I don't understand, I haven't lied to you.'

'Mr Spender, you told me that on the afternoon that the Russian went missing you were working here in your workshop.'

'Yes, I was.'

'You were seen going along the riverbank to your boat during that afternoon.'

Barry Spender looked blank and then his face cleared.

'That wasn't until after four. I thought you meant earlier. I'd put in a good three hours' work and I'd had enough. It had stopped raining by then and I decided to nip home whilst it was fine.'

'Did you meet anyone on the way back?'

'No one I knew, just a couple walking a dog.'

'You didn't see Dennis Coleman?'

'No – did he see me? Was that who told you?'

Roland ignored this. 'Are you sure you didn't see anyone else?'

'Look, I was tired and preoccupied. There may have been other people around but I certainly didn't recognise anyone. The only reason I remember the couple with the dog is because the damn' thing jumped up at me and left muddy pawmarks all down my jeans.'

'I see.' Roland picked up a tuning fork, looked at it and put it down again. 'You were surprised to find Mikhail Rabinovich missing when you got back?'

'Yes, I was. As far as I knew he didn't go far when we weren't there, but I thought he must have gone ashore to stretch his legs.'

'What about his missing belongings?'

'I didn't notice they weren't there. I made myself a nice cup of tea and started to prepare the evening meal. It wasn't until Jonathan returned about an hour later that I began to wonder where Mikhail had got to, then Jonathan realised that all his things had gone.'

'What did you think had happened to him?'

'We thought he'd decided to move on. Rather rude, just clearing off without so much as a by your leave, but what else were we to think?'

'So what did you do then?'

'We celebrated, Inspector.'

'She's bonkers!' said DC William Evans, reversing out of the parking space. 'Off her trolley. I don't know how she ever holds down a job here. For a start, you can't understand half of what she's saying.'

'She may have had a similar problem with you,' said

Roland innocently, who knew that Evans' Welsh accent increased in direct proportion to time spent in the Suffolk force. 'What did she have to say for herself?'

'Too much, and very little of it relevant. She seemed completely unconcerned about the fact that she could be under suspicion of murder. All she was bothered about was how crazy her husband had been to go to the police.'

'You can understand that if she thinks he's guilty. After all, if he had done it we'd never have got on to him if he hadn't walked into the station. We wouldn't have known he even existed.'

'Which surely means he *can't* have done it or he *wouldn't* have spilled the beans.'

'Unless he's covering up for her. If he thought she'd done it and someone could finger her, he might be trying to drag an almighty red herring across the trail. Do you think she'd be capable of the act?'

'And how! But she'd be more likely to have taken a cleaver to him. She's very excitable.'

'Did she tell you how she and her husband got to know about the Russian's defection in the first place?'

'She overheard Laura Nelson and Stella Lingard discussing it in the supermarket, or so she says.'

'It could well be the truth. Have either of the Rakosis an alibi for the relevant time?'

'They were at home in their house, she cooking and he working on one of the musical instruments he makes,' said Evans in disgust. 'Of course, nobody saw them and they didn't see anyone the entire afternoon.'

'You got her dabs?'

'That's another thing – she went almost hysterical when she realised she'd got to have them taken.'

'Don't forget, Evans, she was a refugee herself. She fled the Hungarian revolution with every reason to be terrified of the police in her own country. It's something you never forget.'

'Yes, sir, but you'd have thought we were going to brand her and clap her in jail for the rest of her life.'

'Mmm. If she thought that cello concerto had been written for her husband and he'd been cheated out of it all these years, you can understand her wanting to get her hands on it. It gives her a powerful motive.'

'But I thought you said, sir, that it wasn't written for him but for that other cellist living in the States.'

'Yes, it's a tangled web.' Roland sighed and drummed his fingers on the fascia board. 'Greed, revenge, jealousy . . . we can find plenty of motives for this murder but we've no proof to tie in any of our suspects with it. Plenty of conjecture but no hard proof.'

'So what can we do to get proof?'

'I'll tell you what you are going to do. When we get back I want you and Lucas to start a house-to-house.'

'A house-to-house?' groaned Evans.

'Or, rather, a dog-to-dog.'

'Sir?'

'I want you to visit all the households in the area who have a dog. Find out the people who walk their dogs regularly along the river wall. I know people without dogs also go walkies but it was stinking weather that day; dogs have to be exercised no matter what the weather but I shouldn't think anyone who didn't have to was taking a constitutional then. As I say, check if anyone was along the river wall that Tuesday afternoon and if they saw or noticed anything.'

'It's going to take ages. We'll have to go to every

house to find out if they own a dog in the first place,' grumbled Evans.

'Yes, you will, won't you? So while you're checking whether they have a dog you can slip in a question about their recreational habits. In that way we'll cover the entire population of the villages.'

'Villages?'

'Start with Woodford and then New Blund, and when you've got through them we'll have to consider Old Blund. Don't forget the houseboats but you needn't bother with the "dog-who-walks-himself".'

'The what?'

'You'll find out what I'm talking about,' said Roland with a grin.

Chapter 7

Laura Nelson hummed to herself as she prepared for her dinner party. Barry wasn't a confirmed vegetarian but this meal was really for Jonathan's benefit. As she pounded nuts and chopped vegetables she went over in her mind the difficulty she had had in tying them down to a specific evening. They had professed themselves delighted to accept her invitation but either one or other of them, or she herself, had an engagement for every suggested date. In the end they had decided on this evening but even this had presented problems. There was a jazz group appearing in a pub in Woodford that night that Barry and Jonathan wanted to hear. They would go on to that later and had suggested that she join them. She had declined. As a member of the Blund Festival Choir she herself had a scheduled rehearsal for later that evening which she had intended ducking. In the circumstances, she would now be able to attend; she would have her dinner party and when Jonathan and Barry left she would slip along to rehearsal.

It had been another blisteringly hot day, more like July than September, and she had toyed with the idea of eating outside but on second thoughts had dismissed it. There would be too many midges and moths blundering about, and besides it got dark so early. No, they would have sherry in the garden first but would eat in the house. She had opened all the doors and windows as soon as she got home and hopefully the dining room would be reasonably cool by the time they sat down to eat.

She wiped her brow and checked her watch. She must leave time to have a cool shower before she dressed. She had finished most of her preparations by now. They were having Dolmadis as the main course. Unable to obtain vine leaves, she had substituted cabbage leaves and parcelled up the savoury stuffing in them, hoping the result would be satisfactory. There was nothing more she could do now, the rest was last minute business. She put a bottle of wine in the fridge and searched for the bottle opener.

Jonathan would appreciate what a good cook she was. He would see her in her home surroundings in a romantic setting – she had made posies from pink dahlias and roses for the table, and there were matching napkins and candles – and would have second thoughts about throwing in his lot with Barry Spender. What a pity she couldn't get him on his own but she had realised that she must ask them as a pair; after all, she was returning their hospitality. It could work to her advantage. Barry would see that Jonathan was interested in her and would realise that he had made a mistake.

She didn't like him and it wasn't because he was so obviously a queer. He reminded her of the other one. It must be his hairiness. *He* had been hairy too . . . Uncle Frank. There, she had said his name aloud after trying to suppress all thoughts of him over the last few years. Uncle Frank, her father's younger brother, who had lived with them after some scandal involving a wife who had run off and left him for another man. She shuddered. She mustn't think about him, but suddenly the floodgates of her memory were open and images tumbled in, thick and fast. Uncle Frank, who had cuddled and tickled her when she was a young girl and had gone on doing it after she had arrived at puberty. Uncle Frank, who came home late at night with little gifts that he had insisted on going up to her bedroom and giving her, even if it had meant waking her up. He would hide them behind his back and advance on her bed, tweaking aside the bedclothes and whispering: 'What have I got for my girl today?' One evening he had got in to bed with her and the gift had been something new and strange and disgusting . . .

The chiming of the clock shattered the old nightmare and brought her back to the present. It was a long while since she had allowed herself to dwell on the past. Forget it now, she told herself, and concentrate on getting ready for her dinner party. She took off her apron, checked the table settings and went upstairs to dress.

'So who *does* the bloody manuscript belong to?' Superintendent Lacey stomped into Roland's office and leaned forward on the desk, glaring at his inspector.

'It's a delicate question,' said Roland, carefully moving a sheaf of papers out of the way. 'It's supposed to be gifted to Rostropovich but God knows what the legal situation is. We're going to have to tackle the Russian angle.'

'I know, I know, but that's a different ball game altogether, it can wait. I'm not bringing the Russkies into this and risking an international incident whilst I've got an unsolved murder on our hands and a killer at large. Whoever it belongs to, it is vital evidence in this case and I'm holding it until we solve this murder.'

'I thought you'd see it that way, sir. Have you read my report?'

'Why do you think I'm here? I don't like it at all. Not at all. You seem to have made a complete balls up of it so far. How long is it since the body turned up? And you're no nearer pinning it on someone.' He thumped on the desk and Roland diplomatically moved his chair back a few inches.

'And not only that,' continued Lacey, 'not only do we have a murderer in our midst, but all manner of self-confessed criminals are roaming at large!'

'Sir?'

'This librarian bloke – you could have him on any number of charges. And your second Russian – even if he didn't top his fellow countryman, he's been living here illegally for yonks and breaking all sorts of laws, besides corrupting our youngsters.'

'I don't quite follow you, sir?'

'He teaches, doesn't he? Didn't you tell me that he taught people to play the fiddle?'

'Cello. Well, yes, but I can't see what that has to do with . . .'

'You're getting soft, James, that's what. All this domestic bliss is blunting your edge. I'm asking you, why are they still at large?'

'I thought that I had made that clear, sir. Until we get more proof I don't want to alert anyone.'

'Yes, this proof – proof of what? You would have me believe the Russian was killed by somebody in order to get their hands on the manuscript. Now you say this librarian – and I don't know why you should believe what he tells you – saw someone knock him off and run away *without* the manuscript. How do you explain that?'

'I still think that he was killed for that reason but the murderer was disturbed. He may have heard Coleman approaching the boat or something else alerted him and he ran off intending to go back later and pick up the manuscript, but Coleman beat him to it.'

'And are you getting any nearer to proving this?'

'I'm working on it.'

'Well, I suppose you know what you're doing, you always did work in an unorthodox way, but it's not just me who's asking for answers. The CC is not at all happy. So far all we have officially is an unclaimed Russian who was put to bed in the river. So far, so good. But if any of this other stuff that's come to light gets public, we – and you in particular – are in big trouble. What about this journalist – who I also think you could run in on suspicion? How do you think you're going to keep him buttoned?'

'Fortunately he's not a stringer for the tabloids. He's a serious investigative journalist and I think we understand each other.'

'That's an expression that makes me quake in my boots, Inspector. It's usually a recipe for disaster.'

Roland had once had a bet with a colleague that Lacey couldn't utter a single sentence that didn't contain at least one cliché; and he had almost won.

'How's Evans coming along?' Roland blinked at the change of subject but assured his superior that the young detective constable was progressing favourably.

'Will we ever make a detective out of him?'

'I don't see why not, he shows originality.'

'I don't employ men to show originality,' growled Lacey. 'I tell you one thing, he'll never make a good copper-in-disguise. Ha ha! Not with that red hair and Welsh accent – he sticks out like a sore thumb.'

Even as a young man, the superintendent's enormous bulk and steam-roller manner must have marked him out from his fellow men, thought Roland, but it hadn't stopped his upward rise. He had ambitions that way also but couldn't see himself getting further up the ladder whilst Lacey was his boss. Lacey had done it the hard way and had no time for what he called 'white-collar dicks with university degrees'. There was sour grapes in this attitude but also fear that Roland, with his superior brain, could up-stage him.

'Don't you agree?' barked Lacey, and Roland snapped to attention.

'Yes, but he doesn't look like your average policeman either.'

'Well, I can't spend any more time discussing today's youth. Was there anything else you wanted to see me about?'

Roland forebore from reminding him that he had instigated this discussion.

'No, sir.'

'Right, then get on with it, James. I want results. I'll give you a few more days but if you haven't come up with the goods by then I shall think seriously about bringing someone else in on the case. We don't want anyone else knocked off.'

* * *

'Hello, love, a big box of chockies for you.'

'Oh, Barry, thanks, but you shouldn't have.' Laura Nelson accepted the box he held out to her and tried not to recoil when he kissed her cheeks, but he noticed her reluctance.

'Don't worry, darling, you're safe with me.'

She flushed and turned her attention to Jonathan Cade who, also gave her a quick hug and kiss. ''Lo, Laura. You're looking ravishing tonight – good enough to eat.'

She was wearing a blue and mauve flowered dress with a full skirt and nipped-in waist which complemented her slim figure, and had swept her hair back into an elaborate coil low on her neck and anchored it with a filigree gold barette.

'I'm not on the menu tonight, but I hope you'll do justice to the food. I thought we'd have a drink outside first before we eat. Is sherry all right?'

She had bought a patio set earlier in the summer, a wooden table with attached bench seats, and now she regretted it as she watched Jonathan trying to coil his long legs between the edge of the seat and the table top. Why hadn't she waited until she had saved up a little more money and then she could have invested in a white-painted wrought-iron table and matching chairs, so much more classy than this mass-produced, Sunday Superstore offering. She poured out the sherry and handed it to them. Barry looked around him appreciatively.

'This is a pleasant garden, you must work hard in it. That's one of the things I miss living on a boat – nowhere to relax and stretch out on a sunbed.'

'That didn't stop you today.' Jonathan turned to Laura. 'He came home early and lay prone on the deck in the full sun. Don't you think he looks par-boiled?'

'You do look a bit red, Barry.'

'We can't all go that delightful honey-gold colour,' said Spender, giving his partner the eye.

'I must go inside and put the finishing touches to the meal. Help yourselves to a refill.'

She left them with the sherry bottle and went back into the kitchen and took the wine out of the fridge. She drew the cork and stood the bottle on the table, served up the starters and went out to collect her guests.

'That's a charming brooch you're wearing,' said Barry looking at the Victorian piece she had pinned to her shoulder. It was oval in shape, made from seed pearls and enamel fashioned into an intricate swirl of flower patterns. 'It would look good on your shirt, Jonathan.'

The younger man was wearing a turquoise shirt that emphasised his suntan and tawny hair.

Laura swallowed. 'Dinner is ready, shall we go inside?'

'Sounds good news. Something smells marvellous.'

It was still very hot. The flowers on the table were wilting and the air hung heavy and oppressive in the small room. Laura wished that she had prepared a cold meal.

'If I had lighting outside we could have eaten out there but it gets dark so early. There's a harvest moon tonight but it's hidden behind the other houses.'

'It's unbelievable weather. You think you're in the middle of a summer heatwave and then it's seven o'clock and nearly dark and you realise that autumn is almost upon us.'

They discussed the weather some more and Laura was complimented on her cooking. She gathered the dishes together and asked Jonathan to pour the wine whilst she fetched the next course to the table. The dolmadis made him recall a holiday he had spent in Greece island-hopping as a student.

'Have you ever been, Laura? It was a marvellous experience. The sea really is wine-dark and there are these incredibly white buildings sandwiched between the sea and the sky; whole villages clinging to the summit of rocks rising sheer out of the water. It was very hot but somehow it's a different heat to that which we get here in England.'

'It is hot tonight.' Barry mopped his face and took a long draught of wine. His face was very red and he looked sticky and flustered.

'No, I've never been to Greece,' said Laura, 'it's one of the places I've always wanted to visit but the nearest I've been is a fortnight in Majorca.'

'Well, we all have to start somewhere,' said Barry maliciously, running his finger round the inside of his collar and undoing another button on his shirt.

'Where do you go for your holidays?'

'Haven't had one for a couple of years, but we're remedying that soon, aren't we, Jonathan? We thought of going to Amsterdam for a few days in October to check out the scene there.'

'I have been there. I went on one of those coach-trips that takes in the bulb fields. There are some good museums there, the Rijksmuseum and the Van Gogh gallery. I'm surprised you haven't been there, Jonathan, as you're an artist.'

'I've spent time in Paris and Italy catching up on

art studies but this will be new to me. I'm particularly looking forward to the Van Goghs. Are you interested in that period?'

Jonathan and Laura had a lively discussion on the Impressionists and Post-Impressionists whilst Barry fidgetted and look uncomfortable. His friend suddenly realised he was taking no part in the conversation.

'Are you okay, Barry? You look a bit flushed.'

'I . . . I think I overdid the sun today. I think I've got a bit of sunstroke.

'Oh, Barry, you do look rather red,' said Laura, looking at the older man's countenance which was almost peony colour. 'Have some more wine, it will cool you down.'

He accepted another glass of wine. 'Sorry, Laura, I'm not doing justice to your lovely meal. The heat doesn't usually affect me like this. I feel all hot and yet shivery at the same time.'

'Sunstroke can do that to you. You feel hot one moment and cold the next. You'd better keep out of the sun for the next few days. Would either of you like any more ratatouille or rice?' Both men declined and Laura served up the dessert. 'This is delicious,' said Jonathan after he had eaten a few spoonfuls. 'You must give us this recipe, mustn't she, Barry?'

Barry Spender put down his spoon and gulped. 'I'm sorry, Laura, I feel rather sick – may I use your loo?' he blundered to his feet and gripped the edge of the table, swaying slightly.

'Of course. It's upstairs, first on the right.' After he had left the room she turned to Jonathan. 'Had he been drinking before you came?'

'Drinking?'

'I thought perhaps he'd had too much to drink.' She gave an embarrassed little laugh.

'He had a beer when we got back after work. He may have had a couple, but he hasn't had much here, just sherry and a couple of glasses of wine. I wouldn't have thought that was enough to affect him. I've never known him like this before.'

'But you haven't known him very long, have you?'

'Long enough,' he said shortly. 'I'm sure he's not drunk. It must be too much sun and possibly the alcohol has exacerbated the situation.'

There was an awkward silence and then Laura got to her feet.

'I'll just put the coffee on.' She went out to the kitchen. While she was filling the percolator she heard Barry totter down the stairs and the two men talking together. When she went back into the room she was horrified by Barry's appearance. His face had been very red and flushed before but now it had darkened to an almost purple floridness and he was shaking.

'Oh, Barry, you do look ill. Would you like to lie down for a while? The bed is made up in the spare bedroom.'

'Sorry to make such an exhibition of myself,' he mumbled, 'but I think I'd better go home. A touch of the sun. I shall be okay tomorrow.'

'Well, it's up to you but won't you have coffee first? And how about a brandy – it will help to settle your stomach,' she added.

He shuddered. 'No thanks, Laura, had enough. Must get home.' He was slurring his words and she gave Jonathan a meaningful look.

'Right, old chap, we'd better get you home,' he said, looking worried.

'You can't walk, not with him in that condition. I'll get a taxi. Look, Jonathan, help yourself to a coffee whilst I ring for one.'

'Don't wanna taxi, a walk will help to clear my head.'

'Are you sure?' Jonathan asked his partner.

'Yes, can't go in a taxi. Might be sick over the up . . . upholstery.'

'I'll come with you. The two of us should be able to manage him.' Laura gathered up her handbag and locked the back door.

'I'm very sorry about this,' said Jonathan, 'after all the trouble you went to to cook such a super meal.'

'We can do it again some time,' she said lightly, 'and you enjoyed yours, didn't you?'

'Can't go to the jazz tonight,' muttered Barry. 'Sorry, old love.'

'Don't worry about that, there'll be plenty more gigs.'

'You must go, can't spoil your evening.'

'We'll see. Let's get you home.'

Together they got him out of the house and, supporting him on either side started the trek back to the *Painted Lady*. As they crossed the bridge and went towards the footpath they met Dennis Coleman on his way to the Maltings. He eyed them with concern and hurried over to them.

'Is anything wrong?'

'Barry is unwell, we're taking him home,' said Laura, trying not to cringe as his full weight seemed to rest on her right shoulder.

'He doesn't look too good. Would you like me to get my car and run you round to Woodford quay? It's not so far to walk from there.'

'Thanks, but we'll be okay,' said Jonathan. 'By the time you could do that we'll have him home.'

'Well, if you're sure . . . can you see where you're going?'

'The moon is nearly as bright as street lighting and the night air will help revive him.'

'I'm just going to the rehearsal,' said the librarian to Laura.

'I hadn't forgotten about it. I'll be along later.'

'Well, if you're sure I can't help you, I'll be getting along.'

After a last doubtful glance at Barry Coleman he went on his way and they heard his footsteps receding into the distance.

The journey back to the *Painted Lady* was a nightmare. As Laura was so much shorter than Jonathan she seemed to be supporting more of the sick man's weight. They stumbled and slithered along the grassy path with Barry slung between them, a dead weight. To their left the river sucked and slurped at the muddy strand. The tide was full, just starting to go down, and there were two harvest moons; one rosily flushed like a Chinese lantern, diminishing rapidly as it climbed the sky; the other pale and glittering in the black water like a giant, submerged silver coin. The reedbeds were a spiky, etiolated jungle and from them issued rustles and squeaks as the inhabitants scuttled about their night-time business. Everywhere was the smell of the river; an odour compounded of mud and seaweed and rotted vegetation, overlaid with the sharp tang of salt, a reminder that the sea lay only a few miles distant.

Laura hadn't been aware of how isolated the *Painted Lady* was until they came upon it, a squat, moon-bleached ark, floating in solitary splendour a considerable distance from the huddle of houseboats and barges moored farther downstream nearer Woodford. Barry groaned as they helped him across the companionway.

'Do you think you ought to get a doctor?' whispered Laura to Jonathan. Barry heard her.

'Don't want a doctor. I shall be all right after I have had a night's sleep.'

They got him into the cabin and he collapsed on to the bunk and rolled over on to his back.

'There's nothing wrong with me, just too much sun and booze and rich food.' He closed his eyes and Laura looked across to Jonathan.

'Do you think we should get him out of those clothes? His pyjamas?'

'Leave me alone.' He opened his eyes and focused on Laura with difficulty. 'No woman is going to undress me.'

'I didn't mean . . . Oh, well, I don't suppose it will matter if he sleeps in his clothes for once.'

'Look, Laura, thanks awfully for your help,' said Jonathan, 'but I can manage him now. Will you be okay walking back to your place? I'll stay with him and . . .'

'No,' interrupted Barry, struggling to sit up. 'You go to the gig, you know you badly wanted to go. I shall be perfectly all right on my own. I feel better already. I shall have a good night's sleep and be as right as rain in the morning. You take Laura home and go on to the

gig.' He lay down again and appeared to be drifting off
to sleep. 'Nice girl, Laura . . . can't have her wandering
about on her own at night. Not safe . . .'

Jonathan shrugged. 'Well, I suppose he'll be all right.
He can't come to much harm here.'

'He'll be quiet here, it's probably better to let him
sleep it off. Have you got any calomine lotion on board
for his sun burn?'

'God knows, probably not. It's not worth disturbing
him to find out.'

They were talking in whispers and Jonathan grinned
at her. 'Come on, we'd better do as he says. He's going
to be very embarrassed in the morning when he realises
what's happened; at least he won't feel so bad if he
knows that I went to the gig.'

After a last look at his recumbent friend, Jonathan
switched off the light and they went back on deck.

'Look, Jonathan, if you're going into Woodford for
this gig it's pointless your coming back along the footpath with me, it's in the opposite direction. You go
along the towpath. I'll be all right on my own.'

'Don't be ridiculous. Of course I'll see you back to
the village. I'll go on my bike into Woodford. I left it
at the Maltings.'

As they walked back along the footpath Laura told
Jonathan about her part in the Blund Festival Choir
and the forthcoming concert they were rehearsing for.
Jonathan held her hand and she felt absurdly happy.
If only she hadn't told him about the choir practice he
might have asked her to accompany him to this jazz gig.
The moon was high in the sky now and every blade of
grass, leaf and twig was picked out in glittering detail.
There was not a breath of wind, a most unusual feature

in that district where the cold east winds howled in over the marshes from the North Sea in the autumn and winter and where it was very rare, even in the summer, not to feel any breeze at all, especially at night.

As they approached Laura's house, Jonathan spoke.

'You're going back to face a horrible mess. Let me come in and help you to wash up.'

'No, it's okay, Jonathan. I shan't tackle that tonight. I'll just collect my music and go straight across to the rehearsal.'

'Are you sure? Well, thanks for a super meal, I appreciated it even if my partner didn't. I apologise for him.'

'Don't be silly, it wasn't your fault. And poor Barry couldn't help it. I hope he feels better tomorrow.'

She opened the gate and slipped inside. He bent over and kissed her on the forehead.

'Goodnight Laura – and thanks.'

Once inside, she looked with dismay at the pots and pans littering the worktops in the kitchen and the remains of the meal on the dining-room table. Perhaps she should have accepted his offer of help. But, no, that wouldn't have been right. She scraped the left-over food into the bin and dumped the dirty crockery in the sink, putting in the plug and filling it with water so that they would soak overnight; then she tidied herself up and searched for her music.

Stella Lingard bit her lip and stared at her reflection in the dressing-table mirror. All dressed up and nowhere to go. She removed her earings, heavy glittering globes, rubbed her ear-lobes and ran her fingers through her fringe. She didn't believe Nick Blackstone was ill, she had been stood up. They had been going out for a meal and on to a pub in Woodford afterwards that ran jazz sessions on certain nights during the week. He had rung earlier to say that he felt under the weather and was going to have an early night instead but she was sure that he was lying.

Ever since he had returned from his sojourn in London, about which he had been remarkably reticent, she had noticed a change in him. She couldn't quite pin down what it was exactly, she wasn't even sure if it was connected with her. He was preoccupied and yet in some way excited as if he were gloating over a secret known only to himself. He had told her about his brush with the police – perhaps it was something to do with that but he hadn't seemed worried about it, amused rather. No, he'd probably got another woman, a new lover who was now occupying his thoughts, and this broken date was the forerunner to the big brush-off. He was probably with this new conquest now, maybe even entertaining her in his home on the other side of the village.

At this thought she jumped to her feet, switched off the light and went over to the window. She tweaked aside the curtains and looked out over the lane that ended just beyond her house and the fields beyond. The scene was bathed in moonlight; it was a night for lovers, a night for wandering over the dew-drenched grass hand-in-hand. She couldn't bear it any longer, she had to know what Nick was up to. She would go round to his place and spy on him.

She grabbed a shawl from the back of a chair, flung it round her shoulders and let herself out of the house. She didn't need a torch, the moonlight was so bright it could have been midday. She walked briskly down the road, took a short-cut across the churchyard and ended up outside the Old Smokehouse panting and out of breath. She paused by the gate and then slipped into the garden and looked up at the house. No lights showed at the windows, just the cold glare of moonlight reflecting off the black glass. The place looked deserted, there was no sound, no movement. He wasn't there.

The cheating louse! He *had* lied to her. But no, perhaps he really was unwell and even now lying upstairs in bed in a darkened room. How could she find out? Her fingers itched to ring the doorbell to see if he would come stumbling to the door in his dressing-gown to answer the summons. But she knew she mustn't do that. What would she say, what excuse could she make for her presence on his doorstep? He would know that she had been checking up on him.

She went round the side of the house to the garage. It wasn't a proper garage, but an old lean-to shed that had been utilised for that purpose. The door was permanently propped open and through it she could see Nick's car, a maroon Montego. She crept nearer and in the quietness heard faint clicking and sibilant sighs. The car had been used recently. She edged her way between the vehicle and the wall and laid her hand on the bonnet. It was still warm. He had been out! He had probably only just got back, had only returned to the house a short while ago, or maybe he had put the car away and gone off again on foot.

She moved back and her shawl became hooked on a projecting nail. As she struggled to free it her elbow knocked against a pile of apple trays and they crashed to the ground, making what seemed to her a deafening noise. At the same time there was an unearthly shriek. She leaned against the wall with pounding heart and saw the cat streaking across the lawn. There was no other movement. No lights came on in the house, no Nick Blackstone appeared at the door to see what was happening. She stared up at the house and the windows glimmered blackly back at her.

What was she doing here? How could she have sunk so low as to come spying on her lover? She had never felt like this before; all choked up with an emotion which she supposed was jealousy. In previous affairs she had always been the one to call time, now it looked as if the situation was reversed and she was to be at the receiving end of a rebuff. What was it about Nick Blackstone anyway that had reduced her to this pass? She had no illusions about him, but even knowing what he was like did nothing to dampen her ardour. She was smitten with him and didn't intend giving him up without a fight. But why couldn't she be more like Laura Nelson whose notion of a love affair was cerebral romance rather than physical commitment? Other people managed without it too. Take poor Dennis Coleman; he couldn't have much going for him these days. He must have loved that ghastly Helen once, she supposed, but his love-life must be non-existent now and he was not the sort to take his pleasures elsewhere, more fool him. When she thought about it she knew a lot of lonely, repressed people, or perhaps they just weren't as highly sexed as herself.

She turned her back on the house, slipped through the gate and started the walk home. Her feet were soaked with dew and also the hem of her skirt. It clung damply to her legs, hampering her movements, and she shivered and wished herself home. She retraced her steps and as she recrossed the churchyard heard someone coming in the other direction along the second footpath that ran alongside the row of boundary yews. She slunk behind a gravestone and crouched there, feeling like a heroine of a Victorian melodrama, until the footsteps receded. Then she straightened up and continued on her way. She hadn't seen who the other person was but she had the feeling that whoever it was had been as keen as she not to be seen. There had been something furtive in the movements, something clandestine.

'Omnes, omnes generationes,' sang the altos and the basses and second trebles, 'Omnes, omnes generationes,' echoed the first trebles as Laura Nelson slipped into the hall and took her place amongst the sopranos. The notes of the Bach 'Magnificat' soared upwards, echoing round the hall, and the singers, hot and flushed and with pulsating throats, followed their conductor.

She found her place in the score and joined in, wishing that she could have run through a few scales as a warm-up. Dennis Coleman was across the aisle from her with the tenors; she thought how ill he looked. He always wore an air of perpetual harassment as if life were one big worry but now he looked positively grey, quite haggard. The choir reached the fortissimo at the end of the *'omnes generationes'* and the conductor rapped on his music stand.

'Right, we'll skip the two solos and go on to No. 7: "*Fecit Potentiam*" I know it's hot this evening but do try and get a little feeling into it. We'll break for coffee afterwards.'

* * *

Dennis Coleman came over to her as they collected their cups from the trolley.

'What was wrong with Barry Spender? He looked as if he had had one too many?'

'I'm not sure. They came for a meal and he was taken ill towards the end. He didn't have all that much to drink at my place but I think he'd been drinking earlier. He reckoned he'd got sunstroke.'

'Poor old fruit. So you've been entertaining our gays? Don't tell me you're still hankering over Jonathan?'

'Don't be ridiculous, Dennis, I was just returning their hospitality. It's a shame that Barry was taken ill.'

'So where he is now, tucked up on board the *Painted Lady* with his friend in attendance?'

'We put him to bed, yes, but Jonathan's gone into Woodford. They were supposed to be going to some jazz do and Barry insisted that he keep to the plan.'

'Doesn't seem a very kind way to behave. I always thought that men of that ilk were supposed to be very caring and supportive.'

'I wish you wouldn't talk like that, Dennis. Barry just wanted to be quiet and undisturbed. It seemed the sensible thing to do, to leave him on his own.'

Dennis Coleman drained his polystyrene cup and put it down.

'Well, I must love you and leave you.'

'Aren't you staying for the rest of the rehearsal?'

'No, Helen's not too good and I promised I'd be home early. Besides, we've done the "Magnificat" several times before and I know it inside out.'

'I saw Helen today. Her friend was wheeling her round the shops.'

'Mrs Maudsley? She's a real gem, I don't know what we'd do without her.'

'Helen hinted that you were giving up work soon to look after her.'

'She *what*?'

'Maybe I got it wrong, but she gave the impression that you'd come into some money and wouldn't need to work.'

'Wishful thinking on her part, I'm afraid. We most certainly *do* need my salary and I can't think of . . .'

He left the rest of the sentence unfinished but Laura knew what he had nearly said.

'It must be very difficult for you, Dennis, you need your outside interests like this.'

'It helps to keep me sane,' he admitted. 'I'll slip out now before you start again.'

As he left the hall the strains of 'Fecit Potentiam: The Lord hath shewed strength' followed him across the courtyard. I wish the Lord would show me strength, he thought as he walked through the archway and set off home.

Barry Spender shuddered and pulled himself into a sitting position on his bunk. A short while ago he had been so cold that he had been unable to stop shivering; now he was so hot that he thought he would burst. He felt as if the blood was rushing round his head and his skin was too tight to contain it; at any moment it would burst through and his head would explode. He also felt terribly sick. He must get some air. If he stayed down below any longer he would suffocate.

He swung his legs to the floor and stood up, clutching the bulkhead for support. The sweat was prickling on his forehead, and upper lip. He must get out. Somehow he fought off the dizziness and dragged himself up on deck where he took great gulps of the night air. The moon glimmered on the water and on the boat, throwing monstrous shadows across the deck. The whole scene was like a negative print; black on white, white on black. He knew that he was going to be sick, horribly sick.

As he leaned over the side there was a pressure between his shoulder blades and he felt himself falling . . . falling . . .

The black turgid water closed over his head. He did not resurface.

Chapter 8

Laura Nelson was awakened by the sound of knocking on her front door She struggled up the bed and squinted at the luminous dial of the alarm clock on the bedside table. It said 12.45 am. Had she really heard a noise or had she been dreaming? Even as she lay down again and prepared to go back to sleep she heard a voice calling her name, softly but urgently. She swung out of bed, grabbed her dressing-gown, hurridly donned it and went over to the window. She had left it open when she went to bed and now she pulled back the curtains and leaned out. Jonathan Cade was standing in the middle of the path looking up at her.

'Jonathan! What's the matter? Was that you banging on the door?'

'Yes. Is Barry with you?'

'Barry? What on earth do you mean?'

'He's disappeared. He wasn't on the *Painted Lady* when I got back and I just wondered if he'd come back here.'

'It's the middle of the night! Look, I'll come down. Wait a moment.'

She tied the sash of her dressing-gown, thrust her feet into her slippers and ran down the stairs. Jonathan loomed up in the porch as she unlocked the front door.

'I'm sorry, Laura, it was a crazy idea. I was clutching at straws.' He looked distraught and followed her up the hall in a daze.

'You mean he really has disappeared? But I don't understand . . . Where can he have gone?'

'I got back just after midnight and he wasn't there. I thought he'd be asleep on the bunk but he just seems to have vanished.'

'But what can have happened to him?'

Jonathan said nothing but stared at her in misery. As comprehension dawned she stared back at him in horror.

'Oh my God! You don't think he's fallen in the river?'

'He was all befuddled, he could have slipped over the side.'

'But surely if he fell in the water would have revived him and he would have swum ashore.'

'He can't swim, remember?'

'He can't have fallen . . . perhaps he wanted a breath of air and went for a walk?'

'There's not a sign of him anywhere, I've looked all round. I should never have gone and left him.'

'Oh, Jonathan, I'm sure nothing's happened to him. There's probably a simple explanation . . . he'll turn up again soon.'

'I wish that I could believe that.'

'I'll put the kettle on and make a pot of tea, you look frozen.'

'It is cold out there now. Thanks, Laura, but I'd better get back.'

'It won't take a moment. What are you going to do if he's not there? Don't you think you ought to phone the police?'

'I don't know what to do. There may be a perfectly simple explanation for his absence, and if he comes back and finds I've brought in the law he's not going to be very pleased. On the other hand, perhaps they could organise a search.'

'They wouldn't be able to do that until daylight, would they?'

She poured the boiling water into the teapot, stirred it and filled the mugs. He accepted one, took a gulp and gasped as the hot liquid burned his throat.

'Maybe he did go for a walk and he's slipped and broken a leg or something and is lying somewhere helpless. I must go back and have another search.'

'Shall I get dressed and come with you?'

'No, it was unfair of me to knock you up. I just had this mad idea that maybe he'd come back here later after I'd gone into Woodford.'

'Why should he have done that? And besides, I wasn't here. I went on to rehearsal when I left you.'

'Yes, I'm not thinking clearly. Look, I'll go back to the *Painted Lady*, he may have turned up. If he's still missing in the morning I'll alert the police.'

'Are you sure you wouldn't like me to come with you?'

'No, there's nothing you can do. Thanks for the tea, I'm sorry I woke you.'

She opened the door and watched him walk down the path.

'Jonathan, be careful, won't you? Mind you don't slip and fall in the river.'

After he had gone she eyed the dirty crockery in the kitchen and made a decision. She was wide awake now, there was no way she would get to sleep. She might as well get on with the chores. She ran hot water into the sink, fetched a clean tea-towel and got down to the task of washing up her dinner party dishes. As she scrubbed and rinsed she tried to subdue the little glow that started to flicker deep down inside her. If Barry had really gone missing Jonathan would be all hers. She tried to thrust the thought away; it was wicked to think like that but she couldn't help it. Perhaps the gods were on her side after all.

Ginny Roland also had a disturbed night. The baby was very active and always seemed to choose the times when she was recumbent to start kicking and making its presence felt. She had also had a bad attack of cramp which had kept her and James awake until the small hours, for which she felt very guilty. He had been working all the hours God had given him on this latest case, coming home exhausted and frustrated; he didn't need the extra complication of a restless wife who needed her back massaged in the middle of the night. At six o'clock, knowing that she wouldn't get any more sleep, she struggled out of bed, careful not to wake James who was lying on his side, dead to the world, and padded downstairs.

As she crossed the hall she remembered to reconnect the phone.

James would be furious if he knew that she had deliberately unplugged it a few hours earlier to ensure that nothing else disturbed him. She put the kettle on and looked out of the kitchen window. A heavy mist, shot through with pink and gold, wreathed the garden. It was going to be another hot day, but now, at this early hour, there was a distinctly autumnal feeling in the air. Myriads of gossamer cobwebs shimmered across the dew-drenched lawn. She had picked mushrooms from it yesterday; there might well be another crop today. Faience had heard her moving about and appeared from the mist, bounding across the grass leaving dark pawprints like bruises on the silvery surface. She rattled through the cat-flap and wound in and out of Ginny's legs.

'Hey, Faience, you're soaking! Don't do that!' She bent down with difficulty and poured milk into the cat's saucer. A little niggle of pain ran through her from back to front as she straightened up. Warm-up contractions they were called at her ante-natal class and she had been having them for several days. This baby was going to be early. Simon had been, she remembered, despite being a first baby. She had not told James. Time to worry him when labour started in earnest.

She made herself a mug of tea and was sitting down sipping it when the phone rang. She answered it immediately and Patrick Mansfield's voice came booming down the line.

'Ginny? I didn't wake you?'

'It's all right, Patrick, I'm up and about and I've taken it downstairs. I suppose you want James?'

'Yes, I've been trying to reach you for quite a time. Is there something wrong with your phone?'

'I think it's playing up,' she said vaguely, 'I'll call him.'

'No need, I'm here.' Her husband appeared in the

doorway, his black hair sticking up in wedges, a dark shadow round his jaw.

Whilst he held a terse conversation with his sergeant she fetched another mug and started to lay the table for breakfast. He put down the phone, and stretched and yawned.

'Is anything wrong?'

'One of the chief witnesses in my case has disappeared.'

'You mean he's done a bunk?'

'Met with an accident or something more sinister. I must get dressed, Patrick's coming straight round to pick me up.'

'Have you time for breakfast first?'

'Just some toast. What are you doing up so early? I didn't hear you get out of bed.'

'You were sound asleep, I didn't want to disturb you.'

'Cramp again?'

'His Nibs had decided that I'd been lying still long enough.'

'You should have woken me, I'd have brought you a cup of tea in bed.' He gave her a quick hug and kiss. 'I'm supposed to be looking after you, not the other way round.'

'I'm fine, James, don't worry about me. Is this latest development going to help you solve your case?'

'I've been moaning about things being at stalemate; now it looks as if they're moving again, but this is something I was not anticipating. I may have to rethink it all.'

'You go and get dressed whilst I make the toast and coffee.'

Patrick Mansfield arrived as Roland was finishing his hurried breakfast and Ginny let him in.

'How are you keeping, Ginny?'

'Fine, but I shall be glad to get rid of the bump. Have you time for a coffee?'

'Grab a cup whilst I finish dressing,' said Roland, 'I'll be two minutes.' He pushed back his chair and ran upstairs.

'How's young Simon? I haven't seen him about lately?'

'Moaning about being back at school but he's buckling down to work. I think he's just realised that his GCSE's are next year and not in some distant future. It's time he was up.' She glanced at the clock. 'I must wake him.'

'Not doing the paper-round now?'

'No, he's given it up, what with the extra homework and his hobbies. Is Jean still keeping you to this diet?'

'I'm just a shadow of my former self, haven't you noticed?'

Ginny considered him. 'You don't exactly look thinner, but certainly more healthy. You suit your build. You wouldn't look right if you were thin and boney.'

'Can I have that in writing?'

James thundered down the stairs. 'Okay, let's go. You can give me the gen in the car.'

He gave Ginny a kiss. 'Now be careful, don't do anything silly.'

'What do you think I'm going to do? Dig up the garden?'

'I wouldn't put it past you. Just take things easy, I'll be back as soon as I can.'

After they had gone Ginny poured herself another cup of coffee and called up the stairs to Simon. Perhaps she would go blackberrying later on. That was a nice gentle occupation and there would be no time for such things once the baby was here.

'Jonathan Cade turned up at Woodford Police Station at the crack of dawn and they got straight on to us.' Mansfield winced as the early morning sun struck through the windscreen. He hurriedly pulled down the sun-visor. 'Apparently he was in a terrible state. Seemed to think that Spender had fallen overboard and drowned.'

'Not another one! I don't think I could swallow another identical accident.'

'That's what I thought. He's back on the *Painted Lady* now in the company of Evans and I've organised a search party along that part of the riverbank and marshes.'

'Why wasn't I informed straight away?'

'Your phone was on the blink. I had a hell of a job trying to raise you.'

Roland frowned. 'What did he have to say?'

'Just the garbled tale I told you over the phone. I've left the real questioning to you.'

'When did Spender go missing?'

'Last seen about 10pm last night.'

'Christ! If he fell in the river then and hasn't turned up since, there's not much hope of still finding him alive.'

Being early, there was little traffic about and Mansfield did the journey in record time. They left the car at the head of the towpath and hurried along the river wall. Evans was waiting for them on the deck of the *Painted Lady*.

'Where is he?' asked Roland.

'Down in the cabin. Cade's in a right old taking – seems to think it was his fault. The search party has found no sign in the immediate area. They've moved on to Blund lagoon.'

'He's more likely to be in the water.'

Jonathan Cade had heard their voices and burst on deck. The change in him was startling. His movements were un-coordinated as if he were sleep-walking and his skin looked pinched and yellow. There were dark circles under his eyes.

'Why aren't you *doing* something!' he demanded of the two detectives.

'Calm down, Cade, and tell us what has happened.'

'I've already told the police, you're wasting precious time . . .'

'Look, Cade, if you want us to find your friend tell us in your own words just what happened last night.'

In stumbling sentences he told them of the events of the previous evening. Roland did not interrupt until the other man finished up in an anguished whisper: 'I should never have gone off and left him. It wouldn't have happened if I'd stayed here with him.'

'You think he fell overboard?'

'Don't you understand what I've been telling you? He wasn't well. He was feeling ill and I went and left him . . . He probably didn't know what he was doing. He wouldn't have stood a chance if he went in.'

'Surely he could swim?'

'No.'

'You mean he lived on a boat and he couldn't swim?'

'No – I mean, yes. He used to say that in the olden days sailors never learnt to swim. They reckoned it prolonged the agony if they were shipwrecked . . .' He moaned and turned away, doubled up with grief.

At that moment Roland became aware that someone else was running along the riverbank towards the *Painted Lady*. It was Laura Nelson. He went ashore and intercepted her.

'Miss Nelson, why are you here?'

'Has he turned up? No, he can't have done or you wouldn't be here. Oh God!'

Roland led her along the towpath, away from the *Painted Lady* and Jonathan Cade.

'I believe you were with Barry Spender last night. Tell me what happened?'

'Hasn't Jonathan told you? Surely . . .'

'I should like to hear your version, Miss Nelson. Understandably, Mr Cade is somewhat overwrought at the moment. I'm relying on you to give me the true picture.'

'Well, they came to my house for a meal – Jonathan and Barry. I'd prepared a special vegetarian dinner because Jonathan is a vegetarian. We'd nearly finished eating when Barry was taken ill.'

'What do you mean? How was he ill?'

She hesitated and looked embarrassed and then blurted out: 'If you really want to know, I think he was drunk! No, not drunk exactly, but he'd had too much. I know I shouldn't say things like this, especially as he may . . . may be dead, but I think drink was the cause of it.'

'Are you saying he was tiddly when he arrived?'

'No, but he'd been drinking before he came –

Jonathan said so afterwards – and he had sherry and wine with the meal.'

'Mr Cade seems to think that he was suffering from sunstroke.'

'Yes, I think it was a mixture of the two. His skin was very red.'

'So what happened?'

'He said he felt sick and dizzy and he certainly looked awful. I wanted him to lie down but he insisted on going back to the *Painted Lady* so Jonathan and I took him back. He sort of collapsed on his bunk and said he wanted to be alone and he would sleep it off so we left him.'

'And Mr Cade went off to a jazz concert in Woodford?'

'You make it sound as if he didn't care but it wasn't like that at all.'

'So how was it?'

'They were both supposed to be going to this gig after they left me. Barry insisted that Jonathan keep to the arrangements and we thought he'd be okay, quiet and undisturbed . . .'

'Spender and Cade came to you for a dinner party and yet had made arrangements to go on to another "do" the same evening? I find that rather odd, Miss Nelson.'

'It was a prior arrangement. As I too was supposed to have a rehearsal later that evening, we agreed to eat and go our separate ways afterwards.'

'Rehearsal?'

'I belong to the Blund Festival Choir and we're rehearsing for a concert.'

'So you went to this rehearsal – what time would that have been?'

'About nine-thirty. I got there just before the coffee break. They usually have one half-way through
the evening.'

'They didn't have their interval until after nine-
thirty? Your rehearsals must start late.'

'We usually start about seven-thirty but this was
scheduled for later because the hall was being used
by another group earlier in the evening.'

'I see. So you were at rehearsal from nine-thirty
until . . . ?'

'About ten-forty-five. I went straight home when
it finished.'

'Did anyone see you and Cade bringing Spender
back here?'

'Yes, we bumped into Dennis Coleman. He could
see that Barry was under the weather and offered to
get his car out and run him back but we told him we
could manage and I explained to him later what had
happened.'

'Later?'

'He's in the choir too and I had a word with him in
the coffee break.'

'So you and Dennis Coleman were both rehearsing
for the rest of the evening?'

'Yes . . . well, actually, no. Dennis had to go home
early because Helen wasn't very well. He left before
we started rehearsing again after the break.' Roland
looked at her thoughtfully and she burst out:

'Look, we're wasting time – we should be looking for him!'

'If he fell in the river last night he's beyond our help.
His body will turn up eventually and in the meantime
my men are searching the area.'

'Yes, I'm sorry. I must see Jonathan . . .'

'All in good time, but you haven't finished telling me about last night yet.'

'I've told you everything I can remember.'

'Why are you here this morning?'

She looked at him as if he had taken leave of his senses.

'To find out if Barry has turned up!'

'Miss Nelson, if you went straight back from rehearsal to your home last night, how do you know that Barry Spender has gone missing?'

'Oh . . . didn't he tell you? Jonathan knocked me up in the night.'

'To tell you that Spender had disappeared?'

'He wanted to know if by any chance he'd come back to my house. What put such a crazy idea into his head I can't imagine but he was in a dreadful state and checking out any possibility, I suppose.'

'What time was this?'

'After midnight . . . nearer one o'clock. I offered to get dressed and go with him to look for Barry but he refused. I suppose we should have gone to the police then?'

'I don't think it would have made any difference, Miss Nelson. I think it will turn out to be just one of those unfortunate accidents. You mustn't blame yourself.'

'May I speak to Jonathan now?'

'I can't stop you but I think it would probably be more tactful if you left him alone.'

'I . . . no, I must see him.'

Roland shrugged. 'Just one more question, Miss Nelson. Did you know that Barry Spender couldn't swim?'

'Yes, I thought it was very stupid of him to live on a boat. It's easy enough to slip and fall overboard even when you're sober and I don't think there was even a lifebouy on board.'

Roland put out a call for PC Scoggins and when he turned up he questioned him closely about tides and currents.

'I don't think there's any doubt that he went overboard late yesterday evening – that would have been after nine o'clock. Where would he be most likely to fetch up?'

'It was high tide about quarter to eight so he would have gone in on an ebb tide. He would have gone in the opposite direction to the last one.'

'Downstream?'

'Yes, sir. It was another full tide, he could be way down by now. A dog fell off a yacht further upstream than this last year and he turned up on the beach at Felstone a few days later.'

'You mean, he could have been swept through the mouth of the estuary and out to sea?'

'If he gets as far as the mouth it's quite likely, there are nasty currents and cross-tides near the bar, but I think he'll probably get entangled in something before he reaches there.'

'I hope you're right, we need to find him quick. A lot hinges on whether he was attacked before he ended up in the drink.'

As if on cue, William Evans came hurrying up.

'We've found him, sir, I think. A report has just come through that a body has turned up in the Marina, fouling an anchor chain apparently.'

'Well, it doesn't look as if we're going to need you any longer, Constable,' said Roland to Scoggins. 'Thanks for your help.'

After Scoggins had gone Roland, Mansfield and Evans piled into Roland's car and drove over to the Marina which was situated below Woodford but on the same bank of the river.

'Is it our man? Did they get him out?'

'It's a man's body, that's all I know, and an amateur diver was involved.'

'Amateur diver?' Roland groaned.

'The owner of one of those luxury super-yachts. He tried to up-anchor this morning and realised that something was caught up in the chain, so, as he dabbles in diving, he went down to see what was wrong and found the body. I believe he released it.'

'I thought all those yachts were moored at berths. What was he doing lying at anchor?'

'Apparently all the berths were occupied yesterday, it's a very busy time of year, so he anchored out of the way round the other side of the jetty.'

There was a large police presence at the Marina and it was needed. There seemed to be hundreds of people milling around trying to get as close as possible to the cordonned-off jetty.

'Hell! We're never going to keep this one under wraps. Where have they all come from – I thought this Marina was private property?'

'There's over a hundred boats berthed here and most of them have at least two people, mostly four, on board.'

'Right, if I drive through is there room to turn the car?'

Roland drove through the police cordon and parked the car beside the crane that reared up, black and sinister, from the end of one arm of the jetty.

The body was lying inside a makeshift screen. It was Barry Spender. Roland stared down at him with a horrid sense of déjà-vu. It seemed only a short while since he had been looking at the other body fished out of the river. That one had definitely been murdered, this one could be an accidental death; how did this affect his case, was there a tie-up? He crouched down beside the body and made a cursory examination. There was no visible wound on Spender.

'Where's the bloke who found him?'

'He's on his boat, sir,' said the uniformed sergeant on duty, 'very shaken up by the experience.'

'One of those over there?' Roland straightened up and looked out over the sea of gleaming hulls neatly arrayed in symmetrical lines in the yacht basin.

'No, it's the one moored at the other end of this jetty, the *Spindrift*. His name is Clarke and he and his wife and son and the son's wife are on holiday here. He and his son do a lot of scuba diving in the Mediterranean.'

'He's not local then?' asked Roland as they walked along the jetty.

'Comes from Essex but says he spends most weekends sailing these waters.'

'They don't seem to have heard of the recession around here,' said Mansfield looking at the yachts. 'One of those would set you back at least fifty grand.'

'More like a hundred, I should think, and mooring and membership fees won't be peanuts either.'

* * *

218

There was a middle-aged man dressed in a wet suit sitting with a uniformed constable in the cockpit of the *Spindrift*. He was knocking back a tumbler of amber liquid which Roland reckoned was neat brandy or whisky. He set it down with shaking hands and stood up as Roland introduced himself and Mansfield and Evans.

'Mr Clarke, I understand you found the body?'

'Yes, it was horrible. I had no idea when I went down that it was anything like that.'

'You were diving on your own? I thought there was a rule that there should be at least two people present for safety reasons?'

'I wasn't diving, Inspector, we don't do much around here. The water is too murky.' He looked down at his body encased in yellow-banded, black rubber. 'I'm dressed like this because Danny and I – that's my son – had been water skiing earlier this morning.'

He gestured over the stern of the yacht and the detectives saw the dinghy, lying low in the water under the weight of its powerful outboard.

'Was your son with you when it happened?'

'No, he'd taken Debbie – that's his wife – and my wife into Woodford to get supplies and I decided to move into a berth as there was one vacant.'

'Just a minute. Presumably he took your dinghy to get ashore, how come it's here now?'

'They've been back since then, but I sent them off, with your constable's permission, to the Clubhouse. I thought they'd be better out of the way. My wife has a very nervous disposition. She'll have nightmares for weeks after this. I reckon I will too. I had to have a drink to calm myself. Can I offer you one? But I suppose you can't drink on duty.'

'So, you were on your own and decided to weigh anchor and move to a berth – isn't that a difficult manoeuvre for one person to achieve?'

'No, it's a simple enough operation. I intended moving under power not sail and everything is mechanised.'

'What happened?'

'The anchor chain was winding up smoothly and then it seemed to jam. I looked over the side and I could see this . . . this object in the water not far below the surface. It was large and I thought it was a sack or something like that. I had no idea . . .' He picked up his drink and took a deep gulp. 'I didn't want to hang around waiting for Daniel to return, so I decided to go down and see if I could disentangle it on my own. I thought it would be a simple matter. I put on my gear and went over the side.'

He shuddered and ran his hands through his thick, greying hair, scattering drops of water over the policemen. 'It was heavy, that's what I couldn't understand. I thought it was a piece of sacking or tarpaulin. I could see it had got tangled up in the chain but when I touched it it swung round and bumped against me. I'd got my knife with me and I started to saw through the piece that was caught up and then this . . . this face seemed to swim through the water towards me and I saw a hand . . . I realised then that it was a body.'

'What did you do?'

'I was so shocked I nearly dropped the knife. I grabbed hold of the chain and that movement must have released him . . . there was this whoosh and we both came up together. There was a tender chugging nearby and I hailed it and we got him on board and alerted the police . . . and you know the rest.'

'A nasty experience for you, Mr Clarke.'

'You can say that again! I suppose I should have left him down there until you arrived?'

'It makes no difference. We know who he is, and where and when he went in.'

'You do?' he had perked up a little and was beginning to show curiosity.

'We've been waiting for him to turn up. Now, Mr Clarke, are you intending staying around?'

'We were going to Maldon tomorrow.'

'Is that where you live?'

'No, I live at Hatfield Peverel – will I have to be a witness?'

'Yes, you'll have to attend the Inquest.'

'This one definitely drowned, James, not a mark on him.' George Brasnett looked over his glasses at Roland. 'You don't seem very pleased.'

'It all fits in with the evidence, he fell overboard accidentally whilst feeling sick and dizzy, but its *too* neat, *too* coincidental.'

'Too much alcohol, too much sun, and on top of that he couldn't swim. Wouldn't have stood much chance, I should have thought.'

'How much alcohol?'

'A fair amount, about 80 ml. Not enough to render him insensible and if he was used to drinking those quantities the impact would be less, but taken in consideration with the other factors . . .'

'What about stomach contents? I'm wondering about dope.'

'You think someone dropped him a Mickey Finn?'

'No, I was thinking more along the lines of something self-administered. Perhaps he was a user.'

'There's no sign of drug taking.'

'I don't mean he was an addict but maybe had had the occasional smoke or popped a pill. Could have been on an LSD trip.'

'Surely his companions would have known if he was up to that caper?'

'His lover had only been living with him for a few weeks, he needn't have known, and the girl was only a casual acquaintance.'

Roland mooched round the mortuary, his hands thrust deep in his pockets. 'We're going to have to check. I shan't be happy until I know. I want samples sent up to Huntingdon and they can run a check for barbiturates and what have you.'

'I think you're wasting your time, James.'

'Possibly, but I've got to make sure.'

Patrick Mansfield was also sceptical about the value of the move when he and Roland were milling over Barry Spender's death in the latter's office.

'Suppose the results are positive and he was drugging? Unless it's going to lead to the uncovering of a drug ring – and that's unlikely – I can't see the point of the exercise. It will still be accidental death. He fell overboard whilst under the influence of whatever it was.'

'Supposing he was helped?'

'But there was no sign of any physical violence on him.'

'Bear with me. Let's say that our murderer intends

to knock off Spender in the same way that he killed the Russian. He chooses a moment when he knows that Spender is alone and creeps on board intending to crack him over the skull and tip him into the river; but when he finds Spender in the state he was in he doesn't need to use violence – a little push would be all that was needed.'

'You'll never prove it and why should anyone want to kill Spender?'

'I've been thinking about that and going through everyone's statements again. Dennis Coleman said that when he was returning from the *Painted Lady* on the afternoon of the murder he saw Barry Spender on his way back to the boat. If he saw him it's quite likely that the murderer did too and may fear that Spender saw *him* and could finger him. For all we know Spender may have been blackmailing the murderer ever since and that's why he was killed.'

'So that lets Coleman off the hook. It couldn't have been him who did the killing or he wouldn't have told you that he saw Spender.'

'He may have been afraid that Spender saw him and mentioned it to us to cover himself. Besides, Coleman absented himself from the second part of his rehearsal when he learnt that Spender was alone and ill on the *Painted Lady*. We're going to have to interrogate all our original suspects again anyway and we'll also check their alibis for the time of Spender's death. We know it was between nine-thirty and midnight. We'll start with Coleman.'

'What about Cade?'

'He's taking it hard but he seemed almost relieved when I broke it to him that Spender's body had turned up. I think he'd been expecting the worst, bracing himself for it, and when it actually happened it was almost an anti-climax.'

'On the other hand he could have been expecting him to turn up because he knew that he was in the river.' Mansfield pointed the stem of his pipe at Roland. 'Suppose it was a lover's quarrel. They had an almighty row and Cade shoved him overboard.'

'He's genuinely devastated, I'll stake my life on that.'

'Oh, I'm sure he didn't mean to kill him, he was probably horrified when he realised what he had done. Probably half this grief business could be guilt and remorse.'

'I suppose its possible.'

'He did go to this jazz concert at Woodford?'

'He says he met people there who are casual friends. I haven't had it checked yet but presumably they must be able to give him an alibi or he wouldn't have mentioned them. Of course, he could have done the deed either before he went or after he returned. Let's go and see what Coleman has to say about the latest developments.'

As they drove into the Maltings complex they saw Dennis Coleman crossing the courtyard. Roland hooted and the librarian hurried over to the car. He looked worried when he saw who it was.

'Did you want me, Inspector?'

'Yes, I have a few more questions. Get in the car, Coleman, we can talk in private here.'

Mansfield swung open the door and he got inside. Roland drove over to the far corner of the car park and stopped in front of the high brick wall that bounded the quay area.

'You know that Spender's body has turned up?'

'Yes, it's a terrible business, a tragic accident, and I feel partly to blame.'

'Why is that?'

'I should have insisted on driving them home that evening. The poor chap was obviously suffering from heart trouble. That long trek across the marshes in his condition was too much for him. It brought on a heart attack later and he fell overboard.'

'What makes you think he had heart trouble?'

'His complexion, Inspector. He was this awful purple colour. I've been feeling guilty ever since it happened.'

'You went on to a rehearsal in the hall after this meeting I believe?'

'Yes, I belong to the Festival Choir. Rehearsals are stepping up with the concert only a few weeks away.'

'You didn't stay for all of it. You left half-way through, not long after Miss Nelson arrived and told you what had happened back at the *Painted Lady*?'

'What are you getting at?' He was getting agitated. 'I had to get back home. Helen had been alone all day and I promised her I would leave early and go home and play a game of backgammon with her before we went to bed.'

'You went straight from the hall to your house?'

'Yes.'

'Can you prove that? Did you see anyone on the way home?'

'No, I didn't see anyone, it's only a short distance. Helen will tell you what time I got home, I don't see . . .'

'Don't get excited, Coleman, I'm just wondering where you were at the time Barry Spender met his death.'

'But it was accidental! You're not suggesting it was anything else?'

'I'm not suggesting anything. The Coroner has yet to give his verdict and I have an open mind on the subject.'

'But it was accidental surely? His heart?'

'Barry Spender died from drowning, there was no sign of heart trouble.'

The librarian stared at them and licked his lips.

'Thank you, Coleman, that will be all for now, don't let us detain you.'

He hesitated and looked from one to the other as if he wanted to pursue the subject further, but on receiving no encouragement from them he fumbled with the door handle and started to get out of the car.

'Just one moment. Cast your mind back to Mikhail Rabinovich. In your opinion how did he rate as a musician?'

The librarian blinked at the change of subject.

'He . . . he was principal cellist with the St Petersburg.'

'I know that. That wasn't what I asked you.'

'He was an adequate musician.'

'Adequate? That seems an odd way to describe a musician.'

'Well, since you ask, he had definitely gone off since his visit in 1975.'

'How do you mean?'

'Then he was brilliant; on this latest visit he seemed to have lost his touch – to tell you the truth I don't think the Russians will have been too upset at losing him. I think his days as a cellist were numbered.'

'He was expendable.'

'I don't know what you mean. And what's that got to do with Barry Spender?'

'That's what I'm trying to find out.'

Coleman stared at him suspiciously but Roland ignored him and pulled the starter.

'You've got him worried,' said Mansfield, watching him walk away. 'Who's he trying to kid, suggesting that Spender had a bad heart?'

'I think he's putting red herrings in our path. I wonder why?'

Chapter 9

Stella Lingard was not at the craft centre. They were told by the rather frumpish young assistant working there that she had the day off and should be at her home.

'Good, that suits our purposes better,' said Roland as they strolled back to the car park. 'We can have an uninterrupted interview. We'll go there now. There's no one else here I'm anxious to speak to at the moment. I've already seen Laura Nelson.'

'What about the Rakosi woman?'

'Yes, it's time I caught up with her. But I'd rather see her in her home environment and we need to talk to Rakosi again.'

'Perhaps Stella Lingard is entertaining her lover?'

'Good, then we can kill two birds with one stone.'

Stella Lingard was on her own. As they walked up the path to her house they could see her in the sun lounge that had been built on to the south wall of the house. She was sitting at a table that held a large embroidery frame and a sewing machine and was surrounded by piles of fabric. She saw them approaching and slid open the patio door and waited for them to cross the lawn, leaning against the glass in a way that enhanced the contours of her body. She was clad in multi-printed harem trousers and a matching top and her magenta-red hair was piled on top of her head in a style similar to one Ginny often wore. But there the likeness ended, thought, Roland, glad of Mansfield's solid presence by his side.

He introduced his sergeant and she asked them in. As they stepped inside the room both men were captivated by her work. The embroidery frame held a collage she was setting up and all round the room were examples of wall-hangings and embroidered pictures. They had an ethnic quality about them, reminiscent of Peruvian and Chilean folk art, bold and colourful like their maker.

'This is all your work?' Roland gestured round the room.

'Yes, you could call it my hobby.'

'Do you sell them at the Maltings craft centre?'

'I display a few there but I mostly do commissions or work for friends.'

'Your Ginny would be interested in this, wouldn't she?' said Mansfield, peering at a couple of wall-hangings that depicted jungle animals.

'Yes, she would.'

'And who is Ginny, do I know her?'

'My wife. She is – was – an art teacher.'

'You don't seem very sure.'

'She's expecting our first child,' said Roland coldly.

'Congratulations, Inspector. My husband never managed to get me pregnant, not that it ever bothered me. I'm not the maternal sort and I shouldn't want to be encumbered with children now. Perhaps you'd like to commission me to do a wall-hanging for the nursery?'

'Fascinating as all this is, Mrs Lingard, we didn't come here to discuss your hobbies.'

'Of course you didn't. I stand corrected, Inspector. But I'll give you one of my cards in case you change your mind.'

'What were you doing on the evening before last?'

'That was the night poor Barry died. Don't tell me you think there's something suspicious about his death?'

'I'm asking the questions. Would you mind answering.'

'I was here.'

'Are you quite sure of this?'

'Are you suggesting that I'm lying to you?'

'Mrs Lingard, you were very economical with the truth last time I was checking your alibi.'

'What do you mean?'

'The day the Russian was murdered. You assured me that you had spent the entire afternoon here, in the company of Mr Blackstone, but I find out later that not only was this untrue but that Blackstone actually visited the *Painted Lady* that afternoon.'

'I knew that it was an innocent visit and I didn't want you to get the wrong idea.'

'You can understand my problem; much as I should like to believe you I have to wonder if you are still perjuring yourself.'

'No, I was here.'

'Alone?'

'Yes, alone. If you must know, I was stood up.'

'Really? That must be an unusual experience for you. Are we talking about Mr Blackstone.'

'Yes,' she said shortly, and then, as the two detectives waited: 'He was supposed to be spending the evening with me but he phoned to say he wasn't well.'

'Presumably one can't help being ill.'

'I think it was a convenient illness.'

'You mean you think it was an excuse and he was either avoiding you or had something else on?'

'I think he had made other arrangements for the evening.'

'What makes you think that? Have you any evidence or is it just intuition?'

'. . . I just think that he had something else on.'

'Are we straying from the truth again?'

She flounced round the room and ended up against the table, running her fingers through the boxes of different coloured beads that ranged alongside the sewing machine. As they trickled in rainbow streams from her hands she flashed them a brooding look from her dark, heavily made-up eyes.

'I suppose I was seen in the churchyard. I was recognised by the other person walking through. Who was it?'

Roland and Mansfield exchanged glances. 'Perhaps you'd like to start again and tell me just what you were doing that evening?'

She shrugged. 'All right, I did go out, but only for a short while. I was here most of the evening. If you must know, I went round to Nick's.'

'Checking up on him?'

'Yes, it sounds horrible put like that, but I just had to know. I tell you, Inspector, working at the Maltings seems to put a jinx on one's love life; we all seem to be in the same boat. I seem to be in danger of losing Nick and Jonathan has lost Barry. There's poor Dennis Coleman lumbered with Helen – I know that sounds callous and I suppose he must have loved her once,

232

but she's a millstone round his neck now. And poor Laura Nelson is suffering from unrequited love.'

'Could we keep to the point, Mrs Lingard?'

'I'm sorry. Well, I decided I'd just pop over to his house and see if he was there. It was a beautiful evening and I felt so restless.'

'And was he?'

'I don't know, but I think so.'

'You didn't actually see him or speak with him?'

'No, I didn't want to advertise my presence.'

'So why did you think he was there?'

'The house was in darkness so I presumed he really must be ill and in bed.'

'Surely he could equally as well have been out, which was what you suspected?'

'His car was there,' she said quickly.

'He could have gone somewhere on foot, somewhere local.'

'No, I mean . . . he was back. I mean . . .'

'Just what *do* you mean, Mrs Lingard?'

'He had been out, the engine was still warm.'

'You checked? What a suspicious mind you have.'

'I feel horribly embarrassed. I'm not in the habit of doing this sort of thing.' She fiddled with her rings.

'What time would this have been?'

'About nine-thirty, perhaps a little later.'

'So you came to the conclusion that Blackstone had been out but had returned and was in bed?'

'Yes.'

'You didn't knock on the door or try and rouse him?'

'No, I told you, I didn't want him to know that I was spying on him.'

'What did you do then?'

'I came home, by the short-cut through the church-yard.'

'Where you met someone else?'

'Someone else was hurrying along the other footpath towards the east gate that leads down to the river.'

'You didn't see who it was?'

'No, they were hidden by the trees, but I got the impression that whoever it was didn't want to be seen or recognised either.'

'Are you sure you didn't go out again later that evening? You didn't pay a visit to the *Painted Lady*?'

'No, I did not. I went straight to bed and knew nothing of what happened to Barry until yesterday. Surely his death was a tragic accident?'

'I wish I could be as sure of that as you are,' said Roland as the two men prepared to leave. She came with them to the door, looking very worried.

'This business of Nick being out earlier that evening – it can have nothing to do with Barry and what happened to him.'

'Perhaps not, but it will have to be checked, if only to eliminate him from our enquiries.'

'You won't tell him *I* dropped him in it, will you? That would really get a poor woman into trouble.'

'I can make no promises.'

'I'm sure you'll be tactful, Inspector. You wouldn't want to screw up my love life, would you? I tell you what . . . I'll make an embroidered picture for your baby. When is it due?'

'Bribery will get you nowhere, Mrs Lingard.' Roland paused by the gate. 'By the way, did you by any chance try to ring Mr Blackstone after you got back?'

She looked at him as if he were clairvoyant. 'Yes, I did, but the line was engaged every time I tried. I think he'd left the receiver off the hook.'

'Well, at least she's open about the vagaries of her love-life,' said Roland as they drove through the village on the way to Nick Blackstone's. 'No false modesty. She wants him and she's going to fight to keep him.'

'Do you think that hint she dropped about Dennis Coleman and Laura Nelson is the truth?'

'That they may be having an affair? I suppose it *is* possible. You can hardly blame him although he's old enough to be her father.'

'Yes, but she would appeal to him. They're both somehow old-fashioned and inexperienced, whilst someone as blatantly sexual as Stella Lingard would scare the pants off him. And they share an interest in music.'

'Yes, well good luck to them, but I wonder if it has any bearing on our case?'

'Can't see how, except as another reason for him wanting to get his hands on more dough.'

Jonathan Cade flung himself down on the riverbank and stared into the water. Nearby a group of ramblers shared their packed lunches and laughed and chatted amongst themselves but he did not hear them, too engrossed in his own misery. It was his lunch break and he should be eating but the thought of food nauseated him. Why had this terrible thing happened? Why, just when he had come out and was feeling peace of mind after years of doubt and guilt, had this ghastly accident robbed him of the instigator of this newfound contentment?

Barry was dead but he just couldn't take it in. He

couldn't believe that he would never see him again, would never hear his cheerful voice or see his ugly, attractive face, or laugh with him over his dietary lapses and slovenly housekeeping. Barry was dead and it was his fault. If he hadn't gone off and left him alone Barry would still be alive; it would haunt him for the rest of his days. He kicked savagely at the grass and a clod broke off and tumbled down into the water, sinking below the surface in a cloud of bubbles. Just so had Barry disappeared, ill and unable to swim, falling to a watery grave. Christ! What was he doing down here by the river? Why, of all the places around the Maltings, had he come here, to the rotten, treacherous river that had claimed his lover only forty-eight hours ago?

He started to get up when a shadow fell across him and someone spoke.

'Hello, Jonathan. May I join you?'

It was Laura Nelson and she was staring down at him, apprehension and pleading in her face.

'Suit yourself, it's a free country.'

'Jonathan, I'm terribly sorry about Barry. I know how you must feel, I'm blaming myself too.'

'You couldn't possibly know how I feel and there is no need for you to feel guilty. You did all you could to help him.'

'I know you're feeling ghastly but . . . but you will get over it in time. I mean, you hadn't known him all that long . . .'

'What's that got to do with it? What do you know about it?'

The raw anguish in his voice flicked her like a whiplash. She longed to put her arms round him and comfort him but knew that it would be fatal.

She sat down beside him on the grass and after a few minutes' silence, said tentatively: 'Have you eaten? Would you like to share my sandwiches – they're cheese and tomato?'

'I'm not hungry, I don't want anything.'

'Jonathan, you must eat. It's no good making yourself ill. Please have something.' She held out her lunch box.

'Okay, I'll have an apple. Will that keep you quiet?'

He bit into it and nearly choked as his gorge rose. He ate about half of it and threw the remains into the river where it bobbed along with the tide. But not for long; a black-headed gull swooped down with a harsh shriek and made off with it. A single white feather culled from the bird's breast trembled on the surface like a speck of foam.

Laura quietly munched her sandwiches by his side and when she had finished packed the empty box away in her bag and cleared her throat.

'What are you going to do, Jonathan? My offer still stands.'

'What offer? What are you talking about?'

'To come and live with me in my cottage.'

He stared at her. 'I'm staying put on the *Painted Lady*. Barry has – had – a sister who lives in the States. I suppose she will eventually inherit his stuff but in the meantime I'm staying there and looking after it.'

'You really ought to get away from it all, it can't help still living there with all his belongings around.'

'I'm staying.'

'Well, perhaps later, when it's all sorted out.'

'Laura, I don't think you understand. I've just discovered my true identity. I don't want to cloud the issue by moving in with a woman, you or anyone else of your sex.'

'I know you think that now but you may change your mind when you get over this trauma. Barry seduced you but that doesn't mean you'll always be . . .'

'Barry did *not* seduce me,' he snarled. 'And it's none of your damn' business!'

Seeing her stricken face, he continued more gently:

'You're a nice girl, Laura. I know you mean well, but don't dabble in something you don't understand. I bet there are men around who would give their eye-teeth to date you. Don't waste your time on me.'

'I don't consider it a waste of time but I'm sorry if I've upset you, it was too soon to speak.'

She got to her feet and swung her bag over her shoulder.

'Perhaps you'll change your mind later.'

She walked away with dignity and he stared after her in dismay. He couldn't seem to get through to her. She had latched on to him and wouldn't take no for an answer. He couldn't seem to make her understand that he wasn't interested in her or any girl in the way that she wanted. Christ, what a muddle! But she was right in one thing – he needed to get away. Away from the river and the Maltings and everything that screamed 'Barry' at him whichever way he turned. He must leave the district, leave Suffolk, and try to make some sort of life for himself in another part of the country. Would the police let him go?

* * *

'Where were you, Mr Blackstone, between nine o'clock and midnight on Thursday evening?'

'Here, what's all this about? I thought you were investigating the Russian's murder?'

'There has been another death since then, haven't you heard?'

Nick Blackstone had been in his kitchen getting himself a snack when Roland and Mansfield arrived at the Old Smokehouse. This snack consisted of a slab of bread and cheese and he had answered the door waving a fork on which was impaled a pickled onion.

'Not the rozzers again! What is it this time?'

He had spoken with his mouth full, spraying crumbs around, and had accompanied it with a gentle belch. Roland had ignored the display of bad manners. He knew that the journalist came from an upper-middle-class background and had probably been educated at a minor public school, if not a more well-known one. He was an erudite, well-spoken man and if he had hoped to get a rise out of the two detectives by his behaviour he had not succeeded. They had walked into the kitchen and gone straight into the attack.

'I know that one of your gays has managed to drown himself,' said Blackstone, sitting down at the table and spearing a lump of cheese on the end of his knife. 'Would you two gentlemen care to share my repast? I can do you bread and cheese, or bread and pickle, or pickle and cheese, and there's . . .'

'Cut the crap, Blackstone, and answer my question.'

'Thursday evening? I was here in bed, nursing a migraine.'

He looked at the two impassive faces and sighed. 'You're not very sympathetic. Migraine is a very painful affliction.'

'Stop wasting out time. Your car was seen in Woodford,' said Roland trying a long shot. 'Or are you going to tell me that someone took it for a joyride?'

'Okay, Inspector, I'll come clean. I was in Woodford that evening but I was certainly back here before ten o'clock. Probably nearer nine.'

'I shall have to ask you what you were doing in Woodford and who you were with.'

'I wasn't with another woman, if that's what you're thinking. I'm not two-timing the gorgeous Stella Polaris.'

'I am not interested in your love life, Blackstone, or only in so far as it affects my investigation. Where were you?'

The journalist lumbered to his feet. 'I'm going to make some coffee – there should be some milk in the fridge. We're all going to need a cup. You're not going to like what I'm going to tell you but as you'll probably find out what I've been up to anyway, there's no point in keeping quiet.'

'You've leaked a story to the tabloids?' said Mansfield after a glance at his superior.

'Would I do that after I'd given my word?' Blackstone said reproachfully. 'No, if anything appears in the Press it's not my doing, but I *have* been following up a story.'

He spooned coffee into three mugs and put the sugar bowl on the table.

'What are you talking about, Blackstone?'

'You're not the only ones carrying out an investigation. I've been doing some inquiries off my own bat and I've uncovered an amazing saga that started way back in 1975.'

He gazed quizzically at the two detectives and Roland said heavily:

'Go on.'

'I was intrigued by this business of the Russian's defection, I knew there would be a good story in it for me, but I hadn't realised just how good. I went up to town and nosed around, seeing what I could discover that end. I have some friends who are Russian Jews – musicians who got out about six years ago – and when I told them what had been happening here they told me a tale. How the real Mikhail Rabinovich had gone missing at the end of the 1975 European tour of the St Petersburg Orchestra and how someone else had been schooled to take his place, to assume his name and identity. It was this person who decided to seek asylum here a few weeks ago and got killed for his pains, so I got to wondering what had happened to the *real* Mikhail Rabinovich. I learnt from my Russian friends that his wife had been Hungarian and that some members of her family were still living here in Britain, so I got in touch with the Hungarian community.'

The journalist unplugged the kettle and poured boiling water into the three mugs which he pushed across the table, indicating the milk bottle and sugar bowl.

'You seem to have some very useful contacts, Blackstone,' said Roland drily, pouring milk into his coffee.

'In my profession it pays to have friends in many different camps. Do I need to go on?'

'I'm amazed. Please continue.'

'Well, to cut a long story short, I discovered that the real Mikhail Rabinovich is still alive and well, remarried to his first wife's cousin and living, believe it or not, a few miles from here under the alias of Miklos Rakosi. What was I to think?'

'Don't keep me in suspense.'

'I thought it was too much of a coincidence to disregard. There must be a connection between these facts and the events of the last few weeks.'

'Are you telling me that you think Miklos Rakosi is responsible for the Russian's death?'

'Far be it for me to tell you your job, that is not my concern, but there must be a tie-up somewhere. I'll tell you something – they hated each other's guts. He admitted it.'

'A fascinating tale.'

'You're not going to deny it, Inspector? Come on, I don't know why you've kept the true facts under wraps, but we know that what I've just told you is the truth. Hell, man, I've spoken to Rakosi – that's where I was the night before last!'

'In Woodford visiting the Rakosis?'

'I discovered that the wife actually works at the Maltings – another coincidence – and Stella told me that she has a very volatile temperament so I decided I'd rather catch Rakosi on his own. I phoned him and he told me that she always goes to the cinema on Thursday evenings, so I arranged to go and see him then.'

He put down his coffee and pushed back his chair. 'So there you have it, my full confession.'

'Not quite. You haven't told me what you discussed.'

'You don't expect me to tell you that? Suffice it to say that he confirmed what I'd uncovered and he was no more eager than you for me to publish.'

'A wise man, with a regard for his continuing well-being.'

'You don't think he's in danger?

Roland ignored this.

'Blackstone, I don't know what you're hoping to get out of this but my warning still stands – you publish a word of this and I'll have you up on a charge of obstructing the police, if not of attempted murder. You haven't a leg to stand on.'

'Keep your cool, Inspector. I'm quite prepared to sit on it for the time being. After all, the game's still in play, isn't it?'

'Very true. So you were with Rakosi until after nine o'clock. You didn't by any chance round off the evening by paying a visit to the *Painted Lady*?'

'No, I did not. What are you getting at anyway? Surely Spender's death was an accident?'

'All I know is that he fell overboard and drowned. I'm keeping an open mind.' Roland turned to Mansfield. 'Anything else we need to ask Blackstone before we go, Sergeant?'

'There's just the little business of the Shostakovich manuscript,' said Mansfield, taking up the questioning. 'Did your Russian friends know anything about that?'

'No, they didn't. It was new to them, although they said that it was rumoured in musical circles at that time that he had been working on a large-scale composition just before he died. They were very excited to learn that it had been completed. If you ever turn it up there's going to be a great deal of interest shown from all manner of people.'

'I'm sure there will be,' said Roland, pausing in the doorway, 'and I'm giving you one last warning

– keep out of my case. What's done is done but if I discover you're still interfering with my investigation, you're going to be in big trouble.'

'Just one thing, Inspector. You haven't told me who saw me in Woodford on Thursday evening? It couldn't have been Stella because she thinks I was ill in bed.'

'Does she? I shouldn't underestimate her, Blackstone.'

With that parting shot the two men walked back to the car.

'Naughty! Naughty!' said Mansfield as soon as they were out of ear-shot. 'You've probably really set the cat amongst the pigeons.'

'Petty of me I know, but he riles me. I know his attitude of being on a higher intellectual plane is deliberately put on to annoy us, but he's a mischief-maker and I can do without that. This case is baffling enough as it is.'

'What a change in the weather,' said the other man, looking about him as he zipped up his jacket. 'There wasn't a cloud in the sky when we arrived.'

There was a heavy mist rolling in from the river. It had blotted out the sun and as it moved inland, creeping over the marshes and reedbeds like an aerial tide, it brought with it a chill dampness. The UHF radios in the two men's pockets crackled and boomed in the atmospheric distortion and the windscreen was veiled in moisture when they reached the car.

'Where to now?' asked Mansfield, fastening his seat belt whilst Roland started up the car and switched on the heater.

'To the Rakosis. Let's hope we catch them both in.'

As they drove towards Woodford the foghorn at the mouth of the estuary began its mournful tolling. The fog was coming in off the sea and those sailing craft still under way on the river were gradually becalmed as a thick pall settled over the water, deadening noise and stiffling motion.

It was fine when Ginny Roland left home early in the afternoon to go blackberrying. She had decided to visit the old sand pit where the brambles grew in profusion around the perimeter; it was only a short walk across a couple of fields and the exercise would do her good. She had felt restless and energetic that morning and had given the bedrooms a thorough clean before preparing Simon an early lunch. He had rugger practice that afternoon and as she set off along the footpath towards the quarry with the sun beating down on her she felt sorry for him. It was too hot for such activities, it was still cricket weather.

The stubble was spiked with chamomile and corn marigolds and paler toadflax nestled in the grass verges. Ginny hummed to herself as she walked along the rutted path, a basket over her arm. She was probably crazy going blackberrying on a Saturday; everyone would have the same idea. The best time was mid-week when the bushes had had a chance to recover from the depredations of the weekend pickers. But when she reached the quarry there seemed to be no one else around. She wandered over the rough ground, gradually filling her basket. The berries were small and rather hard, due to the long, hot summer, but there were plenty of them and her fingers were soon stained purple. She heard the sound of a motor-bike over on the far side of the pit and voices coming from behind the screen of gorse bushes that colonised the upper reaches of the sloping banks; she could not see who was there but did not think they were fellow pickers.

After a while she sat down on a grass tussock and munched at the apple she had put in her pocket. It had been more exhausting than she had thought and she would call it a day. A veil had crept over the sun and it was now a shrouded disc glowing pinkly in the encroaching mist. She got to her feet and looked around her. Over to her left, a particularly fine patch of brambles straggled down to a tangle of hawthorn bushes and nettles. The blackberries looked larger and juicier than any she had so far picked and she decided to collect a few of these before returning home. Typically the finest fruit was growing in the topmost briars and as she reached up to pick it she over-balanced and toppled forward.

She clutched at the hawthorn branches to save herself but what had seemed a solid wall of scrub parted before her weight and she started to slither down the slope, gaining momentum as she fell. Her basket flew out of her grasp scattering blackberries in all directions and brambles tore at her as she plunged downwards towards the black, scummy water that lay in the bottom of the pit. All she could think about as she fell was how furious James would be at her foolhardiness and that the baby would be drowned. She snatched desperately at the sparse vegetation to try and break her fall and just as it seemed as if nothing could save her from an immersion, her foot struck a projecting root and she pitched forward into the fork of an elder bush that clung to the very edge of the water.

Her lower limbs actually splashed below the surface as she hung on frantically to the green whippy branches and as she hauled herself back on to the crumbling sandy bank the pungent smell of the elder was rank in her nostrils. The fall and the jolting arrest had knocked the breath out of her and as she clung to the sapling and tried to regain her equilibrium a sharp pain raced through her from back to front. Oh no, not the baby! She couldn't be starting the baby here, now! She had forgotten how savage labour pains were, how overwhelming and all consuming. She closed her eyes and fought panic, trying to control her breathing.

When she opened them again she saw a line of leather-clad aliens scrambling down towards her like a line of monstrous black spiders and she thought she had flipped. She squeezed her lids tightly shut and fought against the waves of dizziness that assailed her. Next time she looked the creatures had resolved themselves into a group of youths in motorbike leathers. They were coming to her rescue and as they got nearer she recognised them as sixth-form members of the school where she had, until recently, been teaching. They slithered and crashed down the steep sandy slope and she sent up a silent prayer of thanks that somebody had noticed her predicament.

'Miss Dalton! I mean, Mrs Roland . . . are you all right?'

'Er . . . yes. I lost my balance and fell. Silly of me.'

'Can you walk?'

'I think so, Kevin, but it's rather steep for walking.'

'We'll get you up, don't worry.'

Somehow they manhandled her up the side of the pit, passing her from hand to hand, hauling her painfully up the steepest parts. It was undignified and she should have felt horribly embarrassed but she didn't. If ever anyone again moans about the youth of today I shall flatten them, she thought, gritting her teeth and trying not to gasp as another contraction struck her. At the top she leaned weakly against a tree trunk, fighting for breath, and the four youths regarded her anxiously.

'I'm fine, thank you, boys. It's lucky you were around.'

'We often come here,' volunteered the smallest one, who was Andrew Redmore, the son of a local dentist. 'We're trying to organise a scrambling circuit around the sand hills.'

Normally a remark like this would have brought instant condemnation from Ginny who was very conservation-minded, but now it fell on deaf ears.

'I must get home.' She thought of the two fields she had to cross. They assumed frightening proportions in her mind and she wondered if she could make it.

'We'll give you a lift home,' said Kevin Connor, who appeared to be the ringleader. 'It won't matter about you not having a crash helmet. We won't have to go on a main road.'

Ginny thought about the motion and resulting jolting and shook her head. 'I don't think that's a very good idea.'

'Look, if you sit on the pillion of one of the bikes we'll *push* you home.'

'Do you think you could?'

They all agreed it was no problem and went off to get their bikes which were over on the far side of the sand pit. Ginny waited for them and tried to practise the breathing exercises which had been taught to her at the

ante-natal classes. She was very aware of the damp folds
of her dress clinging to her swollen belly and her arms
and legs were covered with scratches and the raised
pimples of nettle stings. She shivered. She was cold
not only because of her partial ducking but because
the weather had changed dramatically since she had set
out earlier in the afternoon. The sun had disappeared
completely behind the curtain of mist which had rolled
across the countryside insidiously, shrouding the trees
and bushes and deadening sound.

The four youths appeared out of the fog, chugging towards her on their motorbikes, and as they
dismounted she looked with dismay at the gleaming machines and wondered how on earth she could
possibly mount one of them.

'Do you think you could sort of sit side-saddle?'
asked Kevin, whose bike was the pride of his life and
just that little bigger and more powerful than those of
his companions.

'That's a good idea,' said Ginny firmly, 'I think I
could manage that.' She looked down the side of the
quarry. 'I've lost all my blackberries.'

'We could try and pick them up for you,' said
another of the youths doubtfully, 'but they'll be covered in sand.'

'No, don't bother, I shan't have time to process them
anyway, but if you could rescue my basket?'

A short while later, after a great deal of heaving
and even greater loss of dignity, Ginny was perched
side-saddle on Kevin's pillion and they set off across
the fields for her house. Every jolt and bump over the
uneven ground echoed through her body, magnified a
hundred times, and she shut her eyes and willed herself

to reach home without revealing to her escort that she was in labour.

Simon Dalton had just returned from his rugger practice and was putting his bike away when the little cavalcade turned in at the gate. He gaped at the sight of his mother, pale and bedraggled, in the company of that select band of sixth-formers whom he worshipped from afar, and seated on one of the shining machines that he lusted after with all his heart.

'Mother! What's happened?'

'You mum fell down the quarry.' Kevin Connor regarded the fifth-former with disdain.

'But what were you doing there?'

'I was blackberrying and I slipped. There's nothing to worry about, Simon, just help me off this machine.'

'We happened to be around and we got her out and brought her home,' said Kevin, flexing his muscles and kick-starting his bike as Ginny slipped off the pillion helped by her son and one of the other riders.

'Take care, Mrs Roland. Bye for now.'

Her thanks were drowned as the four motorbikes roared into action and accelerated back down the road.

'You're all wet – you didn't fall in the water?' Simon helped her up the path and into the house.

'Only half of me. I'll tell you all about it later.' She sunk into a chair beside the kitchen dresser and gripped the arms.

'What on earth were you doing blackberrying in your state?'

Accusation and anxiety vied in his voice.

'Don't scold. I shall get enough of that from James.'

'But are you all right?'

'Actually I think you had better ring James. I think your brother or sister is going to make an early appearance.'

'You mean it's started? The baby's on the way?' He looked horrified and there was a tremor in his voice.

'Don't panic, there's plenty of time, but try and get hold of James.'

Simon rushed into the hall and picked up the phone.

'Ring Felstone HQ,' called Ginny, 'they'll know where he is.'

A couple of minutes later he re-appeared.

'They're putting out a call for him. He's over in the Blund district and the Woodford Station will have to raise him on their wavelength. He should be in radio contact with them so they're going to ring back in a few minutes. What can I do to help?'

'Make me a cup of tea. That's just what I need.'

As Simon crashed around in the kitchen she surreptitiously counted the intervals between her contractions; they were coming every five minutes. Simon had actually made the tea and was pouring it out when the phone rang and he plunged into the hall.

'They can't find him, he's out of radio contact.' He eyed his mother anxiously. 'Will you be all right?'

'Yes, but I don't think we can wait for James. You'd better ring for an ambulance.'

Chapter 10

'What number is it?' Roland and Mansfield were cruising down Bent Lane in Woodford looking for the Rakosis' house.

'Number 32. It must be down the far end, there are only about fifteen houses each side.'

Bent Lane was on the outskirts of Woodford and one side was backed by open countryside; contrary to its name it was as straight as a die. At one time it had been part of a separate hamlet and the houses reflected this. They ranged from a three-hundred-year-old-cottage to solid Victorian villas, and the modern houses and bungalows which interspersed them were the result of in-filling in recent years.

As Mansfield had predicted, number 32 was at the far end of the lane and seemed to have more garden than its neighbours. There was a wide tract of land on three sides and several outhouses. By now the sea mist had turned to fog, more reminiscent of a November afternoon than a September one, and the dahlias and michaelmas daisies in the flowerbeds dripped with moisture whilst the tops of the fruit trees were blotted out entirely. When the two men got out of the car the atmospheric interference on their UHF radios was so bad that by unspoken consent they both switched them off.

Màrta Rakosi answered the doorbell and Roland was surprised by her appearance. For some reason he had imagined a small, dainty person but the woman who faced him was of above average height and although not heavily built, looked strong and wiry; she dwarfed her husband. She was dressed in a grey linen skirt with a dipping hem and a multi-coloured cardigan which displayed her rolling breasts to disadvantage. She could have done with some under-pinning, thought Mansfield, but her bra-less state was surely not due to Woman's Lib and all that caper? She regarded the two men with suspicion and they introduced themselves.

'Why have you come here harassing us? We have done no wrong.'

'I am conducting a murder enquiry and I want the answers to some questions. I hardly think that is harassment, Mrs Rokosi.'

'What you want to know?'

'Could we come in, please? Is your husband here?'

'You cannot disturb him, he is working on very important job; he makes the cello for very important client.'

'Who is it, Màrta?' called a voice from inside the house, and with a venomous look at the two detectives, she hissed: 'Police!' making it sound like 'Gestapo.'

A door opened and closed and Miklos Rakosi joined his wife on the doorstep.

'The Inspector! Come in, sir, and your good assistant.'

'This is Detective Sergeant Mansfield. We have a few more questions to put to you.'

'But of course. Come in, come in.' He beamed at them as he ushered them inside.

He seemed positively pleased to see them, thought Roland, a situation they didn't meet with very often in the course of their work, and he was sure that it was genuine, unless the man was an exceptional actor. Surely this meant that he could be crossed off their list of suspects? He wouldn't welcome them so warmly if he were in any way guilty of the murder they were investigating. But his wife was another matter. Dress her in trousers and a jacket and conceal that grey haystack of hair and she could easily pass for a man. She glared at them as they entered the sitting room and stood, arms akimbo, daring them to sit down. The two men very pointedly sat themselves in the chairs that her husband indicated.

'What is it you want?' she demanded.

'I have told you everything about my past and what I know about the man who stole my identity and got himself killed,' said her husband.

'I'm more concerned with what you told somebody else,' said Roland. 'I am checking up on your movements on Thursday evening, two days ago. I believe you, Mrs Rakosi, went to the cinema?'

'How . . . ? Yes, I go every week. It is art form I study,' she said grandly.

'You do not accompany your wife?' he asked Rakosi.

'No, it does not interest me. Why do you wish to know?'

'Barry Spender died that evening.'

'But it was an accident surely?'

'It is unlucky ship,' said his wife. 'Two peoples die already – there will be more! It has a curse on it – it should be sinked!'

'Màrta!'

'Is true. I know what I say, Inspector. That ship has been cursed, it has the evil eye put on it – you mark my word!'

'Màrta, we must offer the inspector and his sergeant our hospitality. You will go and make the coffee and some of your new cake?'

'But I . . .'

'That would be much appreciated, Mrs Rakosi, if you would be so kind?'

She flounced off to the kitchen, muttering under her breath, and her husband leaned forward and spoke confidentially.

'You must not mind Màrta. She have unfortunate experience with the police when she is a young woman in Hungary. It make her a little . . . paranoid.'

'I understand. Now, I believe you had a visitor that evening?'

'Yes, but Màrta does not know.' He cast an agonised glance towards the kitchen.

'So I gather. A certain Mr Blackstone, who happens to be a journalist, visited you for the purpose of uncovering your past. Did you tell him what you told us?'

'He did not need the telling. He already knew. We had discussed it before.'

'Before?'

'He had been to see me before – also when Màrta was out of the way. He had found out all about my past and he wanted confirmation from me. It frightened me Inspector, how easily he had found out what had been secret for so long.'

'When was this?' asked Roland sharply.

'I . . . I'm not sure.'

'Was it before you came to us?'

'Yes,' he said unhappily.

'Before the Russian was killed?'

The man looked even more unhappy and Roland rapped out: 'Well?'

'Yes, it is so.'

'I see. This puts a different complexion on things, doesn't it, Rakosi? I think I understand now just *why* you walked into the Station that day and spilled the beans. You knew that Blackstone had uncovered your past and that when we got to hear of it we would very naturally think that you had a very good reason for killing the Russian, so you tried to hoodwink us by getting in first with a disarming tale about not wanting to live a lie any longer.'

'You are right, Inspector, I was afraid. I knew you would suspect me so I had to tell you the truth. I am innocent man. I did not kill Temirkanov, so I come to you and tell you all about my past.'

'It's a pity you were not so open about the present.'

'Please?'

'You deliberately concealed the fact that a journalist – a *journalist*, Rakosi – was on the trail, and there's also the fact that you denied all knowledge of the manuscript.'

'That is because he did not tell me about that.'

Roland and Mansfield exchanged looks. 'Do you really expect me to believe that Blackstone and you discussed your past and the present situation, and he didn't mention the manuscript?'

'No, it is truth. I know nothing about it until *you* tell me, Inspector. I think he did not know.'

'Oh, he knew about it.'

'Then, I do not understand . . . why did he not mention it?'

'A good question, Rakosi. I fear that Mr Blackstone has been as sparing with the truth as yourself. Perhaps you would now like to tell me why he re-visited you on the evening that Barry Spender died?'

'It was to check up on some details. He wishes to write up the truth about what happened. As you say, Inspector, he is a journalist and he is following up the story but he must get his facts right before he publish. This time he *did* ask me about the manuscript – I thought he had only recently found out about it – and he wished to learn what I knew about it.'

'How long was he here on the second occasion?'

'I'm not sure. Quite a long time.'

'Let's put it another way. What time did he leave you?'

'After nine. Perhaps nine-thirty? It was before Màrta got back.'

'And you're sure she knows nothing of Blackstone's visits?'

'No, I think it best not to tell her, she get so . . . so excited.'

'But she knew about Temirkanov leaving the orchestra and going to stay on the *Painted Lady*?'

'Yes, she heard about it through the grapevine. In fact, she tell *me* originally.'

'And she knows about you and he being enemies and rivals?'

'How you mean?' He was indignant and getting agitated.

'I understand there was bad blood between you. It

must have seemed a golden opportunity to get your own back after all these years?'

'You do not understand! In the old days we were rivals, I admit, we did not like each other. But as you say in this country, it was all water under the bridge, a long time ago. I make myself new life here. It was different to what I had planned but I am happy. *He* was still having to live under the System. Oh, I know what they say about life being so different in Russia now, but it cannot be all that wonderful or why did he leave?'

'Your wife?'

'Please to keep Màrta out of this. She . . .'

As if hearing her name, Màrta Rakosi came back into the room bearing a tray on which were set out steaming mugs of coffee and a very rich-looking gateau. That would play havoc with his diet, thought Mansfield, his mouth watering, but Jean would never get to know and it was all in the course of duty. The Hungarian woman produced a wicked-looking knife and as she sliced through the cake he felt sure that she would rather be carving them up than feeding them. After they had tackled the enormous slices that she thrust at them, Roland turned his attention to her.

'What film did you see on Thursday evening, Mrs Rakosi?'

She mentioned the film which was currently showing at the only cinema in Woodford. It was an American teenage saga and he didn't think it could have held much interest for her.

'Were you on your own?'

'Yes. Sometimes a friend go with me but this week I am alone.'

'Did you see the whole programme through?'

'But of course, what else should I do?'

'You didn't leave the cinema early and go over to Blund?'

'You think I'm crazy? I work at Blund in the daytime, I do not go back there at night.' She was derisory but there was a shrewd gleam in her eyes which he noted.

'Do you drive, Mrs Rakosi?'

'Yes. Why for all these questions?'

'And did you drive to the cinema on Thursday evening? I suppose it would be within walking distance from here?'

'I take the car. My poor feet are tired after day at work.'

She picked up the cake knife and flourished it. 'You have another piece of cake?'

'It was delicious, but no more, thank you.'

'What about you?' She turned her attention to Mansfield. 'You have big frame to feed.'

'Sergeant Mansfield is on a strict diet,' said Roland, 'don't encourage him to backslide any further.'

'You English and your diets!' She flung out her hands in a very foreign gesture. 'When you have the food you should eat. So many are hungry.'

'Màrta, *I* shall have another slice,' said her husband, 'it is very good.'

'It certainly is,' said Mansfield, 'but I must not have any more.'

'Where do you make your instruments?' Roland looked round the room which was spotlessly clean and uncluttered. 'Have you got a workshop?'

'Yes, it is built on to the garage. Would you like to see it?'

On the affirmative he took the two men outside and

over to the detached garage which was some distance from the house. The workshop had a separate door and he unlocked this and took them in. They were immediately assailed by the smell – compounded of wood and varnish and linseed. There was a large worktable in the middle of the room with an anglepoise lamp and templates scattered on it. On the benches round the walls were woodmaker's tools, many that Roland could identify but many more he couldn't put a name to; packets of what he took to be coiled strings; and many copies of the *Strad* magazine. There were also racks on the wall which supported sections of half-finished instruments and completed whitewood instruments hanging up to dry and looking curiously naked as they awaited varnishing. Large sheets of wood were also propped up at the far end of the room and Rakosi explained their use.

'This is maple, the back and sides of the instrument are made with this and also the bridge, and the front is sycamore or pine – see here. The rosewood is for the pegs and the fingerboard is this hard wood, ebony. Also I make the tailpiece from ebony but now is the fashion to have tailpiece made from metal.'

The two men were impressed. This was no amateur hobby. He was a dedicated craftsman and his work was of a fine quality.

'How much is this going to cost your client?' Roland indicated the cello he was working on.

'About three thousand pounds, and the bow will be another six to seven hundred pounds but I do not supply them. They are made elsewhere by another expert.'

Mansfield looked thunderstruck and Roland was taken aback.

'How long does it take to make an instrument from start to finish?'

'About six to eight months. I have several on the go at once. They have to be left to dry out at certain stages.'

'How did you acquire this skill? You trained as a musician, a performer.'

'I teach myself mostly and I read up about it, and because I am a musician I know what is required of an instrument, what the end product must be.'

'I am impressed, Rakosi. Tell me, do you regret the end of your career as a cellist? You seem to have compensated for it.'

The stocky little man considered this and there was a far-away look in his eyes.

'Sometimes I think of what might have been and I am saddened, but I have good life here as I have told you. I am still helping to make beautiful music and Màrta is a good wife. I am content. I do not want it to be different, you must believe me.'

'Perhaps you are content now that you have settled an old score?'

'No, no! It was not like that!'

'Well, what did you make of that?' asked Roland as they walked back to the car a little while later.

'He's a funny little cove and you can't help liking him, but he could have done it and it would explain why the murderer didn't take the manuscript.'

'Yes, he knew nothing about it so he would just

have bashed his old enemy over the head and ske-
daddled. Likewise it could have been his wife. Did
you get the feeling that she was acting a part? I
thought she was too over the top to be true. It
was a caricature of an eastern European woman of
uncertain years.'

'Yes, she really let it all hang out, but I agree
that I don't think she's as emotional as she made
out.'

'No, underneath all those flamboyant gestures she
was cool and collected and I think she overdid the
fractured English.'

'So either of them could be the killer? Well, if so,
that really puts paid to your theory that Barry Spender
was also murdered.'

'Not necessarily. As we've already conjectured, he
could have noticed him or her on the way back to the
Painted Lady that afternoon and afterwards realised
that he had seen the murderer. He may have been
putting the screws on. Blackmailers are prime victims
of murder.'

'And what about our journalist friend?'

'What about him indeed? He's getting up my nose,
playing with the truth, deliberately trying to mislead us.
He's up to some game of his own and I intend finding
out just what it is.'

'Maybe he's the murderer.'

'Hmm.' Roland thought about this. 'Suppose it happened like this: he goes to the *Painted Lady* that
afternoon intending to face the Russian with the facts
he had uncovered and hoping to get corroboration
about the past. For some reason Temirkanov won't
play ball with him and they quarrel. It turns into a fight

and in the heat of the moment Blackstone snatches up a weapon and bashes him over the head?'

'That doesn't fit in with what Coleman said he witnessed. If *he* was speaking the truth, the murderer crept up on his victim unawares.'

'Yes, I'm afraid we can't pin it on him,' said Roland regretfully, 'the very fact that he's still poking around and following up his own story points to him being in the clear. I can threaten him all I like but if he's innocent he know's he's got nothing to fear.'

'So we disregard him?'

'No way. He's not getting away with this, misleading the police, interfering with our witnesses. I intend having further words with Mr Nick Blackstone and he'd better come up with some truthful answers.'

'Where the hell is your boss?'

William Evans was collared as he went past the control room at Felstone headquarters.

'He's up at Blund interviewing suspects in our case.'

'I know that's where he's supposed to be, it's on the list, but neither we nor Woodford Station can raise him. He's out of radio contact.'

'Has something come up?'

'Personal business. I don't know why I'm worrying but I've had his son on the phone and he sounded upset. Wanted to get hold of his father, said it was urgent.'

'His stepson it would be. God, I wonder if it's his wife! She's expecting a baby any minute now.'

'Well, she won't be the first police wife who's pupped without her husband around to hold her hand.'

'He ought to know, he's only been married a year.'

'It happens, laddie, it happens.'

'When did the call come through?'

'It was logged at 16.04 hours. Are you on your way out?'

'Yes,' said Evans, making a quick decision. 'I have some information he ought to have. I'll try and catch up with him at Blund.'

'Are you taking a car?'

'I'll go in my own, I'm off duty now.'

'I should be so lucky!'

The mist was clearing as Evans drove over to Woodford. As suddenly as it had come it started to disperse into wisps and the low sun shimmered through the rents in the ghostly curtain. He caught up with Roland and Mansfield as they sat in the former's car outside the Rakosis' house in Bent Lane. He slammed on the brakes, performed a screeching U-turn in the narrow road and snarled to a halt, his bonnet just an inch away from Rolands's.

'You bloody fool! This isn't the Sweeney. What are you playing at?'

'I've been trying to find you – you've been out of contact.'

'Well, you know what the weather's been like this afternoon, or hadn't you noticed?'

'This is important.'

'We've heard from Huntingdon and the results are positive?'

'Yes, they've faxed through the results but they were all negative – not a trace of any drug in his mortal remains.'

'It was worth a try but you didn't burn up the road just to tell me this?'

'Your stepson's been trying to get hold of you – said it was urgent.'

'Simon? What's wrong?'

'I don't know, that was the message passed on to me. I thought maybe your wife . . . ?'

'It's not due for another ten days, is it?' asked Mansfield, seeing the expression on his superior's face.

'Christ, no! There must be something wrong!'

'Maybe it's putting in an early appearance. It does happen, you know. You may soon be a proud father.'

'I'm going straight home. You go back to the Station with Evans.'

The young detective constable opened his mouth to protest that he was off-duty and then thought better of it. James Roland was not a man to cross, especially when he was in this mood. He slipped the lock on the passenger door and Mansfield climbed in. Before he had fastened his seat belt Roland had reversed and roared back up the lane in a good imitation of Evans' ton-up.

Afterwards Roland had no recollection of that drive back to Wallingford. The roads must have been busy but he didn't notice, he drove on automatic pilot. Once home, he flung open the gate and ran up the path. The back door was unlocked and he rushed inside calling out Ginny's name. There was silence. A half-full mug of cold tea stood on the table and a bag containing Simon's rugger gear had fallen off a chair, spilling its contents in a wide arc across the floor. Ginny and Simon were not in the house. He pounded upstairs and into their bedroom. The case, which had been packed and ready for weeks and kept beside the dressing-table, was missing. She must have started labour and gone into hospital.

He slammed the door behind him and ran back down the path. Mrs Higgins, their next-door neighbour, put her head over the hedge.

'Your wife's gone off in an ambulance!'

She was a busybody, always poking her nose into other people's business and the Rolands found it difficult to remain on cordial terms with her. This had worried Ginny who prided herself on establishing good relationships with all her fellow men, but in view of Mrs Higgin's nature they had avoided contact as much as possible and tried to keep their affairs private.

'How long ago?'

'About an hour – she looked terrible!'

'Was Simon with her?'

'Yes, and he looked even worse than his mother. It's not right, a boy his age having to deal with something like that.'

Roland ignored her but she was determined to have the last word.

As he opened the car door she called over the hedge: 'She came back on a motorbike earlier in the afternoon.'

'She *what*?'

'I think you'd better get to the hospital, Mr Roland, I reckon it's serious!' And she popped back out of sight, leaving him speechless.

The cottage hospital, which housed the local maternity unit, was situated on the outskirts of Felstone, not far from the school where Ginny had taught. The core was an old rambling Edwardian building on to which had been added new wings containing various clinics, theatres and wards over the intervening years. The maternity wing was on the north side and there was a visitors' car park at the side adjacent to the courtyard that led into the building. The sky was an angry red, torn by purple streaks as he drove on to this car park and amethyst and violet clouds were piling up in the east. The wind had risen and the fog and mist had departed, a thing of the past. It would be a stormy night.

The first person he saw, once through the double doors, was Simon. The boy was mooching around the reception area looking at the posters on the walls. He glanced up as Roland arrived and his face lit up with relief, only to be replaced immediately with a look of anger and what Roland could only call hatred. Ginny might forgive him for not being there when needed; Simon wouldn't.

'What's happened? Your mother . . . ?'

'You let her down! We couldn't get hold of you!'

'I came as soon as I got the message. What's happened?'

'She had a fall and the baby started to come so I sent for an ambulance, and now she has to have an operation!'

'An operation? What's gone wrong?'

'I dunno, they won't tell *me*.'

Roland brushed him aside and strode over to the desk. The nurse behind it had already seen him coming.

'Are you Mrs Roland's husband?'

He confirmed that he was and she continued: 'The doctor will be out to see you in a moment.'

'But what's wrong? My wife . . . ?'

'Your wife is fine, Mr Roland. If you would just wait I'll see if the doctor is available.'

She disappeared through the door behind her and returned a few minutes later with a young intern in tow. He looked as harassed as Roland felt.

'Look, will someone tell me what's wrong with my wife!'

'She had a nasty fall and it triggered off labour. There was some foetal distress so it was decided, in the circumstances, to perform a Caesarian section. It is quite a normal procedure, Mr Roland.'

'But will she be all right? What about the baby?'

'Both will be fine. You weren't here to sign the consent form . . .'

'I got here as quickly as I could. Can I see her?'

'She's in the theatre. Don't worry, you'll soon be a proud father.'

'But what . . . ?'

'I suggest, Mr Roland, that you get a cup of tea and try not to worry. I'm sure your son could do with one. We'll let you know as soon as there is any news.'

He went off and Roland had to be content with that. The nurse eyed him with sympathy. 'Try and relax, Mr Roland, I haven't lost a father yet!' She chuckled and gestured at the kiosk over on the far side of the room where refreshments were on sale. He collected Simon, bought two cups of tea, and sat him down at a table.

'Now tell me exactly what happened.'

'She fell down the quarry.'

'The quarry? You mean the old sandpit at the back of the village?'

'Yes.'

'But what in God's name was she doing there?'

'She went blackberrying. I don't know what happened but she somehow lost her balance and fell.'

'She didn't go into the water?'

'Not completely. There was a bush or something that broke her fall. Kevin Connor and some mates from my school were around and they got her out and brought her home.'

'Is he one of the young hobos who roar round the village on a motorbike?'

'Yes.'

'My God!' Enlightenment dawned. 'He didn't bring her home on his bike?'

'They wheeled her home. She just sat sideways on his machine.'

'So Mrs Higgins was right!'

'Did Ma Higgins see her? She would do! I bet she made the most of it.'

'It's made her week – she couldn't wait to tell me. Did your mother hurt herself when she fell?'

'I don't think so, she was just shaken up.'

'Thank goodness you were there when she was brought home.'

The boy flushed and looked as if he were going to make a retort, but said nothing.

'Do you want another cup of tea or something to eat? They've got some chocolate biscuits. I don't know how long we're going to be here.'

'No thanks. Why is it taking so long?'

'They had to prepare her for the theatre, it all takes time. She won't actually be under for long.'

'Suppose something goes wrong?'

270

'It won't, she's in good hands. This Caesarian is really a precautionary measure.'

Women don't die of childbirth nowadays, he told himself sternly as he tried to comfort Simon, but there was always the odd exception . . . And what about the baby? Maybe the cord had got looped round its neck or perhaps the afterbirth had started to come away and it had been starved of oxygen . . .

'Mr Roland?'

So engrossed had he been in his thoughts that he hadn't noticed the door open again nor the man who entered. This doctor was older and was still robed in his theatre gown. Both he and Simon got to their feet.

'You've got a lovely daughter, Mr Roland. And you've got a little sister, young man.'

'A half-sister,' muttered Simon, but his face lit up.

'My wife?'

'She's fine, and so is the baby – a healthy three kilograms.'

'May I see my wife?'

'Just for a little while. She's still under the influence of the anaesthetic.'

'What about me?' demanded Simon.

'Later. We mustn't tire the patient.'

'I won't be long, and I'll give her your love,' said his step-father, and followed the doctor through the door.

'They'll be bringing her down shortly, they're just cleaning her up and making her comfortable. She'll be a little sore to start with. In the meantime, here's your daughter.'

The nurse who had taken over from the doctor

had brought him into one of the side rooms that led off the main maternity ward. She went over to the cot from which were issuing little sniffles and snuffles. He followed her, hardly daring to breathe. All he could see was a mop of red hair and a little wrinkled-up face that rivalled the hair in colouring.

'She's ginger!'

'And so she is, and what's wrong with that?' The nurse had a fine Irish brogue and Roland now noticed belatedly that she also possessed auburn hair. 'They always lose their first hair. The second crop may be another colour altogether.'

'Is she really all right? The doctor said something about foetal distress?'

'She's as healthy a baby as I've seen. And here comes your wife.'

Ginny was wheeled into the room and he hurried over to her.

She smiled at him woozily and he bent over and caught hold of her hands.

'James, I'm so sorry – it was a daft thing to do.'

'Shush, it's I who am sorry. I wasn't there when you needed me. Will you ever forgive me?'

'You couldn't help it, and Simon coped marvellously. Have you seen her?'

'Yes, she's beautiful, just like her mother, and she's got your lovely hair. I don't know what colour her eyes are – whether they're odd like yours.'

'All babies are born with blue eyes,' she said sleepily. 'Are you sorry she's not a boy?'

'Certainly not. A daughter suits me fine, and Simon's tickled pink. He's waiting downstairs. They wouldn't let him come up too.'

'We've got to decide on a name . . .'

'Plenty of time. Are you all right? Does it hurt?'

'I'm still dopey but I think I'll feel sore later.'

'What are those scratches on your arms?'

'I got them when I fell down the sandpit. Did Simon tell you what happened?'

'Yes, it brings me out in a sweat just to think about it. Thank God there was someone around to rescue you.'

'It was some boys from the sixth form – did he tell you? They were magnificent. You'd have expected them to be horribly embarrassed but they took it in their stride.'

'The nurse came back into the room.

'Are you ready to hold your baby, Mrs Roland? She's a bonny lass.'

Roland marvelled at her tiny fingers and shell-like ears and was astounded by her powerful lungs. It was a very bemused man who returned to his stepson a little while later.

'I want to pull the plug on this case. I made that clear at the last briefing.' Superintendent Lacey glared at Roland out of his piggy eyes.

'There has been another death since then.'

'Quite. It all ties in.'

'Sir?'

'The Russian chappie was killed in a private quarrel by one of our poofs on the *Painted Lady* who has now accidentally drowned. No one can be brought to trial – end of case.' He sat back and watched Roland's reaction.

'What are you getting at?'

'That maybe he *was* bumped off by one of his fellow countrymen, with official connivance.'

'This isn't a Len Deighton thriller.'

'I know, I know, and normally I would agree with you, but there are special circumstances in this case. This Russian was not who he appeared to be. There was a big cover-up seventeen years ago and they wouldn't want that to come out. He could have been killed to stop that can of worms being opened. If we take *my* line, the case is satisfactorily concluded and no one loses face.'

'You call it satisfactory to let a murderer off the hook? Someone who has definitely killed once and possibly twice?'

'You haven't an atom of proof that Spender was killed. It's just wishful thinking on your part. My officers investigate facts, not flights of fancy.'

'I can't believe his death is unrelated to the case.'

'You had him checked for drugs, didn't you? No coke, horse, hash or acid.' He scowled down at the report in front of him. 'Wasting police resources.'

'I'm going to ask for an adjournment at the inquest.'

Lacey heaved himself to his feet and stomped over to the window. He gestured with a podgy fist.

'Out there, in that seething mass of humanity, are numerous criminals carrying on their illegal business – and you and some of my most promising officers are wasting time and manpower in cloud-cuckoo land. You're a thorn in my flesh, James.'

'Yes, sir.'

'How's the missus and the kid?' he continued with one of his lightning volte-faces.

'They're both doing fine.'

274

'What's this I heard about some complication?'

'Ginny had a fall and went into premature labour and they had to perform a Caesarian Section, but the baby's okay and Ginny is recovering well.'

'What are you calling her?'

'We haven't finally decided, but probably Katherine.'

'Hmmm. Pity it's a girl. You have my sympathies, James. They're nothing but trouble from start to finish. You won't have a minute's peace till she's safely married and off your hands – twenty years of hard labour!'

As Lacey had no daughters of his own, only three sons who were all married and living far from Felstone, Roland took this remark as sour grapes.

'I expect I shall survive, sir.'

'How long will she have to stay in hospital?'

'About ten days.'

'And I suppose you'll be wanting time off?'

'After she comes out of hospital.'

'Well then, you've got ten days in which to button up this case.'

Helen Coleman lay propped up on the sofa and regarded her husband peevishly.

'How much longer have we got to wait before you do something about the manuscript?'

'Helen, I've told you over and over again, the police are investigating a murder. We'll have to sit on it for at least a year or two. They mustn't be able to trace it back to me.'

'I shall probably be dead by then! Couldn't we just set things in motion? Put out some feelers in the States?'

'Not yet, you must trust me. It's safe where it is, and when the time is ripe I'll . . . I'll take action.'

'We need the money now, Dennis. I can't go on like this much longer, relying on hired help. It would make all the difference. You could give up work and we could be together all day long. I wouldn't have to be on my own any more.'

Dennis Coleman pushed up his glasses and tried not to groan out loud. His hands shook as he put down the newspaper he had been trying to read.

'Be patient, Helen, things will work out.'

'Will they? I've been watching you, Dennis, over the last few weeks. You're really going to pieces. You want to pull yourself together. I would never have thought you would have had the guts, but you did and now we're going to reap the benefits. I don't want you getting a bad attack of conscience and confessing to the police. Why shouldn't we get something out of this? We deserve a break.'

'Yes, we do,' he said soothingly. 'Shall I make the cocoa?'

'I think I'll have mine in bed. I feel tired.'

She looked tired, he thought. There were dark circles under her eyes and the paper-white skin was stretched tightly across the contours of her face, revealing the skull underneath. Heavens knows what she had been doing to tire herself, he was the one who did all the physical work . . . As usual he ended up feeling guilty. She led a hell of a life and what was going to happen to them now? He pushed these thoughts aside and prepared her for bed. As he carried her upstairs he tried to stifle the revulsion he felt as he held her bony frame. She was a skeleton, like the carcass of a young bird that has fallen out of the nest. She was a *living* carcass.

He performed his caring duties, and when she was duly tucked up in one of the twin beds in their bedroom made cocoa for them both in the kitchen and carried it upstairs.

'Do you want one of your sleeping pills?'

'No, I think I shall be able to sleep without one tonight.'

'I'll put them in the cupboard.' He bent down and put the bottle in the bedside cabinet. At the same time he helped himself to her box of painkillers which was on the shelf. He tucked them away in his pocket without her noticing.

'Aren't you coming to bed now?'

'No, there's some reading I want to catch up on. I'll do it downstairs so that I don't disturb you.'

'Don't be long. You'll only disturb me when you do come up.'

'I'll try not to make a noise. Goodnight.' He dropped a kiss on her forehead, switched off the light and left the door ajar before returning to the living room.

It was ten-thirty. He looked at the clock and then down at the box of painkillers in his hand. When full it contained ten packs each holding ten pills. There weren't many left, only one and a half packs, but he thought it would be enough. He put them down and buried his head in his hands. How had he got into this disastrous situation? Why had he given in to temptation. Just one mad impulse on the spur of the moment and it had landed him in all this trouble. He wasn't cut out to be a criminal, the world of murder and larceny was completely alien to his nature. He was a law-abiding man who had suffered a momentary brain-storm and now he had to pay for it. And not just him, Helen too.

What would she do when she found that the police had the manuscript and they would not get a penny of the money she was already spending in her imagination? and supposing he was arrested for the murder – what would happen to her? Even if he escaped a murder rap there were other charges hanging over him, there was no way out. He couldn't go on another day living out the life he now led with Helen like a giant incubus around his neck. There was no future.

He picked up the foil packets and pressed out the pills, fifteen of them. Oblivion. That was what he sought and he had the means here in front of him. With him out of the way Helen would be taken into hospital or some sort of institution where she would be cared for far better than he had managed by trained people who knew how to cope with her needs and temperament. No more lies, no more subterfuges, no more quaking each time the doorbell rang or a visitor asked for him in the library.

He fetched some sheets of paper from the bureau and tried to compose a note, but after a few abortive attempts he screwed them up and flung them into the wastepaper basket. He didn't know what to say or even what he wanted to say. It was all a gigantic muddle. Let them sort it out for themselves, he didn't care what they thought. He went into the kitchen and got a tumbler of water which he took back with him into the living room. He selected a record from his collection beside the record player, put it on the turntable and dropped the arm.

As the fateful, dynamic notes of the *Dies Irae* from 'Verdi's Requiem' soared round the room he picked up a handful of pills and raised the tumbler of water to his lips.

Chapter 11

'Have they decided what they're going to call her yet?'

Jean Mansfield was curled up in an armchair knitting squares for an Oxfam blanket when her husband came home that evening.

'I think they've finally settled on Katherine.'

'It's a nice traditional name, won't give her age away when she gets older like some of these fashionable names that are all the rage for a short time and then date you terribly. How is James taking it all?'

'He's like a dog with two tails, and I've got news for you – we've been asked to be godparents.'

'Have we really? How nice.'

'Neither of them has any close relations and I think they thought we were as good as anyone. Young Simon will be the third one.'

'That's good. How is he reacting?'

'Nearly as infatuated as James, from what he says. That baby is going to be horribly spoilt if they don't watch out.'

'Thank God he's taken it like that. He was so aggressive and mutinous before they married that I didn't think the marriage would survive the first few months.'

'He seems to have accepted it and settled down now

and he's certainly thrilled with his baby sister. I've got a message for you – Ginny would love to see you if you would like to visit her in hospital.'

'Oh, good. I was going to drop in anyway but I was afraid she might get overtired if she had too many visitors. I've been knitting matinée coats for the baby.'

'Is that some of it?' Mansfield nodded at the red and green striped knitting hanging from her needles.

'No, of course it isn't, silly. I've had hers finished and put on one side for ages. Do you want some supper?'

'Just a coffee and perhaps a biscuit?'

'Biscuits are out, you know that.'

'Then why did you ask?' He was aggrieved.

'I thought perhaps some fruit or maybe a salad?'

'At this time of night? You're ruining my digestive system, woman.'

'Nonsense, you know you feel better.

Whilst she was in the kitchen making coffee he raided the biscuit tin that was standing on the sideboard. It was empty and he replaced the lid in disgust. How was a man supposed to keep up his strength and carry out his professional duties half-starved?

'I think we should ask James and Simon over for a meal whilst Ginny is still in hospital,' said his wife, coming back into the room with a laden tray. 'It can't be much fun having to cope by themselves and she went into hospital so suddenly that I don't expect she had a chance to prepare much for them.'

'Good idea. What are those?'

Mansfield looked disbelievingly at the plate she was lifting off the tray.

'Cheese scones. I've taken pity on you. But you're not to have butter with them.'

'You're a good cook, Jean,' he mumbled a little while later, his mouth full of scone. 'It's a shame not to practise your skills.'

'The day you go without a proper square meal is the day you can start complaining. How's the case going?'

'It isn't. We seem to be at a standstill. Lots of theories but no facts to back them. We're at a proper stalemate.'

'I bet that's upsetting James, he doesn't take failure lightly.'

Mansfield shrugged. 'Between you and me, I think he's lost his touch over this case. It may be because his mind isn't fully on the job, what with his home situation, but he's floundering. He's always worked in a contrary manner – thinking up theories and then trying to fit the evidence to them, instead of the other way round – but this time it's not working. I don't think we're going to solve this case and the Super's breathing down out necks.'

'So where does that leave you?'

'Out on a limb with our James.'

'That's not going to do your chances any good. It's time you got promotion.'

'Now, don't start on that theme again, Jean. I know my limitations. I've got as far as I want to go in that direction. I'm a damn' good sergeant and I'm content with that. I don't want the hassle and responsibility that goes with a higher grade. James and I make a good team.'

'And he gets all the kudos whilst you do the hard slog.'

'Not this time. He's bogged down and trying to dig himself out by making suppositions without a shred of solid evidence to back them. Hey – where are you taking those scones?'

'You're not having any more. They're for Jane's lunchbox tomorrow.'

'I see. I starve whilst my daughter increases her puppy-fat.'

'She hasn't got puppy-fat, she's got a nice little figure. I noticed the appreciative looks she was getting from the younger male population of Felstone when we went shopping last Saturday.'

'Jean, doesn't it worry you, strange young men ogling our daughter?'

'No, I think it's rather sweet.'

'Sweet!' He thought of the sexual urges rampant in most young men's breasts, or rather loins, and his blood ran cold. Jean was an innocent. She didn't come across the sexual harassment, the assaults and actual rapes that he met in the course of his duties. He was far more worried about Jane's safety than she was.

'It makes me feel quite envious. I remember the catcalls I used to get in my youth. There's nothing like an appreciative catcall to raise a woman's spirits.'

'Things are different now. It doesn't stop at catcalls. They're just the prelude to far nastier things. We live in a different climate now.'

'Okay, so I'm middle-aged and out of touch, but I'm glad I'm not cynical like you.'

'I didn't mean it like that. I still fancy you. Let's go to bed.'

A short distance away, James Roland lay in his solitary bed and turned over in his mind similar thoughts to those Patrick Mansfield had just expressed to his wife.

This damn' case was getting him down. It had looked so cut and dried at the beginning; an obvious motive, obvious suspects – it should have been a doddle. But here he was, weeks later, with a still unsolved murder on his hands and what he feared was probably a second murder too. There again, he was up against opposition; with only a gut feeling to go by; he was convinced that Barry Spender's death had been contrived, was no accident, but no one else shared this belief. His sergeant thought he was barking up the wrong tree and he set great store by what Mansfield thought. They had worked together now on many cases and he had always had the full support of the older man. They worked well in tandem, bouncing ideas off each other, but this time Roland felt that he was on his own. Not that Mansfield had actually said anything or behaved other than in his usual scrupulous fashion. He carried out the instructions given to him and appeared to be backing his chief but Roland knew that he was unhappy with the situation.

For the umpteenth time he went over in his mind's eye his list of suspects and their stories. The crux of the matter was, he believed their tales. He was sure that Dennis Coleman had been telling the truth; much against his will he also thought that Nick Blackstone had finally explained his part in the situation as it had actually happened; as for the Rakosis – it would be so easy to subscribe to the theory that they had killed the Russian out of revenge, but he couldn't see the little man in that role though his wife was a different matter . . . And what about the other women in the case, Stella Lingard, Laura Nelson, Helen Coleman? He had no reason to disbelieve their evidence. Christ, if Lacey was aware of his thoughts he would really think his inspector had flipped! If there was one precept that Lacey adhered to it was this: you didn't believe a word anyone told you, especially murder suspects; you certainly didn't take their evidence at face value.

Roland groaned and turned over in bed, heaving at the duvet. Barry Spender had been helped to his end, he was sure of it. What he had to do now was to find some evidence that definitely linked the two deaths. Perhaps they had been concentrating on the wrong motive. On the other hand, perhaps it was so obvious that they had overlooked it? Convinced that he was not going to sleep a wink that night, he buried his head in the pillow and allowed his imagination to run riot. He was not sure when sleep took over from reality, when his thought processes gave way to dreams; distorted, crazy dreams in which Nick Blackstone was conducting the investigation, solving the case and publishing his result in Hansard. A Nick Blackstone who jeered at him and insisted that Ginny had been his mistress in a past life.

Shuddering and sweating, Roland clawed himself back to full wakefulness. Faience had jumped onto the bed and was kneading his shoulder with unsheathed paws. He pushed her away, and when she yowled dismally he snapped on the light, gathering her up under his arm and stumbled down to the kitchen with her. He gave her a saucer of milk, made himself a cup of tea and returned to bed as the clock struck three. This time he fell into a deep sleep, undisturbed by dreams, and didn't wake again until Simon called up the stairs to tell him that it was eight o'clock.

* * *

Helen Coleman came to with a start. She had been dreaming that she was back in the corps de ballet at Covent Garden. They were performing 'Romeo and Juliet' and the Montagues and Capulets were strutting across the stage in a ritual dance to the strains of Prokofiev's haunting music. She gave a little moue of distress and twisted her head on the pillow. She hated it when she dreamt of the past, when she re-lived the dancing and music that had meant so much to her. But the music was continuing, great crashing chords that tore round the room. It wasn't her imagination, she really was hearing music; some choral work that expressed anguish and triumph and made the hairs rise on the nape of her neck. What did Dennis call it – the tingle factor? It was too bad of him, playing records at this time of night and disturbing her rest.

She struggled up in bed and looked at the luminous dial of the bedside clock. It was twelve-thirty. What the hell did he think he was doing? Then another factor struck her. It was the same few bars of music playing over and over again. The record was stuck. Why didn't he do something about it? She fumbled for the walking stick that was kept by the bed so that she could summon Dennis by thumping on the floor, but her clumsy agitated fingers slipped off the polished knob and it crashed sideways out of reach. Nearly weeping with frustration she clasped at the light pull and managed to switch on the overhead light. The music was still repeating itself inanely and she felt panic sweeping through her. Dennis would never let a record be ruined like that. He had gone and left her! She was alone in the house, he had run out on her!

Even as she assimilated this thought it was taken over

by another fear. Supposing he had had a heart attack? He hadn't left her, he had been taken ill. He was lying downstairs dead or dying and she was helpless! What could she do? Even if she managed to swing her legs out of bed she could never drag herself across the room without the walking stick, and even if she did there was no way she could cope with the stairs.

She must summon help. The phone? Gritting her teeth she pulled herself into a more upright position and stretched out for the phone that sat on the bedside table. The sweat was trickling down her face before she dragged it close enough to reach the buttons. Who should she call? The police? The doctor? No, she would ring Pam Maudsley. She lived nearby and she had her own key to the house. She would come. She MUST come!

'Ken! The phone's ringing!' Pam Maudsley dug her elbow into her husband's back and he rolled over and grunted.

'Ken! Did you hear me?'

'Well, answer it then, woman,' he mumbled and burrowed deeper into the bedclothes.

She sat up in bed, her heart pounding. Downstairs the phone continued to shrill. There was something wrong. She hated it when the phone rang in the night, it always meant bad news. Someone was ill, there had been an accident, something had happened to one of the family . . .

She struggled out of bed and pulled her dressing-gown from the hook on the back of the bedroom door. She couldn't find her slippers and padded downstairs in bare feet, shrugging into her dressing-gown as she went. Terrible images swept through her head. Kevin had smashed up his car and himself with it; the twins had had an accident; there had been a fire or explosion at Clare's cottage . . . She tripped over a coat that had been left in a pile on the bottom step and nearly yanked the telephone cord out of its socket as she grabbed for the receiver.

'Who is it?'

'Pam? It's Helen. Something's happened to Dennis!'

'What do you mean?' The voice that came over the line was so disturbed that she had difficulty in recognising the caller but when she did she sat down heavily on the stairs and listened to what the distraught woman was saying.

'What do you want *me* to do?' she asked when the other woman had finally run out of words. 'It's the middle of the night!'

'Please come over, Pam – I don't know what to do!'

'What – now?'

'Please, Pam. I'm afraid something terrible has happened!'

'All right, give me time to get dressed. I'll come as quickly as I can. Don't panic, and don't do anything till I get there.' Which was as stupid a thing as anyone could have said, she thought as she rang off, the poor woman was helpless.

She stumped back upstairs and switched on the bedroom light. Her husband glared at her, blinking.

'What the hell do you think you're doing?'

'There's something wrong over at the Colemans.'

'What do you mean?'

She explained to him what had happened as she started to dress. 'You're not going over there? Can't

289

it wait till the morning? That woman thinks you're at her beck and call, day and night!'

'Ken, the poor woman is a cripple. She can't even get out of bed on her own.'

'I suppose I'd better come with you,' he grumbled, getting out of bed himself. 'Though I can't see why she doesn't ring the police if she thinks there's something wrong.'

A short while later the two of them let themselves out of the house and set off for Mill Close.

'How are we going to get in?'

'I've got my own key. I do hope nothing's happened to Dennis. Whatever will she do?'

'Well, you're not getting involved. You do too much already. Let the Social Services do their whack, that's what the Welfare State is for.'

'She's a difficult woman, and don't I know it, but I feel sorry for her. Just put yourself in her place.'

'You've got a husband and a family of your own to look after, you can't take on someone else's problems.'

It was a dark night and the moon was hidden behind cloud. There were no street lights in the village and the Maudsleys were glad of their torch as they hurried down the deserted street. The Colemans' house was the second one along in the Close and as they approached they could see that the lights were on in the sitting room and in one of the upstairs bedrooms.

'Oh, Ken, I'm frightened. I wonder what we're going to find?' Pam Maudsley clutched her husband's arm as they reached the gate.

'You wait out here while I go and see what's wrong.'

'No, I'll come with you. Here's the key.'

She handed it to him and he unlocked the front door. They stepped inside and music immediately assailed their ears. It was coming from the sitting room. There was no light on in the hall but a band of light showed beneath the door.

'Mr Coleman – are you there?'

There was a muffled noise from upstairs and Pam Maudley threw a worried look over her shoulder as her husband pushed open the sitting room door.

Denis Coleman was sitting slumped at the table, his head and shoulders and one arm resting on the top, the other arm hanging limply down by his side. A tumbler had rolled across the table and rested on its side, poised on the very edge, and there were splashes of water on the surface.

'My God! He's collapsed! He's dead!'

Pam Maudsley stood rooted in the doorway but her husband was made of sterner stuff and pushed past her.

'Turn that bloody noise off!'

She stumbled across to the record player and switched off the turntable. The sudden silence was shattering.

'Is he dead?' she demanded of her husband who was attempting to raise Dennis Coleman's head off the table.

'I don't know, help me lift him up.'

She moved across to him and trod on something that crackled underfoot. She bent down and picked it up. It was a foil packet that had contained tablets, a 'popper-pack', and she read the name stamped on it: CO-PROXAMOL.

'Ken, these are Helen's painkillers – it's empty. I

reckon he's taken them. He's taken an overdose! What are we going to do?'

'He's still alive. We must get a doctor – an ambulance!'

'The phone's over there. Oh, poor man! The strain of looking after her has been too much for him!'

Whilst her husband phoned for help, Pam went upstairs to deal with Helen Coleman.

Roland learned about Dennis Coleman's suicide attempt quite by chance the following afternoon. He had been to visit Ginny and as the car park by the maternity wing was full had to drive onto the main car park to find a parking space. He was returning to his car when he saw Laura Nelson hurrying across the tarmac. She looked very agitated as if she had received some bad news and he wondered whom she had been visiting or whether she herself had been receiving treatment at the Out-patients Department. There were a couple of matters he wanted to check with her and he decided to intercept her. She looked up startled as he fell in step beside her.

'Miss Nelson, are you all right? You look upset.'

'Of course I'm upset. And now I suppose you're going to pester him? You policemen are like ghouls, homing in on tragedy – anyway, I thought you couldn't be prosecuted for it nowadays!'

'Miss Nelson, what are you talking about?'

'Attempted suicide – it's not a crime any longer.'

Roland felt a stab of foreboding. He stared down at her.

'Suicide? Whose suicide?'

It was her turn to stare. 'Do you mean you hadn't

heard? Dennis Coleman tried to commit suicide last
night. He's in Intensive Care and they won't let
me see him!'

He made a quick decision 'My car's just over there,
we can talk inside.' As he led her across the questions buzzed round in his head. Had Coleman tried
to kill himself because he was guilty of murder? Had
Coleman left a confession, and if so why hadn't he been
informed? He unlocked the passenger door and got into
the driver's seat.

'Who found him?'

'Mrs Maudsley, the woman who does for them.
Apparently Helen woke up in the night and suspected
that something was wrong. She rang for Mrs Maudsley
and she and her husband went over and found Dennis.
He'd taken an over-dose and was unconscious.'

'So where is Mrs Coleman now?'

'She's been taken into care for the time being. Poor
Dennis, I can't believe it.'

Roland remembered the suspicions they had had
about her and Dennis Coleman.

'You seem very distressed. I know Mr Coleman is a
fellow employee at the Maltings but I'm wondering if
you and he have a closer relationship.'

'What *do* you mean?'

'I put it to you that you are, or were, lovers?'

She flushed and her voice trembled. 'How could you
suggest such a despicable thing!'

'Are you denying that you and he were having
an affair?'

'I most certainly am. The idea is preposterous! He's
married and takes his responsibilities seriously. He's
never let Helen down.'

'Wouldn't he be doing just that by doing away with himself?'

She glared at him. 'I should hate to be a policeman, always thinking the worst of people, distorting facts, digging the dirt!'

'Why do you think he did it then?'

'Because it all got too much for him – the strain of looking after Helen, this murder business. He must have had a brain-storm – he's been looking ghastly just lately, really haggard and run-down.'

'Tell me, Miss Nelson, who else knows about his suicide attempt?'

'I suppose most people at the Maltings will have heard. You know how bad news gets around.'

'Who told you?'

'I can't remember.'

'Can't remember? I find that hard to believe.'

'Oh, it was someone who works in the library – Miss Parker. They've had to cover for him today.'

'Thank you, Miss Nelson, I mustn't detain you any longer.' He reached across her and undid the door, aware in that close proximity, of the palpable waves of fear that were emanating from her.

'Is there anything else you want to tell me?'

'No. No, of course not. What else would there be?' She hesitated and he thought that she was going to say something further but she changed her mind and slipped out of the car before saying defiantly: 'You're not going to pester him, are you?'

'Are you telling me my business? And shouldn't you be at work?'

She flushed again and slammed the door, and when Roland continued to sit there unperturbed, turned on her heel and hurried off across the car park. He waited until she was out of sight and then got out and went back into the hospital.

The sister on desk duty in Intensive Care was quite emphatic even when Roland explained who he was and that Dennis Coleman was involved in a murder enquiry he was conducting.

'You cannot see the patient today. He's far too ill.'

'Is he going to recover?'

'Yes, he's a lucky man, though he may not think so when he's sensible again. He was found only a couple of hours after he had taken the overdose and was brought straight in here. If he'd been left till morning . . .' She shrugged.

'What had he taken?'

'Distalgesic – Co-proxamol tablets. They contain paracetamol as well which can cause irreversible liver damage, but we got him in time.'

'I understand the home help found him?'

'Yes, her husband phoned for an ambulance straight away.'

'When can I question him?'

'Not until tomorrow. He should be out of IC by then but I don't know how much sense you'll get out of him.'

'I'll come back first thing tomorrow. In the meantime, let me know if there is any change in his condition.'

He extracted from her the address of Pam Maudsley. As he was preparing to leave an alarm bell rang out and immediately the area was a scene of activity with doctors and nurses appearing from nowhere and rushing through the door into the unit.

'It's not . . . ?' he asked the sister who was also joining the exodus.

'No, it's one of our heart patients.'

Somewhat shaken, he looked at the door as it closed behind her. On the other side a life-and-death struggle was going on to resuscitate the victim of cardiac arrest. He hoped the poor devil survived, whoever he was.

Pam Maudsley was in her kitchen cooking when Roland called and her husband was cutting the lawn in the front garden. He willingly relinquished the lawnmower when the detective introduced himself and led him round the side of the house to the back door.

'He hasn't pegged out, has he?'

'No, he's expected to make a full recovery, thanks to you and your wife's prompt action.'

'We only did what anyone would have done but I'm glad to hear that. The wife's in such a state about it, anyone would think they were close relations instead of her employers.' He banged on the kitchen window as they walked past and his wife looked up startled and hurried to the door.

'It's the police, Pam, come about Coleman.'

'He hasn't . . . ?'

'No, I was telling your husband, he's going to be fine. I just want to ask you some questions about last night and what happened.'

'You'd better come in. I was just going to make Ken a cup of tea. I expect you'd like one too?'

A little while later Roland had finished his tea and learned how the Maudsleys had been involved in the events of the previous evening.

'Did he leave a note?'

'A note?' Pam Maudsley looked blank.

'It is usual for a suicide to leave a note behind.'

'No, I didn't notice anything, did you, Ken?'

'No, there was nothing like that in the room, I'm sure of it.'

'Have you still got your key, Mrs Maudsley? Would you take me round the house?'

She looked doubtful. 'I don't know if I should . . .'

'I can get an official search warrant but we don't really need to go to all that bother, do we? I just want to check if there is anything lying around that might embarrass Mrs Coleman or him when he recovers.'

'Oh, I see. Yes, well, I'll take you round there now. It's only round the corner.'

'I ought to have seen the warning signs,' she confided to Roland as she unlocked the door and they went inside the Colemans' house. 'He's been looking awful just recently but I hadn't realised he was at the end of his tether. She was a difficult woman – God help her now, poor dear – and I did what I could, but Ken didn't like me to get too involved and Dennis bore the full brunt of it, day and night. This is where I found him.'

She indicated the table which stood over near the bay window.

Roland made a quick search of the room. He found what he was looking for almost immediately; two crumpled-up pieces of paper in the waste paper basket which stood in the hearth. He unfolded and straightened them. A single half-finished sentence was written on each. One said: 'Dear Helen, this will be a shock to you, I am sorry,' and the other: 'I can't go on any longer.'

'Poor man, he really meant it,' said Pam Maudsley, looking over his shoulder.

'Could he have completed a third note and left it where his wife found it?'

'No, there was nothing like that. She kept saying she couldn't understand it, that he seemed perfectly all right when he put her to bed.'

Unease gripped Roland again. Surely the pills had been self-administered and Coleman hadn't been helped to his near-demise? Well, if he had, the plan had backfired and he would learn the truth tomorrow morning.

'What will happen now?' asked Pam Maudsley. 'Do you think I should clean the place up?'

'I should leave it just as it is for the time being. If you leave the key with me I'll drop it by later. I want to check upstairs before I go.'

After she had gone he explored the rest of the downstairs rooms and then went up to the bedrooms. The rumpled bed with the covers thrown back, the walking stick lying where it had rolled under the bed, the receiver half hanging off the phone so that the dialling tone purred into the silence of the deserted room, all told the same tale. Roland sat in the bedside chair and imagined himself in Helen Coleman's place. How terrified and helpless she must have felt, you could not help but pity her, and yet, if her husband was guilty of murder, she had driven him to it. If he were a violent man surely he would have administered the pills to her rather than to himself? No, this was a classic case of a man driven by despair to try and end it all and he, Roland, was partly to blame for hounding the man.

He went downstairs again, avoiding the wheelchair which stood at the bottom. You would have expected one of the ground floor rooms to have been turned into a bedroom to accommodate her state. Coleman must have had to carry her up and down each day and although she was a frail thing he wasn't exactly a robust man. In fact, it was surprising how few things in the house were arranged for the benefit of a cripple. Perhaps they had refused to acknowledge the gravity of her illness or maybe she had deteriorated suddenly in the last few months. There was nothing more he could do here. He locked up, dropped the key at the Maudsleys' and went back to the Station to bring his sergeant up-to-date with these latest events.

'You say Laura Nelson denied having an affair with him? Did you believe her?' Mansfield scraped out the bowl of his pipe and banged it against the ashtray to get rid of the last traces of dottle. His superior watched the operation with exasperated resignation.

'Methinks the lady did protest too much. We'll have to have it out with him in the morning. Maybe they had been having an affair and she got fed up with the hole-in-the-corner aspect and cried off, and that was the last straw as far as he was concerned.'

'So, if it hadn't been for that record getting stuck in the groove, he would have had it?'

'No doubt about it.'

'You'd have thought, him being a music buff, that he would have been into CDs and all that jazz.'

'Probably couldn't afford it. The record player was very similar to the one we've got.'

Mansfield cocked an eyebrow. 'The hard-up police officer? Don't make me weep.'

Roland grinned. 'It's Ginny's birthday soon and I've

been toying with the idea of buying her a CD player. The only trouble is, we've got such a huge collection of LPs between us and they'd all have to be replaced.'

'When does she come out of hospital?'

'Wednesday, if all goes well.'

'You'd better make the most of the next few nights, they'll be your last undisturbed ones for a long time. How are you and Simon making out in the grub stakes?'

'We're keeping the local take-aways in business.'

'Jean said you were to come round for a meal. How about Tuesday evening as long as nothing comes up here?'

'Fine, as long as she knows we may have to cry off at the last moment. Still, she should know the score by now.'

'What's next on the agenda?'

'Get off home, Pat, and have an early night for once. There's nothing more we can do here. I feel as if I'm going round in circles. None of our suspects' alibis for the Russian's murder can be proved or broken. Evans and Lucas have checked every household in the three villages and have come up with a complete blank; nobody saw or noticed anything untoward at the time – any one of them could have done it and we've got no leads at all. And then there's Spender's death – does it tie in with the first murder? The evidence all points to its being accidental but I've got this hunch . . .'

'You want a break. Forget about it for a few hours and perhaps you'll be struck with inspiration.'

'It's what we need. Hard graft is getting us nowhere.'

Roland got to his feet and replaced some of his

papers in the filing cabinet. 'I'll pick you up at eight-thirty tomorrow morning, and let's hope he's well enough to be interviewed.'

Dennis Coleman was still attached to various tubes and drips when they arrived at the hospital the next morning. He had been moved out of Intensive Care into a room of his own and lay there looking pale and drained and oddly defensive without his glasses. They had had strict instructions from the sister on duty that they weren't to tire him and could only have a short time with him.

'How are you feeling, Coleman?'

'I made a balls up of that too, didn't I?'

'Why did you do it?'

He closed his eyes and made no reply and Roland tried again.

'Was it guilty conscience?'

'You don't give up, do you?' he said wearily.

'Put yourself in my place. Wouldn't you think it was an admission of guilt if one of your chief suspects decided to end it all?'

'I didn't kill the Russian, I know I didn't, and I just don't care any more what anyone else thinks.'

Roland stared down at the man and told himself he mustn't feel pity. He tried another tack.

'Were you having an affair with Laura Nelson?'

The man's eyes snapped open.

'Whatever gave you that idea? Of course I wasn't! I've never cheated on Helen.'

'I've been told that Miss Nelson has formed an unsuitable attachment to someone, which I presume means that she's fallen for a married man.'

'Then that shows how wrong you can be.' A travesty
of a smile crossed his gaunt features and he closed his
eyes and appeared to drift off.

Damn, thought Roland, another theory aborted
before he'd hardly had a chance to examine it. He
gestured to Mansfield to take over the questioning and
went across to the window.

'Was it your idea to take an overdose?'

Coleman opened his eyes. 'What do you mean?'

'You weren't persuaded by someone else?'

'I don't know what you're getting at.'

'You weren't slipped a Micky Finn unawares yesterday evening?'

'No, I deliberately tried to take my own life whilst
of sound mind. There – does that satisfy you?'

'Did your wife . . . ?'

'Oh, my God, Helen! What will happen to her?'

'I understand she's being well looked after,' said
Roland, strolling back to the bedside. 'It's only a stroke
of fate that she's not a widow now.'

'And do you think that's a reason for rejoicing?
Why couldn't they have left me? Why did they have
to bloody interfere?' There was a mutinous look on
Coleman's face as he turned his head away from
them and Roland knew that they would get no more
answers. The sister returned at that moment and
insisted that they leave and with a last look at the
troubled man they stepped outside and walked back
down the corridor.

'Do you ever feel ashamed of your profession?'
asked Roland, stepping aside to avoid a trolley. 'I
feel we are partly responsible for his state, that we
drove him to it.'

'You think he's in the clear then, as far as the murder rap is concerned?'

'I wish I knew. All I'm sure of is that I'm not sure of anything any more.'

Which coming from Roland, the bright-eyed and bushytailed DI, was quite an admission, thought Mansfield, and one that he would probably regret when he had recovered his aplomb.

By the next morning James Roland was feeling less dejected and had decided to take Mansfields advice and try and put the case out of his mind for a few hours, and what better way than by gardening? It was not a task he had taken much interest in before his marriage but Ginny was a keen naturalist and gardener and some of her enthusiasm had rubbed off on him. The garden had been overgrown and neglected when they had moved in and they had re-planned it and were gradually tackling it, piece by piece. Until recently she had done most of the work with him lending a hand with the really heavy spadework, but over the last few weeks it had been left unattended. Fortunately the dry summer had meant that the lawn had needed very little cutting and even the weeds had stopped growing. They had built a patio at the back of the house which faced south, levelling the ground and laying slabs of York stone, and intended furnishing it with shrubs and flowers in ornamental containers, but so far it remained bare and horribly new-looking.

Roland had an idea. He went inside and spoke to Simon. 'We'll go over to the Garden Centre and buy some tubs and spring bulbs and set them up on the patio. It will be a surprise for your mother when she comes home. What do you say?'

Simon was full of enthusiasm, eager to grasp at any diversion to avoid his homework, and after a scratch lunch they set off towards Woodford. Many other people had had the same idea and the Garden Centre was crowded. They had difficulty in parking and were both surprised by the large variety of plant stock and garden furniture available.

As they wandered up and down the rows of container-grown plants Roland got quite carried away and began to understand how visiting gardening centres was fast becoming one of the great Sunday afternoon pastimes of the British public.

'You can even buy fair-sized tree in containers,' he pointed out to Simon. 'We could really go to town and transform the garden over-night.'

'They're ever so expensive,' said Simon, 'and Mum always says that a real gardener never buys anything – you beg, borrow or steal.'

'Does she now?' He suddenly remembered a handful of cuttings that she had produced from a pocket after they had visited a stately home in the spring. 'Well, we're not begging, borrowing or stealing tubs. Let's go and look at some. I think they are over there.'

The selection of tubs, pots and bowls was quite daunting. Roland favoured a pair of urns that looked as if they were made from weathered stone, with ornamental handles and carving round the brims, but Simon was dismissive.

'They're too fancy. Mum would like something more natural-looking and plain – like those ones over there.'

'Yes, I think you're right,' he said, looking at the collection of terracotta pots. 'Bulbs would look good in them, and geraniums in the summer.'

They chose two shallow terracotta bowls and two Ali Baba pots and then Simon nudged his step-father. 'How about one of those for fun?' He pointed to the collection of garden gnomes which was standing nearby.

'Your mother would think we'd taken leave of our senses.'

'It would be a good joke. Can you imagine her face if she saw one of those on the patio? One that looks as if it's fishing. We could stand it beside the washing-up bowl full of water.' He giggled and Roland grinned back.

'My God! I can't get away from you.' The heavily sarcastic voice broke in on their banter and Roland looked up to see Patrick and Jean Mansfield standing near them.

'Don't tell me you're into this gardening lark too?'

'She twisted my arm,' said Mansfield gloomily.

'Rubbish, you're just as keen as I am,' said his wife. 'Hello, James, Simon, how are you?'

'We're decorating the patio to give Ginny a surprise when she comes home.'

'Not with garden gnomes?' She was horrified and Simon gave a hoot of laughter.

'We thought we'd get one for a joke.'

'So that's what you were laughing about. It would be an expensive joke though – have you seen the price?'

'I can't believe people actually buy these things,' said Roland.

'Oh, they do, they're quite a cult. I suppose some of them are rather engaging. You want to come round this side and look at them. From the back they all look alike with their hoods up, huddled over their rod and line, but their faces have all got different expressions.'

Roland stared at her and Jean Mansfield laughed.

'What's the matter? You're not seriously thinking of buying one, are you?'

'It would be more than my life was worth. Come on, Simon, let's go and pay for these pots and get some bulbs and potting compost. It's not too early for planting bulbs, is it?' he asked Jean.

'It is rather but I don't suppose it matters. They'll be able to advise you at the check-out.'

'What are you here for?'

'Roses,' said Patrick Mansfield, 'but we can't agree on whether to concentrate on HT's or floribundas.'

'The HT's have far superior blossoms and are fine for cutting but the floribundas make a much better display and go on blooming for longer,' said his wife.

'Why not a few of each?'

'Very tactful, James, we shall probably end up doing just that. Pat says you're coming for a meal on Tuesday?'

'Yes, if that's all right with you. I'm sorry, Simon, I forgot to tell you.'

'I have a lot of homework on Tuesday evenings,' he said ungraciously.

'Don't worry, I'm not expecting you to stay around and listen to us old ones talking. I'll just feed you and then you can go off and do you own thing.'

'Thanks, it will be good to have a proper meal for a change.' He gave his father a sly grin.

'We've managed very well so far and I'm now going home to endeavour to cook you a Toad-in-the-Hole.'

'Frog-in-a-puddle? Yippee! Can we have beer with it?'

* * *

James Roland was very preoccupied for the rest of the day. He cooked Simon and himself a meal, and after they had cleared away and washed up he drove them over to the hospital to visit Ginny and the baby. Afterwards he dropped Simon back home and prepared to return to Felstone.

'I've got to go back to the Station.'

'You're not on duty on a Sunday evening?'

'It's nothing to do with being on duty. I've just had an idea connected with the case I'm working on and I want to check my notes. I shouldn't be too long, don't wait up for me.'

'You sound as if you're talking to Mother,' said Simon sagely.

Roland shut himself up in his office and got out the statements connected with the case. As he read them through yet again a thread of excitement ran through him. Was it possible that they had been looking at this from the wrong angle? Could this new theory that was forming at the back of his mind have any substance? It had been triggered off by that remark of Jean Mansfield's: 'They all look the same from the back.' He held his head in his hands and closed his eyes and tried to picture the scene of Mikhail Rabinovich's murder.

He visualised the dumpy figure, clad in jeans and kagool, hunched over the fishing rod, his hood pulled up over his head as the storm clouds gathered in the sky and the rain-spattered water flowed in full spate past the boat. Roland brought his fist crashing down on the desk. Anyone approaching from behind could have thought the man was Barry Spender. Had the Russian been killed in mistake for Spender? Had Spender been the intended victim all along?

Chapter 12

It had been staring him in the face all the time and he hadn't seen it because there had seemed to be so many possible reasons for the Russian's murder and so many people who could have wanted him out of the way. Yes, it had seemed so obvious that he hadn't looked any further. Roland drummed his fingers on the desk and explored his startling new theory.

They *were* alike. Both were short and stocky, wide across the shoulders with powerful arms. From a distance even their faces had a fleeting resemblance, broad across the temples with deepset dark eyes. In fact, you could include Miklos Rakosi in the count and say that the three of them were superficially similar. And the Russian had been wearing Spender's clothes, his jeans and kagool. His murderer had crept up behind him, bashed him over the head causing him to fall into the river, and had probably not even realised that he had killed the wrong man. What a shock he must have had when Spender turned up alive and well afterwards.

Roland rifled through the statements in front of him. Had anybody seemed unduly startled when they'd been interviewed? But no, they had all known that the Russian had been found dead long before he spoke with them. So what had happened next? Realising that he had failed, the murderer had planned a second attempt. He had kept watch on Spender and had been lucky enough to find him alone and unwell one evening. All he had had to do was give him a helping hand over the side.

Roland stood up and walked over to the window. As he stared out unseeing into the dark night he argued with himself. Was he spinning fantasies? Was he so eager to make a break-through that he was concocting imaginary scenarios in his head? Or had he at last hit on the truth? There had been something about this case all the way through that had niggled away at him like an aching tooth. Something that he hadn't been able to put his finger on but which had fluttered at the back of his mind casting a shadow over his reasoning. Lacey had pooh-poohed the idea of Russian drop-outs and missing manuscripts as being too over-the-top right at the beginning; perhaps he had been right.

He looked at his watch: ten o'clock. Mansfield wouldn't thank him for dragging him out at this time on a Sunday evening just to have a theory expounded to him. It would have to wait till the morning. Perhaps if he slept on it he would have a better idea as to whether this new idea was viable or just a load of old codswallop. Mansfield, with his solid, phlegmatic manner and his feet firmly entrenched in his native Suffolk soil, was very good at bringing one down to earth.

He listened carefully the next morning to Roland's reasoning, sucking on his unlit pipe and making non-committal grunts until his superior had finished.

'The wrong man, eh? I suppose it *is* possible. Remember, I never saw the Russian, dead or alive, but I take your word for it that the likeness was there.

The stumbling block is, why should someone want to kill
Spender? What was the motive if he was the intended
victim all the time?'

'I know,' groaned Roland, 'I've been up half the
night trying to work that one out and I haven't got very
far. Let's go through the list of suspects and see if you
can throw any light on the matter.' He referred to the
papers in front of him. 'There are the three women –
Stella Lingard, Laura Nelson and Màrta Rakosi – what
possible reason could they have for killing Spender?
I didn't include Helen Coleman because she couldn't
physically have done it unless she and her husband
planned it together and he actually did the deed.'

'I can't see Coleman as a murderer, I never have.
He hasn't got the guts to kill anyone.'

'It takes guts to try and kill yourself.'

'Yes, but I think that points to his innocence. He'd
rather kill himself than someone else.'

'Then there's Miklos Rakosi – why should he want
Spender out of the way? And the same for Nick Black-
stone. The only person on our list who's a possibility is
Jonathan Cade.'

'A lover's quarrel? He seems genuinely cut up about
his lover's death but who knows how their minds work?
Maybe it was someone from Spender's past.'

'We're going to have to dig deep into that. It may be
something to do with the gay faction. Another possibility is that Spender had got something on Blackstone
and was blackmailing him.'

'You're not suggesting that Blackstone is connected
with the gay scene?'

'Certainly not if his current lifestyle's anything to go
by, but it could be something else that Spender had

discovered. Of course, the other thing is, it doesn't have to be anyone on our list of suspects. We originally drew it up from people who worked at the Maltings and knew about the Russian going to live on the *Painted Lady*. If Spender was the real victim it doesn't have to be someone who works there or even who lives locally. It could be someone from way back in his past of whom we know nothing.'

'Surely it must be someone who's living locally and was able to keep tabs on Spender?'

'Yes, I suppose so, but it could theoretically be anyone living in the local community.'

'I reckon it's a well-nigh impossible task. I'm not saying you're wrong but where are you ever going to get proof to back up your theory? Where do you start?'

'With Jonathan Cade. We'll go right over there now and ask him some more questions, different ones this time.'

'Is the Super going to wear this?'

'To speak in his idiom – We'll cross that bridge when we come to it.'

As Roland drove over to Blund, Mansfield sat silently beside him, pondering this latest quirk in his superior's reasoning. The wrong victim? It wouldn't be the first time a would-be murderer had killed the wrong person, either through bungling or circumstances beyond his or her control. Was this the case here? It was always possible, but Spender was a far more unlikely victim than the Russian and he couldn't see how Roland could justify this latest bee in his bonnet. These hunches were all very well, and Roland had been proved right against all the odds in previous investigations on which they had worked, but you had to have *some* solid evidence to go on. You couldn't spend police resources chasing after pie in the sky . . .

He was suddenly aware that the man beside him had asked a question and was waiting for an answer.

'Come again, I was thinking.'

'Don't overdo it, Patrick, you look positively pained.'

It was Jonathan Cade's day off and they found him on the *Painted Lady* working on a large canvas he had set up in the cabin. It was a swirl of colour with yellow and orange predominating and although it was an abstract Roland could pick out shapes of musical instruments suggested in the composition: a trumpet and a saxophone and what looked like a thread of musical notes twisting in and out of a treble clef.

'It's a tribute to Barry, he was very fond of jazz,' said Cade, flinging his brush down and wiping his hands on a paint-stained rag. 'I've got to do something.'

'You hadn't known Spender very long, had you?' asked Roland.

'What's that got to do with you? What do you want?'

'Some information about Spender. How long *had* you known him?'

'Since I came to work here in June. We actually lived together for only a few weeks.'

'Are you sure you didn't know him before? Perhaps you came to work at the Maltings because he was already here?'

'No, I didn't, to both questions, and what is this inquisition about anyway?' He was beginning to get annoyed and Roland pressed on.

'I'm not satisfied that Spender's death was accidental. I'm trying to build up a picture of his past life.'

'He warned me about this! How the police try to make us into scapegoats. How could his death have been anything but accidental? How could it be connected with Rabinovich's murder?'

'I'm asking the questions, Cade. Presumably he had had other lovers before you came on the scene. Do you know of any?'

'Yes I do. He had a very close friend whom he lived with for years before he died.'

'Died?'

'Yes, and it wasn't Aids, Inspector. He died from leukaemia.'

'How long ago was this?'

'Three or four years. Barry wasn't promiscuous. He and this friend were together for many years and since then I'm the only one who meant anything to him.' His voice shook and he glared at the two detectives.

'Are you sure that Spender was not in contact with anyone from his past? Someone who could have cut up nasty about his new life with you?'

'Yes, I've told you.'

'Had he come into any money recently?' asked Mansfield, taking up the questioning and with his mind on the matter of blackmail.

'Look, what are you getting at?'

'I don't know how well paid his job was but did he seem flush in the short while you lived with him?'

'He made a living, we had enough. Money didn't mean much to Barry.'

'People only say that when they have no money cares.'

'I don't know what you're insinuating . . .'

'Who benefits by his death? Did he leave a will?'
asked Roland who was admonishing himself for not
having checked this out before.

'There's a sister in Canada. *I* don't want to benefit
by his death!'

'Presumably this boat now belongs to her?'

'I'm just looking after it until everything is sorted
out. I shall be quite happy to move somewhere else.
There are too many memories here for me.'

'Right, Cade, that will be all for now. We'll leave you
to get on with your painting. What do you intend doing
with it when it's finished?'

'Why, keep it, of course. *This* is my memento mori,
Inspector, not Barry's worldly goods.'

'What now?' asked Mansfield as they left the *Painted
Lady*.

'We're going to have to check out the local gay
community, I'll get on to my contact. But right now
we're going back to the Maltings to see Mrs Marilyn
Proctor again. She presumably employed Spender in
the first place. She may know something of his background and past.'

'What happens in the winter at the Maltings? They
have the festival in the spring and the summer proms
but how do they keep going the rest of the year?'

'The music school operates all the year round and
there are concerts arranged throughout the year and
musical workshops and so on, and the complex itself
is a little mecca for tourists – what with the specialist
shops and the river trips.'

'Yes, I suppose the Americans lap it up. It's handy
the Bases being near.'

As they walked back to the car a strengthening breeze tugged at their hair and clothes and rustled the marram grass. The river was beginning to get a deserted look. Laying-up time was here and although the weather was still holding out many boats had already been taken out of the water. A flock of oyster-catchers swept up from the water's edge, their metallic piping mingling with the snapping halyards of those boats still moored nearby. Soon the Sunday sailors would all have gone into winter hibernation and the only vessels left would be the handful of houseboats and those craft whose owners plied a living on the river.

'He'd been here about four years. Do you want me to find you the exact date?' asked Marilyn Proctor.

Roland declined. 'How did he come to be employed here? Did he answer an advertisement?'

She looked puzzled. 'He wasn't employed, he rented the premises for his piano workshop.'

'I thought that all the people who worked in the complex were employed by the Trust?'

'No, it's rather ambivalent. The art gallery and craft centre and the shops are run by us, and we employ the people who work in them, but Barry Spender was a freelance. As I say, he rented the premises and set up his piano workshop. The garden centre is run on the same lines.'

'So you know nothing of his background?'

'I know that he was a very respected craftsman, Inspector,' she retorted crisply, 'and he had made quite a name for himself in the area. I should imagine it was quite a lucrative business. People used to come from far away to consult him. He will be hard to replace.'

'Do you happen to know where he came from? Where he had lived before he settled here?'

'I have no idea, but I understood that there had been a tragedy in his past and he was trying to build a new life for himself.'

'A life in the gay community? You did know that he was gay?'

'Yes I did, and I fail to see how that affected his ability as a craftsman.'

'Some members of the public are very prejudiced about that sort of thing.'

'Well, I'm not,' she retorted. 'Working as I do in the Arts I meet a lot of that fraternity and most of them are very gifted, charming people. They're not all camp and limp wrists – but surely I don't have to tell you that?'

Roland changed the subject. 'I'm anxious to trace anyone who may have known him in the past.'

She misunderstood this. 'You mean for inheritance purposes – didn't he leave a will? I thought he had a sister living in the States, but maybe I'm mistaken. Jonathan Cade's the one who would be most likely to know. Maybe he's in line, but I shouldn't think so. They hadn't been together very long.'

'Well, thank you, Mrs Proctor. I'm sorry we've wasted your time and ours.'

The two detectives got to their feet.

'I really don't understand why you're so concerned with Barry Spender, tragic though his death is. Shouldn't you be concentrating on the Russian's death? Are you any nearer to solving that?'

'We are following up several lines of enquiry.'

She saw them to the door, still talking. 'I'm beginning to think that there's a jinx on this place. First the Russian, then Barry Spender, and now poor Dennis Coleman.'

Who else had expressed the same thoughts to him recently? thought Roland, as Mrs Proctor continued: 'I feel partly to blame for that. Poor man, you could see it coming. I should have done more to ease his workload, but of course he didn't want that.'

'No?'

'The time he spent in the library was the only time he got away from his wife. I know I shouldn't say this – and I ask myself how I should like to be stricken down in that way – but she really is a dreadful woman. Oh dear, I do hope you're not taking this down in evidence, Inspector?'

'Completely off the cuff,' Roland assured her, 'and you are not the only person to express such sentiments.'

'When illness strikes like that it is a terrible tragedy but how does one deal with it? Possibly, I should respond in the same way. You can understand her being bitter.'

'I presume his job is being kept open for him?'

'But of course, Inspector, we must look on this little episode as a temporary abberation. To all intents and purposes he is on sick leave due to stress and overwork.'

'Well, we're not much further forward, are we?' said Mansfield as they returned to Felstone HQ. 'Are you still holding to this new theory?'

'You think I'm crazy, don't you? We shall see, we shall see. I'm in Court all day tomorrow on that Clifton case and Ginny comes out of hospital on Wednesday and I intend being there. Perhaps if I give it a break for a couple of days I'll be able to get things in perspective and not feel that I can't see the wood for the trees. In the meantime, you and Evans can follow up the queries I've indicated.'

Nick Blackstone was rattled. He slumped in an armchair, beer can at the ready, turning things over in his mind. He had spent the last few weeks following up a story that had to be one of the best things he had ever investigated: mysterious Russians, missing manuscripts, devious goings-on – it had all the ingredients of a spy-thriller apart from one thing, it was the absolute truth, and as such was an utter gift. He had tackled it from different angles, unravelling the tangled threads and weaving them into a cohesive strand. He was ready to publish, his editor was breathing down his neck, but he refused to be pressurised. He had his reputation to think about. Not for him the innuendos, the half-truths, the blatant misinterpretation of facts that his despised colleagues of the gutter press went in for; he was known as a purveyor of the truth. When he broke a story on the unsuspecting public it was accepted as a certainty, a proven fact. He had never been sued for libel yet and he had no intention of risking it now. There was one last thread that was still out of place. He had not been able to find out what had happened to the Shostakovich manuscript. It had vanished without trace and the police seemed to have lost interest in it. Was this because they knew where it was? Every likely trail he had followed in his efforts to trace it had finished in a dead end and he was horribly frustrated.

He got to his feet and went over to the window where he stared out over the garden with unseeing eyes. He had been expecting either one or both of the Rakosis to be under arrest by now. The police, with their superior facilities and technology, must have arrived at the same conclusion as himself, but nothing had happened. They were still at large and the police seemed to have turned their attention to the death of the gay piano wallah. Why? Had some new facts come to light of which he was ignorant? Had the Bill stolen a march on him? In an effort to discover just what was going on he had sought out Jonathan Cade but his timing had been wrong. He'd fallen foul of Roland and his sergeant, been accused of interfering with the course of justice, and knew that he had come within a whisker of being charged with obstructing the police.

That damned inspector! His side-kick was your usual plodding flatfoot, the stereotype of a Suffolk yeoman; slow, methodical, reliable, but incapable of acting on his own initiative. Roland was different. He recognised the sharp, probing mind that was capable of making quantum leaps and joining up apparently disparate snippets of information, a skill equally prized in journalism. He had enjoyed pitting his wits against the other man in an endeavour to get there first but he was too bloody handsome. He knew that Stella fancied him. She hadn't said anything, she hadn't needed to, he knew the signs. She was definitely interested and, whilst he had no intention of making their affair permanent, yet he was damned if that bloody inspector was going to cut him out.

He went over to his desk and sat down, pushing aside the neatly typed notes that mocked him even as he wondered if he would ever get to publish anything. Perhaps Stella knew more than she had let on. Perhaps he hadn't gone to the right source for the information he needed. Next time they got together there would be more than bed on the agenda . . .

The day that Ginny returned from hospital the weather finally broke. There was a storm in the night followed by a grey, cold dawn. The swags of dessicated leaves that had clung to the trees, burnished gold and copper against the cobalt skies of the last few weeks, had fallen overnight in great masses and there were sodden heaps strewing the pavements and filling the gutters. The rain continued to fall in a steady, monotonous drizzle and as the wind dropped a dank mist formed in low-lying areas and the landscape took on a monochrome appearance.

Roland found himself caught up in a big embezzlement job at Felstone Docks that occupied practically the entire local force for a few days but he dropped home whenever possible, even if they were only fleeting visits, to see his wife and new daughter who was flourishing. Her hair was a thick, bright orange cap and Ginny assured him that hers had been that colour as a child and Katherine's would tone down with age. She was a contented baby, only waking for one feed in the night and confining her crying to a period during the afternoons when her father was usually not there. He was besotted with her and Simon was too. He rushed home from school eager to see his baby sister and assisted at bathtime as well as helping around the house when Roland was at work.

Roland hoped the situation would continue. It had been a difficult fifteen months in many ways since their marriage, due mainly to Simon's trouble in accepting him as a stepfather. He had put himself out to win the boy over, being careful not to monopolise Ginny and trying to find a common ground on which they could meet. Simon had been polite and distant, grudging of his affections and wary of showing enthusiasm for any of the ideas that his step-father put forward. But gradually over the last few months he had mellowed and since the birth of the baby he seemed to have been won over completely. Roland began to think that he had gained a son as well as a daughter and was discovering that a teenage boy could be a good companion. Simon even consulted him about his homework which flattered his ego and actually led to the break-through he had been hoping for.

After days of trying to work out the ramifications of his latest ideas he felt that he had got nowhere fast. Barry Spender was not known in the local gay community, he appeared to have had no enemies and Roland could find no evidence linking him with either Blackstone, Cade or Coleman in the past. He had no proof whatsoever to back up his theory except an overwhelming feeling that he was on the right track at last, but unless he could put some facts before Lacey, the superintendent would treat his suggestions with derision. Equally, he was no nearer solving the problem if the murderer *had* meant to kill the Russian. He had a horrible feeling that this was going to be one of those cases that would never be resolved satisfactorily, that the file would remain open, a nasty reminder that he had failed, that one had got away. And then a chance remark from Simon provided the clue that pointed him in the right direction.

He had finished his school project and Ginny was reading it through.

'This is good, Simon, you've covered a lot of ground. Read it, James, and see what you think.'

'It's more up your street than mine, I don't know much about natural history and conservation.'

'You'll learn more if you read this. It's a good study of Blayden's Glebe.'

'Is that the area you've covered?' Roland asked Simon.

'Yes, it's not very big but it contains lots of different habitats. There's a bit of woodland, a natural meadow with a stream running through it and some ancient hedgerow. Did you know that you can tell how old a hedge is by the number of different species in it?'

'No, is that a fact?' Roland took the folder from Ginny and started to read. Simon had illustrated his survey with drawings and paintings of the various plants, insects and birds he had recorded, and Roland was impressed. Simon had obviously inherited his mother's artistic flair, he hadn't realised that. He paused at the page showing a red toadstool with white spots.

'"Fly Agaric." Is that what it's called? That's the one that's always used in fairy tales isn't it? Can you really find it in Blayden's Glebe?'

'Yes, under the silver birches at the edge of the wood. There's Death Cap in the woods as well.'

'Death Cap? Are you sure?'

'Well, I'm not sure if it's the real thing or the False Death Cap, but that's pretty poisonous too.'

'Actually, there are not many fungi that are really poisonous,' put in Ginny, 'but you have to be careful because they can be mistaken for harmless ones. Take the Death Cap – in its early stages it can look like a Field Mushroom or an immature Puffball.'

'You've got me worried. I thought we had wild mush-rooms the other week that you had picked?'

'Don't worry, the Death Cap grows under trees. These were growing in the middle of the lawn.'

'It would be a good way of bumping someone off,' said Simon enthusiastically. 'Have you ever had a case when someone's been murdered that way, James?'

'No, sorry to disappoint you, though I do remember a case when I was a young constable in Oxfordshire when a whole family were wiped out because of eating some poisonous mushrooms. I suppose that must have been the Death Cap or something similar.'

'But it would be a good way of killing someone, wouldn't it?' persisted Simon.

'You'd be found out. It would show up in an autopsy.'

'But you could eat a small amount yourself, not enough to kill you but enough to make you ill, and then everyone would think it was accidental.'

'Too risky, only a very small amount is fatal. You'd probably end up poisoning yourself as well.'

'Yes, but you could have something else.' Simon had really got the bit between his teeth. 'There are other mushrooms that could make you sick and ill but they wouldn't kill you. You could give your victim Death Cap and you could have one of the other ones. Look, it tells you all about the different ones here.' He picked up the reference book on British Fungi which was lying on the table. 'Which ones are poisonous and which ones are edible. I remember reading about one . . .' he rifled through the pages '. . . this is it, the Common Ink Cap. It's supposed to be good to eat but you mustn't have alcohol with it.'

324

'Why what happens?' asked Ginny, looking up from her knitting.

'You suffer nausea and palpitations,' read Simon, 'you sweat and go hot and cold and your face and neck go red and purple. I say, wouldn't it be a joke to feed some to someone and then make them drunk!'

'Nasty,' said his mother, 'not my idea of a joke. Why, what's the matter James? You look as if you've seen a ghost!'

'Give me that book.' He practically snatched it out of Simon's hands and hurriedly read through the relevant passage. 'Look, can I borrow this? You don't want to use it this evening, do you?'

'No,' said Simon, looking bewildered, 'but . . .'

'I'll take good care of it.'

'James, where are you going?' exclaimed Ginny.

'I've got to go back to the Station. I can't explain now.'

He snatched up his coat and rushed out of the house, slamming the door behind him. As they heard the car start up, mother and son stared at each other and Ginny shrugged.

'I don't know what you said but you've obviously started up a hare.'

Roland sat at his desk and read through the paragraph on Common Ink Cap in Simon's library book. The sentence warning of the after effects if eaten with alcohol leapt out of the page at him: 'Nausea, palpitations . . . flushed skin.' It was there in black and white. For the second time in less than a week, again late in the evening, he searched through the statements of his witnesses. 'He said he felt sick and dizzy and he certainly looked awful, his skin was very red,' Laura Nelson had said, and she had thought that he was drunk. Cade had mentioned several times that Spender had felt sick and had appeared to be un-coordinated and hot and bothered. He had put it down to sunstroke. And what had Coleman Said? Roland pulled out his statement: 'The poor chap was obviously suffering from heart trouble. His complexion, he was this awful purple colour.'

Was it possible? He re-read the last sentence in the book which described the symptoms as being similar to the effect caused by taking Antabuse, which is sometimes prescribed for the treatment of alcoholism, and his pulse quickened. Antabuse? Was it possible that he had put his finger on the cause of Spender's distressing symptoms on the night he had died? He looked at his watch: ten-thirty. Could he get hold of Doc Brasnett? He picked up the phone and dialled his number.

George Brasnett was in the middle of a game of bridge and was not pleased at being disturbed. His voice came booming down the line.

'Couldn't this wait till morning, James? I'm just about to play a vital point, this has really broken my concentration.'

'It won't take long. If I say "Antabuse" to you, does it mean anything?'

'Antabuse?' There was a pause. 'It's used for treating alcoholism. Produces frightening symptoms which are supposed to put the victim off drink for life.'

'Would it show up in an autopsy?'

'Depends if you were looking for it, I should say.'

'Cast your mind back. Barry Spender: were there any traces in his body when you did the PM?'

'You insisted on samples being sent to Huntingdon

to check for drugs – did you ask them to look for
it?'

'No, only the usual abusive drugs.'

'Well, there's your answer. You know how hard-
pressed they are, they only check out the substances
requested.'

'But it would be possible to find traces if they
were present?'

'Yes, if they tested for it. Look, what is all this
about?'

'Will they still have his samples around?'

'What is it – a week or two since they received them?
You should still be lucky.'

'Thanks, Doc, I'll explain later. Have fun, and don't
trump your partner's trick.'

He put the phone down and sat back and knuckled
his eyes. What did this mean? Had Spender been an
alcoholic who had been prescribed Antabuse? No, that
didn't make sense. He and his companions would have
known the effect if he had taken alcohol. Had someone
slipped him some Antabuse – in what form did it come?
– or had he eaten Ink Cap? What had they had to eat
at the meal Laura Nelson had prepared? Had it been
mushrooms of some sort? Had she picked them wild
and inadvertently included some Ink Cap by mistake?
But if so, why hadn't they all been affected? Perhaps
Spender had been unfortunate enough to get the only
portion containing the Ink Cap and had been drinking
more heavily than the others. He must check what they
had had to eat that evening.

But suppose Spender *had* mistakenly eaten some Ink
Cap causing Antabuse poisoning – what then? It would
account for his symptoms and was a plausible reason

for his having fallen overboard accidentally, but so what? Sunstroke or Antabuse – what difference did it make? It didn't go any further towards proving that Spender had been murdered. Or did it? Perhaps he had been deliberately fed the substance, knowing how he would react and seeing it as a way of getting rid of him when he was in a vulnerable state. This would point to Laura Nelson, but what possible reason could she have for killing Spender? And anyway, surely the drug wouldn't act so quickly? He must have been given it earlier in the day.

Roland snapped his fingers impatiently. There were so many questions to ask and he would have to wait till the morning. He could do nothing more that evening and he felt horribly frustrated. Apart from questioning Laura Nelson and Jonathan Cade, he needed to check the reference library and he must get back to Forensics at Huntingdon. He put the papers back into his filing cabinet and locked it, picked up his jacket and walked down the stairs deep in thought.

'Nasty night, sir,' said the duty sergeant on the front desk looking up as Roland crossed the foyer.

'Yes, autumn has come with a vengeance. Goodnight.'

'Goodnight, sir.'

It had been raining lightly when Roland had driven to the Station but he had been so engrossed in his thoughts that he had hardly noticed it. Now it was bucketing down. He picked his way between the puddles that reflected back puckered chequers of yellow from the Station's windows and turned up his collar as he made a dash for the car. As he got in and started the engine a flurry of sodden leaves slammed against the windscreen and slid down the glass in slimy rivulets. He switched on the wipers and the heater. How different it was from the night when Spender had died. Then it had been hot and still with a harvest moon and the only moisture had come from the soft, milky dew dropping gently over the landscape. As he drove through the deserted streets the questions chased themselves round his brain. Had Spender been drugged prior to ending up in the river? And, if so, had it been accidental or intentional?

The next morning found him down at the *Painted Lady* before eight o'clock. Jonathan Cade was in the middle of shaving and came up on deck clad only in jeans, his lower face covered in foam.

'What is it now?'

'Some more questions. Shall we go below?'

Cade shrugged and led the way down the companionway. He wiped his face with a grubby towel and pulled a sweatshirt over his head.

'Don't you people ever sleep?'

'I wanted to catch you before you went to work.' Roland looked round the cabin. Barry Spender's belongings were still in evidence and the lid of the piano was open. 'You haven't sorted out Spender's things yet?'

'They're not mine to sort out, and what the hell is it to do with you?' Cade ran his hands through his hair and slumped on to the bunk. 'I'm sorry, I guess I haven't come to terms with his death yet. If only we could have a funeral . . .'

'I'm still investigating the circumstances surrounding the death. What did you have to eat at Laura Nelson's dinner party?'

'To eat? God, I can't remember.'

'Please try. It could be important.'

'It was a vegetarian meal, I'm a vegetarian.'

'And was Spender too?'

'Most of the time but he lapsed sometimes when he thought no one would know.' The half-smile that formed at the memory turned into a grimace of pain.

'So what did you have?'

'Dolmadis. That's vine leaves stuffed with . . .'

'Yes I know what Dolmadis are. Did you have real vine leaves?'

'I think they were cabbage leaves but she'd stuffed them with a very tasty nut mixture.'

'What did you have with them?'

'Rice and ratatouille, she'd done some delicious stuffed peaches for afters.'

'And is that all you had?' asked Roland in disappointment.

'We had some sort of pasta dish for starters, pasta shells with mushrooms.'

'Mushrooms? Are you sure?'

'Yes,' said Cade, looking surprised at the tone of the detective's voice. 'She'd cooked them in a cream sauce and they were really good.'

'And all three of you ate them?'

'Yes, of course – what are you getting at?'

'How did she serve them up, Cade, can you remember?'

'How do you mean?'

'Did she serve it up at the table from a dish?'

He puzzled this one out. 'No, she brought it to the table in individual dishes. They were those shell-shaped ones we sell in the craft centre – scallop shells made in pottery.'

He looked at Roland and comprehension dawned. 'Look, are you saying that Barry could have been poisoned, that it was something he ate that made him ill?'

'It is a possibility.'

'But we all had the same. And what difference does it make if he *was* suffering from a tummy upset – it won't bring him back!'

'It may make all the difference. Tell me, how did he spend the day before you went to Laura Nelson's?'

'He was at work, of course.'

'Morning and afternoon? What else would he have had to eat that day?'

'We had orange juice and toast and coffee for breakfast. I don't know what he had at lunchtime.'

'You didn't spend it together?'

'Sometimes. Not that day. Actually I remember now, he told me that Màrta Rakosi had been in to see him. She probably took him a snack. That's what I mean, Inspector, about him not being a strict vegetarian. She knew that he still hankered after meat and she used to tempt him with these little titbits she concocted from her Hungarian cookbooks.'

'You mean the woman who works in the boutique?' Roland tried to keep the excitement out of his voice.

'Yes. I believe her cooking is quite something if you go for this spicy continental stuff. She uses herbs and things she grows herself and a lot of paprika.'

'Did he know her well?'

'Not really. It was her husband Barry was friendly with.'

'Miklos Rakosi?'

'Yes, have you met him?'

'He has figured in my enquiry. So Spender was friendly with him?'

'Well, more in the way of them being fellow crafts-men. They both make – made – musical instruments. Rakosi turns out string instruments and I believe they are very fine pieces of work, and he's almost entirely self-taught. He and Barry used to talk shop.'

Of course! thought Roland. He should have guessed that they would have known each other. So there was yet another tie-up in this tangled web.

'Did they ever come to the *Painted Lady*?'

'Not since I've been living here but they may have done in the past.'

'I see. By the way, did Spender smoke?'

'No.'

'So he wouldn't have been taking anything to cure him of the habit?'

'No. As far as I know he had never smoked, he was very anti.'

'Well, thank you for your time, Cade. I'll see myself ashore.' The rain of last night had cleared away leaving a pale turquoise sky smudged with feathers of pink and white cloud. The wet grass squelched under his feet as he walked back to the car and wreaths of mist steamed gently from the sodden ground. He glanced at his watch; it was eight-thirty, too early to try Huntingdon and the library wouldn't be open yet either. He would go to the Station and bend the ear of his sergeant.

A couple of hours later he and Mansfield were mulling over the case in his office.

'So you really think that he was fed Antabuse and that's what made him feel ill, or appear drunk or whatever?' said the latter, stuffing tobacco into his pipe and dribbling shreds of it all over the desk.

'We shall soon know. I've been on to Huntingdon and asked them to run a test for it and they promised to get back to us as soon as possible. I've also been to the library and checked all their books on fungi. This business of alcohol reacting with Common Ink Cap is mentioned in all of them and the symptoms described certainly tally with those Spender seemed to be displaying that evening.'

'So you reckon that Laura Nelson did it either accidentally or on purpose?'

'I don't see how she could have done. I've been on to Brasnett again and he reckons it would be at least an hour or two after ingestion before it took effect. The mushrooms would have to be broken down by the stomach acids and absorbed into the system. He must have eaten it earlier and Cade says that it is quite likely that Spender spent the lunch-hour with Màrta Rakosi and probably shared a packed lunch with her.'

'Màrta Rakosi, eh?' Mansfield took an immoderate puff at his pipe and started a paroxysm of coughing. 'So we're back to her, which means that Spender wasn't the intended victim originally.'

'I'm keeping an open mind about that, following up both lines of enquiry, but for the moment let's concentrate on Màrta Rakosi.'

'You think she could have deliberately poisoned him – why?'

'Because, as we've conjectured before, he saw her near the *Painted Lady* on the afternoon the Russian was killed and he was either black-mailing her or she knew he'd seen her and knew she would never be safe until he was silenced.'

'It seems a very hit or miss way of doing it. She couldn't know exactly how he would react or whether she'd be able to take advantage of his state later to finish him off.'

'Actually it was rather clever. She must have known about Laura Nelson's dinner party and knew that he would probably drink a fair amount of alcohol. All she had to do was to be around later and she had the perfect alibi with her weekly date at the cinema. Also, if we happened later to get on to the fact that he had been poisoned, she would think that we would naturally put it down to something he had eaten that evening at Laura Nelson's. She must think that she has covered her tracks nicely and that we could never trace it back to her.'

'But this is all guesswork.'

'Too true. We're going to have to tackle her and see what she says.'

'Okay, what are we waiting for?'

'A call from Huntingdon. I'm not sticking my neck out without anything to back my hunch.'

The call, when it came, confirmed Roland's theory.

'Traces of Antabuse definitely present,' he announced triumphantly to Mansfield. 'Quite a fair amount actually, and also partly-digested mushrooms of some sort. How about that? I reckon I was right, Spender *was* murdered.'

'You can't be certain. The Ink Cap could have got in with the mushrooms accidentally and it needn't have anything to do with Spender's falling in the river later.'

'It means, whether the Ink Cap got in accidentally or deliberately, they must have been picked wild and not bought in a shop. That's a starting point. Come on, let's pull in Màrta Rakosi.'

'You're going to grill her here?'

'Yes, I want to lean on her. We can do it better here. Find Evans, he should be writing up his reports.'

William Evans was only too glad of the chance to exchange his report writing for a piece of the action.

'I want Màrta Rakosi brought here now,' Roland instructed the young DC. 'If she's not at home she'll probably be working in the boutique at the Maltings. You can put the fear of God into her but make sure she understands that she is not being arrested. And don't take no for an answer!'

'I reckon I should get danger money.'

'Don't tell me, Evans, that you're scared of a middle-aged woman. Take Lucas with you as back-up.'

Whilst he waited for Evans' return Roland caught up with his own paperwork. Lacey was going to demand an up-date at any moment now and he wasn't going to like what he read.

'Why for you bring me here?' Màrta Rakosi was frightened but belligerant when she arrived at the Station.

'Thank you for coming, Mrs Rakosi,' said Roland, 'please sit down.' He indicated the seat opposite him and after hesitating for a few seconds she sat down and leaned her elbows on the table.

'I demand to see my lawyer! That is right, is it not? I can have lawyer?'

'That is your prerogative, Mrs Rakosi, but you are

not under arrest. Surely Detective Constable Evans didn't give you that impression? I just want a little chat with you and I thought it would be more private here. You don't want your employers learning all your private business, do you?'

Evans had found her at work in the boutique and extracted her with some difficulty.

'What you want?'

'When we spoke with you before you did not tell us that you were a personal friend of Barry Spender?'

'I not understand, he was friend of my husband.'

'And you also, surely?'

'I know him, of course, we both work at Maltings and he visit our house to discuss the instruments with Miklos.'

'I have it on good authority that he also frequently spent his lunch-breaks with you and you were in the habit of feeding him.'

'What is this?' She was thoroughly alarmed.

'Mrs Rakosi, did you spend the lunch-hour together on the day that he died?'

'I may have done.' She feigned indifference.

'Yes or no?' snapped Roland.

'I think I did, yes.'

'And did you also share your lunch with him?'

'Yes, what harm in that? Poor Barry, he do not like all this vegetable food. He say to me: Màrta, you save my life, it is not good this . . .'

'Yes,' Roland cut her short. 'What did you have to eat that day? Did you buy sandwiches in the snack bar?'

'Dear God, no! That is rubbish food also. I make the pasties. I am very good at the pastry bake, Inspector.

You must have the cold hands and the warm heart for to make good pastry and I, Màrta Rak –'

'What was in them?' At a signal from Roland, Mansfield interrupted and took over the questioning.

'Some meat, good beef, and the vegetables and herbs.'

'What vegetables?'

'Carrot and onion, a little garlic, I think, and some mushrooms.'

'Mushrooms? Where did you get the mushrooms?'

'I buy in the supermarket at Blund.'

'You're quite sure? You didn't pick them yourself wild?'

'How you know I gather my own mushrooms and herbs? You are clever man, Sergeant. You English do not make the use of all the good things that grow in the wild. Why, in Hungary now, at this time of the year, we have big expedition to pick mushrooms. All the family go. It is holiday and we pick the morels and chanterelles and boletus and . . .'

'I thought you just said that you bought the mushrooms in the supermarket?' said Roland.

'This time, yes. I have not the time to go out and find them so I buy them in shop, but they are not the same. Little hard knobs, they have not the taste of the wild ones.'

'Are you sure that you bought them? This is important and, remember, we can check at the supermarket that you *did* purchase them.'

'I am telling you, am I not? Why you want to know all this? What has this to do with Barry's death? He fell off the ship, the so unlucky ship.'

'It is possible that he was poisoned before he fell.'

Roland watched her closely to see how she would react.

'Poisoned? You say *I* poisoned him? No, this is all lies. We have the pasties and they are good. He is not ill, I am not ill! You bark up wrong bush!'

'Mistakes can be made with mushrooms.'

'I do not make the mistakes and I tell you, those mushrooms come from the shop. If he was poisoned it is *she* who has done it!'

'Who?'

'She. That Laura Nelson. They go there for the meal, for the dinner party that evening.'

'How do you know?'

'Barry tell me. She invite them for the splendid dinner party – huh! She is not good cook like me, it is her to blame!'

Chapter 13

Roland and Mansfield drove Màrta Rakosi back to the Maltings. They had been unable to shake her story. She insisted that the lunch she had shared with Spender could in no way have made him ill and she stuck to this with much hyperbole and dramatic gesture. Seeing that he was getting nowhere, Roland acknowledged temporary defeat and took her back to work with the intention of catching Laura Nelson and checking her version of the dinner she had cooked for the two men. He was defeated in this also. Laura Nelson had the day off to go up to Norfolk to visit a sick relative.

'Damn and blast!' said Roland. 'Well, now we're here let's go to the pub and get a beer and something to eat.'

The Eel and Jug was doing a brisk lunchtime trade. It was a homely little pub which had altered little in appearance in the four hundred years since it had been built. It was a free house and had thus mercifully escaped the modernisation and improvement schemes which had befallen so many of the local taverns owned by the big breweries. The ceilings were low and so smoke-stained that they were almost as dark as the heavy oak beams that supported them, and the flooring was the original stone flags, worn and uneven, with a few dark red turkey rugs overlaying them. There was a large inglenook fireplace at one end of the lounge bar and a roaring fire burned in the grate. It was a real fire, Roland noted with pleasure, not one of those imitation gas fires that were betrayed by the gas pipe snaking round the fire basket. This one crackled and spluttered and smelled of the logs which were piled up nearby and there was a scattering of grey ash over the hearth. A few copper pans hung from the plastered walls; they looked as if they had been hanging there for centuries, genuine antiques, not modern tat.

The two men ordered their meals; Roland chose lasagne and, after a defiant look at his colleague, Mansfield settled on steak pie and chips. They collected their pints from the bar and sat down at a table not far from the fireplace to await their food. How different from the time when he had come here with Ginny and Ellen Gascoigne, thought Roland, although only a few weeks had lapsed. Then, they had been glad to get out of the heat into the comparative coolness of the low, shadowy bar; now he was glad of the warmth from the fire and the pub was a snug little haven in the raw autumn countryside.

It was here that he had first set eyes on Nick Blackstone. The man hovered round the perimiters of the case but he couldn't really tie him in with the action. Pity, he thought, I'd like to get something on him, something that would deflate his ego. But he knew, as a good policeman, that he must push such thoughts away. Fair and strictly impartial, that was his role, but Blackstone's half-veiled derision and the way he preyed on Stella Lingard got up Roland's nose. An attractive woman like her should have no difficulty in finding another partner, but such was the way of the world that she and other like women seemed doomed to fall for the likes of Blackstone with his lazy charm and amoral attitudes.

She was a fool, mused Roland, and then did a double-take as he caught sight of her between the people crowding the bar. At first he thought he had conjured her up out of his imagination but Mansfield had also seen her.

'That's Stella Lingard, isn't it?' he asked, leaning forward to see her better.

'Yes, she must frequent this place. Can you see who she's with? Is it Blackstone?'

'Good God! It's Dennis Coleman, he must be about again.'

Stella Lingard noticed them and raised a hand in greeting but when her companion saw who she was acknowledging he shrank back in his chair and ignored them. It was here, in this bar, that Ellen Gascoigne had fingered him, thought Roland, and he had been convinced that he was well on his way to solving the case. By now he was sure that Coleman was innocent of the crime of murder; he hadn't enough bottle.

Their meal arrived and as they ate they mulled over the latest developments.

'What do you think of Màrta Rakosi's part in it now?' asked Mansfield.

'Well, leaving aside the fact that I'm still rooting for the idea that Spender was always the intended victim, I reckon she's a good contender for the role of murderer, or rather murderess. It would seem to be in character, the way she went about it. She fed him the Ink Cap in her pasties knowing full well that he was going out for a meal later that day where he would be sure to drink alcohol – by the way, did I tell you, if you drink alcohol a day later the symptoms will return – and she hung around the *Painted Lady* later that evening then hey presto!'

'It's all a bit "iffy", isn't it? How could she know that he would be alone on the boat or even that he would return there at all?'

'She probably overheard that all three of them had planned to do other things later that evening, she's the type to listen in to other people's conversation, and she took a chance. If she had failed that evening she would have made another attempt later.'

'How are you going to prove it?'

'That, Pat, is the million dollar question.'

Stella Lingard and Dennis Coleman got up from their table. He made a point of detouring round the room to avoid them, pushing between customers and wending his way between tightly packed tables and chairs, but Stella Lingard came over to speak to them.

'Inspector Roland, I must have a few words with you to put things right. I think you misinterpreted something I said and poor Dennis Coleman has enough to cope with at the moment.'

'Please join us.' Roland stood up. 'Can I get you something?'

'No, thank you, I'm on my way back to the Maltings. I'm afraid I'm interrupting your lunch . . .'

'Not at all, we've just about finished.'

She sat down at their table and a wave of her sultry musk perfume flowed over them, overpowering and overstated.

'How is Coleman?' asked Mansfield.

'As well as can be expected in the circumstances. I suppose his problems are still with him.'

'And his wife? Is she back with him?'

'She comes back this week and the authorities are making efforts for them to get more support from the social services, etc.'

'It is an unfortunate situation.'

'That's a meaningless phrase, Inspector, *I* would call it tragic. He's lumbered with Helen but he's never so much as looked at another woman.'

'You gave me to understand that he was having an affair with Laura Nelson.'

'I don't know how that happened, we really got our wires crossed, didn't we? He's got enough on his hands without being accused of being unfaithful to Helen, though I don't see that it is any business of yours anyway.'

'We're talking about Laura Nelson. You insinuated that she was in love with a married man and Dennis Coleman's name came up in the course of the conversation.'

'That just shows how careful one must be, how easily reputations are made or broken. You certainly got the wrong end of the stick. Laura Nelson is in love, or so she thinks, but Dennis Coleman is certainly not the man.'

'No?'

'No, nothing so simple as that. She's infatuated with our Jonathan.'

'You mean Jonathan Cade?'

'Yes, she won't listen to any of the advice her well-meaning friends give her. She's convinced that she can win him back to straight sex, especially now there's no Barry around.'

'Really?' Roland kept his voice neutral and avoided looking at his colleague.

'Yes, she's convinced that his homosexual relationship with Barry was a temporary aberration and that underneath he's a hetero. I feel quite sorry for him, she won't leave him alone, won't take no for an answer. Poor old Barry's accident was tragic, but Laura for one isn't sorry he's out of the way, I'm sure.'

'I understood she was friendly with both of them. They had dinner with her the evening Spender died.'

'Yes, well, as I say she didn't give up. If she couldn't have one without the other she did her best to make Jonathan draw comparisons between her and Barry, hoping he would see the error of his ways and realise that she was the one for him. Crazy, wasting her time on one of his ilk, but that's Laura for you. She's really screwed up underneath that calm exterior.'

'Oh?'

'I probably shouldn't be telling you this but I don't want you to get the wrong idea about her and Dennis Coleman. I think she's incapable of relating to any man. I bet if Jonathan started showing an interest in her she'd run a mile.'

'What makes you think that?'

'Something she once hinted at, some nasty episode in her past. If you ask me I think she once had an unpleasant sexual experience and it's left her flawed. She doesn't really like men at all and she's only kidding herself about Jonathan because subconsciously she knows he won't respond and she feels safe.'

'Very interesting, Mrs Lingard.' Roland kept his voice neutral. 'Thank you for telling us.'

She glanced at her watch and got to her feet. 'I must fly. I've enjoyed out little chat and I hope that I've put the record straight.' She gave both men a provocative smile and then paused.

'By the way, there's something else I've been meaning to mention. That night when I went over to Nick's house, the night that Barry died – I told you that I heard somebody else crossing the churchyard as I returned. Well, I've been thinking about it and I'm pretty certain that it was a woman. It couldn't have been Nick, he blunders about like a bull in a china shop, but these footsteps were light – not the tramp of a man's feet. I don't suppose it's important but I didn't want you to think that I was trying to incriminate Nick.'

'Weren't you?'

'Oh, Inspector, I know that I was a bit miffed about his behaviour that evening but you mustn't take it seriously, I was just being unreasonable.'

'Is that so?'

'Yes. And to change the subject – tell me, has that baby arrived yet?'

'I have a daughter.'

'Congratulations, but don't spoil her. She needs to learn from an early age that this is a man's world.'

They watched as she wended her way sinuously to the door and then Roland exploded.

'Laura Nelson! How's that for a motive?'

'Surely it's too far-fetched?'

'What's far fetched about it? You and I know that over half the homicides committed in the course of a year are because of love, sex, passion – call it what you will. Laura Nelson wants Jonathan Cade and is convinced that she can win him so long as there are no gay affairs getting in the way. And if Stella Lingard is to be believed she's warped and unbalanced. What could be more straightforward? And it also verifies my theory that Spender was always the intended victim – the Russian's death was just an unfortunate accident.'

'Put like that . . .' Mansfield was dubious and didn't mind showing it. Roland was making galloping assumptions again and roaring along with the bit between his teeth.

'There's just this question about timing. Let's say she killed the Russian, thinking he was Spender. Looking back, don't you remember how excessively shaken she appeared the first time we interviewed her when we told her that Rabinovich had been murdered? She'd already had the shock of discovering she'd killed the wrong man but she must have hoped that we'd think it was an accident. She was horrified to find that we were treating it as murder, but we thought she was just an over-sensitive nice young woman! When she realised her mistake she planned another attempt. She doctored the mushrooms Spender ate knowing that they would make him ill and appear drunk so that when he "fell" overboard later no one would be surprised. But how did she get them to work so soon?'

'Because he'd been drinking beforehand? But she wouldn't have known that, would she? And he was also suffering from sunstroke. But again, she wouldn't have known that.'

'Come on, let's go and see Cade again. Perhaps if we press him he can throw some more light on it.'

They finished their pints and left the Eel and Jug. It

was now nearly two o'clock and Jonathan Cade should be back at the gallery. They left the car and walked back to the Maltings. The wind whistled over the bridge and flags of angry looking cloud streamed across the sky. It was low tide and the reedbeds were sombre swamps against the vast expanses of grey, leaden mud. The tourist season was over and there were few visitors about apart from a short queue outside the box office where a poster proclaimed the forthcoming visit of a famous American dance company.

Jonathan Cade was sitting in the office attached to the art gallery, his feet up on the table, desultorily reading a magazine. He glanced up as they came in and a look of resignation settled on his features but he said nothing.

'Mr Cade, just a few more questions about that meal you and Spender had with Laura Nelson.'

'What do you want to know?'

'The mushrooms you had for starters, did . . .'

'Those bloody mushrooms!' he interrupted. 'Why do you keep harping on about them! All right, they may have made him ill but so what? he's dead and you can't bring him back!'

'Bear with me, please, there is a reason for my interest. Do you happen to know where Miss Nelson got the mushrooms from?'

'From a shop, I suppose, where else?'

'She didn't pick them from the fields? This is the season for the wild ones.'

He looked non-plussed for a few seconds and then enlightenment dawned.

'Actually, now you mention it, she *did* pick them wild. She made a joke about having got up at the crack of dawn and picked them in the dew, but they were beautiful mushrooms. There was nothing wrong with them, although they were a funny colour.'

'Funny colour? What do you mean?'

'The flesh was very dark but that was because of the way she had prepared them; she said that she had been marinating them for over twelve hours in brandy and it certainly paid off, they were delicious.'

'Thank you, Cade, that's all we wanted to know.'

'But . . . I don't understand. What is this all about?'

'You've just confirmed my theory. Please don't mention this conversation to anyone – do you understand?'

They left behind a baffled Jonathan Cade and hurried back to the car.

'*That's* how she did it,' said Roland, once they were in the privacy of the car. 'She soaked the Ink Cap in brandy so that by the time he came to eat it the alcohol had had all those hours to interact with the chemical composition of the fungi. What with that and the booze he had before and during dinner, is it any wonder that he started displaying symptoms before they had finished the meal?'

'But how would she have known about the Ink Cap and its strange properties?'

'Have you forgotten where she works? She sells books on natural history in her shop. There are books on fungi there; in fact, she has in stock the very title that Simon was using for his homework – I checked the other day.'

'But even if you're right, how are you ever going to prove it?'

'I'm certain I'm right. Don't look so dubious, Pat,

it's all falling into place. We've got a motive and we've just found out how she managed the poisoning. We're nearly home and dry.'

'Except for one little thing: you haven't an atom of proof. Even if your conjectures are right you haven't got a hope of pinning it on her.'

'There's only one way of getting proof – we'll have to set a trap!'

Roland spent the rest of that day and half the following night trying to work out a plan of action. He was still awake and in the little downstairs room at home that he used as a study when Katherine awoke and started crying for her night feed. He heard Ginny moving about above him and yawned and rubbed his eyes. He looked at his watch. God! He must have dozed off, it surely couldn't be 3am? He was cold and cramped and got to his feet with difficulty. He stretched and then padded upstairs to their bedroom.

Ginny was sitting up in bed, propped against the headboard with her eyes half-closed and her daughter firmly attached to one blue-veined swollen breast. Her eyes snapped open as he blundered into the room.

'James! You're still dressed. Good heavens, I was so tired I was out like a light the minute I hit the pillow – I hadn't realised that you hadn't come to bed!'

The baby, momentarily dislodged from her feeding supply, made little distressed sucking noises and searched blindly for the nipple. When guided back by her mother, she clamped on to it like a limpet with a loud, guzzling sigh. Ginny smiled down at her daughter and Roland felt his insides dissolve with love.

How beautiful she looked with her hair falling like a curtain round her shoulders, glowing apricot in the light from the bedside lamp, her eyes smudged with sleep and her beautiful breasts peeping out of the white lacy nightdress. She looked like a Pre-Raphaelite painting; some nymph captured by Burne-Jones or Millais.

'What's the matter, James?'

'I was just wishing that *I* was the artist in this family and could get you down on canvas.'

'That's very poetical for this time of the morning. Have you really been working through the night?'

'Trying to, but I can't do any more now. My thoughts aren't making sense.'

'I shouldn't think so. Would it help to talk it through with me?'

So whilst Ginny finished feeding Katherine, winded her and changed her nappy, Roland brought her up to date with his case and discussed the course of action he had arrived at.

'Do you think it will work?' she asked, returning the baby to her cot whilst he undressed.

'Probably not, but can you think of anything better? It's a gamble. If it doesn't come off we'll have to think of something else.'

'Poor girl, poor misguided girl.'

'You're not feeling sorry for her?'

'I'm so lucky, I've got so much – you, Simon, Katherine – and she's got nothing, just a doomed obsession. You can understand her being repressed and unbalanced.'

'If I'm right she killed two men in cold blood!'

'Yes, it's dreadful, and she must be stopped before there's another tragedy.'

'Don't say that – there must be no more deaths.'

He hesitated and tried to quell the uneasiness that still lapped the perimeters of his mind. 'It all makes sense to you – what I've just told you?'

'Why, yes, what do you mean?'

'You don't think my reasoning is suspect? That I've concocted a fantasy out of thin air because I'm so keen to make a breakthrough in this case?'

'Is that what Lacey thinks?' she asked shrewdly.

'It's not just the Super, it's Patrick. I'm not getting the backing I hope for from him.'

'You mean he's not supporting you?'

'His heart isn't in it. You know Patrick, he would never contradict me openly or try to prove a theory of his own at the expense of mine – it's just that we're not on the same wavelength over this case. He thinks I'm wrong, though he's trying not to admit it even to himself, but it makes for an uneasy relationship.'

'Patrick is a very logical person,' said Ginny slowly, trying to express what she was thinking, 'he progresses from A to B and hasn't got your flair for seeing beyond the immediate objective. I shouldn't let it worry you. If you're convinced that you're right, and I think deep down you are, you've got to push on regardless and try to get your proof.'

'Words of wisdom, O Goddess wife. What would I do without you?'

'Do come to bed, James. You can't do any more tonight and you'll be fit for nothing in the morning if you don't get any rest.'

The next morning Roland had a long discussion with Superintendent Lacey which resulted in both men becoming heated but ended with Roland achieving grudging support for his plan. He then held a briefing with Mansfield and the other men in the team and finalised details of date and time. This done, he paid another visit to Jonathan Cade who agreed to do what Roland requested although he was not told the reasons why.

The detective then went over to Woodford and ran Miklos Rakosi to ground in his workshop, deliberately calling at a time when he knew Màrta would be away at work. Because of the part Roland wanted the man to play he had to reveal more details of his plan than he had to Cade but Rakosi remained in ignorance of the true facts and who it was the detective was hoping to entrap.

Having done all this, Roland could only wait and hope that the weather would co-operate. It had to be a Tuesday afternoon when most of the Maltings employees had their half-day off and conditions had to resemble that other occasion. If it rained all day it would be impossible, but the odd shower would be perfect. He went over the scheme again and again in his mind. Had he forgotten anything? No, the pieces would all be in place on his chessboard, it just remained for fate to move the right ones.

Laura Nelson held the sheet of paper in her hand and read it through again. If she had received this a few days ago, even as late as Sunday afternoon, she would have been overjoyed and thought she was getting somewhere at last. But the events of Sunday evening had shattered her confidence and she had suddenly come face to face with the fact that she was on a hiding to nothing.

The Paul Taylor Dance Company from the United

States was on tour in Britain and was giving three performances at Blund Maltings. She had managed to get two tickets for the Sunday evening performance and had asked Jonathan to go with her. At first he had demurred, saying that he was in mourning and it wouldn't be right and he didn't feel like it anyway, but she had persisted and in the end had persuaded him to join her. He had never been to a ballet before and was not sure what to expect but she had assured him that he would enjoy it. And how, she thought, her face twisting in pain at the memory.

The first half had passed without incident; a folk ballet based on themes from Copland's Appalachian Spring, followed by a short divertissement involving all the members of the company. During the interval, in which Jonathan bought her a glass of wine and they strolled round the foyer, he admitted that he was enjoying it and looking forward to the second half. The opening piece was a work for six male dancers set to part of the Brandenburg Concertos. There was no story line, just a changing pattern of form and movement and the dancers were clad in brief leotards and tights that left nothing to the imagination. Laura happened to glance at Jonathan during the middle of this performance and the expression on his face made her guts twist.

You couldn't call it desire, it went deeper than that; it was a look of naked longing mixed with wonderment and excitement. She had known in that moment that he would never be hers, that she had never had a chance and was treading on alien territory. She had felt sick and empty and had wanted to rush home and hide herself away and nurse her grief. The rest of the performance had passed in a blur. At the end, Jonathan, looking dazed, had taken her home and she had said goodnight briefly and had not asked him in for coffee.

And now she had received this note from him asking her to come to the *Painted Lady* this afternoon. What for? Why was he inviting her over? Perhaps he wanted her to help him sort out Barry's belongings though it was strange that he hadn't mentioned it on Sunday. Her first instinct was to refuse. Her feelings were still raw and she didn't want to twist the knife in the wound, but she couldn't stay away. She had to go although she knew that she was a fool, exposing herself to further hurt. The note said come between two and three so at just after two she let herself out of her cottage and took the footpath to the river.

It was a typical autumn day, heavy showers mixed with sunny periods and the wind was from the east, cutting across the marshes like a scythe, mowing the reeds this way and that and hurling the clouds across the sky. She shivered and turned up her collar and wished she had worn boots as her feet squelched along the path that had become a quagmire overnight. As she neared the houseboat she noticed yet again, as Roland had earlier, how hidden it was from public view. The twist in the bank and the screen of willow hid it from sight until you were right upon it.

She rounded the bend and dropped down from the towpath – and froze. She was only a few yards from the *Painted Lady* and there, sitting on deck, his back towards her, was a figure dressed in a kagool with the hood pulled up, bending over a fishing rod. This was how it had been before. This was how it had been on that fateful day in September – it couldn't be happening again! She felt a rush of blood to her head and something snapped.

She hurled herself up the gangplank and across the deck. She grabbed the figure by the shoulders.

'It can't be you! I killed you! You've come back to haunt me!' She shook the man and the hood slipped off his head revealing the startled features of Miklos Rakosi. She screamed.

Other people came on deck and she swung round. Jonathan Cade appeared in the doorway and for a few seconds they stared at each other and then he croaked: 'Laura!'

Another figure appeared beside him. It was William Evans, his red hair flattened by the wind and clashing horribly with his red anorak. He put a hand warningly on Cade's shoulder and Laura saw the gesture and misread it.

'You shan't have anyone else!'

She flung herself towards him and in those split seconds somehow snatched up an old marlin spike that had lain for ages, rusty and unnoticed beside the hatch cover. With the weapon in her hand she attacked Cade who was so dumbfounded that at first he did nothing to defend himself. The two figures swayed together and Evans moved over to part them, skidded on the slippery deck and measured his length on the wet boards.

She seemed to possess a superhuman strength and Cade, who had been trying to fend her off and prevent her hurting herself, found himself fighting for his life as he tried to avoid the arm that was making murderous attacks with the deadly spike. They rolled against the side and she stabbed upwards, catching him in the chest. He gave a cry and tried to push her away, but she clung to him and drew back her arm for another thrust, and as the other detectives rushed towards them they overbalanced and plunged over the side.

Cursing himself for being taken unawares Roland dashed to the side. Beside him, Mansfield croaked: 'So you were right! Christ, she's mad!' as he leaned over the rail. Cade was floundering in the river below, a red tide leaching into the murky water. Laura Nelson had been caught in the current and was already being swept away.

'Get him out!' Roland shouted, and dragging off his jacket and kicking off his shoes, dived into the river. It was still quite warm but the tide was running strongly and the shock of the surging water temporarily paralysed him. He gasped and spluttered and then struck out in her direction. Being that much heavier the undertow carried him rapidly towards her and he was soon within grappling distance.

She fought like a demon, threshing around in the water, but she was not still in possession of the marlin spike. Roland realised that she was fighting to avoid being rescued and so determined was she that she nearly drowned both of them. Somehow he got his fingers in her hair and, twisting and twining, managed to push her head up out of the water. As her white, rigid face surfaced he made a supreme effort and slugged her on the jaw.

He could not fight the current and swim back to the *Painted Lady*. Instead, towing her body, he let the tide carry him downstream to the little curve of beach that marked the boundary of Woodford. As he staggered out of the water with her in his arms Mansfield was waiting for him. Beside him, Bob Lacey rocked backwards and forwards on the balls of his feet at the water's edge. There was a grim expression on his face.

Chapter 14

'Criminal incompetence,' barked Lacey. 'Didn't you search the boat before you set up your trap?'

'It was an oversight on my part,' admitted Roland, 'I accept full responsibility for not noticing the marlin spike.'

They were in the Superintendent's office where Lacey was, as he put it, 'Making *my* case rather than yours, and dotting the i's and crossing the t's.'

'She could have killed him in full view of you. How is he?'

'He'll be okay. It didn't penetrate very far and missed any vital organs. The hospital was more concerned with the rust than anything. You must agree the trap worked beautifully.'

'So well that it caught you all unawares. You were lucky, James. If she hadn't admitted it in front of witnesses you'd never have pinned it on her. I see she's confessed to the second murder.'

'Yes, it happened almost exactly like I thought.'

'You're convinced that the first murder was unpremeditated?' He tapped Roland's report which was lying in front of him on the desk.

'Yes. I think she was visiting the *Painted Lady* on her afternoon off hoping to find Jonathan Cade at home.

Instead, she saw a man she thought was Barry Spender fishing over the side. On the spur of the moment she grabbed a convenient weapon – one of the stakes lying around – crept up on him and brought it down on his head, knocking him into the water, without realising that it wasn't Spender she had attacked.'

'Must have had a shock next time she saw him.'

'Yes, but the fact that everyone thought the Russian had been killed because of the manuscript played into her hands. She thought that she was safe and also realised how easy it was to kill someone like that.'

'So she plans another attempt, a cold-blooded one this time.'

'Yes, I think she was so infatuated with Cade by this time that she became completely unbalanced.'

'Women! Can't understand them!'

'She's one of these quiet, introspective types who are as neurotic as hell underneath; fatally flawed, but able to hide it from everyone with whom she came into contact.'

'They're always the dangerous ones. I suppose her defence will plead diminished responsibility or some such crap. So, next time she doctors the mushrooms?'

'Yes, she picked wild mushrooms *and* Common Ink Cap and served up the mushrooms to herself and Cade and the Ink Cap to Spender. Because she'd marinated them in brandy for hours beforehand the effects of the Antabuse started to appear before they finished the meal. She made a point of suggesting to Cade and Dennis Coleman, when they met on the way back to the *Painted Lady*, that he had had too much to drink and put the same idea into my head the next day when I questioned her. They left Spender on board feeling

groggy and returned to the village. As soon as Cade
left her at her cottage, Laura Nelson doubled back to
the *Painted Lady*. Spender had been feeling so hot and
nauseous that he'd gone up on deck. He was probably
leaning over the side being sick when she helped him
into the water. He probably never knew that he was
being pushed. He couldn't swim, and what with that
and the effects of the Antabuse, didn't stand a chance.
It was a straightforward case of drowning.'

'And naturally everyone thought it was an accident.'

'Yes, even Cade was convinced of that right up
until the little drama yesterday. Anyway, afterwards
she slipped back the way she had come, taking a
short-cut through the churchyard where Stella Lingard
heard her. Unfortunately they didn't come face to face
so Mrs Lingard didn't know who it was.'

'So how did you get on to the fact that Spender was
the intended victim all along?'

'It was a remark that Mrs Mansfield made – about
garden gnomes.'

Lacey snorted. 'I know that you're trying to baffle
me, James, and I shan't play into your hands by asking
you to explain it.'

'It was just a chance remark she made about something completely unconnected with our case that suddenly made me realise how alike Spender, Rakosi and
the Russian were. From the back they could easily be
mistaken for each other. I should have got on to it
before, it was staring me in the face all the time, but
there seemed to be such an obvious motive for the
Russian's death and I didn't look any further.'

'So you set Rakosi up as a decoy.'

'He agreed to wear Spender's jeans and kagool and

sit on the deck of the *Painted Lady* with his back to the shore pretending to fish. He certainly could have passed for Spender as far as I was concerned and Laura Nelson thought it was the person she had attacked before she freaked out.'

'And nearly finished off a third victim!'

'She thought Evans was Cade's new lover.'

'What in God's name was Evans doing when she attacked Cade?'

'He tried to separate them and slipped over. It had been raining only a short time before and the deck was like an ice rink.'

'I can't believe I'm hearing this! One frail, half-crazed woman seems to have brought the local Force to its knees! I'm speechless, James! And what about that bloody journalist? How the hell did he come to be on the scene?'

Nick Blackstone had witnessed the entire drama that had taken place on the *Painted Lady* from an observation point behind the nearby bank of scrubby willow. Just how he had happened to be there at the appropriate time Roland didn't know. Perhaps he had been keeping vigil for days hoping for something to break, perhaps he had had a tip-off, although Roland had sworn everyone concerned in the operation to secrecy and he couldn't believe there had been a leak from within the Force. He had been noticed as he had tried to sneak back to his car and although Mansfield and Evans had tried to intercept him they had been too late, arriving at the derelict yard where he had parked his car just as the journalist swung his vehicle round the corner and roared off back down the road. Mansfield had reported that he had given a thumbs-up signal as he swept past them.

'I don't know, sir,' said Roland woodenly.

'You bloody should know! You set up the operation – but perhaps you invited the Press so as to have more witnesses?'

There was nothing subtle about Lacey's sarcasm and the detective inspector stayed silent under the tirade.

'It's going to be all over the papers tomorrow, you realise that? The headlines will be screaming it out in capitals.'

'Yes, I'm afraid they are.'

'You seem very calm about all this, James.'

'Blackstone has been following up this story right from the start, it's a miracle it hasn't leaked before. There's no way you can stop him from publishing, but at least he'll get the facts right.'

'Christ! And I'm supposed to be grateful for that? Thank God we've established that the Russians had nothing to do with it and that bloody manuscript is not involved.'

Lacey glared at his inspector over steepled fingers.

'Yes, that will certainly make life much easier.'

'Easier? When do we policemen ever have an easy life? Is there anything else I should know?'

'I think I've brought you up to date with everything.' Roland collected his notes together and got to his feet. Lacey waited until he had almost reached the door before speaking again.

'There's just one little thing you haven't told me. How did you get on to this business of the Ink Cap?'

'That was because of another chance remark by Simon, my stepson. Sheer serendipity.'

'Get out, James!' roared Lacey.

'Yes, sir.'

Ginny was horrified at how close James had come to drowning and he hastened to reassure her later that day. He was feeling that curious mixture of relief and anti-climax that always overcame him when a case had been solved. This one had dragged on for some time and he had despaired of ever bringing it to a satisfactory conclusion but now that it was over, although he was trying to unwind, he couldn't let go. Ginny realised this and was encouraging him to talk and get it out of his system. For the first time in over a week he had eaten his evening meal with her and Simon and now he was sipping coffee and reminding himself that he didn't have to go out again that evening.

'There was no danger of me drowning,' he said, pushing away his cup and stretching. 'I'm a strong swimmer, but Laura Nelson tried very hard to resist my efforts to save her. She wanted to die. I nearly let her go. I felt a monster dragging her back to face the consequences. Perhaps it would have been better for everyone if I had let her die, but I couldn't, Ginny. It went against all my training and principles.' He ran his fingers through his hair and appealed to her. 'What would you have done in my place?'

'I don't know, I'm glad that *I* didn't have to make the decision. But don't let it haunt you James. After all, she had killed two innocent people who happened to get in her way.'

'True, O Wise One, but she needs help not punishment. Her counsel will argue that she's unfit to plead. She completely cracked up when we got her out of the water, didn't seem to know what had happened and certainly didn't take in the official caution or understand that she was under arrest. She just kept gabbling about "Uncle Frank" and WPC Linda Barrett was the only one who could do anything with her. It all came pouring out when she was taken into custody. Apparently she was regularly sexually abused as an adolescent by this "Uncle Frank" who lived with her family.'

'Oh, James, how awful!'

'Her father and mother never knew and she never told anyone else but bottled it all up and tried to suppress the memory. Of course, it damaged her psychologically, she couldn't have a normal relationship with a man, which is why she latched on to Jonathan Cade.'

'You mean she deliberately chose someone who was a no-go in that area?'

'It wasn't deliberate. She wanted to lead a normal life and get married and have a family, but subconsciously she picked on a person who wouldn't fulfil such a relationship.'

'Men have a lot to answer for. So to all intents and purposes she was an ordinary young woman and nobody knew what a mess she was inside?'

'Strangely enough Stella Lingard guessed that there was something like that in her background and even said as much to me. She's an astute woman underneath that sexy exterior.'

'You're making me jealous.'

'Don't be silly, that blatant sexuality is a turn-off as far as I'm concerned, but I wonder if Nick Blackstone has got beneath the surface and knows just how fly a woman he is tangling with.'

'That's the journalist?'

'It is and his name will be a national by-line tomorrow. He just "happened" to be around and witnessed everything that took place down at the river today.'

'And Lacey hasn't eaten you for dinner?'

'He's waiting to see just how it breaks. I may yet be thrown to the wolves.'

'Oh, that's so unfair, James. It was your intuition, though I know you hate me using that word, that led to the breakthrough in this case. You didn't give up although nobody else wanted to back your hunch. Why should you be disciplined?'

'It all depends on how the CC takes it – whether he thinks the solution outweighs the publicity. I'm not bothered, I've got the satisfaction of knowing that I cracked it even though it's left a nasty taste in my mouth. It's not just the killer and the victim who are involved in a murder enquiry. A train of events is set off that draws in many other people.'

'What will happen to the librarian?'

'Dennis Coleman? Nothing. The Super has agreed that there's no point in pressing charges, the poor chap has been punished enough already. The theft of the manuscript had nothing to do with the case in the end and so isn't needed as evidence. That little episode will be quietly shelved and forgotten.'

'What is going to happen to it?'

'Edwin Cheyney, the Director of the Maltings, is to be given Power of Attorney to liaise with Rostropovich and Shostakovich's son Maxim over it. They're both in the States but he's hoping it will eventually be premiered over here at Blund.'

'That will be a feather in his cap. Do you think he'll bring it off?'

'He's hoping that he will. How would you like to attend that concert?'

'A music-lover's dream. You'd never get tickets!'

'I shall do my damndest when the time comes.' He lifted his head. 'Isn't that Katherine crying? I'll go and get her.'

'Too late, Simon's got there first!'

A rather sheepish Simon blundered down the stairs and into the room clutching his half-sister to his chest.

'She started crying and I thought her feed was due so I've brought her down to save you having to go upstairs.' He jiggled her in his arms and laid his cheek against hers.

Ginny watched with amusement as her husband curbed his eagerness and refrained from snatching the baby from Simon.

'This girl,' she said, eyeing her two menfolk, 'is going to be spoilt silly.'

The lights dimmed and a buzz of excitement ran round the auditorium. From their seats at the back of the concert hall, Patrick Mansfield hissed to his wife: 'Do you think I'm going to enjoy this?'

'You'd better, this is an historic moment. It's a shame that James and Ginny are missing out on it but lucky for us.'

It was the following spring and Shostakovich's 3rd Cello Concerto was being premiered at Blund Maltings after much negotiation on the part of Edwin Cheyney. He had managed to secure two tickets for Roland as a thank you for his part in retrieving the manuscript but at the last moment the Rolands had had to cry off. Simon, who usually looked after Katherine on the rare occasions when they went out together, had an important table-tennis match that evening at school and the plan to get another babysitter was cancelled when the baby started teething problems a few days before. She ran a fever and grizzled and cried all evening long and they had reluctantly decided that they must forego the concert and passed on the tickets to the Mansfields.

It was a gala occasion and the Press was there in force, also the television cameras. Mansfield had noticed Nick Blackstone drinking in the bar beforehand with a handful of fellow journalists. He looked very distinguished in his dinner jacket, not at all like the lazy, uncouth man they had had to deal with the previous summer. There was no sign of Stella Lingard and Mansfield wondered if they were still together. Màrta Rakosi had swept past a few minutes before with her husband in tow. She was swathed in a dark red velvet dress, all drapes and folds, and her grey bird's-nest hair was piled up in an intricate chignon. Beside her, her husband looked insignificant and uneasy as if he were wearing a borrowed suit that was too big for him.

The first violin walked out on to the stage and the audience clapped enthusiastically. He acknowledged this and sat down and then there was a pause which whipped up the anticipation and excitement which was seething round the concert hall. Maxim Shostakovich, the guest conductor, walked out leading Mstislav Rostropovich, and the audience erupted in a frenzy of clapping. The composer's son stepped on to the rostrum and waited for his soloist to tune up and indicate his readiness to begin. But Rostropovich walked to the edge of the stage and peered out into the auditorium. He saw the person he was looking for and beckoned to him.

As Miklos Rakosi got to his feet and stumbled along the row, Rostropovich spoke to the audience.

'There is an old friend of mine here tonight who should be up here playing with me. I wish him to join me here on the platform and take part in spirit in this so wonderful work of our dear friend.'

He walked towards the steps at the side of the platform and held out his hands as Rakosi tottered eagerly on to the stage. Just as the two men were about to embrace, Rakosi clutched his chest and dropped to the floor like a stone.

The entire assembly was shocked into silence.

The phone rang just as the Rolands were settling down for a well-earned rest. Katherine had whined and cried for nearly three hours, ramming her little fists against her hot, flushed face and kicking and struggling in their arms. They had walked the floor with her, trying to pacify and soothe her, and at last she had fallen into an exhausted sleep and had been tucked into her cot.

Ginny sat in a low chair in front of the fire and James sat on the floor and rested his head against her, watching the leaping flames and relishing the silence. When they had been house-hunting Ginny had insisted that the place they chose must have an open fireplace and he was glad that they had managed to find one. The house had full central heating but they lit a fire on cold evenings as a top-up. It was cold that evening; it might officially be springtime, but the long, chill winter lingered on and forecasters even spoke of the possibility of further snow.

Ginny sighed as the phone rang.

'Surely it's not work again, James? Are you expecting a call?'

'No. Perhaps it's a wrong number.'

He scrambled to his feet and picked up the receiver. Mansfield's voice boomed down the line.

'It's Mansfield here.'

'Patrick! I thought you were supposed to be at the concert?'

'I am. It's the interval and I'm ringing from the Maltings.'

'Is anything wrong?'

'You obviously haven't been watching the box?'

'No, we've been otherwise occupied. To tell you the truth, we'd forgotten all about it. Has something happened?'

'You could say. He's croaked in front of an audience of millions.'

'Who? Who are you talking about?' A sense of foreboding gripped Roland.

'Miklos Rakosi. Rostropovich called him on to the platform before he started playing and he collapsed and dropped down dead in front of our very eyes.'

'It was natural causes?' asked Roland sharply.

'Yes, apparently he had had a bad heart for years and nobody knew about it except for his wife and his doctor. The excitement was too much for him.'

'Good God! What happened? Did they cancel the performance?'

'No Màrta insisted that they carry on. She said he would have wished it.'

'So it turned out to be a requiem.'

'Do you know something?' Mansfield's voice crackled over the line. 'He wasn't meant to hear that concerto, was he?'

More Compelling Fiction from Headline:

TESSA BARCLAY

THE FINAL PATTERN

'Tessa Barclay always spins a fine yarn . . .
gripping and entertaining'
Wendy Craig

Jenny Armstrong, mistress of the thriving Corvill and Son
weaving business, returns to her native Scotland
determined to achieve prosperity and comfort for her
reunited family. But the death of her brother Ned brings
disruption and harm . . .

Once again young Heather Armstrong is caught up in her
widowed Aunt Lucy's machinations; Jenny's rekindled love
affair with her husband Ronald is threatened and
strangers lurk in doorways to spy on the Armstrongs and
their friends. Jenny uncovers a terrible secret in Lucy's past
that still demands vengeance, and there is an unknown
enemy to be reckoned with . . .

THE FINAL PATTERN is the compelling sequel to
A WEB OF DREAMS and BROKEN THREADS –
'Just what a historical novel should be' Elizabeth Longford
'Filled with fascinating historical detail and teeming with
human passions' Marie Joseph
– also available from Headline.

FICTION/SAGA   0 7472 3542 2

A selection of bestsellers from Headline

FICTION

STUDPOKER	John Francome	£4.99 □
DANGEROUS LADY	Martina Cole	£4.99 □
TIME OFF FROM GOOD BEHAVIOUR	Susan Sussman	£4.99 □
THE KEY TO MIDNIGHT	Dean Koontz	£4.99 □
LEGAL TENDER	Richard Smitten	£5.99 □
BLESSINGS AND SORROWS	Christine Thomas	£4.99 □
VAGABONDS	Josephine Cox	£4.99 □
DAUGHTER OF TINTAGEL	Fay Sampson	£5.99 □
HAPPY ENDINGS	Sally Quinn	£5.99 □
BLOOD GAMES	Richard Laymon	£4.99 □
EXCEPTIONAL CLEARANCE	William J Caunitz	£4.99 □
QUILLER BAMBOO	Adam Hall	£4.99 □

NON-FICTION

RICHARD BRANSON: The Inside Story	Mick Brown	£6.99 □
PLAYFAIR FOOTBALL ANNUAL 1992-93	Jack Rollin	£3.99 □
DEBRETT'S ETIQUETTE & MODERN MANNERS	Elsie Burch Donald	£7.99 □
PLAYFIELD NON-LEAGUE FOOTBALL ANNUAL 1992-93	Bruce Smith	£3.99 □

SCIENCE FICTION AND FANTASY

THE CINEVERSE CYCLE OMNIBUS	Craig Shaw Gardner	£5.99 □
BURYING THE SHADOW	Storm Constantine	£4.99 □
THE LOST PRINCE	Bridget Wood	£5.99 □
KING OF THE DEAD	R A MacAvoy	£4.50 □
THE ULTIMATE WEREWOLF	Byron Preiss	£4.99 □

All Headline books are available at your local bookshop or newsagent, or can be ordered direct from the publisher. Just tick the titles you want and fill in the form below. Prices and availability subject to change without notice.

Headline Book Publishing PLC, Cash Sales Department, PO Box 11, Falmouth, Cornwall, TR10 9EN, England.

Please enclose a cheque or postal order to the value of the cover price and allow the following for postage and packing:
UK & BFPO: £1.00 for the first book, 50p for the second book and 30p for each additional book ordered up to a maximum charge of £3.00.
OVERSEAS & EIRE: £2.00 for the first book, £1.00 for the second book and 50p for each additional book.

Name ....

Address ....

....